THE KILL CALL

STEPHEN BOOTH

The Kill Call

HarperCollins*Publishers*

HarperCollins*Publishers*
77–85 Fulham Palace Road, London W6 8JB

harpercollins.co.uk

Published by HarperCollins*Publishers* 2009

1

Copyright © Stephen Booth 2009

Stephen Booth asserts the moral right to
be identified as the author of this work

A catalogue record for this book
is available from the British Library

ISBN 978-0-00-724345-7

Set in Sabon by Palimpsest Book Production Limited,
Grangemouth, Stirlingshire

Printed in Great Britain by
Clays Ltd, St Ives plc

Mixed Sources
Product group from well-managed
forests and other controlled sources
www.fsc.org Cert no. SW-COC-1806
© 1996 Forest Stewardship Council

FSC is a non-profit international organisation established to promote the responsible management of the world's forests. Products carrying the FSC label are independently certified to assure consumers that they come from forests that are managed to meet the social, economic and ecological needs of present and future generations.

Find out more about HarperCollins and the environment at
www.harpercollins.co.uk/green

As with all my previous books, this story would never have seen the light of day without the hard work and support of a whole team of people. This novel is particularly dedicated to my agent, Teresa Chris, to my editor, Julia Wisdom at HarperCollins, and to long-suffering copy editor Anne O'Brien, all of whom have been involved with Cooper and Fry for almost a decade.

1

Journal of 1968
In those days, there were always just the three of us. Three bodies close together, down there in the cold, with the water seeping through the concrete floor, and a chill striking deep into flesh and bone. The three of us, crouching in the gloom, waiting for a signal that would never come.

And what a place to wait and watch in. Seven feet high and seven feet wide – it might as well have been a giant coffin. But slam down the lid and blot out the sun, and we'd survive. Oh, yes. For fourteen days, we'd survive. Thinking about all the things we'd hoped for, and the way our lives could be snuffed out, just like that.

One night, Jimmy looked up from his bunk at me and Les, and he said we were like the three little pigs, or the three billy goats gruff. Well, I don't know about that. Three blind mice, maybe – it would be more fitting. If it all kicked off, the three of us would be as good as blind. Blinded by a million suns. Blind to the people dying.

A few of the details are a bit dim now. Age does that to you. But other things are as bright and stark in my mind as if they'd been burnt there by a lightning flash. Faces and eyes are what I remember most. Faces in the dark. Eyes turned up towards the light. That look in the eyes a second before death.

Yet all we had down there was a miserable six-watt bulb. I don't think they even make bulbs that small any more, do they? No wonder your sight could get damaged. Then, every ninety minutes, the switch would pop and it went totally dark. Black as a cat in a coal hole. I always hated that. Even now, complete darkness is what frightens me most. You never know what might be coming up right next to you in the dark.

But it's amazing how you can adapt to it, for a while. With that one little bulb, we could see pretty well in the murk, well enough to read and do what was necessary.

The place was shocking damp, too. I don't know what they'd done wrong when they built it, but Les said it hadn't been tanked. Les was our number one, and he might have been right, for once. The water seemed to soak right through the walls from the soil. It was particularly bad in the winter, or after a heavy rain, which happens a mite too often in Derbyshire. Some nights, if it were siling down, it would be all hands to the pump.

And that was the three of us. Me, Les, and poor old Jimmy. Always three, except for the time that we didn't ever talk about.

A lot of things seem to come in threes, don't they? The Holy Trinity, the Three Wise Men, the Third World War. There must be something magic about the number. Perhaps it's to do with the Earth being the third planet from the Sun. Or the fact that we see the world in three dimensions – even if your world happens to be only seven feet wide and seven feet high.

Well, times change so much. The years pass and the world turns, and suddenly no one cares, and no one wants you any more. They take away your friends, your pride, your reason for living. But they can't ever wipe out your memories. Sometimes, I wish they would. If only they could take away

2

the nightmares, free me from the memory of those damp concrete walls and the icy darkness, and the memory of a face, staring up at the light.

And that's another funny thing. They say bad luck comes in threes, don't they? I think I always knew that.

But here's something I didn't know. It turns out that people die in threes, too.

2

March 2009, Tuesday
Old buildings drew Sean Crabbe like a bee to honey. The more neglected they were, the better he liked them. He couldn't really explain the appeal. It might have been something to do with the history that clung to the walls, the lives of long-dead people written in the dust, their stories forever trapped in cobwebs hanging from broken ceilings.

That was why the old Nissen huts above Birchlow were one of his favourite places. He made his way there whenever he got the chance, bunking off from college or just disappearing on a weekend, when no one cared what he was up to. No one else ever went up to the huts any more – not since the homeless man had died there, wrapped up in a roll of plastic sheeting with empty cans scattered around him, a cold morning light glinting on the last drops of his beer as they dribbled across the floor.

Sean had been there on that morning, had found the old derelict lying in his pool of Special Brew, and had walked away to try somewhere else. Next day, he'd watched from the hillside as the police and paramedics made their way to the site. He wondered why they'd sent an ambulance when any fool could see that the man was long since dead.

Some folk said that the place was cursed now, haunted by the ghost of the drunken vagrant. So that was why Sean was always on his own at the old huts. And it was just the way he liked it.

There was one big building that was almost intact, with damp brick walls and corrugated-iron sheets banging in the wind. Its purpose was a mystery to him, but he didn't really care. There were a few small rooms that might have been offices, a kitchen that still had a filthy sink in it, and a bigger space with a concrete floor and shelves along the walls, like a workshop. He liked the narrow corridors best, the floorboards that had warped from the damp and seemed to move with him as he crossed from room to room, and the peeling paint of the doorways where he could imagine anything waiting behind them to be found.

In a way, whenever he pushed open one of those doors, he was entering a different world, stepping through into the past. He wondered if the past had been a better world than the one he was in right now.

This morning, Sean's need to escape had been urgent. His BTEC course at the further education college was turning out to be a waste of time, useless for his chances of finding the media career he'd dreamed of. The money he'd saved doing holiday jobs had long since run out. All those hours washing caravans and picking up rubbish hadn't kept him in course fees for long, and now he owed his parents for a loan to see him through. His girlfriend had dumped him weeks ago, because she said he was mean. If he could call her a girlfriend. Most of the girls thought he was geeky. But, if he was a geek, why wasn't he cleverer at passing exams and doing assignments?

And, to cap it all, a bunch of kids had mugged him last night outside the pub and nicked his phone. Lucky he didn't have his iPod with him at the time, but losing the Nokia was a real pain. His parents had shelled out for it, and he couldn't face telling them that he'd lost it.

It was pity there was no sun, though. A patch of thin, lattice-like wood had been exposed up there in the roof space, and when the sunlight shone through, it cast shadows across the floor. Then Sean could pretend he was a child, avoiding the cracks on the pavement. Here, he could step from light to light, avoiding the dark shadows as if they were traps, holes where evil lurked. Step from light to light, and avoid the shadows. If only life was so easy.

But there was no sun today. Just the rain clattering on the corrugated iron, blowing through the splintered windows, streaming down the walls. He was already wet when he arrived at the huts, and the chill made him shiver inside his parka.

Mouldy, fusty, stale and mildewed. Those were the familiar smells of the hut. If the weather was warm, he could scent an underlying odour of oil or grease, saturated into the concrete from whatever had gone on in here. That smell must have lasted decades. Fifty, sixty years? The buildings must be from about that time. They were so old-fashioned, so last century. It was hard for him to imagine what anyone might have done up here, stuck on an empty hillside in Derbyshire.

Now and then, he smoked a spliff up here at the huts, but he couldn't afford that now. Instead, he plugged in the earphones of his iPod and selected some Coldplay. A feeling of peace settled over him as he listened to Chris Martin's plaintive vocals coming in on 'A Rush of Blood to the Head'. He could forget everything else for a while once the music was playing.

Today, though, Sean knew something was different. He tugged out the earphones and stayed completely still, his eyes tightly closed, his ears straining for a sound. The scurrying of a mouse under the floorboards, maybe, or a bird scratching a nest in the roof. But there was no sound.

He squinted at the dust swirling slowly around him, disturbed only by the current of his own breath. The room looked the same as always. Nothing had been moved or disturbed since his last visit. It was always a worry that someone else would find the derelict buildings – another vagrant sleeping rough, a couple of kids finding a place to have sex or take drugs. Or, worst of all, the owner coming to check on his property, or a builder with a plan to demolish it.

Sean closed his eyes, trying to recapture the moment that had been lost. But he finally had to acknowledge that something really was different today. It wasn't a sound, or anything that looked out of place. It was in the very quality of the mustiness, an underlying odour that was too sweet to be oil or grease. He couldn't deny the message that was hitting his nostrils.

The difference was in the smell.

It had been raining for six hours by the time they found the body. Since the early hours of the morning, sheets of water had been swirling into the valley, soaking the corpse and the ground around it. Pools of water had gathered in the hollows of the fields below Longstone Moor, and a new stream had formed between two hawthorns, washing their roots bare of earth.

Detective Sergeant Diane Fry wiped the rain from her face and cursed under her breath as she watched the medical examiner and an assistant turn the body on to its side. Rivulets of blood-soaked water streamed off the sleeves of a green coat the victim was wearing. A crime-scene photographer crouched under the edge of the body tent to capture the moment. Big, fat drops bounced off his paper suit, ricocheting like bullets.

Shivering, Fry made a mental note to find out the manufacturer of the victim's coat. Her own jacket was barely shower proof, and it would never have withstood the amount of rain that had fallen during the night. Her shoulders already felt damp, though she'd been standing in the field no more than ten minutes. If she didn't get back to her car soon, her clothes would be sticking to her all day, with no chance of a hot shower for hours yet. She'd be unpopular back at the office, too. No one liked sharing their nice, warm working space with a drowned rat.

'Haven't we got any cover up here yet?' she said. 'Where's the mobile control unit?'

'On its way, Sarge. It's a difficult spot to get to.'

'Tell me about it.'

She'd left her Peugeot way back somewhere in a muddy gateway, two fields off at least. Her trek to reach the scene had been across hundreds of yards of damp, scrubby grass, dodging sheep droppings, hoping not to twist an ankle in the treacherous holes that opened up everywhere in this kind of area. The remains of old lead mines, she'd been told. The legacy of thousands of years of men burrowing into the hills like rabbits.

And then, when she arrived, she'd discovered a delay by the first officers attending the call to get a body tent up. The FOAs' vehicle had been short of the required equipment. What a surprise.

An officer standing nearby in a yellow jacket looked at the sky to the west and said something about the rain easing off a bit. He said it with that tone of voice that a countryman used, pretending to be so wise about the ways of the weather. But that was one thing Fry had learned about the Peak District during her time in Derbyshire – there was nothing predictable about the weather.

'Could you find something more useful to do than pretending to be Michael Fish?' said Fry.

'Yes, Sarge. I expect so.'

Fry watched him walk back towards the gateway to direct an arriving vehicle. Even if the officer was right, it was already too late. She felt sure about that. There was a limit to how much water even a limestone landscape could absorb, and this crime scene wouldn't take much more of a soaking.

Continuous heavy rain did an effective job of destroying physical evidence at an exposed crime scene like this one. And exposed was the right word. She was standing in the middle of a field of rough, short-cropped grass, with no real shelter in sight except a distant dry-stone wall. Right now, she would be glad to huddle behind that wall, even if it meant sharing with the sheep she could see standing hunched and miserable at the far end of the field.

Crime-scene examiners put their faith in the theory that anyone present at a crime scene took traces away from it, and left traces behind. It was called Locard's Principle. But, in this case, one half of Locard had been rendered practically worthless by the weather. During the past few hours, blood had been washed away, fingerprints soaked off, shoe marks obliterated. Whatever traces an attacker might have left behind were dissolving into the soil, his unique DNA absorbed into the landscape.

Fry took a step back and felt something soft and squishy slide under her heel. Damn it. If only traces of these bloody sheep disappeared from the landscape so quickly.

For a moment, she gazed across the valley towards Longstone Moor. According to the map, the nearest villages of any size were Birchlow and Eyam. But if they were ever visible from here, she'd chosen the wrong day to enjoy the view. Grey clouds hung so low over the hills that they seemed to be resting on the trees. A dense mist of rain swept across the part of the valley where Eyam was supposed to be.

Fry already hated the sound of Eyam. That was because she'd been corrected about its pronunciation. It was supposed to be said 'Eem', they told her – not 'I-am', which was the way only tourists pronounced it. Well, sod that. She felt inclined to say it the wrong way for the rest of the day, just to show that she *was* a tourist, at heart. Yes – deep down, she was just a visitor passing through, taking a break from civilization to study the ways of primitive hill folk.

A gust of wind blew a spatter of rain in her eyes. That was one thing you could say for a city. Any city, anywhere. There was always a building within reach where you could get out of the rain. In the Peak District, the weather would always catch you exposed and vulnerable. It could bake you one minute, and drown you the next. It was like some big conspiracy, nature combining with the remains of ancient lead mines that lurked under your feet to trip you up.

When Fry turned away from the view, she found the crime-scene manager, Wayne Abbott, standing in front of her, as if he'd materialized out of the rain. He was a damp ghost, glistening in his white scene suit as if he was formed of ectoplasm.

'There doesn't seem to be much physical evidence in the immediate area around the body,' he said, when he'd got her attention.

'I'm not surprised.'

'And I can't even see where the approach route might have been. We'll probably have to do a fingertip search over the whole field.'

'How many people on the ground would we need for that?'

'I don't know. It's a big field.'

'Thanks a lot.'

Fry could imagine the arguments about overtime payments and the hours spent frowning over the duty rota. Luckily, she could pass that problem up to her DI, Paul Hitchens.

The information so far was too scanty for her liking. A sighting of the body had been called in by the air support unit at nine forty-five a.m., a sharp-eyed observer on board Oscar Hotel 88 spotting the motionless figure as the helicopter passed overhead en route to a surveillance task. The zoom facility on his video camera had confirmed the worst. Paramedics had attended, along with uniforms from Bakewell, the observer keeping up a running commentary to guide units to the location. With death confirmed, the duty DC had been

10

called out, and gradually the incident had begun to move up the chain. Her DI, Paul Hitchens, would be on scene shortly, and he would become the officer in charge.

But Fry could see that this was already looking like a difficult one. According to the control room, there were no overnight mispers, not so much as a stressed teenager who'd stayed out all night to wind up Mum and Dad. Neighbouring forces weren't any help, either. She'd held out hopes of Sheffield, who usually had a bunch of drunks gone AWOL, even on a wet Monday night in March. But no such luck.

So there was going to be a lot of work to do getting a story on the victim, even with a quick ID. If this did turn out to be a murder enquiry, the first forty-eight hours were absolutely crucial.

Fry shivered again as a trickle of water ran down her neck. And it didn't help much when Mother Nature decided to spend the first six of those forty-eight hours re-enacting the Great Flood.

A miserable figure was making his way across the field, slithering on the grass and dodging strips of wet crime-scene tape flapping around him in the wind. Detective Constable Gavin Murfin wasn't cut out for country treks, either. But, in his case, it was for a different reason. No matter how many memos did the rounds from management about the fitness of officers, Murfin had been unable to lose any weight. Recently, Fry had noticed that he'd compromised by taking his belt in a notch, which had succeeded only in producing an unsightly roll of spare flesh that hung over his waistband.

Murfin had a comfort-eating problem, and Fry could relate to that. If only he didn't leave so many crumbs in her car.

'Gavin. How are things back at the office?'

'In chaos. Have you seen that Branagh woman? She's empire-building already.'

Fry shrugged. 'That's the name of the game at senior management level.'

11

'God save me from promotion, then.'

'I don't think you need God's help, Gavin.'

Murfin shrugged. 'I notice you've been doing your best to keep out of her way. So I don't suppose you're exactly her number one fan, either.'

Fry didn't answer. She still had some instinct for diplomatic silence.

Murfin pulled a face as he took in the fields and the distant stone walls.

'Witnesses are going to be a bit thin on the ground, Diane.'

'Yes.' Fry eyed the sheep suspiciously. 'There are plenty of those things, though.'

Murfin nodded. 'Sheep see a lot of things. You'd be surprised. One day, some clever bugger at Ripley will come up with a scheme for surveillance sheep. Imagine them wandering about with miniature video cameras strapped to their heads, like hundreds of little woolly PCSOs.'

She tried to picture some of E Division's community support officers with the faces of sheep. But her imagination failed her.

'The mind boggles,' she said.

'A bit of boggling now and then never did anyone any harm, in my opinion.'

Fry sighed. 'Where is everyone, Gavin?'

'Oh, am I not enough for you?'

'What about Hurst, and Irvine? Where are they?'

'Processing.'

'Still?'

'It's the price of success.'

Fry didn't need to ask any more. Sunday had been E Division's strike day. Not a total withdrawal of labour in protest at their latest pay deal, as some officers would have liked, but a pre-planned operation targeting known criminals. Search warrants had been executed in various parts of the division. Arrests were made for assault, theft, burglary, going equipped, supplying Class-A drugs, and money laundering. Officers had recovered drugs, cigarettes, and a large amount of cash. Not a bad haul for the day, and the chiefs were happy. Intelligence-led, proactive policing at its best. But the consequent mountain of paperwork was horrendous. There were so many stages that followed from an arrest – prisoner handling, interviews, witness statements, case-file preparation . . .

'And Ben Cooper –' said Murfin.

'Yes, I know. He's got himself a cushy job.'

Murfin nodded casually at the body tent. Apart from the coat, about all that could be seen of the victim was a pair of muddy brown brogues that almost protruded from the tent into the rain.

'We've got cars out trying to locate a vehicle,' he said. 'Reckon he must have got himself out here somehow, mustn't he? He isn't a hiker, not in those shoes.'

'No luck so far?'

'No, sorry.'

'It'll be parked up in a lay-by somewhere. Unless he was brought out here by someone else, of course.'

'By his killer. Right.'

Fry didn't answer. One of the other downsides of policing a rural area was the lack of CCTV cameras. One of the many downsides. If she'd still been working back in Birmingham, or any other city, they'd have caught the victim's car on half a dozen cameras as it passed from A to B, registered his number plate at a car-park entry barrier, and probably got a nice, clear shot of him walking along the pavement to wherever he'd been going. And then they could have scanned the CCTV footage for possible suspects, grabbed images of a face from the screen for identification.

But out here? Unless their victim had been idiot enough to go more than ten miles an hour over the limit on a stretch of the A6 where the speed cameras were actually operating, his movements might as well have been invisible.

'If someone else took his car,' said Murfin, 'they might have dumped it and torched it by now.'

'If they have, it'll turn up somewhere.'

Murfin was wrestling with a decrepit Ordnance Survey map. Normally, he swore by his sat-nav, and never took driving instructions from anyone but TomTom, or his wife. That wasn't much use when you'd left your car two fields away, though Fry knew that Wayne Abbott had a GPS device to map the location of a crime scene precisely.

'We're somewhere about here,' said Murfin, stabbing a finger at a square of damp plastic. 'Longstone Moor that way, the nearest village is Birchlow, over there. A few more villages across the valley. And a load of quarries all around us, some of them still in use. There's a big mill down in that dip. Not textiles, it processes stone from the quarries.'

'A tricky area, then?'

Murfin shrugged. 'The lads are checking any pull-ins on the A623 or this back road over here between the villages. But, as you can see, there are quite a few unmade lanes and farm tracks in this area. So it could take a while, unless some helpful punter phones in.'

'The victim's shoes are muddy, so he could have walked some distance, at least.'

'Eyam at the furthest, I'd say,' suggested Murfin, pronouncing the 'Eem' correctly. 'There's a car park that tourists use, near the museum. I've asked for a check on any that have outstayed their parking tickets. He's been dead for an hour or two, right?'

'Three hours, according to the ME.'

'He might be due for a fine, then. Poor bugger. That's the last thing he needs.'

'That's not really funny, Gavin.'

'Oh, I thought those were tears of unrestrained hilarity running down your face. Maybe it's just the rain, after all.'

The officer nearby was listening to a call on his radio, and became suddenly alert. Fry looked at him expectantly.

'What's the news?'

'Not good, Sergeant. The control room says a 999 call was received about twenty minutes ago.' The officer pointed towards a distant stone building. 'A unit has been despatched to the old agricultural research centre, about half a mile away in that direction. They thought we'd like to know. There's been a report of another corpse.'

Fry cursed quietly, squinting against the downpour.

'I've heard about showers of frogs,' she said. 'But I've never heard of it raining bodies.'

3

Detective Constable Ben Cooper ran his hand down the glass of the passenger window, clearing a path through the condensation. But it was wetter outside than inside the car, and all he saw was a blurred reflection of himself – a pair of dark eyes, fragmented against the streets of Edendale. Automatically, he swept back the stray lock of hair that fell across his forehead, before focusing beyond his own image to the side door of the house across the street.

'Someone home, I think.'

'There'd better be. The boss won't be happy if it's all a wasted effort.'

Despite the rain, Cooper would always prefer to be outside, rather than shut up in the office with a mountain of paperwork. That was why he'd managed to talk himself into this assignment, though he hadn't anticipated finding himself trapped inside a car instead, with the atmosphere growing stale and his breath steaming the windows.

'We'll get into the property, whatever,' he said.

'We need an arrest, though.'

'Right.'

He could feel an itch developing under his stab-proof vest. Right underneath, where he had no chance of reaching it without taking the thing off completely. No amount of twisting his body and squeezing a hand into the gap would do the trick. That was the trouble with sitting doing nothing, waiting for the action to start. You began to develop unreachable itches. You began to think about things.

His colleagues were fidgeting and grumbling beside him in the car, trying to reach itches of their own, or ease the cramp in their legs. They might have been better waiting outside in the rain, except that Kevlar was said to disintegrate when it got wet. Cooper didn't know whether that was true, or just a canteen-culture myth that had survived the death of the canteen. He had no urge to be the first one to try it out, though. An itch was better than a knife in the guts.

'What are we waiting for now? Who's running this show, anyway?'

'Laurel and Hardy, by the look of that entry team.'

'Jesus. They've got the Michelin Man on ram.'

Cooper watched four officers in overalls and riot helmets exiting their unmarked van and approaching the house. Well, no one looked good in a stab vest; Cooper had an uncomfortable feeling that he had put on a few pounds in the wrong places himself. Despite the muscle he'd been building up in the gym, too much good food had staged a kind of counterattack and his waist was now pushing uncomfortably against the inside of the vest. That would be Liz's fault, he reckoned. She wasn't a bad cook, and every time she made a meal for him, he felt obliged to return the favour with a visit to a decent restaurant. What a fatal spiral. At this rate, he'd be the Michelin Man himself before too long.

He watched the bulky figure of the entry team officer swing back the ram. The big red key, they called it. It opened any door, if you used it right.

A couple of liveried Traffic cars moved into position to close off the road. Cooper had done his five years in uniform before he joined CID, but he'd never been tempted by Traffic.

Funny, when it was the job that got you out and about the most, instead of wearing out a chair in the CID room. Even without his twelve years in the force, he had more local knowledge than the rest of his shift put together. Well . . . one day, maybe, when the paperwork finally wore down his resistance.

'Here we go, lads.'

And then suddenly everything was happening at once. Cooper threw open the door and jumped out of the car. Immediately, he was surrounded by noise – the thump of boots on the pavement, an Alsatian barking furiously, a radio crackling with messages, and the first shouts of 'police' as the entry team burst into the hallway of the house. As he ran, he could hear his own breathing, feel his heart pounding in his chest. This was the moment many police officers lived for – the sudden rush of adrenalin, the surge of excitement, the blood pumping through the veins at the scent of danger. It was like a high for some of them, a feeling they couldn't get enough of. Dangerous, in its own way.

Almost before he was inside the door, he caught the distinctive odour. An officer at the top of the stairs signalled a find. So intelligence had been on the mark, after all. Upstairs, a bedroom would have been converted into a small-scale cannabis factory, with its windows boarded up, an air vent protruding from the attic, possibly hundreds of plants under cultivation, releasing that unmistakable smell. There was no way of disguising all the tell-tale signs in a suburban street like this one. How did they think they could fool anyone? Well, he supposed they relied on a code of silence, the closing of ranks against the authorities. No snitching.

And that was why more than sixty per cent of cannabis sold in the UK was home-grown now. Latest bulletins showed an average of three factories a day raided around the country. The owners of this house would appear at magistrates' court tomorrow charged with cannabis cultivation, and would probably be remanded in custody.

Cooper entered the living room, where two male suspects were already being handcuffed by the entry team. Somewhere in another room, a female suspect was screaming – a hysterical, high-pitched noise that penetrated the walls and rattled the windows. He helped the sergeant in charge of the operation to search one of the men, removing keys and a mobile phone from a pocket. Vital seizures, these – the keys would lead to a vehicle containing more evidence, the phone would provide contacts for the enquiry teams to follow up.

'Can you escort a prisoner, Ben?' asked the sergeant.

'No problem.'

Cooper looked around the room while he waited for the man to be read his rights. He could hear the woman sobbing now, in between outbursts. For him, this was the worst moment. After that surge of adrenalin at the start of a raid, there was this uncomfortable feeling that came over him when he found himself standing in someone's home, an intruder into their lives, turning over the belongings and poking into the hidden corners. He always felt he had to avoid the accusing eyes, though he knew the feeling of guilt was irrational. He always prayed there would be no children in a house like this. Children were the worst. No amount of explanation would make it right for the children.

But this was something he couldn't really share with his colleagues. He looked at them now, more of them entering the house, intent on their jobs, professional and calm. Did any of them experience the same feelings?

Long before his prisoner was in the car, the female suspect had stopped screaming. Yet the sound still seemed to echo in Cooper's head long after the shouting had died down and the barking had stopped, and the adrenalin surge had drained from his body.

By the time the ME and the crime-scene manager allowed her to get near the body in the field, Diane Fry was glad to climb into a scene suit. She followed the line of stepping plates laid down by the SOCOs and examined the victim as closely as she could. There would be much more detail in the SOC and ME's reports, and in the photographs. But personal impressions could still be vital, whatever the benefits of science.

The first thing she noticed was how much blood there was on the victim. His hair was matted with it, and it had run down his temple and into his ear. His shirt collar was stained, and the waxed cotton was darkened by more than rain.

'The victim is in his mid-forties,' said Murfin, rustling alongside her with his notebook. 'He seems to have been in reasonably good health, though a little overweight. Well, that describes a perfect specimen of manhood, if you ask me.'

Fry glanced at him, noting the way his scene suit bulged and sagged unflatteringly around the middle.

'Matter of opinion, Gavin.'

Murfin sniffed. 'Approximately six feet tall, brown hair, brown eyes; the blood is from a rather nasty head wound.'

'I can see that.'

Scalp wounds always bled dramatically, even a surface cut. But in this case, Fry could see the damage to the skull, where it had been crushed a few inches above and behind the left ear.

'No ID in his pockets,' said Murfin. 'That's the bad news.'

'Nothing?'

'No wallet, no chequebook, no car keys. And no mobile phone.'

'A robbery victim? Out here?'

'Could be. Or it might have been an attempt to prevent us identifying him.'

'The postmortem might find something for us. It would be useful if his fingerprints or DNA are on record, of course.'

The body had been moved by the ME during his examination, but now lay on its back, face turned upwards to the rain, which was being deflected by the roof of the body tent. The coat the man was wearing turned out to be one of those green waxed affairs, similar to one that Fry had seen Ben

Cooper in sometimes, though this one looked a bit newer and probably more expensive. Underneath the coat, there was a blue body warmer and a cotton shirt with a thin green check. Dark blue corduroy trousers led down to that pair of nice brown brogues. Dark blue and brown never went well together in Fry's opinion, but the shoes looked much too good for yomping across sheep-infested hills.

'Logic would suggest that his car must be somewhere within easy reach,' she said. 'He wasn't really dressed for hiking, was he?'

'He was wearing a rainproof coat,' pointed out Murfin. 'So he must have expected to be outdoors for a while, at least.'

'But no boots. Just the sort of shoes he might wear at the office. Of course, somebody else could have brought him here.'

'And there's no visible blood spatter on the ground,' said Fry. 'That could be thanks to the rain, or because he was killed somewhere else.'

'So if he came here in someone else's car, he might still have been alive when he accepted the lift.'

'Do dead people accept lifts?'

'Probably not,' conceded Murfin.

'And no ID on him at all? What was in his pockets?'

'Some loose change,' said Murfin. 'Comb, tissues, a pair of reading glasses in a metal case. I suppose we might be able to trace him through the optician, if necessary.'

'Which optician?'

'SpecSavers, but no branch name on the case.'

'Blast. They're everywhere.'

'Yes, I suppose he could be a tourist,' said Murfin. 'Even in March.'

'Great.'

'Oh, and there's a receipt from somewhere called the Le Chien Noir. It's a restaurant in Edendale. Quite upmarket, I believe. Expensive, anyway.'

'Not the sort of place I'm likely to know, then.'

Murfin held up the evidence bag and squinted at the receipt. 'The print is a bit faint, but it looks like dinner for two.'

'What date?'

'The ninth. That was last night.'

Fry nodded. 'The condemned man's last meal. I hope the chef was up to scratch.'

'This restaurant is a long way from the crime scene,' said Murfin. 'Eight or nine miles, or more.'

'So how did he get from dinner at Le Chien Noir to a field near Birchlow?'

Fry looked down at the victim again. Rain still glinted on his face from the lights set up inside the tent. Blood was darkening rapidly in his hair, smears drying on the sleeve of his nice waxed coat.

Despite the difficulties presented by the location and the weather conditions, the crime-scene examiners would have followed all the protocols for evidence collection. Trace hairs and fibres first, then bloodstains, any possible tool or weapon marks, visible fingerprints or footwear patterns. Finally, latent patterns that required powder or chemical enhancement. Not much chance of some of those in the monsoon season.

Although Fry had been given an estimate by the ME, she knew that time of death should be based on witness reports and not on physical evidence. Measuring body temperature was prone to error, and the degree of rigor mortis wasn't as accurate as it was sometimes cracked up to be. But in this case, her stiff was, well . . . hardly stiff at all. The corpse had been pretty fresh when it was first spotted.

She looked across the moor. Somewhere over there were the remains of the agricultural research station. Although units had been despatched in response to the 999 call some time ago, the airwaves had been ominously quiet since then.

'Let's see what we've got across the way then,' she said. 'With luck, body number two might explain everything.'

*   *   *

22

It took Fry so long to find her way to the collection of derelict buildings on the hill above Birchlow, the site had already been searched by uniformed officers, and Wayne Abbott had moved on from the field to supervise the scene.

Most of the site consisted of little more than cracked foundations, weed-grown concrete yards and broken fencing. The surrounding bracken and gorse were gradually encroaching on to the site, and weeds had burst holes through the tarmac road.

She stepped through a door sagging from its hinges and gazed at the scene of dereliction inside. The buildings hadn't been occupied for many years, of course, and the site had reverted to the landowner. Health and Safety might have something to say about the lack of security, though. No locks, no warning signs, no measures to prevent anyone from suffering injuries through collapsing roofs or broken shards of glass.

'There's no body here, Sergeant,' said an officer who had been searching the building. 'But we've found what look like bloodstains on the concrete in the largest hut.'

Fry turned to gaze back across the fields in the direction from which she'd come. The white body tent was clearly visible from here.

'Well, unless we've got a dead man walking, this call wasn't to a body at all. Our victim was still alive when he came in here – and then he made it across at least two fields before he gave up the ghost.'

'Why would someone phone in and give this location for the body, then? It doesn't make sense.'

'Perhaps,' said Fry, 'whoever else was here believed the victim was already dead.'

Murfin came up alongside her, shaking himself like a dog. 'It seems the 999 call was made from a mobile,' he said. 'The caller refused to give a name, but we've traced the number, and the phone is registered to a Mr Patrick Rawson, with an address in the West Midlands. Control have tried calling the number back, but it just goes to voicemail. The phone is switched off, probably.'

'Has anyone checked the barn over there?'

At that moment, the sight of Wayne Abbott making his way towards her again through the rain came as a relief to Fry.

'No drier up here, is it?' he said.

'Who'd live in England?' said Fry.

'It rains in other countries, you know. I went to Texas for a conference once, and it rained the whole week.'

'Somehow, that doesn't sound too bad.'

Fry was wondering how CSMs managed to get sent to conferences in Texas. Perhaps she'd been in the wrong job all this time. No one had ever suggested sending her to Swindon for a conference, let alone the USA.

'Have you found something?' she said.

Abbott pushed back the hood of his scene suit. The last time Fry had seen him at an incident, he'd had a shaved head. Now, his hair had begun to grow back in ragged patches, so that his skull looked like an old tennis ball that had been chewed by the dog.

'Well, we've got a series of impressions in the soil within a two hundred-yard radius of the hut,' he said. 'Quite a lot of impressions, actually.'

'Shoe marks?'

'Well, sort of.'

'I thought the rain would have obliterated them by now.'

'In the usual way of things, yes – that's what I would have expected, too. Light prints on soft soil like this would have deteriorated beyond use. But these prints are a bit different.'

'Different how?'

'The amount of weight behind the shoe marks has imprinted them deep enough into the ground to preserve them in the drier subsoil, where the rain hasn't affected them so much.'

'Weight? That makes such a difference?'

24

Abbott nodded, a knowing smile on his face. 'This amount of weight does. That, and the fact the shoes in question were made of steel.'

Fry found herself starting to get irritated. She was too wet and uncomfortable to tolerate people playing games.

'Steel? What on earth are you talking about, Wayne?'

'Horses,' said Abbott. 'I'm talking about horses.'

4

There was still a lot of processing to do, of course. With his prisoner safely in the hands of the custody sergeant at E Division headquarters in West Street, Cooper made his way reluctantly from the custody suite, dodging the rain to reach the walkway that led into the main building.

In the CID room, the rest of the team were hard at work over their paperwork. DC Luke Irvine and DC Becky Hurst had been given the desks closest to his. They were the newest members of E Division CID, and they made him feel almost like a veteran now that he was in his thirties. They were eager to impress, too – anxious to get every last detail right in their reports and case files before their supervisor saw them. He had to give credit to Diane Fry for that. She had the new DCs with their noses to the grindstone. No one wanted to get on the wrong side of her.

'Hi, Ben. How did it go?' called Irvine.

'Great. A good result.'

'Wish I'd been there.'

Irvine was a bit too eager, his face still reflecting his excitement in the job, even when he was buried under paperwork. That wouldn't last.

As he stripped off his stab vest, Cooper felt the last of

the tension fall away. Suddenly, he felt bored again. He stared out of the window at the rooftops of Edendale, dark with continuous rain. His mind drifted back two days to the previous Sunday, and he realized the source of his restlessness.

There was a moment when he had been sitting in his brother Matt's new Nissan 4x4 on the way back from Staffordshire. He recalled the sound of Phil Collins suddenly filling the car. 'Another Day in Paradise'. The music had broken a painful silence that had lasted since he and Matt, and their sister Claire, had left the National Memorial Arboretum, near Lichfield.

As always, Matt had been gripping the steering wheel as if he was at the controls of a tractor, pushing the John Deere 6030 across a ploughed slope on a Derbyshire hillside, muscles tensed in his forearms as though power-assisted steering had never been invented. He was getting so big now that he could probably pull the plough himself, like a shire horse.

'We're not late,' said Ben. 'We don't have an appointment to meet. Personally, I'd rather get home alive.'

'Oh, am I driving too fast?'

'Just a bit.'

'Sorry. I forgot the KGB were in the car.'

Matt had insisted on driving them down from Edendale that morning, because he desperately wanted to show off the new 4x4. In the visitor centre at the arboretum, the first thing Ben had noticed was a huge, carved police officer standing just inside the entrance. It must have been about twelve feet high, like a giant totem pole. A bobby complete with tunic and helmet, but made out of some sort of copper-coloured wood.

After picking up a guide book, they had taken advantage of a break in the rain to cross Millennium Avenue to the plinth marking the start of The Beat, a long avenue of chestnuts. At the top of it was their destination, the Police Memorial Garden.

As they walked down The Beat, it had seemed to Ben that the entire history of Britain's armed forces must be recorded here, in one way or another. There was a memorial to the Rats of Tobruk, the Iraq and Afghanistan willows, and trees planted for the First Army Veterans. Everyone from the Kenya Police to the Women's Auxiliary Air Force was remembered.

The guide book said that chestnuts had been chosen for The Beat because the first police truncheons were made from their wood, chestnut being particularly durable – not to say hard, if you were cracked across the skull with it. Several of the trees had been grown from conkers taken from Drayton Manor, the home of Sir Robert Peel himself. Who knew that the founder of the police service had grown his own chestnut trees?

Ben saw that Matt and Claire had reached the Memorial Garden before him. He supposed he must have been dawdling, subconsciously delaying the moment. Yet he'd promised himself he'd face up to everything he had to deal with from now on. Nothing was to be gained from shutting his memories away and slamming the lid down tight.

Startled by a sound behind him in the office, Cooper looked around guiltily, remembering where he was. For the first time, he became aware of the atmosphere in the office, a little bit more relaxed than usual.

'So where's DS Fry?' he asked Irvine.

'Call-out to a body.'

'Suspicious?'

'Sounds like it.'

'Have we got some details?'

'Here somewhere,' said Irvine.

Cooper read quickly through a copy of the incident log. The Eden Valley Hunt? What were they doing with the hunt? Saboteurs? That could be tricky. Fry would be totally out of her depth.

Without even bothering to sit down at his desk, he made

a call to a familiar mobile number, but only got the recorded voicemail message. Irvine and Hurst watched him in amazement as he headed back out of the office.

'Diane? I think you'll need me. I'm on my way.'

'Don't forget,' said the uniformed inspector, surveying the small group of officers he'd been allocated that morning, 'it's perfectly OK for them to be killed – as long as they're shot.'

Standing on a roadside near Birchlow, Diane Fry watched the inspector at work. Like a practised mind reader, she could tell what he was thinking. With luck, they wouldn't be called on to do very much today, except watch.

Officers nodded and shuffled their feet. They adjusted their high-vis jackets and tucked in the scarves they hoped would stop the rain from trickling down their necks. Fry thought some of them looked bored already. With luck, they'd be even more fed up before the morning was over. Their presence was supposed to be a deterrent, rather than anything else. It was policing as a spectator sport.

The inspector's name was Redfearn, a grey-haired veteran approaching his thirty years' service, twelve of which had been spent in the Met before he returned to Derbyshire. Fry always wondered how he'd managed to maintain an unruffled, pragmatic manner all that time. It was great for dealing with young bobbies, but there had been times when she'd wanted to prod him into some kind of response. Being in CID, she didn't have too much contact with him, but today was going to be different.

'They can even use dogs, provided it's no more than two,' said Redfearn. 'But the actual killing has to be done by shooting. Or by a bird of prey, if there happens to be one present. That's legal.'

The inspector paused, glancing at the vehicles already gathered in a field and along the grass verges as far as the eye could see. No doubt he was thinking that the rain might keep the numbers down. But it was late in the season, and intelligence had suggested a confrontation could be expected.

'From past experience, it's probably the sabs you'll have to watch out for,' he said. 'But we don't take sides, all right? We're here to uphold the law, but mostly to prevent public order offences and ensure all parties can go about their lawful activities. So keep your eyes open, and your wits about you. Oh, and try to keep your feet dry.'

As the officers dispersed, Fry introduced herself to the inspector. She didn't envy him his job. Keeping public order was often a thankless task, especially when you found your-self thrust between two groups who each had the right to go about their peaceful activities. Hunt duty wasn't an assign-ment that many would want.

The Eden Valley Hunt met twice a week, and Fry felt it was surely no coincidence that today's meet was so close to her potential murder scene. In fact, she realized now that the air support unit's surveillance task was connected with the hunt. The helicopter was visible hovering over a copse a couple of fields away.

'You think one of the hunt supporters might know some-thing about your body?' said Redfearn when she explained.

'Someone left hoofprints all over my crime scene, Inspector. In fact, it looks like more than one horse to me. Your oper-ation here is less than half a mile away – I could see you from the scene down there. It seems to me you might have some potential witnesses for me.'

'There are quite a lot of them, you know. There are horse boxes and trailers parked all the way back from here to Birchlow.'

'We're going to have to talk to them, and find out who was here first this morning.'

'What time?'

'Around eight thirty a.m., the ME says.'

'You want the huntsman, or one of the whippers-in, then.

They'd be here with the hound van, early doors. Oh, and a couple of hunt followers would have been out laying the artificial scent.'

'Where are they now?'

Redfearn looked around. 'God knows, Sergeant. In one of these fields somewhere. They'll turn up later on.'

'I need to grab them as soon as poss.'

'Understood.'

The inspector used his radio, asking for someone whose name she couldn't catch to come to the control point and speak to Inspector Redfearn. Well, they would do for a start. Impatient though she was to get on with the job, Fry was well aware that she didn't yet have the manpower to start interviewing dozens of hunt supporters. She glanced at the lines of horse boxes. Was it dozens, or scores? Or even hundreds?

'And what about your saboteurs, Inspector?' she said, when he'd finished with his radio.

'What about them?'

'I'm wondering if one of them might be missing. It would be useful to talk to them.'

He shook his head. 'Well, the sabs aren't very forthcoming, you know. It's difficult enough getting their own names and addresses out of them. Understandably, because if their identities get known, they can be subject to repercussions. But we'll try to rope in a couple for you, if you like.'

'I'd appreciate it.'

Fry turned at a clatter of hooves and saw a bunch of riders rounding the corner. Red coats, black coats, mud-spattered boots, gleaming horses. They trotted towards her as if they'd just fallen out of a time warp. Because surely those scarlet coats charging across the landscape were a throwback to a world of pub prints and Victorian Christmas cards. Hard to believe that it still went on, so far into the twenty-first century, and after all that fuss about the legislation to ban it.

31

'Are you expecting much trouble?' she asked the inspector as the riders passed.

'Hard to tell. There's a cyclical pattern to these things, though. Tension builds up over the hunting season between September and March. Niggling resentments from the start of the season can lead up to minor assaults and scuffles around Christmas, then more serious incidents tend to happen at the end of the season. Both sides get a cooling-off period during the summer, you see.'

Seasons and cooling-off periods; it all sounded like one big game to Fry. She wondered what constituted a goal for either side. A fox killed, or a fox saved. A black eye or a successful prosecution. Then they all went home with their stories to tell, and met up again next September. Amazing.

They stepped to one side of the road to allow another a horse box to pass. A late-comer, since the rest of the hunt had already assembled and scattered across the fields.

'Before the Hunting Act, we did have a lot of violent confrontations between sabs and hunt supporters,' said Inspector Redfearn. 'More than we do now. The Eden Valley Hunt was unpopular, and it attracted a lot of protests. Sabs travelled hundreds of miles to be here.'

'Have you always been on hunt duty?'

'No, but it comes round regularly. Ironically, the turn-out for the hunt has increased since the ban. Their support is booming. On the other hand, the anti-hunt groups lost a lot of members, people who thought the battle was over when the act came in. Now there's just the hardcore left, and they have to try that much harder to make their presence felt.'

'And are the saboteurs local?' asked Fry.

'We think we've got three different groups today. Our own local group we see quite regularly, and they're generally peaceful. The trouble makers seem to come from other parts of the country, and they're of a rather more aggressive nature. It generally starts with the foot followers being given grief, then someone gets spat at, a girl's pony gets sprayed with an unidentified substance. It can take less aggro than that for incidents to kick off big time.'

'The Eden Valley don't hunt foxes now, though,' said Fry.

'Their official policy is to observe the law. But you know there are exemptions under the Act.'

'Of course. I heard your briefing.'

'Well, even if they don't catch foxes any more, their opposition still turn out. Only now some of them call themselves "hunt monitors" and they're armed with video cameras, aiming to catch infringements of the law. We never condone vigilante groups, no matter what their cause, so we watch the sabs carefully.'

Fry nodded. She didn't know who her victim was, yet she already seemed to have an array of potential witnesses, suspects and associates, all milling around the landscape having what passed for fun in these parts. Well, as much fun as you could have in the rain.

A lone rider cantered down the road, a woman in a red coat who dug her knees into her horse's flanks to turn it as she approached them. The mare trotted over the last few yards of wet grass, hooves thumping on the soft ground, steam spurting from its nostrils.

The rider's boots and jodhpurs were splattered with mud and her face was red from exertion and the cold air.

'What's the problem, Inspector?'

'This is Detective Sergeant Fry,' said Redfearn. 'She's investigating a suspicious death in this area.'

'I saw the activity across the way. Thought your people had just got lost.'

'This is Mrs Forbes,' Redfearn told Fry. 'Joint master of the Eden Valley Hunt.'

Fry didn't think she'd ever been quite so near to a horse before. She knew absolutely nothing about them, except that they bit at one end and kicked at the other.

She explained to Mrs Forbes what she wanted. As she spoke, the rider looked down at her with an expression she'd seen on the faces of the hunt supporters when the saboteurs got too close. An unmistakable hint of contempt, probably just the instinct of the mounted person looking down from a great height on the lowly pedestrian.

'You think any of our members might know something about this?' said Mrs Forbes. 'What nonsense.'

'If we could just speak to the people –'

'I can't allow you to speak to anyone. It's just some mad story made up by those antis.'

Fry could feel the horse's breath blowing from its nostrils in warm jets. She suspected that the animal regarded him with much more benevolence than its owner did.

'One way or another, I'll speak to your huntsman, and anyone else who was in this area at around eight thirty this morning,' said Fry. 'If you prefer, we can stop the hunt altogether while we do that.'

Beside her, Redfearn cleared his throat nervously, but said nothing. Mrs Forbes stared from one to the other, her hands gripping the reins tightly, as if it was her horse that was on the verge of getting out of control, rather than her own reactions.

'Do what you like,' she said finally. 'Who is this person who got himself killed?'

'We don't know yet.'

Mrs Forbes snorted, and pulled at her reins. 'I'll give Widdowson instructions.'

Fry watched her go, the mare's tail flicking from side to side as if bothered by invisible flies.

'Widdowson?' she said.

'The huntsman,' said Redfearn.

The inspector's radio crackled, and he listened for a moment.

'This body of yours, Sergeant,' he said. 'Did I understand that he died some time this morning?'

'About eight thirty. Why?'

'Funny thing, that's all. One of my officers is reporting that some of the sabs got a bit over-excited. They said they heard three long, wavering notes on a hunting horn. It sounded to them like the signal that calls in the hounds to kill the fox, or the terrier men to dig him out. That got them all worked up. But it was too early, the hunt hadn't even moved off. So I think they must have been mistaken.'

Fry had lost interest, but tried to appear polite. 'Well, thank you for your co-operation, Inspector.'

Redfearn looked offended. 'Well, I just thought you should know. In case it was relevant that some of the sabs say they heard the kill call.'

Fry turned back. 'The what?'

'That's the name of it,' said the inspector. 'Three long, wavering notes. It's known as the kill call.'

5

A few minutes later, Diane Fry was sitting in her car and fuming. She had gone barely a few yards out of the gateway before she met the entire hunt coming back from the direction of Birchlow. Horses, dogs, people in Land Rovers and vans, others trailing behind on foot. It was a complete carnival.

Traffic was brought to a halt at a crossroads on the A623 while the hunt went by. As the horses passed, the sudden clattering of hooves on tarmac was uncomfortably loud inside the Peugeot. For a few minutes it completely drowned out the mutter of her idling engine and even the efforts of Annie Lennox, who was hurling *Songs of Mass Destruction* at her from the CD player. As the hunt pressed around the car, a powerful whiff of sweating horse crept in through the driver's window, followed by a rich aroma of saddles, cotton jodhpurs and manure.

Many of the mounted hunt supporters seemed to be young girls, wearing their hard hats and pony-club complexions, bright-eyed and eager for a twenty-mile hack. What was really amazing, though, was that there were still so many middle-aged businessmen who sat comfortably on horseback. Surely most members of the business community had never been nearer to a horse than the grandstand at Uttoxeter race course, or the counter of the betting shop in Clappergate, depending on their degree of commercial success.

But the joint master, Mrs Forbes, looked confident and well in control of her mount as she led the main body of the hunt. A long tail of riders was still making its way across a field from the direction of Foolow, kicking up clods of dirt as they cantered towards the road.

One particularly large horse came a little too close to the Peugeot for comfort. Its rear end swung round and it began to prance sideways, edging nearer to the car until the muscles of its haunches were almost pressed against the window, twitching and glistening in the rain. The sweating hindquarters were level with Fry's face, and she could see quite clearly that it was an ungelded stallion.

Fry closed her eyes, waiting for an impact, the crunch of hooves on metal. But no collision came. When she opened her eyes again, the horses were disappearing beyond the next bend, the clatter of hooves growing quieter.

So the motley bunch of people tagging along in a little group at the back must be the saboteurs. Some of them looked like students, glittering with piercings and tattoos, and one even had a red mohican, which was exactly how she would have pictured them, if asked. But a few of the protestors were middle-aged women, positively respectable looking, wearing walking boots with thick socks rolled over their ankles, and carrying little rucksacks. They reminded her of the Greenham Common women who had impressed her when she was a small child, because they always seemed to be on the TV news.

A couple of the sabs were carrying video cameras, others had mobile phones they were using to take photographs. Maybe they were also keeping in touch with another group somewhere, with a person in charge of co-ordination. Or perhaps they really were just a disorganized rabble letting off a bit of steam.

On the other hand, she could see now that video cameras and mobile phones weren't the only equipment the protestors were carrying.

She saw Inspector Redfearn, and wound her window down.

'Inspector, do you know some of those animal rights people are carrying whips?'

'Yes, it's usual. Its one of their tactics for confusing the hounds.'

'Shouldn't you seize them? Wouldn't you consider them offensive weapons?'

'Ah, but look at the huntsman, and half of the riders. They all have whips or riding crops. We can't seize them from one side and not from the other.'

'So it's all in the cause of impartiality?'

'Yes, Sergeant.'

Fry shook her head. If the two sides had both been armed with baseball bats, knives, or AK-47s, there'd have been no question how the police would react. But nice, middle-class people couldn't have their whips taken off them, could they?

The inspector's radio burst into life, and he listened for a moment.

'Uh-oh. It seems to be kicking off on the other side of that copse.'

'So there is another group of sabs.'

'Sounds like it. This lot are probably just the diversion.'

Fry got out of her car and waited to see what would happen. It was so difficult to tell what was going on. A confusion of shouting, horns blowing, car engines revving, hooves clattering on the tarmac. She smelled a chemical spray on the air, almost as if tear gas had been fired. Four police officers ran down the track from where she'd last seen the hounds. A radio crackled, someone uttered a short, sharp scream.

She walked a few yards further up the track, feeling completely out of her depth.

'Do you need help?' she called.

'It's usually all over and done with in a few minutes,' said the inspector. 'It'll just be a question of who's left with the most bruises.'

Four men in camouflage jackets trotted past her. They were all big men, bulky under their jackets, and one of them was carrying a pickaxe handle. He gave Fry a hard stare as he went by, and she felt sure she'd seen him before, possibly in court, or occupying a cell in the custody suite. If she'd seen those four sitting in a car within fifty yards of a bank, she would have been tempted to call in the response team to arrest them on suspicion of planning an armed robbery. Today, though, they all wore baseball caps that said HUNT STEWARD. The unmistakable scent of violence hung on the air.

'I see the hunt have their own heavies, Inspector,' said Fry.

'The stewards, yes. They were stood down for quite a while, but they seem to have been re-formed for the occasion.'

'Looking for a chance to teach the protestors a lesson, I suppose.'

'We do try to keep an eye on them. But with an event like this, things can be spread over a wide area. The hounds are in one place, the riders another, and the car followers all over the shop. That's why we tend to watch the sabs. The trouble happens where they are, one way or another.'

An officer came up and spoke to the inspector.

'OK, thanks.' He turned back to Fry. 'It seems some hunt supporters blocked the sabs' van in with their vehicles and let the tyres down. That's pretty tame stuff, really.'

'What about all the shouting and screaming?'

'Oh, one of the joint masters got a bit aggravated and chased the sabs down the road.'

'When he was on horseback?'

'That's "she". Two of the Eden Valley joint masters are women. Yes, she was mounted at the time. A horse can be a bit terrifying when it's coming towards you at a canter. That's one reason we use them ourselves, of course.'

A moment later, two young women ran through the trees and on to the road towards the police. One of them had blood streaming down her face and into her hair from a cut above her eye, and the other was holding a hand to her mouth, wincing in pain.

'That doesn't look like tame stuff to me.'

'I'll get an ambulance here.'

'Good luck getting it through, Inspector.'

But the two women were soon telling their story in the back of a police car while they waited for the ambulance.

'It's often the female sabs who get hurt,' said the inspector, when he returned.

'Funny, that.'

'To be honest, I think they're probably the most provocative. Though I suppose I shouldn't say it.'

Fry made her way back to her Peugeot, carefully stepping over heaps of steaming horse muck on the road, and the muddy ruts left by the wheels of the transporters. She was just in time to see a stray foxhound, its tongue lolling, cocking a leg to urinate on her car.

'Oh, wonderful,' said Fry, to no one in particular. 'Another slice of country life.'

Sean Crabbe was surprised to have made it home safely. He was still trembling and sweating by the time he arrived at the house, and he had to pretend that he'd been running. Then he had to make up some excuse to explain why he wasn't at college, which he'd forgotten all about.

If only he could afford to get a place of his own, this would never be a problem. He was twenty years old, for Christ's sake. He ought to be independent, earning his own living, free to come and go when he pleased, without making explanations.

But instead he had to mutter something vague about not feeling well, before disappearing to his room. His mother looked at him suspiciously, but she would probably decide that he must have 'flu coming on or something. What he needed most was to have a shower, and to check whether he had any traces of blood on him.

Sean couldn't believe he'd done something so stupid. Maybe he could blame Coldplay; 'A Rush of Blood to the Head'. Damn right. That was exactly what had happened.

In that moment of anger at the intrusion into his territory, the invasion of his sanctuary among the derelict buildings, he'd acted without thinking things through. Just because no one else ever came up to the huts, because he was so confident that he wouldn't be seen, he'd done something he would never have considered in the ordinary world. He wasn't a criminal, in fact he hated the junkies and yobs and thieves he saw every night in the streets of Edendale. He never wanted to be part of their world. So why had he done it?

Sean stripped off his clothes, holding his parka and jeans up to the light from his bedroom window. No sign of blood. But what about his trainers? Soil and dust trapped in the pattern of his soles, a few small pieces of stone. If the police got hold of them, they would probably be able to piece together exactly where he'd been, the way they did on *CSI*.

He scrubbed the soles of his trainers in the sink, then showered and put his clothes into the wash basket. No telling when Mum might collect them, but there was nothing he could do about that, except hope she did it soon. If he mentioned it to her, she'd know something was wrong.

While he dried himself, he went through the sequence of events again. From the first scent of that sweet smell in the hut, the knowledge that someone else was present, to the panicky call he'd made to the emergency services. And then hurling the phone as far as he could into the first suitable place he came to.

Well, that was stupid. He should have thought more carefully about where he disposed of the phone. The call was

41

probably a mistake, too. But they couldn't trace him from that, could they? It wasn't his phone, after all. He'd tried to wipe it clean before he got rid of it. Fingerprints were one thing he did know about.

It was just that momentary opportunity, the desire that had overtaken him when he'd seen the phone just lying there, and the bulging wallet with all that money in it. All that money. The temptation had been too much. Anyone else would have done the same.

But he hoped the man wasn't really dead. After the incident with the vagrant, he'd assumed that he recognized death. Assumed, too, that he could clear out and watch the action, with no one any the wiser. No one to know that he'd been there.

Sean shuddered as he re-lived the moment the corpse had seemed to come back to life. Like a scene from a horror movie. A bloodied zombie with a hole in the head, but sitting back up and reaching out blindly, gripping his arm with fingers that dug deep into his skin.

That had been what made him run. He'd run from the old huts until his breath was ragged and a stitch jabbed unbearable pains into his side. He seemed to have run for a long, long time through the rain before he stopped. For a few minutes, he'd actually tried to think logically, wondered whether he ought to go back, so he could do the right thing and sort everything out. But he'd looked at his watch and realized how long he'd left it. Far too long for him to look innocent.

Then he'd finally made the call. As quick as he could – no name, no location, no return number.

And Sean had discovered that he was on the moor, in the middle of the dark heather and the capped mine shafts. And he'd known where he could dispose of the phone. He'd climbed the fence and watched it tumble out of sight, heard the smash as it hit the rocks on the bottom. No one would be calling that phone again.

It was a pity, though. It had been a nice new Sony Ericsson with video calling and everything. At least he still had the money.

Sean was feeling calmer now. He dressed in clean clothes, wished that he had a smoke available to steady his hand, then lay down on his bed to wait until he was called. He plugged in his iPod again. Not Coldplay this time, but the Kaiser Chiefs: 'I Predict a Riot'.

And Sean finally allowed himself to dream about what he could do with the money he'd taken. The money that had belonged to the dead man.

6

When Fry finally got back to her body on Longstone Moor, she found her DI, Paul Hitchens, waiting for her. He hadn't even bothered walking all the way to the scene, but was leaning against a car at the rendezvous point.

'Death verified, Diane?' he said.

'The paramedics were here first. The ME has confirmed.'

'Life pronounced extinct, as the old boys used to say.'

'Yes, sir.'

Fry knew that police officers weren't officially trusted to verify death. Not unless death was obvious. Since procedures failed to define 'obviously dead', it generally meant decapitation or an advanced stage of decomposition before any officer could exercise judgement.

'Cause of death?' asked Hitchens.

Fry shook her head. 'There's an obvious head injury. But we'll have to wait for the preliminary PM report.'

'It could have been a fall, though? Wet grass, plenty of stones lying around. Or a slippery cow pat – I've done it myself. What did he have on his feet? Appropriate footwear?'

'No, sir,' admitted Fry.

'And the emergency call – that could have been some passer-by not wanting to get involved. It happens all the time.'

'In the town, maybe. But out here? It's difficult to imagine a passer-by up at those old huts, anyway.'

'The owner of the phone that the call was made on – he's from out of the area, right?'

'Yes. We'll track him down, of course.'

'So have we really got suspicious circumstances here, Diane?'

She hesitated. The expense of calling in a Home Office pathologist was only justified when there was substantial evidence of suspicious circumstances, the proverbial foul play. The DI wouldn't want to get caught out trying to justify the expense in the face of an 'accidental death' verdict by the High Peak coroner.

'This body has no ID. That's a good indication of suspicious circumstances in itself, isn't it?'

'Maybe.'

Fry noted his reluctance. The decision was his at this stage, as the senior officer present. Personally, she had a strong feeling about the body in the field, but she was wary of talking about feelings. The notorious detective's 'hunch' didn't fit well with the pragmatic, evidence-based decision-making processes that came with the training. It sounded so old school.

'All right,' she said. 'So he could have left his wallet and car keys at home, if he went out for a walk. He could have worn his nice new brogues instead of bothering to change into something more appropriate. I can see that's possible. But why wouldn't he have taken a mobile phone?'

'He could have walked out of the house in the middle of a row with his wife. Slammed the front door without picking up his keys or phone, and decided not to go back for them.'

Fry turned away. 'Done that yourself, too, have you?'

'What did you say, Diane?'

'Nothing, sir. I was just saying that it was more likely horse droppings than a cow pat. We've got hoof marks all over the scene.'

'There's your first line on a potential witness, then.'

'Yes, I'm on to it,' said Fry. 'But without more resources

out here, it's going to be totally impossible to interview all the hunt supporters. Anyway, I'm convinced they're just going to close ranks.'

Fry thought of the SIOs' mantra: *What do I know now? What do I need to know? How am I going to find out?* On the other hand, her most important question might be 'How much are they going to *let* me find out?'

'Think of another approach,' said Hitchens.

She sighed. 'We could round up the sabs. There aren't anywhere near as many of them.'

'There you go, then. Anyway, a confirmed ID is your first priority.'

'Naturally.'

The DI studied her for a moment, and waited until a SOCO passed out of earshot.

'Are you all right, Diane?' he said.

'Yes, sir. Fine.'

'Good.'

It was well known that Hitchens had been asking everyone in CID if they were 'all right', ever since the arrival of the new detective superintendent. Probably it was a form of caring for staff morale.

'An ID by tomorrow then,' he said. 'Top priority.'

'It's early days, sir.'

'Of course. Early days.'

Fry watched Hitchens walk back to his car, his job done for now. He could go back to his paperwork at the office until another major operational decision was called for.

But he was right, of course. They couldn't get a serious enquiry under way until there was an ID on the victim. An identification would come one way or another – possibly through a missing-person report, maybe through fingerprints or DNA, if the victim had a criminal record. If not, then a trawl around the available dental records, or more likely a tip-off from a member of the public when the media appeals went out.

That all took time, of course. It could be months, if not years, if they had to rely on appeals and bulletins to other forces around the country. And sometimes with an unidentified body, it was more than months and years – it was never. There were old cases lying on the files where no ID had been achieved after five or ten years, or more. Those were the victims with no family or friends to come forward and claim them, people who appeared to have no available lives to be pieced together.

Fry shook her head. The man in the field surely wasn't one of those. This victim was no homeless vagrant, nor a runaway teenager or illegal immigrant. She was convinced he must be a man with a house somewhere, a job, a car, a bank account. There was probably a wife expecting him home, row or not. Or at least a pet waiting to be fed. Someone would have missed him when he didn't come back last night, colleagues would notice that he wasn't at work today. Even if he was a solitary tourist, his holiday would be due to finish some time. It was unfeasible that he could stay unidentified for long.

Fry's phone rang. It was Hitchens on his way back to Edendale, safely in his car and out of the rain.

'Diane, why haven't you got Ben Cooper at the scene?' he said. 'Is he on a rest day, or processing?'

'Processing,' said Fry. 'He's back at the office.'

And it was only then that she noticed a missed call on her phone.

There was always a wind blowing, up here on the moors. Looking across the valley, Cooper could see acres of pale grass rippling on the plateau, clouded by swirls of rain. It was as if the whole moorland was moving, a vast tide rushing endlessly eastwards in the direction of Nottinghamshire.

Because of the number of police vehicles already present, he had been unable to get his Toyota near the crime scene, even with four-wheel drive. So Cooper had to walk the last few hundred yards on a lane that rose steeply from the village of Birchlow.

At the bottom, there had been plenty of evidence of the Eden Valley Hunt meet, and Matt had been tense with the expectation of encountering people he knew. But the main body of the hunt must have been away in the fields somewhere, following their artificial fox-scented trail.

Cooper stopped for a few moments to catch his breath, trying to orientate himself. Near the top of the lane, the views were spectacular, with several gritstone edges dominating the northern and eastern skylines – White Edge, Froggatt Edge, Curbar and Baslow. But, for the most part, Longstone Moor wasn't one of the wild, barren moors characteristic of the Dark Peak further north. Its expanses were positively civilized, with farms, quarries, fields, and a criss-crossing of tracks formed by generations of people crossing the moor.

Ever since he was a child, Cooper had never stopped being fascinated by the layer upon layer of history that formed the landscape he'd grown up in. Thousands of years of history, visible right there in front of him, wherever he went – Neolithic stone circles and burial chambers, medieval guide stoops way out on the moors, the bumps and hollows of the lead mines, whose abandoned workings dated back to the arrival of the Romans. Cooper felt himself to be a part of that history, completely inseparable from it. Those people who'd built the stone circles, who'd worked in the lead mines, and carved the names on the guide stoops – they'd all been his ancestors.

Ahead of him, Longstone Edge itself was carved by the vast, white scars of opencast mining called rakes. Some were abandoned now, great gashes in the landscape as if a series of earthquakes had split the ground open. But open-cast mining was still active here, on a big scale. Longstone Edge had been the subject of a long-running campaign protesting against the extent of limestone extraction, thirteen million tons of Peak

District hillside trucked away every year for roadworks and building projects.

He could see graded piles of chippings awaiting collection near the new haulage road to Cavendish Mill. Some abandoned workings had filled with water, forming the kind of small lake known locally as a flash, its surface seething with rain.

Putting his head down, Cooper carried on walking. If he remembered rightly, the mere names of the tracks in this area were redolent with history. At one time, Black Harry the high-wayman had terrorized travellers crossing the moors around Longstone and Birchlow. His activities had gone on for years before they were cut short on the gibbet at Wardlow Mires. But his name still lived on in Black Harry Lane, Black Harry Gate, and Black Harry House. His memory was preserved forever on the White Peak sheets of the Ordnance Survey map.

In fact, with so many clues to Black Harry's whereabouts, it was funny that the highwayman had taken so long to catch.

Fry found Wayne Abbott loading some equipment back into his vehicle. Abbott was lucky enough to have been given a 4x4 to drive and had managed to get near the scene without having to hike across the fields.

'Those hoof marks,' said Fry. 'When were they left?'

'Ah, I expect you mean pre- or post-mortem? It's difficult to say.'

'Still – ?'

The crime-scene manager shrugged. 'No, really – it's too difficult to say. Unless we find a hoof mark underneath the body, or some other conflicting trace . . .'

'Let me know soonest if you do.'

'Of course.'

'So we still don't know how he got from dinner at the Le Chien Noir to a field near Birchlow,' said Fry thoughtfully.

'On horseback?' suggested Murfin. 'Since we have all these hoof marks.'

Fry shook her head. 'It seems pretty unlikely to me, but forensics will be able to tell us when they get his clothes in the lab.'

'Well, how else do the horses come into it?'

'I don't know. But there are an awful lot of the hunting fraternity hallooing about down there with their fancy jackets and strangled vowels.'

'Ah. The fox-hunting re-enactment society, I call them.'

'I prefer "the unspeakable in pursuit of the uneatable",' said Fry.

'That's not one of my quotes.'

'No, it's Oscar Wilde.'

Fry hated not knowing more about the victim. Was he a saboteur? Could his killers have been members of the hunt? But he didn't look the type to be an animal rights protestor. No mohican, no sabbing equipment. And none of the genuine sabs had any knowledge of him. Or they weren't willing to admit they had. But why were horses' hoof marks found? There had to be a reason for their presence, and the hunt were the obvious suspects.

She turned at the sound of clumsy footsteps clattering on the rocks. She was met by a startled gaze and a snort of alarm from a black muzzle.

'Those damn sheep.'

Then she looked up at the sky in surprise. Well, at least it had stopped raining at last.

Cooper had reached the outer cordon, where blue-and-white crime-scene tape was strung between two gate posts and across the path. He gave his name to the officer at the cordon as he passed through, and saw Fry and Murfin walking back across the field from the body tent. Fry looked cold and tired, her coat and hair filmed with rain.

'Ben – I didn't think you were serious,' she said when he got nearer.

'Why wouldn't I be?'

'Nobody comes out of a nice dry office on a day like this, if they can possibly help it.'

'But I said I'd come, didn't I? Why would I say that, if I didn't mean it?'

Fry shrugged. 'To impress someone?'

Cooper turned away. Though Fry was wrong about his reason, he didn't want her to probe any further.

'So what's the situation?' he said. 'Have you got an ID? Any initial lines of enquiry?'

'Just a minute,' said Fry. 'Before you get carried away – I don't really need you here. I don't want to be responsible for wrecking the duty roster just because you got bored sitting around on your backside.'

'Actually, I think you *do* need me, Diane.'

'Oh? How do you make that out?'

'You said members of the Eden Valley Hunt were involved?'

'They might be. We haven't established that yet.'

'Horses, though.'

'Yes.'

'And what do you know about horses? What do you know about the hunt, or hunt supporters?'

'I can ask.'

Cooper gazed steadily at her. 'You know perfectly well that I can talk to them better than you, and get more information out of them. You'll just get everyone's backs up.'

'What do you mean by that?'

'You know what I mean.'

'No, do tell me. How do I get everyone's backs up?'

'Well, I bet you have your own fixed views on field sports already. Have you expressed any opinions yet while you've been here? Shall I ask Gavin?'

Fry bit her lip. She always seemed to hate admitting that he was right.

'All right, I'll compromise,' she said finally. 'I'll fill you in

51

with what we have so far, and I'll let you look at the scene. If you can contribute anything useful, you can stay, and I'll square it with the DI.'

'Great.'

'Wait. But if I think you're just bullshitting and you've nothing new to contribute, you're out of here and back to your paperwork, no matter how boring you're finding it.'

Cooper smiled. 'OK, Diane. It's a deal.'

She looked at him, evidently wondering whether he was serious. She had never really understood him, and he didn't suppose it was going to be any different today.

Cooper listened carefully while Fry filled him in.

'These hoof marks,' said Cooper when she'd finished. 'You said something about the hunt?'

'As I told you, the Eden Valley Hunt has been out this morning. There was a police presence for the meet. They were expecting trouble from saboteurs. Got it, too.'

'Yes, I saw the hunt.'

'There were so many dogs. Why do they need so many?'

'Dogs?' said Cooper. 'You mean hounds.'

Fry shook her head. 'I know a dog when I see one.'

Cooper sighed. He'd grown up with a different relationship to the Eden Valley Hunt. Not only did the hunt rely on the goodwill of local farmers, it was one of the great organizers of social events. A dinner dance at Hassop Hall, a hunt ball at the Palace Hotel in Buxton, Buck's fizz and a horn-blowing competition, a charity auction in aid of the air ambulance . . . Not many weeks ago, the hunt had thrown their annual Christmas party for farmers' children. Cooper could recollect being taken to it himself a few times, when he was very small. The parties actually took place just after Christmas – but nevertheless involved a visit by Santa, dropping in at Edendale on his way home to Lapland.

'But apart from the hoof marks, you have no evidence anyone from the hunt was involved?'

'Well – that, and all the people milling around on horse-back a few hundred yards away from the scene. It's pretty persuasive circumstantial evidence.'

'Was it the hounds who found the body?' asked Cooper.

'Apparently, they came down this way, but the dog men were on hand – oh, what do you call them?'

'The huntsman? The whipper-in?'

'Yes, them. They called the hounds away, but didn't realize what the pack had found. They assumed it must be a dead sheep or something. It was the helicopter crew who actually called it in.'

'The hounds are supposed to follow a scent trail. I wonder why they would get distracted by a human smell?'

'I don't know. Perhaps he smelled a bit foxy.'

Cooper could see that Fry was getting exasperated. But the light was fading anyway, and there wasn't much else that could be done here. There was just one thing more.

'If he was killed at around eight thirty, it would have been daylight,' said Cooper. 'I wonder who would have been able to see the scene from the surrounding area.'

Fry gazed around. 'Can't tell in this light. There seems to be a farm way over there, past that barn. Maybe a lorry driver on one of the quarry roads. No one in Birchlow – the village is in a dip from here.'

'You might see the lower part of the track, though.'

'If his killers came that way. The SOCOs will try to establish an approach route in the morning when the light is better. And hopefully, the weather.'

Cooper peered through the dusk. 'What about Eyam? Some of those houses are in a direct line of sight to the crime scene. And there aren't even any trees in the way.'

'It's way across the valley,' said Fry. 'Too far away for anyone to have seen anything, surely?'

The southern side of Longstone Moor was occupied only by a few quiet, self-contained farmsteads sheltering behind their walls of silage bags. But on the north side of the moor, it was quite different. Lorries and giant dumper trucks ran backwards and forwards to the quarries on unmade roads, blowing clouds of white dust behind them, as if their wheels were on fire. The rain had carved channels down some of those roads, forcing lorries up on to eroded bank sides. Cooper could hear the booming of the empty wagons, the scream of reversing alarms on the dumpers. Nobody would be out walking in this area – the dust was too thick, too gritty on the wind.

'It depends,' said Cooper. 'It depends on what there was for anyone to see.'

Seventy-five miles away, in the Great Barr area of Birmingham, Erin Lacey was watching her father pack. The Mercedes already stood in the drive, and his laptop was in its case, ready to go.

'How long will you be away?' she asked.

'I'm not sure, love.'

'Will you phone?'

'Of course.'

Michael Clay looked at his daughter. 'I know how you feel about this, Erin. I realize you don't approve.'

'No. And I'm not going to pretend otherwise.'

Erin tried hard to control her feelings. She knew that getting angry wouldn't do any good. Her father could be very stubborn when he got an idea into his head. For a middle-aged accountant, he was remarkably headstrong about some things. And this idea was the most ludicrous one he'd ever had, as far as Erin was concerned.

As he zipped up his bag, she thought about how much he'd changed, not just since her mother had died a few years ago, but after the death of her uncle Stuart. When pancreatic cancer took his older brother last year, Michael Clay had been hit very hard. It had taken him a long time to get round to sorting out Uncle Stuart's possessions, to sift through the memories. She could understand that, of course.

But after that, everything had seemed to happen very quickly. Her father had developed this obsession with what had happened in the past – the very dim and distant past, so far as Erin was concerned. And then this woman had appeared.

Somehow, it was worse when a man of her father's age started to act foolishly. He'd always had such a good reputation for being careful with money, and now he seemed to have lost his head. Unsuitable business associates, doubtful enterprises, a persuasive woman with an eye for the main chance. And this trip to Derbyshire was the last straw.

'I wish you wouldn't go. Haven't you done more than enough for her? Why do you have to go yourself?'

'I need to see her,' said Michael simply.

'Why?'

'To sort a few things out.'

Her heart sank when he said that. 'What things?'

Michael smiled. 'I'll tell you about it when I get back.'

But Erin didn't feel like smiling. She was starting to get more and more upset as she watched her father put on his coat and pick up his car keys. He must have seen it in her face, and felt guilty.

'If you don't want to keep an eye on the house for me, love, I'll understand. I'll ask Mrs Fletcher next door.'

'No, it's all right. But, Dad . . . look after yourself, please.'

'Of course I will.'

Erin kissed him as he went to the door. Her father was trying to sound bright and breezy, as if he was just popping down to the shop for a bottle of milk. But she knew it was much more than that.

Michael Clay got into his Mercedes and waved as he turned on the drive. As she watched him go, Erin Lacey felt a tear in the corner of her eye, as if she was saying goodbye to her father for ever.

7

By the end of the day, the body had been released for collection by the mortuary. Fry watched the anonymous black van crawl away from Longstone Moor in the fading light.

Now there was nothing more she could do at the scene. Inspector Redfearn's men had rounded up as many of the anti-hunt protestors as they could and taken names and addresses, along with statements from any who had been in the area at eight thirty that morning. They had also seized video footage from several cameras, so that might help. The sabs seemed to have filmed anything that moved.

Fry felt uncomfortable about dealing with the protestors in a different way from the hunt supporters. But she supposed the hunt was organized in a more formal way, and there would be no trouble obtaining the identities of any individuals she might want to talk to.

The huntsman, John Widdowson, had finally appeared, looking very tired, and as damp as she felt herself. For a few seconds, Fry had found herself surrounded by the pack, dozens of panting brown-and-white dogs crowding around her legs, pink tongues lolling, the white tips of their tails flicking. Some of them had black patches around their eyes, like burglars' masks, which gave them a peculiarly manic look. They sniffed at her knees and shook water from their coats.

Widdowson's story was that the hound van had arrived outside Birchlow shortly after eight thirty. Although there had been a few horse boxes already at the scene, he had noticed no riders heading off on their own. It wouldn't have been the custom, he said.

'It's a pity the air support unit weren't on station a bit earlier,' said Fry, as she left Inspector Redfearn. 'They could have filmed the whole incident for us.'

'They had a priority call,' said Redfearn. 'A pursuit on the A61.'

'I know. It would just have been nice to get a bit of luck for once.'

Gavin Murfin called Fry before she could reach her car.

'You're on duty late, Gavin,' she said. 'What's up?'

'Thought you'd like to know straight away, boss. We've found a car. A Mitsubishi, 08 reg.'

'Where is it?'

'Way off the road, parked up by the old field barn on the edge of Longstone Moor. In fact, I think you might actually be able to see the barn from the crime scene.'

Fry called up a picture of the scene in her mind. 'It's about a mile away, I guess.'

'That would be about right.'

'So I presume we've done a check on the number. Who's the registered owner?'

'A Mr Patrick Rawson, from Sutton Coldfield, West Midlands.'

'The same man who made the 999 call.'

'Well, the call was made on his phone, anyway.'

'Yes, you're right, Gavin. And . . .?'

'Local police have just called at his address. His wife told them he drove up to Derbyshire yesterday, on business. But she hasn't had a call from him since. And, Diane . . .'

'Yes?'

'Mr Rawson's age and general description match the victim.'

'I thought we might be coming to that conclusion. Whoever was at the huts with Mr Rawson took his phone and wallet, and then made the 999 call.'

'A plain and simple robbery, then,' said Murfin. 'Mugger panicked when he realized he'd hit the victim too hard.'

'Funny place for a mugging,' said Fry. 'Funny place to be doing anything, really.'

'Well, if our suspect uses Mr Rawson's phone again, we can trace him.'

'He'll have ditched it by now, Gavin. More likely he'll try to use the plastic in Mr Rawson's wallet.'

'I'll get on to that.'

'Thanks, Gavin. Scenes of Crime on the car?'

'Soon as they can get there. Wayne says they're going to be a bit stretched, what with the field, the hut *and* the car.'

'I know.'

Fry drove back to the West Street headquarters in her Peugeot, conscious of the water dripping from her clothes on to the seats and soaking into the mats in the floor well. She had the heater going full blast, but all the windows had steamed up immediately she got in, and she had to open the driver's side a crack to clear the condensation. The result was that the lorries passing her on the A623 blew spray on to her face before she was even dry.

In the CID room, everyone had packed up and gone home. On a white-board, someone had scrawled their own bitter slogan:

Sergeant Wilson's Law: lack of resources + shortage of staff = shit hitting the fan.

The paperwork waiting on her desk included a copy of the G28 sudden-death report form, completed by the first officers attending the incident this morning. By the simple act of filling in the paperwork, uniforms would feel they'd effectively passed on a problem to CID.

Fry sighed. It was one of the aspects of CID work that constantly baffled and frustrated her, this requirement for developing a love of paperwork and file preparation, a mania for detail that could border on Obsessive Compulsive Disorder.

True, there were a few moments of excitement, but they were usually in the court room, sitting behind a barrister when a jury brought in a guilty verdict that you'd been working towards for months. There were moments when you had to drop everything and rush off to a critical incident, but those were pretty rare. There were other occasions when you had to deal with families going through the trauma of losing a loved one.

The rest of the job consisted of making lists of exhibits, preparing Narey files, sitting in CPS case conferences, sweating over duty rosters. She spent most of her time worrying about interviews, memos, file upgrades and threshold tests. Being a detective no longer seemed to have any kudos.

Recently, a new Assistant Chief Constable had joined the force from West Midlands Police. He'd even been commander for the Aston and Central Birmingham operational command units, where Fry had once been based. He was now Derbyshire's ACC Operations, responsible not only for territorial divisions, but also for level two cross-border crime, crime support, armed-response vehicles, the task force and dog section.

Fry might have expected to be noticed under the new ACC. But her immediate problem was here in Edendale, in the form of Detective Superintendent Hazel Branagh. Since she'd arrived in E Division, she seemed to have been casting some kind of dark spell, like a female Lord Voldemort.

This morning, Gavin Murfin had referred to Branagh's 'empire building'. Fry was beginning to suspect that she might have no place in Branagh's empire.

She found DI Hitchens still in his office. Hitchens had recently taken to wearing black shirts and purple ties, like a jazz musician. Fry suspected he was letting his hair grow a bit longer, too. Tonight, he looked as though he ought to be sitting in the corner of a badly lit nightclub, nursing a double whisky and a clarinet case.

'Tell me we're on top of this case, Diane,' he said.

'This is no one-day event. Not like turning up at a domestic, lifting the boyfriend and getting an instant confession.'

'Yes, those can get a bit boring,' he agreed. 'Mind you, there's likely to be a mountain of paperwork.'

'True. Well, we think we've got an ID, at least.'

'That's like having one ball in the National Lottery. What about the other five?'

'Five?'

'Cause of death, time of death, motive, means . . .'

'. . . and a suspect?'

'No, no. That's the bonus ball.' Hitchens stroked his tie impatiently. 'There's another one, but I just can't think of it.'

'Where did you get this lottery stuff from, sir?'

'Management training,' he sighed smugly. 'It's a focus aid.'

'A what?'

'A simple concept that helps focus your mind on the essential elements of a task. You break down each task into components and identify them by a mnemonic or a visual tag. It's so that none of the elements gets forgotten or overlooked.'

Fry sighed. 'Time of death is estimated at between nine and nine thirty this morning. We won't get a confirmed cause of death until after the postmortem, of course, but it looked like blunt-force trauma to me. There were certainly serious head injuries.'

'Good. But if you're considering suspicious circumstances, do you have any suggestion of a motive?'

'Not until we've gone into the victim's background thoroughly. We don't know yet what he was doing in Derbyshire, even. That should give us a line of enquiry.'

'An arranged meeting?'

60

'That's what I'm hoping,' said Fry. 'The old agricultural research station is too unusual a place for a random encounter with a mugger. I'll update you tomorrow.'

'Yes, keep me in the loop.'

'More management speak?'

Hitchens looked up. 'Sorry?'

'Nothing, sir.'

Fry made her way to the door, under the impression that her DI had drifted away into some strange seminar-like world of his own, all whiteboards and overhead projectors, with a spicing of motivational role-play.

'Witnesses,' said Hitchens suddenly.

'What?'

'The sixth lottery ball. Motive, means . . . and witnesses. That's what you need, some potential witnesses.'

'I've got a whole posse of them,' said Fry. 'But without enough bodies available, it's impossible to question them all. By now, they could have got their stories straight, anyway.'

Fry turned the Peugeot off Castleton Road into Grosvenor Avenue and pulled up at the kerb outside number 12, a once prosperous, detached Victorian villa nestling behind mock porticos. Her flat was on the first floor – a bedroom, sitting room, bathroom with shower cubicle, and a tiny kitchen area. Strangely, the first floor was regarded as the high-status part of the house, poised between the noisier ground-floor flats and the tiny bedsits in the old servants' quarters on the top floor.

Directly beneath her was a flat full of students. She wasn't quite sure how many of them shared together – three, perhaps four. The number probably changed from week to week, for all she knew.

When she'd first moved into number 12 Grosvenor Avenue, all the other occupants had been students, most of them studying at High Peak College on the west side of town. But in the past year or two, there had been a gradual population shift, with the students packing their rucksacks and heading for smart new accommodation in the halls of residence that had opened on the college campus. Their replacements seemed to be migrant workers of various nationalities. Many of them were as young as the students, but they were out all day, and often all night, working in hotels and restaurants around Edendale.

Fry took off her jacket and shoes and collapsed on her bed. She must have a shower, or she might never feel human again.

Cooper arrived at Welbeck Street gasping for a coffee. He felt as though he hadn't taken a dose of caffeine all day; the briefing before the raid on the cannabis factory seemed so long ago now.

He knew he drank too much coffee when he was at home on his own. He never used to do that – it was a habit he'd developed when he moved out of Bridge End Farm into Welbeck Street. It had begun only gradually, just as something to occupy his attention for a few minutes, spooning the granules from a jar of Nescafé, fetching the milk, filling up the kettle. The routine seemed to take just enough time for the feeling of loneliness to pass. He was deflecting an undesirable emotion with a series of routine actions, switching the brain to a safe little rut.

Cooper went out into the conservatory to see where Randy had got to. The cats at Welbeck Street had been his landlady's pets originally – or, at least, they'd been strays that Dorothy Shelley had taken under her wing and fed whenever they decided to turn up. He'd inherited one of them with the flat – a furry black object who still came and went whenever he felt like it. He didn't know how old Randy was, but it was obvious that he was approaching his later years. He was very stiff when he moved, which wasn't often, and he continued to lose weight, no matter how much he ate. Finally, Cooper noticed one day that the cat was becoming incontinent. Despite his nomadic habits, he had always been a very clean animal, and his condition clearly bothered him.

'Sorry, old chap,' he said. 'It looks like another trip to the vet.'

Mrs Shelley hadn't been well recently, either. It seemed unkind, but Cooper had begun to wonder who would inherit the two adjoining houses in Welbeck Street if and when she should die. She never talked about any children, and rarely had visits from family members, except once a nephew and his wife. The nephew had looked a bit shifty to Cooper, had given the properties too much of a proprietary examination from the street before he went in. But he was probably worrying unnecessarily, and far too early. Despite the casualness of the agreement when he'd moved in, he must have some security of tenancy.

Besides, Dorothy Shelley was the sort of woman who would go on forever – never too strong and always a bit vague, but tottering around long after younger people had given up the ghost. He hoped that was the case. He'd got quite fond of her, in a way. Apart from the question mark it might put over his own future, he'd be sorry to lose her. And he certainly didn't want to see her being taken advantage of by some greedy nephew who didn't care one jot about her.

But then, knowing Mrs Shelley, the problem would never arise. She had probably made a will leaving her entire estate to Cats Protection anyway.

In her sitting room, Mrs Shelley had a stuffed barn owl, so old and fossilized that Cooper could have used its beak as a bottle opener. He'd come to think of his landlady as a bit like that stuffed owl. Rather bedraggled and slightly moth-eaten around the pinions, but likely to last for ever, so long as it was valued.

Cooper looked around the conservatory. At the far end, there were so many cobwebs that the spiders would soon be complaining about overcrowding. He needed to make time for a spring clean. He needed to find time for Liz, too, or she'd be complaining he neglected her. He was supposed to have made time for a holiday.

But time was always a problem. For him, and for Randy, there was never enough of it.

Strange how complications seemed to mount up in your life as you got older. In his twenties, everything had seemed very simple. Now, within a few years, he felt as though the world was on his shoulders some days. Was it the creeping infection of responsibility? He had a steady relationship now. He'd been going out with Liz Petty, a civilian crime-scene examiner at E Division, for several months. He ought to be getting to know her fairly well by this time.

And then there was that old, vexed question of promotion. It had come up in conversation with Liz the other night. Over a glass of white wine and a Bondi Chicken in the Australian Bar at Bakewell, she'd gently quizzed him about his future. Cooper never found it difficult to listen to Liz. She didn't take herself too seriously, and might burst out laughing at him at any moment. He treasured those moments, as a rule. But that evening, she'd been more serious.

And she had been right, he supposed. It was now or never, if he was ever going to go for promotion. Even if it meant some kind of horizontal development, a move to a different speciality – whatever it took to get noticed. You couldn't stand still, or you moved backwards in this world. If he was going to settle down one day and have a family . . . Well that, after all, was what he would do, wasn't it? If he was going to settle down, he couldn't spend his life on a DC's salary, growing cynical and grumpy, like Gavin Murfin. Putting on weight in all the wrong places, too, probably. Oh, damn.

His mother had always talked so much about her grand-children – not only those who already existed, but those that were in the future, yet unborn. They had been the most important thing in her mind in those final years, even when the illness had taken most of her memories. Matt had done that for her, the older brother fulfilling the hopes and dreams. But Ben knew he had failed her. Maybe there was still time to make up for it, though. Still time to tell her that he had settled down, got the promotion, produced those grandchildren she'd talked about. He felt sure she would know, even now, wherever she was. If it mattered enough, you could make it happen.

8

Fry woke with a fuzzy head, and looked around her in confusion. She'd only lain down on her bed for a few minutes to rest, but she must have dropped off to sleep almost straight away. It had been a busy day, but not that bad. There had been many days when she'd put in much longer hours, when the time to go home never seemed to arrive. There could be a few of those days to come, depending on the course of this new enquiry. But not today. Today had been . . . well, average. There was no reason she should feel so tired and groggy, unless she was coming down with something. And that was the last thing she needed.

She sniffed. The smell of soy sauce was drifting up from the flat downstairs. It was one of those smells that seemed to be able to penetrate floors and carpets with surprising ease, as if its spicy aroma could wind its way through the cracks of the floorboards like wisps of smoke.

One day, it had dawned on her that she had plenty of money in her savings account. A police sergeant's salary was perfectly adequate, and there were hardly any major expenses in her life, except for her car and the rent on this flat. Not exactly a lavish lifestyle, was it? Fat chance of that. She ought to be able to think of something she could do with her savings.

Fry made her way into the kitchen and looked at the washing up. There wasn't much of it, not now that she was on her own again, her sister Angie having headed back to Birmingham and whatever sort of lifestyle she led there. So those few plates and pans shouldn't look quite so daunting, sitting there in the sink in that squalid, disapproving way.

What to do with a few thousand pounds? She supposed she could put a deposit down on a house and take out a mortgage. It was the sort of thing that everyone else seemed to do. They'd all tied themselves up in property and debts by the time they got to her age.

Fry hissed between her teeth. A mortgage? She'd rather be chained in purgatory, with eagles pecking at her liver.

She showered, changed her clothes, then pulled on her coat and went out for a walk to wake herself up. The clouds had cleared now, and a crescent moon was shining on the wet street. Music played behind curtained windows as she passed. Tunes that were vaguely familiar, but she couldn't quite hear enough of to name.

She felt like the only person out in the streets tonight. The rest of Edendale was shut up behind its doors and windows, people enclosed in their own little worlds. Sometimes she wished she had a world of her own that she could enter that way, instead of always standing out in the cold, feeling so small and vulnerable under a vast, moonlit sky. At times like this, she craved the crowded intimacy of the city.

After a few months, Fry had finally brought herself to make an effort at getting acquainted with the students. So what if they had nothing in common? She wasn't going to spend the rest of her life with them. But then they had all left. They'd moved away to live in student halls, or had finished their courses and got on with their lives. It was strange how everyone she moved towards always seemed to move away from her. It was as if she was caught up in some old-fashioned dance where no one was supposed to get too close, everyone spinning constantly round the ballroom floor, touching briefly before whirling away to a distant corner where she never saw them again.

She thought of Ben Cooper. The one person, perhaps, who had never entirely drawn away. She wasn't sure whether that was a good thing, or not. It had been so typical of him to turn up at the crime scene on Longstone Moor today. She remembered the moment she'd spotted Cooper approaching the outer cordon – an unmistakable figure striding effortlessly up the slope towards her, shrugging off the wind and rain as if he was a natural part of the landscape, a creature totally at home in its own environment. He always looked vaguely windswept, even in the office, with that infuriating lock of hair that fell across his forehead. Yet he also radiated a kind of intensity that Fry rarely saw in anyone, let alone the police officers and other professionals she worked with day in and day out, people trained to say exactly the right thing in all circumstances. You could rely on Ben Cooper not to do that, at least.

Fry sighed. Of course, Cooper had been right about her antipathy to hunting. She didn't think it was just some kind of class thing, though. At least, she hoped it wasn't. Though hunting was often associated with class privilege and social hierarchy, there had always been a lurking violence at the heart of the sport that turned it into a kind of blood ritual.

When she was a studying at UCE, there had been fellow students who had been deeply involved in animal rights protests, including the campaign against fox hunting. Some of them were the sort of people whose instinct was to be anti everything, but the propaganda had been pervasive, the leaflets handed out, the posters of mutilated animals pinned to the notice boards in the Students' Union.

To Fry, it had been obvious that the demand for a ban on fox hunting in Britain had as much to do with class politics as a love of animals. As any eighteenth-century farm labourer transported for killing a hare could have told you, the hunt was always about the relative status of human beings.

The impression most people had of fox hunting came from its depiction in art. There, hunting had always been portrayed as the preserve of the few, a jealously guarded conspiracy.

There was a painting Fry had seen in the National Gallery once, on a visit to London. A portrait of Lord Somebody or Other, Master of the Hounds. He had been painted dressed in a black hunting outfit, his dark shadow accompanying him in the background, like the spectre of death. His boots had been polished to a high gloss, and he gripped the silver handle of a riding crop as though he was just about to thrash a servant rather than his horse. To the observer, his expression suggested that he was regarding an incompetent groom who'd just dropped a brush.

When Fry had studied the label, she realized that his lord-ship must have been perfectly happy to appear arrogant and potentially violent, since he had given the portrait to the National Gallery himself. Hunting art had always been frank about the cruelty of the sport. These days, everything was about presentation and image. Would there have been the same demand for a ban if hunting had a better image in art?

Yet every stately home and every country pub still had hunting prints rotting from their frames. That bloody symbolism survived.

Cooper stepped outside into the back yard at Welbeck Street, and turned his face up to the rain, wiping a spatter of water from his face. On Sunday, it had been raining at the National Memorial Arboretum, too. Trickles of water had formed on the memorial at the end of The Beat, streaking the surface of the stone. They looked so much like tears that even Matt Cooper had been silenced by the symbolism. Ben had pulled up his collar, hunched his shoulders inside his coat, and regretted ever agreeing to come.

'They've done it nicely, though,' Matt had said. 'Good job.'

'Yes, nice.'

Claire gave Ben an odd look then. What was that look supposed to mean? Ben could never really understand what his sister was thinking, the way he could with Matt. Did she share his own reaction? Did their brother's hearty matter-of-factness have the same effect on her – that sinking feeling of grief and loss that was rammed home by the simple act of watching someone read an inscription on a plaque?

Yes, they'd done it nicely. Written their father's final epitaph in a few strokes of engraving. *Sergeant Joseph Cooper, Derbyshire Constabulary, killed on duty.* Recorded for ever. Permanently set in stone.

'There are so many,' said Claire. 'You don't realize, do you?'

Ben had gazed around the site at all the memorials to hundreds of thousands of service personnel who'd died for their country. Surely one police sergeant who had been kicked to death by drunken yobs on the streets of Edendale was a unique individual, even among so many deaths?

A few months ago, Ben had been asked to join an organization called COPS, one of those convenient acronyms that police services across the country were so fond of. Its initials stood for Care of Police Survivors. Last July, he'd attended their annual service of remembrance, complete with a fly-past by a police helicopter and a cavalcade of motorcycles ridden by the Blue Angels.

He'd come away from that service with mixed feelings. Some parts of it had been moving, like the sight of so many other relatives of dead police officers. But he wasn't so sure about the idea of turning the occasion into a spectacle, as if it was the Edinburgh Tattoo. People grieved in different ways, he supposed. Some preferred to remember their loved ones in a public way, rather than confine their feelings to private grief. Yes, emotions were sometimes easier to deal with in public, when people felt the necessity to behave properly, and not to be an embarrassment.

At the time of the remembrance service, The Beat had been under water and impossible to reach. Hundreds of trees in the arboretum had to be replaced because of the effects of repeated flooding. Not just in winter, either. Last summer, a temporary lake had formed, drowning The Beat. Fifteen inches of water had surged across the site, washing away stakes and flattening trees.

Ben had promised himself that he'd come back one day, and Matt and Claire had jumped on the idea with enthusiasm, much to his surprise. He shouldn't think that they didn't grieve too, just because they didn't always show it. For heaven's sake, *he* didn't show it too much either, did he?

'Perhaps we should go back to the visitor centre,' Claire had said. 'The rain is getting a bit heavy.'

'In a minute,' said Matt. 'Give me a minute.'

Something in the tone of his voice had sounded wrong. Matt's back was to them, and he hardly seemed aware of the rain falling on his shoulders.

Ben turned and walked a few yards away towards the RAF memorial. Alongside it, he saw a smaller grove – two rows of hawthorns supported by wooden posts. They looked to be young trees, seven or eight years old, maybe. They were probably intended to form an arch eventually. Each tree carried a label bearing a curious logo, with a name and number. He saw 7 Group Bedford, and 8 Group Coventry next to it. Before he could look more closely, Matt called to him from the other side of The Beat.

'It's funny,' he said, 'but in Dad's day, we all believed the police were on our side. They kept us safe, protected us from criminals, all that stuff. We respected them for it. Everyone I know would have done their best to help the bobbies because of that. But now it's changed. And I don't know where it went wrong.' He looked up at his brother. 'Maybe you know, Ben.'

Ben blinked. Where the heck had that suddenly come from? What switch had turned on the flow of his brother's resentment so abruptly?

He looked at Claire, but of course she'd been nodding as Matt spoke.

'Well, I know exactly what you mean,' she said. 'It's because the police seem to spend most of their time persecuting law-abiding people for petty infringements of the rules instead of going after the real criminals. They're pursuing government targets and political correctness instead of chasing the bad guys.'

'They do it because it's easier, and it gets their detection rates up,' said Matt. 'A motorist who goes a few miles an hour over the speed limit is a nice soft target. Not to mention all those cases where people tackle yobs causing trouble. If they don't get beaten up by the yobs –'

'Or killed,' said Claire.

'Yes, or killed,' agreed Matt, 'then they get arrested themselves. And yet at the same time you hear stories of police officers standing around doing risk assessments while someone is dying. It's ludicrous. I can tell you, Dad would never have done that. He would never have hung back if he thought he might save someone's life.'

'No.' Claire was quiet for a moment. 'I suppose you hear this all the time, Ben.'

'Pretty much.'

When it had come time to leave the arboretum, Claire insisted on taking a photograph of her two brothers on her digital camera. She posed them near the rain-streaked windows to get the best light, gesturing them to get closer together until their shoulders were touching. Ben tried to smile, but could sense that his brother was as stiff as he was. Not the best family portrait, probably. But Claire didn't seem to notice, flashing off a few shots before pulling up her hood and leading them out into the rain.

'All right,' Matt said. 'I suppose it's just today, visiting this place. Thinking about Dad. About how much things have changed in those few years. He would never have been able to live with it.'

'I know,' said Ben. 'I *know*.'

Ben found he could listen to their comments without even being tempted to argue. There was nothing in them that he hadn't heard before. Yes, it was hurtful that his own family should have these views, but he wasn't surprised by them. Matt read the *Daily Mail* and the *Daily Telegraph*, after all. Stories like these were commonplace. There was some new incident in the media every week. A view of the police as the enemy was spreading rapidly among ordinary members of the public. Like a disease, it passed from one person to another by word of mouth.

And this wasn't the way it had been meant to be. Not in this country, anyway. In Britain, there was supposed to be policing by consent, a partnership between the police and the public. It was never imagined that police officers would be attacked on the street by members of the public just because they happened to be there.

Though it upset him to hear what was said, it was difficult for Ben to summon the enthusiasm to put up any defence. He heard much the same concerns at work day after day, from the people caught in the middle of the trap.

And the worst thing of all was that Matt had been right. Sergeant Joe Cooper would never have stood by while someone was dying. He would have torn up the risk assessment forms and thrown them in the face of anyone who tried to stop him.

In the back yard of his flat in Welbeck Street, Ben Cooper let the rain run down his face freely, no longer caring whether he wiped it away or not.

9

Journal of 1968

I can't remember who first started to call it 'the pit'. Jimmy, probably. But my memories of him are so twisted now, so bent with emotion and blackened with anger, that I don't know what I'm remembering and what I've put in from my own imagination. In my mind, Jimmy is a tiny figure, his pale face turned up to the sky, glasses catching the light, flashing like a signal, until a huge shadow falls across and obliterates him.

Les was a lot older than us, and such a big man. No, big isn't the right word. He was fat, all right? He had double chins like a concertina, and rolls that spilled over the waist-band of his trousers.

Well, I realize none of us exactly resembled Errol Flynn in those uniforms, but Les always seemed as though he'd burst out of his battledress tunic at any moment, as if he'd send those little silver buttons popping all over the place. In winter, when he wore his greatcoat, the belt would slip up over the top of his stomach and pin itself across his chest, until he looked like a badly wrapped parcel. It was a miracle he ever fit in the shaft.

We used to joke about it, Jimmy and me. We said that one

day Les's backside would get stuck in the hatch like a cork in a bottle. And that would be us well and truly trapped for the duration. Never mind what was going on outside, on the inside it would be hell.

Oh, and he had these little piggy eyes, too, I remember. If you did anything wrong, Les would stare at you for ages without saying anything. But you knew he was making a note of it, in case he could use it against you some time. He was like that, Les. He talked all the time about us being a team, but he'd stick a knife in your back at the first opportunity.

Jimmy was totally the opposite to look at. Such a scrawny lad; no kind of uniform was ever going to make him look good. He didn't have the shoulders for it, if you know what I mean. His hair was best described as sandy, and he was growing it long at the sides, so it stuck out from under the elastic brim of his beret in ragged little clumps, which drove Les mad. It was the fashion of the time, of course. Jimmy was even trying for a little moustache, but it was patchy and so pale that you could hardly make it out in a bad light. He wore these wire-framed glasses that were probably supposed to make him look like John Lennon, but didn't. He looked too studious, a proper skinny weed.

But he *was* clever, Jimmy. Really clever. He understood the technical stuff better than any of us. Better than Les, for all his air of superiority.

These days, I suppose people would have called Jimmy a geek. But I liked him, truly liked him. Jimmy was my best friend, you see. He was almost a brother.

And he was also the first one to die.

10

Wednesday

Next morning, when she walked out of her flat to the parking area behind the house, it struck Fry what she could spend some of her money on. Her old black Peugeot could be replaced.

It was obvious, really. The annual MoT and service was starting to get a bit expensive, even though she suspected the garage on Castleton Road gave her a surreptitious discount. Last time, there had been some parts to replace on the suspension system, and French parts weren't cheap.

The Peugeot had served her well for several years now, and it didn't show up the dirt too much when she forgot to wash it for weeks on end. But in the bright sunlight of this clear March morning, Fry could see that it was beginning to look a little scuffed around the edges. Its paintwork carried a few too many scratches from squeezing into odd places, like the field gateway near Birchlow yesterday. Each scratch was minor in itself, but the cumulative effect was of an old tomcat with unhealed claw marks from too many late-night punch-ups.

But, if she was going to trade it in, what would she replace it with? She hadn't the faintest idea.

And she didn't have any more time to think about it this

morning. As she battled through roadworks still puddled with rain, and the cars and buses packed with school children that constituted morning rush-hour in Edendale, she started to prepare herself for the briefing that would start the day.

'OK, our victim appears to be Patrick Thomas Rawson, date of birth twelfth of April 1964. Born in Digbeth, Birmingham, with a current address in Sutton Coldfield, West Midlands. His wife says Mr Rawson is a company director, type of business as yet unspecified.'

Copies of a photo were passed around the CID room, and DI Hitchens placed one on the board next to a shot taken by the Scenes of Crime photographer the day before, and an enlarged map of the scene at Longstone Moor.

'The description fits for height, age, and so forth. West Midlands Police have scanned this photo and emailed it to us. You've got to admire their efficiency.'

The new photo showed a smiling man in his mid-forties, dark-haired and dark-eyed, almost Italian-looking. Then Fry mentally corrected herself. No, not Italian. He was probably of Irish ancestry, one of those dark Celtic types from the west coast. She could practically see the charm oozing from his smile, and hear the lilting brogue. But that couldn't be right, either. Patrick Rawson had been born in the Irish quarter of Birmingham, his Celtic roots overlaid by Brummie. In reality, his accent had probably been not unlike her own.

'It looks pretty conclusive to me,' said Fry, remembering clearly the dead man lying under the body tent in a spreading pool of blood. It was difficult to be sure, but he might even have been wearing the same coat in the photograph sent from West Midlands.

Hitchens nodded. 'Yes, I agree. But the wife will confirm identity. Local police have visited Mrs Rawson, and she's coming up to Edendale today to do the identification.'

'Who's bringing her?'

'A brother, I think they said.'

'So what was a forty-five-year-old company director doing in a field outside Birchlow?' asked someone.

'His wife told the West Midlands bobbies she has no idea. Hopefully, we should be able to get more out of her when she arrives.'

Fry and Hitchens looked at each other. If the death of Patrick Rawson did turn out to be murder, then nine times out of ten the spouse or partner was the obvious suspect. A lot would depend on Mrs Rawson's demeanour, the consistency of her story, and whether she had a compelling motive.

'Over to you then, DS Fry,' said Hitchens cheerfully. 'You were senior officer at the scene most of yesterday. Let's have your assessment.'

Fry stepped up and took centre stage. The faces watching her expectantly were only her CID team, plus a few uniforms they'd been allocated. It wasn't exactly a major spotlight, but it would do for now.

She drew their attention to the map. 'Right now, we're working on the theory that the victim drove up towards Longstone Moor early on Tuesday morning and parked his car, a black Mitsubishi 4x4, close to this field barn, here. It seems likely that he went there to meet with someone. Who that was, we don't yet know. You can probably come up with some ideas.'

'A woman?' suggested DC Irvine.

Well, there was a chip off the old block. But DC Hurst, sitting next to him, raised her hand. 'The person who made the 999 call was male,' she said.

'Yes, Becky. It was a young male voice, local accent. We can hear the recording in a minute.'

Luke Irvine and Becky Hurst were the two youngest DCs, who had been in the department a matter of months. Beat and response officers for a few years, then rushed into CID. That was an indication of the shortage of experienced staff.

78

Fry was conscious of an entire generation coming into the police service behind her, with quite a different attitude to the older officers like Gavin Murfin. All of that new generation were born between 1979 and 1991. They were Thatcher's children.

Despite that, she'd noticed a few signs that Irvine and Hurst were tending to look to the wrong people for role models. Ben Cooper, for a start. Murfin, even.

'The victim made his way from his car to this derelict hut at the agricultural research centre, about two hundred yards away. He sustained a head injury at some point here, because blood was found inside the hut. His mobile phone and wallet were also taken. It seems likely that the person who made the 999 call on the victim's phone was also at the huts, since he told the control room operator that's where the body was to be found. But, in fact, the victim was still alive. Despite his injuries, he managed to get across these fields before he collapsed and died.'

'I wonder why he didn't just head back to his car,' said Hurst. 'That would be the logical thing to do.'

Fry looked at Hurst. 'Yes, but if you see the severity of the head injury, you can imagine that he wouldn't have been thinking logically. In fact, he was probably dazed and disorientated. He would have been suffering from concussion as well as blood loss, I guess. Hopefully, the pathologist will give us a clearer picture after the postmortem.'

Fry saw Superintendent Branagh settling into a chair at the back of the room, trying unsuccessfully not to be noticed.

'SOCOs have been assigned to the car,' said Fry. 'We'll bring it in when they've processed the scene where it was parked.'

'A barn, was it?'

'A field barn. The track to the location is still usable, but the Mitsubishi was parked out of sight of any walkers. We'll be trying to trace Mr Rawson's route from the car to the scene where he met his death, and of course establishing his movements prior to arriving at the barn in the first place.'

'We have two scenes to cover, then.'

'Three, including the hut. And two of them are totally open to the elements. Just our luck to get the sort of weather we had yesterday morning. We also have separate lines of enquiry on this mysterious 999 caller, and on the hoofprints found all over the scene. Some potential witnesses there, I hope.'

'Appeals?'

'Yes, we need to get public appeals out as soon as possible, to encourage these people to come forward with information. Particularly the man who made the call.'

They listened to the recording of the call logged by the control room. It was very brief, just a description of the location in an unsteady voice, as if the caller had been running. An insistence on *'There's a body,'* said twice. Repeated requests from the operator for the caller's name were simply ignored. Listening to the recording for the second time, Fry thought the man might actually still have been running when he dialled the emergency number.

'We won't have the initial postmortem report on cause of death for a while yet,' said Hitchens, sensing the end of the briefing approaching. 'But, given the severity of the head injury, this could be classified as a murder enquiry at any time. So follow procedures, no slip-ups at this early stage, please.'

'The killer seems to have taken his wallet and mobile phone,' said Irvine. 'Could this have been a robbery gone wrong?'

Fry shook her head. 'I can't see it. No, it's more likely they did it to conceal the victim's identity for as long as possible. We were lucky to find the car so soon and get his identity. Our only other lead is this –' She held up the evidence bag. 'A restaurant receipt in the victim's pocket. Le Chien Noir, in Clappergate. If Mr Rawson used a credit card to pay for his meal, it should provide additional confirmation of his identity, even without the assistance of the wife.'

'Diane, are you going to follow that up yourself?' asked Hitchens.

'As soon as we've finished here, sir.'

The DI smiled. 'By the way, I hear you had a bit of trouble at the hunt yesterday?'

'It was nothing. One of those situations where everyone claims to be an injured party.'

Superintendent Branagh waited while the meeting broke up. She was wearing a dress this morning. It was dark blue, with a pattern of enormous white flowers, and it was cut so badly that it made her shoulders look even broader than usual. Watching her stand up and come towards them made Fry think of a window ledge that the plant pots had fallen off.

'I wonder what her vital statistics are,' whispered Murfin. 'She'd look good in the front row of the scrum.'

'Women don't have vital statistics any more, Gavin.'

'Ah. Political correctness. Maybe I should get myself sent back in for re-education again. I obviously need my ten thousand mile service.'

As everyone went back to work, Fry noticed that Ben Cooper had sneaked into the back of the room, too. He looked as if he wasn't sure how welcome he would be, or whether his presence could be regarded as official, even.

It turned out that Branagh had noticed Cooper, too. She turned to Hitchens and Fry.

'DC Cooper is supposed to be on leave, isn't he?'

'Yes, ma'am.'

Fry regarded her with a certain respect. A woman who could memorize the duty rosters must have a ruthlessly efficient administrative brain. Most senior officers wouldn't even have bothered looking.

'He heard we were short-handed and came in to see if he could help,' explained Fry. 'But I can send him home, if –'

'No, why would you do that? We should be encouraging such enthusiasm, DS Fry.'

'Of course.'

A few minutes later, Fry found Mr Enthusiasm himself standing at her desk.

'You didn't mention any trouble with the hunt,' he said.

'It was all a storm in a teacup.'

'Sabs, I suppose?'

'Yes, but there were hunt stewards involved. I didn't like the look of them too much, Ben. There were one or two familiar faces, I'm sure.'

'Customers of ours?'

'Almost certainly. When I get hold of their names, I think there'll be a few counts of affray and GBH on record. Some potential suspects there, well capable of cracking a person's skull. If we could link one of them to Patrick Rawson, then tie it up with the forensics . . .'

'You're focusing on the hunt stewards rather than the saboteurs?' said Cooper.

'The protestors were a motley bunch. But some of them looked as though they wouldn't say "boo" to a goose. They'd probably be too afraid of violating its rights.'

Cooper perched on an adjacent desk. 'The sabs are pretty clever and sophisticated now. They've had a lot of experience over the years. In fact, some people say successful hunt sabotage needs as much knowledge of hunting techniques as hunting itself. You have to understand the direction a scent travels, possible lines a fox might take. And good communication is vital.'

'According to Inspector Redfearn, there are mainly hard-core activists left since the ban. They seem to be convinced that hunts are trying to break the law every time they go out.'

'Not all hunts,' said Cooper. 'The Eden Valley have developed a bad reputation with the sabs. Some of the neighbouring hunts, like the High Peak, are considered pretty clean and law abiding. But, yes, there are definitely some extreme groups. A while ago, there were a bunch called the Hunt Retribution

Squad, who were alleged to have been responsible for a series of fire bombings. That was after the deaths of two young saboteurs in incidents involving hunt vehicles.'

'Deaths? Really?'

'It was a few years ago.'

Cooper had got Fry's interest now, and he could see it. He sat down at his PC and did a quick search, soon coming up with the details.

'Yes, they were both in 1993. One in Cheshire, and one in Cambridgeshire. The sabs who died were aged eighteen and fifteen. The fifteen-year-old was crushed under the wheels of a horse box.'

'That's just a child,' said Fry.

Cooper nodded. 'Funny thing is, the angle of the media reports at the time damaged the reputation of the saboteurs rather than the hunt supporters. There were allegations of children being recruited directly from schools and sacrificed for the "anti" cause, with a few hints at Nazi sympathies thrown in.'

'Which suggests the hunt lobby might have had better PR than the opposition.'

'Maybe.'

Fry tapped a pen on her desk. 'This has been going on for years, then. There could be some old scores to be settled, couldn't there? A young sab in the early nineties might be in his mid-forties now.'

'You're thinking of your victim – Patrick Rawson?'

'It's a theory. There were too many horses at the scene for the hunt not to be involved in some way. And I got a bad feeling from that woman, Mrs Forbes, and the huntsman. I was convinced they were concealing something.'

'They learn to be defensive,' said Cooper.

'Even so . . .'

'Yes?'

'Well, let's be fair,' said Fry. 'There are some fairly aggressive

83

hunt supporters, too. What was that slogan some of them had during the campaign for a ban? "Born to Hunt, Prepared to Fight".'

'Something like that,' said Cooper. 'You didn't enjoy seeing the hunt, did you?'

'I'm not a fan of horses, as it happens. They're too big for my liking – I wouldn't want one of those things to bite me. And there were so many dogs. Why do they need all those dogs?'

'Hounds.'

'Oh, yes – hounds, then.'

Cooper laughed, then tried to look more serious.

'So what can I do, Diane?'

'Are you sure you're free?'

'I've got an appointment to keep at about five o'clock – but otherwise, yes.'

'Got a date?'

'No, I'm taking the cat to the vet's. Have you got some jobs for me?'

'Well, there are a few addresses that need visiting in Eyam and Birchlow. Potential witnesses to speak to.'

'Sure. Give them to me.'

Fry handed him the call logs. 'They're probably nothing, but best to check.'

'OK. Where are you off to yourself?'

'A nice restaurant,' said Fry. 'One of the perks of the job.'

Wednesday was market day in Edendale, and Fry had to go all the way up to the top of the multi-storey car park in Clappergate to find a space for the Peugeot.

Le Chien Noir was in a row of retail premises near the corner of the market place, distinguished from the building societies and mobile phone shops around it by the subdued colours of its décor, the deep gloom visible through the windows, the discreet menu under its own little awning on the wall outside.

Though the restaurant wasn't open for business yet, a frantic bustle of activity was going on. Every time a door from the kitchen opened, a burst of noise filled the empty restaurant: shouting and clanging, voices singing or screaming in several different accents. It occurred to Fry too late that very few workers in the service industry had English as their first language these days. Even if she found the right waitress or barman, she might need to call on the services of an interpreter to get detailed information out of them. And, whatever languages the staff at Le Chien Noir spoke, she was certain French wouldn't be among them. She prayed that she wouldn't have to start racking up additional costs on use of the Interpretation Line.

But, for once, she was in luck. Patrick Rawson had been served by the manager himself, who turned out to be a Scot called Connelly, a slim man in his thirties with close-cropped hair disguising incipient male-pattern baldness. He was wearing a brightly patterned waistcoat and a white apron, with his order pad protruding from a pocket.

She showed him a printout of the photo faxed from Sutton Coldfield.

'Yes, I'm pretty sure I saw that gentleman,' said Connelly. 'It was only . . . what? Monday night?'

'That would be correct, Mr Connelly.'

'Most people I don't remember for very long. If you'd asked me next week, it would probably have gone clean out of my head. I have that sort of mind, you know. I always need something new.'

Within a few minutes, Fry had obtained the credit-card record which would confirm Rawson's identity, and established that there had been no reservation made. At least, none that had been entered in the book. A walk-in, then. Around eight or eight thirty, the manager thought.

'What do you remember about him?' she asked.

'Well, he was rather loud. Not drunk or anything awful

85

like that, you understand. He was just one of those terribly over-confident men. Ridiculously masculine, wanting to be dominant all the time – and wanting everyone else to see it, too. It turns me right off.'

'Interesting.'

Fry smiled at him, feeling a growing surge of relief that she wasn't going to have to dig for details. Connelly's impressions of Patrick Rawson would be as valuable as gold.

The manager warmed to her approval. 'Oh, I suppose he was quite good looking in a rugged kind of way. Knew it, too.' He studied the photograph again. 'Mmm. Has to be the centre of attention all the time. You can see it in his eyes.'

'Was he having dinner with a woman?'

'Oh no, love. His companion was an older man.'

'Can you describe him for me?'

Connelly shook his head. 'We see so many middle-aged businessmen in here. There was nothing about him that would have made him stand out from the rest. Greying hair, clean shaven. A suit and tie. What else can I say? He was a diner. We don't exactly look at the colour of their eyes.'

'Just the colour of their money.'

'The colour of their plastic. Our customers rarely use cash.'

'Had either of these two men been in the restaurant before?'

'I couldn't say.' The manager hesitated. 'I suppose I could go back through the book and see if your chap made a reservation some time, or check the credit-card records –'

'It doesn't matter,' said Fry. 'We can get hold of his credit-card statements ourselves.'

'That must be fun. I'd love to be able to do that.'

Powerful smells of cooking were starting to drift from the kitchen. They made Fry think of garlic bread, which she daren't eat during the day, even if it was offered to her. That didn't stop her salivating, though.

'I'm interested in this second man,' she said. 'Did you hear him speak at all, Mr Connelly?'

86

'Yes – when he ordered, of course. And at the end of the meal there was a bit of an argument about who should pay the bill.'

'Oh? Mr Rawson didn't want to pay?'

'No, no, it was the other way around. Both gentlemen wanted to pay, and they had one of those terribly polite little argie-bargies over who had got their credit card out first. We see it so often in here. It's a sort of ritual they go through. My opinion is, there's a question of status involved. They all want to be the one who paid for the dinner.'

'Did you gain an impression of the relative status between these two, Mr Connelly?'

'Well, I've been doing this job for a long time, love. You'd be surprised how good I've become at judging that.'

'That's why I'm asking you,' said Fry.

Connelly smoothed down his waistcoat in an unconscious preening gesture. 'And, in this case, I'd say the two gentlemen were pretty much equals. They knew each other quite well, I'm sure. It wasn't as if they were meeting for the first time. No ice to be broken, if you know what I mean.'

'Yes, I understand. So they were friendly?'

'Mmm. I didn't say that, did I? On the contrary, I felt there was a little bit of tension. Nothing was said while I was at the table. I'm afraid they were rather too discreet for that. But, watching from a distance, I could see their conversation was getting a bit heated at times.'

Fry looked around the restaurant. Despite its reputation, the tables were pushed fairly close together. Or perhaps that was *because* of its reputation. Restaurants went in and out of fashion all the time. Right now, Le Chien Noir might be the place to eat, but next month the people with the money could be going elsewhere and reservations would dry up. Managements liked to cash in on a spell of popularity. More covers meant more profits.

'Was the restaurant full?' she asked.

'On Monday night? No way. The good people of Edendale like to stay at home in front of the telly most of the week. We get a nice visiting clientele during the summer, but not in early March. Besides, the weather was bad, wasn't it?'

'Yes.'

Connelly followed her glance around the room. 'Ah, you're wondering whether any other diners might have overheard their conversation. Unfortunately, I gave the two gentlemen a nice, quiet table in a corner, with no one too near them. I thought they might be discussing business, you see.'

'And hoped they would be good tippers?'

The manager inclined his head. 'As indeed they were.'

The kitchen door banged, and someone shouted what sounded like a complicated curse. What was the language? Russian? Polish? Something East European, anyway.

'You were telling me about the other man,' she said. 'Did you notice what kind of accent he had when he spoke?'

Connelly shrugged. 'He didn't speak all that much. Local, I would have said. But don't make me swear to it in court.'

'Don't worry, I won't.'

Fry looked at the credit-card receipt. She noticed for the first time that Patrick Rawson had, indeed, been a good tipper. He'd added a hefty gratuity to the bill, rather than leave cash in hand.

'It seems Mr Rawson paid the bill at five minutes past ten. I imagine he and his companion left together shortly afterwards?'

'Certainly.'

'Can you remember whether they arrived together?'

Connelly tapped the photograph dramatically with a long, pale finger. 'I believe this gentleman arrived first, by a few minutes. But not much.'

'Did you see a car outside? Or did they ask you to send for a taxi when they left?'

'No. Neither. Their clothes weren't wet, but I don't think it was actually raining at the time. Just a moment now . . .'

'Yes?'

The manager pointed towards the exit, a smoky glass door looking out on to the market place. For a second, Fry felt disorientated. Her eyes had become accustomed to the dim lighting of the restaurant, her concentration had been on Connelly and what he was saying. This sudden glimpse of blue-and-white market-stall awnings, crowds of people passing by, the brake lights of cars queuing at the traffic lights – they all seemed like an intrusion.

'I do recall them looking out to see what the weather was doing before they left,' said Connelly. 'Customers often do that, spend a few moments deciding whether to wait, or to make a dash for their cars. People who dine here don't like to get wet.'

Fry felt a bit disappointed that Connelly hadn't come up with anything more. He had seemed so promising in the beginning. But perhaps she just wasn't asking the right questions.

'I know your memory is good, sir,' she said. 'So if you do recall anything else about either man, anything at all, please give me a call, won't you?'

She handed him her card, which he glanced at and slipped into his apron pocket.

'Detective Sergeant, it would be a pleasure. And do make a reservation for dinner some time. Would you like to take a menu with you?'

'Not just now, thank you.'

'Well, don't forget. I'll make sure you're given a special table.'

11

They called it the Plague Village. Nice name, thought Cooper. Not the sort of thing you'd expect to be used as a selling point for your house in an estate agent's brochure. Who would want their home to be remembered for an intimate connection with an outbreak of Black Death?

But the name for Eyam must have well and truly stuck by now, since it was still in use more than three and a half centuries after the event. Five-sixths of the village's population had been wiped out, most of them during one deadly summer in 1666. Along the main street, picturesque little stone cottages displayed plaques in their front gardens, listing the names of people who'd died there, killed by the bubonic plague.

Yes, like all the best disasters, Eyam's outbreak of Black Death had been turned into a tourist attraction.

Along with thousands of other children, Cooper had visited this village with a school party. It had been a sort of living history lesson, collecting the work sheets from the museum, gawping at the plague tableaux, looking eagerly for the stocks where miscreants had once been pelted with rotten food. Those were his favourite sort of lessons.

Two hundred and sixty people had died when the plague

hit Eyam. Yet the rector, William Mompesson, had rallied the villagers to a famously selfless act of isolation. He'd told them that it was impossible for them to escape by running away, that many of them were already infected and carried the seeds of death in their clothes. He told them that the fate of the surrounding country was in their hands. They broke off all contact with the outside world for five months, as the plague cut down the population of Eyam, one by one.

For that, Mompesson had been rewarded with the death of his own wife. Now, hers was the only grave of a plague victim to be found in the Eyam churchyard.

Despite its role as a macabre tourist attraction, Cooper could tell Eyam remained a thriving community. It was good to see a village that still had a butcher's shop, for example. A high-class butcher's too, according to the sign. In many villages, the shops had long since gone, the parish church had been converted into a holiday home, and the vicarage was providing bed and breakfast. And, of course, every village post office was now the Old Post Office, selling teas and ice cream instead of stamps and tax discs.

The first address on his list was in Laurel Close, on the outskirts of the village. Cooper could see straight away that Laurel Close was an old people's housing estate. Quiet and well tended, with stone-faced bungalows standing in neat rows behind well-mown grass, like gravestones in a cemetery. The image was appropriate, really. This could be a place where the main topics of conversation were illness and death, and the latest funeral was the highlight of the week.

Ah, well. No more time to be lost. Cooper got out of his car and knocked on the first door.

Deborah Rawson took a long drag on her cigarette. 'Let's get this straight. Are you saying that Patrick was murdered?'

'We don't know that for sure, Mrs Rawson.'

'It's a bit much to take in.'

'Yes, of course.'

When Fry arrived at the mortuary in Edendale, she'd been met by a woman in her late thirties. Short hair, a pale, sharp face. Suspicious eyes. Her brother was somewhere around, having made an excuse to get out into the fresh air. Fry couldn't blame him.

'I'm sorry to have to ask you questions at a time like this,' said Fry. 'But you're quite sure this is your husband?'

'Absolutely.'

Fry watched Mrs Rawson carefully, noting the unnatural paleness that indicated shock. The hand holding the cigarette trembled slightly, and the ash was tapped off a little too often. This was a woman trying to pretend to be calmer than she really was.

'You understand that we need to establish how Mr Rawson died. It would help us a lot if you can give us some information. The sooner we know where to start —'

'Yes, it's all right. What do you want to know?'

'Mrs Rawson, can you tell us why your husband came up to Derbyshire?'

'He visits horse sales. There's one in Derby, isn't there?'

'Is there?'

'I think it's on a Saturday.'

'Today is only Wednesday.'

Mrs Rawson shrugged. 'He came up a bit early, then. He must have had some other business to do.'

The woman was well dressed. Expensively dressed, at least. Fry could recognize designer labels, even when they were worn with more aggression than style.

'And what is your husband's business, exactly?' she asked.

'Patrick has lots of business interests. I could never quite follow all the ins and outs. He owns a share of several companies. You can probably get the names from his papers. Mostly, he buys and sells, then invests the profits in new enterprises. He's been quite successful over the years. But he's the kind of man who's always looking for new things, new ideas to make a profit from.'

Fry had heard lots of people being vague about their 'business interests'. Usually, it meant they were drug dealers, or running a protection racket, or handling stolen property. Buying and selling? Investing the profits? It sounded as though Patrick Rawson's business dealings would take a bit of looking into. And was his wife really so innocent, so ignorant? Or was she being deliberately coy about the fact she'd been turning a blind eye to where the money had come from that bought her those nice clothes?

'We're going to have to go through Mr Rawson's papers,' Fry said. 'Who keeps his appointments diary?'

'Well, I suppose he does.'

'You suppose?'

'I never got involved in the business, Sergeant. Do you think I work as his secretary, or PA? Did you think I married the boss? Well, I didn't. Whatever Patrick does in his business is his own affair.'

There was a shrill edge to her voice now that she couldn't conceal. Fry knew she would have to be careful. People who tried so hard to hide their feelings were often the most likely to crack completely. That made them useless as witnesses.

'Did he not mention anything about who he was planning to meet up here?'

'No.'

'And where were you on Tuesday morning yourself, Mrs Rawson?' asked Fry.

'At home, of course. In Sutton Coldfield.'

Fry noted that Deborah didn't seem to understand the implication of the question. Another sign that she wasn't thinking quite so clearly as she might?

'We need to know where your husband stayed when he was up here. Can you tell us that, at least?'

'Now, I thought you would ask that. Patrick always stays

93

at the same place when he's in Derbyshire. He says it has a nice golf course.' She produced a card from her bag. 'This is it.'

Fry took the card. The Birch House Country Hotel. She wasn't familiar with the hotel, but judging from the address in Birchlow it must be practically within a golf swing of her crime scene.

'Did you ever phone Mr Rawson while he was there?'

'Yes, once or twice.'

'Actually on the hotel number?'

'No, I always call his mobile. Why go through a hotel receptionist?'

Why, indeed? Except that it would have established whether Patrick Rawson really was staying where he told his wife he'd be. A jealous or suspicious partner would have thought of that. But not Deborah Rawson, apparently. Fry wasn't sure she believed it.

'And the number you called would be this one, which you gave to the local police yesterday?'

'Yes. That's the one Patrick used for personal calls, the Sony Ericsson. He had another number for business calls, though.'

'Oh?'

Fry felt a surge of irritation. If those West Midlands officers had discovered that fact yesterday, her team could already have been tracking down all the calls Rawson had made and received. As it was, she would be nearly a day behind on the job. It was time lost that could never be regained. And all because somebody had failed to ask the right question.

Mrs Rawson gave her the second number. 'Pat does his business entirely by mobile phone, because he's always on the move. He might have left the Sony Ericsson behind somewhere, but he would never have been without the iPhone. He hates the idea of missing a business call or an email, and all his contacts are on there.'

'Thank you.'

So there were two phones missing. This was looking less and less like an accident, or even a mugging gone wrong. Fry itched to get the machinery swinging into action, but there was still no confirmation that Rawson's death was due to murder. The postmortem would be starting right now, with the bereaved widow safely out of the way.

'I keep saying "Pat does this" and "he hates that",' said Mrs Rawson. 'I suppose I have to learn to start using the past tense, don't I?'

'It will take a while to come to terms with what's happened,' said Fry, watching carefully for an emotional outburst, which didn't come. 'Would you like me to send for your brother?'

'No, I'm all right. Really.'

'Just one more thing for now, then,' said Fry. 'Why did your husband attend horse sales, Mrs Rawson? Do you ride?'

'I'm not keen myself. But we do have some stables at the house in Sutton. Patrick used to buy horses and sell them on. Quiet rides for novices. He had a good eye for that sort of thing.'

'I see.'

Mrs Rawson looked at her watch. 'If you want to know anything more about the business, you'll have to talk to Patrick's partner,' she said. 'That's Michael Clay. He's a bit boring, but he's very good at managing all the paperwork and so on. He's an accountant by profession. As I said – boring.'

'I'll do that,' said Fry.

And she definitely would. Mr Clay might be a boring accountant, but it was possible that he would also be a bit more forthcoming with the truth.

She escorted Deborah Rawson back down to reception. A man was waiting for her there, a tall and smartly dressed middle-aged man, with unusual grey eyes and a face that was slightly too wide around the jaw line to be called good looking. Fry took him for Deborah Rawson's older brother, and realized that she didn't know what his surname would be.

'Sorry to keep you waiting, Mr . . .?'

The man smiled, creases forming across his cheeks from the too-wide jaw.

'Clay,' he said. 'Michael Clay.'

Fry was so taken aback that she couldn't at first figure out where she had made a false assumption.

'I'm sorry. Are you Mrs Rawson's brother?'

'No. Dennis is waiting outside. He wanted to have a cigarette. I came to see if I could be any help. I hope that's all right.'

'You're Patrick Rawson's business partner?'

'Yes, in some ways. Patrick had other interests that I wasn't involved in, but we worked quite closely. Has Deborah been able to give the information you need?'

'Well, not exactly. We haven't been able to establish why Mr Rawson was in Derbyshire, and who he was meeting yesterday morning.'

'I can't help you there either, I'm afraid. Patrick didn't share the day-to-day details with me. But if your enquiries do turn up a business connection, please come and see me and I'll give you whatever help I can.'

'Thank you, sir.'

Michael Clay gave her his business card, and Fry noted the Birmingham phone number. She also noticed the way he hovered protectively over Deborah Rawson as he began to usher her towards the door.

'I'm not quite clear how you came to be here, sir,' said Fry. 'I understood Mrs Rawson's brother had brought her from Sutton Coldfield.'

'Yes, he did. Obviously, Deborah called to tell me what had happened to poor old Patrick. And since I happened to be in the area, I thought I'd come along to give my support. It's going to be a difficult time for her.'

'Indeed.'

Clay fixed her with his grey eyes. They were strangely cool

and almost emotionless eyes, which emitted a great sense of calmness and confidence. He made you feel as though you'd be ready to trust him with your last penny.

But did Fry feel she could believe him? Was she convinced that he happened to be in the area for an entirely innocent reason? Not on your life.

'I'll be in touch, Mr Clay,' she said. 'Perhaps quite soon.'

Cooper had found himself invited inside number 6 Laurel Close. The resident was an elderly man, probably about eighty years old, but still reasonably upright and mobile, if a little slow. An old soldier, perhaps? Well, if that was case, it would soon come into the conversation.

Cooper had been prepared for residents in these bungalows to take a long time getting to their doors. He knew that stiff joints would have to be levered out of armchairs, walking frames grasped, hearing aids adjusted. And that was before they even got out of their sitting rooms. Then there would be chains on the doors, and his ID to be shown before anyone would talk to him.

All the precautions were justified, too. Laurel Close was the sort of area where distraction burglaries were most common, where opportunist thieves preyed on the elderly, keen to take advantage of their confusion, and their trusting natures.

He was able to hear movement from inside the bungalow for a few minutes before the door chain rattled and the face of the old man peered out.

'Mr Wakeley?'

'Aye.'

Cooper showed his warrant card, giving the old man time to scrutinize it carefully. Not so long ago, there had been several incidents of a thief posing as a police officer to gain access to properties just like this, with the intention of rifling the drawers for some OAP's life savings as soon as their backs were turned.

97

'You reported hearing a disturbance on Tuesday morning. Is that right, sir?'

'Yes, that was me. Responsible citizen, I am.'

The old man laughed, and let Cooper into the bungalow, pointing the way through to a small sitting room. He waved his visitor ahead, and very slowly followed him into the room. He didn't support himself on a stick or a frame, but moved as if he had all the time in the world, and no one was going to hurry him. Cooper was reminded of a giant Galapagos turtle he'd seen on a natural history programme, determinedly placing one foot in front of the other.

The sitting room was filled with too much furniture, and scattered with framed photographs of smiling family members. Biscuit crumbs lay on the carpet. Cooper could feel them crunching softly under his boots. Near the armchair he was given, the crumbs were thicker. He felt as though he ought to offer to do a bit of vacuuming while he was here.

'Early in the morning, it was,' said Mr Wakeley. 'Folk having a row.'

Cooper felt a surge of interest. It was a small thing, and it might be irrelevant. But every detail should be followed up.

'You heard people arguing? What time exactly, can you say?'

The old man glanced automatically at a handsome grandfather clock that stood in one corner. The clock dominated the room, completely out of proportion to the size of the bungalow. Cooper guessed it must have been brought from a former home, a house with larger rooms and higher ceilings, where all the rest of the furniture was heavy and dark. But the clock ticked away steadily, a deep *thunk* of a pendulum echoing gently inside the mahogany case.

'Eight thirty, or a bit later. I couldn't be more exact than that.'

'You were here, in your bungalow? Were people arguing outside in the street?'

Wakeley shook his head. 'No, I went for a walk. I don't sleep too well these days, tend to wake up about five o'clock in the morning. There's not much else to do at that time, I can tell you. No one to talk to, nothing on the telly worth watching. And who wants to sit around with nothing but their own thoughts for company at that time of the morning?'

Not me, thought Cooper. No one was at their best at that time. He decided it might be more fruitful to let the old man talk, rather than trying too hard to pry out the details.

'So you went out when, Mr Wakeley?'

'About seven thirty. I used to go out earlier, at first light – cock crow, if they actually allowed anyone to have a cockerel around here. I can't manage it now.'

'Was there anyone around?'

'Not a soul to be seen on the estate, a few cars moving about the village – commuters, I suppose, off to their jobs in Sheffield.'

Cooper looked at the old man. He had probably been quite a fit person once, perhaps even athletic. But now he was the giant tortoise. It would take him half an hour just to get to the end of his street.

'And where did you walk to, sir?'

Wakeley laughed again, a dry chortle that suggested to Cooper he was making the old man's day, probably his week. He was starting to think that he'd been given the duff job, the visit to the old fogey who just wanted a bit of attention and someone to talk to for a few minutes. There were plenty of them around.

'I only got as far as the bench at the corner of the lane,' he said. 'That's my limit these days. I used to hike up Longstone Edge without batting an eyelid, but they seem to have made it a lot higher and a lot steeper these days. I blame the government.'

'Was it raining at that time?'

'A bit. But a drop of rain never did anyone any harm.'

Cooper nodded. It was what he'd expected. Mr Wakeley was one of that tough breed who had almost died out, even in Derbyshire.

'So these people you heard . . .?'

'Up on the moor,' said Wakeley. 'They must have been a good two miles away. Funny how sounds travels at that time of the morning, when no one's about. If you get the right sort of weather conditions, you can hear a dog bark at Birchlow.'

'I see.'

The old man grinned at him, showing a set of fine white teeth that must have come courtesy of the NHS dental service.

'Nothing wrong with my hearing,' he said. 'You young 'uns expect old folk to be deaf as well as daft, I suppose. But my ears are as sharp as yours. Maybe sharper. I never damaged my ear drums with loud music, you see. Children now, they stick those little ear plugs in their ears and walk around with music blasting all day. Now, *they'll* be deaf as posts by the time they're sixty.'

'If you could just –'

'Oh, aye. I'm getting round to it. I have to take my time these days, as you can see.'

'I'm sorry.'

'I was just sitting on the bench, being quiet, waiting for the birds to start singing with the light coming up. And there were at least two people, shouting. A man and a woman. They went at it pretty good, too. No doubt they thought no one else was about to hear them.'

'Could you hear what they were arguing about?'

'I might have good hearing, but I'm not bionic.'

'No, of course. So where exactly were they? Could you –' Cooper had been about to ask the old man to take him to the bench in question and point out the location, but he realized that it would take all afternoon. There were other jobs waiting for him to do. Shame – Mr Wakeley would have enjoyed it. 'If I showed you a map, could you estimate their position?'

'I'll have a go.'

Cooper fetched his OS map from the car and spread it out on Mr Wakeley's table.

'You would have been around here?'

'Yes, the old silk road, that is. The pack horses used to go that way, to get up over the moor. No cars on that road early in the morning.'

'So the people you heard would be where?'

'Whereabouts is Birchlow on here?'

'Here.' Cooper placed a finger on the map.

'One of these fields, then. Back of the church, near where those trees are.'

The contour lines on the map showed that the location Mr Wakeley had indicated was on the northern slope of the moor. Because of the lie of the landscape, anyone who had been up and about in Birchlow might not have heard the argument. But there would be direct line of sight to the bench on the old silk road where the old man had been sitting. Clear air, except for the rain that had been falling.

'Do you know Birchlow?' asked Cooper.

'Birchlow? Aye, there's a lot of history in Birchlow. Some amount of dry rattle there, if you know what I mean.'

'Skeletons in the cupboard, Mr Wakeley?'

'More than skeletons. If you shake the cupboard too much, half the village will fall out. But you don't want old gossip.'

The old man chuckled, and coughed.

'Are you all right?' asked Cooper, wondering whether Mr Wakeley didn't have quite so much toughness, after all.

'I will be, when I'm dead.'

Cooper smiled. The old man and his clock seemed to be running at different speeds. The clock still ticked away at a regular pace, but Mr Wakeley had slowed down, as if his internal spring was unwinding and losing its tension, no longer

101

able to push his body around at the old rate. He was gradually slipping out of real time.

And one thing was certain. He wasn't going to find out who had been having that argument in the early hours of the morning by standing here in the sitting room at 6 Laurel Close. He would have to follow the trail closer to Birchlow.

Standing in the residents' lounge of the Birch Hall Country Hotel, Fry was impressed by a series of oak bookcases lining the wall. While she waited, she peered through the glass to study the contents. Shelves were full of volumes that were clearly more for display, and creating the right ambience, than for reading. Bound volumes of *Punch*, a complete set of Sir Walter Scott, *Who Was Who 1951–1960*. Their dark bindings formed an impenetrable wall behind the glass.

She'd obtained a copy of Patrick Rawson's account from the head receptionist, who had expected Mr Rawson to be staying at the hotel until the weekend. It wasn't unknown for guests to miss sleeping in their room for a night, but there was always the chance that something regrettable had happened. From the response to her news, Fry wasn't sure whether the hotel would be sorry to have lost a guest, or relieved that they had a scan of his credit card to settle the bill.

A quick search of Patrick Rawson's room had been unfruitful. Clothes, yes. Toiletries, of course. But anything that could provide useful information must have been back home, or in his car. She would have to make sure the room was kept locked until a proper search could be conducted.

When her phone rang, she found that it was Gavin Murfin, calling with the first solid information on Patrick Rawson.

'Has he a record?' she asked. 'Anything on the PNC?'

'A bit of juvenile vandalism,' said Murfin. 'Keying cars, mostly – with a special fondness for the more expensive motors.'

'Oh, early anarchist tendencies, then.'

'What?'

'Never mind. I was kidding.'

She could imagine Murfin staring at the phone in amazement. Diane Fry kidding? Cracking a joke? It was almost unheard of. She sighed ruefully.

'Now we have Patrick Rawson's mobile phone numbers, we can get hold of a record of his calls.'

'Did you say "numbers"?'

'Yes. His wife says he had one phone for personal calls, and another one for business. Sounds like he was the sort of person you'd really hate to be on a train with, listening to him taking two calls at once. I gave both the numbers to Becky.'

'Right.' Murfin seemed to turn away from the phone for a moment. 'I think she's on to it. So when we get the records for Mr Two Phones, what are we looking for?'

'Local numbers, in or out. He must have been in touch with someone up here, both after he arrived and in the days before he came.'

'Got it,' said Murfin. 'By the way, we've got initial forensics on the Mitsubishi. No prints except Rawson's and his wife's.'

'A shame, but no surprise.'

'He did leave a paper trail all over the Eden Valley, though, by using his credit card for everything. Hotel bill, restaurant, petrol station . . . So we know where he slept, where he ate dinner, and which way he was heading. If we hadn't found him already, we'd have a head start.'

'There's a lesson in that, Gavin. If you don't want to be found, pay cash.'

'I'll bear it in mind when I decide to do a runner.'

12

Cooper drove back into the centre of Eyam. Of course, most of the village seemed to have slipped out of real time. The seventeenth century was so powerfully present that he wouldn't have been too surprised to see the Reverend Mompesson striding down the path from the church in his black robes, Bible in hand, filled with unselfish determination to protect his flock. Or what remained of it.

Cooper remembered from his school visit a couple of plague tableaux in the museum. One represented the last days of John Daniel, plague victim number ninety-two. Number ninety-two? A sentence from a TV series had run irreverently through Cooper's head – '*I am not a number.*' The bubos were clear and livid on John Daniel's neck, illuminated by a candle burning at the head of his bed.

But the exhibit that had impressed him most was the long list of all the plague victims. Among all the Thorpes, Syddalls, Rowes and Thornleys were the names of two boys, the sons of a widow who had taken in a journeyman tailor as her lodger. It was a delivery of cloth from London for the tailor that had brought the plague to Eyam. The two sons had been dead within a month.

He looked at his list. Two more calls to make in Eyam,

following up reports of a disturbance during the night. His instinct was to suspect drunks. The timing was surely too early to be related to the death of Patrick Rawson. But Fry was right to give them to him – everything had to be checked at this stage. Next week could be too late.

A horse was being walked through the village, clacking slowly past the Mechanics Institute. A pallet of cured Danish ham stood outside the butcher's shop, and stone dust rose from a new housing development. One day, excavation work for new foundations would unearth some of the old plague victims' graves in Eyam. If it hadn't happened already.

A display of postcards outside a shop caught Cooper's eye. He felt in his pocket for some change, and bought a card with a picture of the Plague Cottage, showing the names listed on the plaque at the gate.

Then he made his way back past Eyam Hall to reach the car park on Hawkhill Road, near the museum. He stopped for a moment to admire the way the honey-coloured stone of the houses blended with the foliage on the hillside. Just occasionally, the handiwork of man and nature seemed to fit perfectly together, complementing each other, creating a very satisfying harmony. It was a rare thing. But it happened more often in the Peak District than in other parts of the world. And it was good to get the chance to just stop and stare now and then.

An elderly lady with mobility problems was waiting to cross the road. Before Cooper could move to help her, someone came out of the shop and gave her an arm to lean on. Two cars had stopped, and one of the drivers even waved.

Cooper realized he was having difficulty remembering that he wasn't on leave any more, because he'd offered to do some jobs for Diane Fry. Get back on duty, Cooper.

Fry had to pass through Eyam to reach Longstone Moor. On the main street, she saw Cooper, his mind clearly somewhere else as usual.

She watched as an old biddy with a stick started to totter across the road, taking her own good time, holding up the traffic for no good reason. Cooper seemed to be about to move towards her. Perhaps he was going to arrest her for obstruction. But someone else got there before him, and the whole performance creaked painfully on before cars were able to begin moving again.

Fry sighed as she turned off the main street towards Longstone Moor. She couldn't even send him home, because he wasn't actually supposed to be on duty. And anyway, you took what resources you could get. No point in complaining.

She changed the CD as she drove through a steep-sided dale. Alison Moyet's *The Turn* came to hand, and she slipped it into the CD player. A solitary guitar, then the familiar bluesy voice singing 'One More Time'. Perfect.

Birchlow was an amorphous cluster of gritstone cottages, laid out according to no visible plan. An organic village, then, thought Cooper. A settlement now barely interesting enough to attract a single tourist, unless they were lost. It had nothing to offer in competition with the attractions of areas to the south and west. Unlike Eyam, it had even escaped the effects of the plague.

Cooper knew tiny villages like this. They were dominated by the older generations, the younger population having moved away to find work, or to live in the cities. Few youngsters had any interest in scraping a living from the land. In Birchlow, the natural instinct would be to distrust the unfamiliar. He could expect politeness on the surface, suspicion underneath. Not to mention a tendency for people to conceal the fact that they were capable of any human feelings.

His other visits in Eyam had proved fruitless, as he'd suspected. But the system had flagged the calls up, and his boots were the ones on the ground right now in this area. If

106

what Mr Wakeley had told him had any significance at all, he would find the answer here in Birchlow somewhere.

He dialled Fry's number to let her know his location.

'It's close enough to your scene,' he said. 'Could be significant.'

'Yes, it's worth following up. But don't knock yourself out, Ben.'

'I'm here, so I'll do the best I can.'

'As you always do, right?'

Cooper passed a small church, which had one spectacular stained-glass window catching the light. A depiction of a saint, dying in great sanctity, with a quiver of arrows through his throat. Bright yellow daffodils grew in the cottage gardens, contrasting with a red pillar box, and a line of dark grey wheelie bins standing at the roadside, waiting for the refuse collectors. Milk bottles had been left out for the milkman, the way everyone had once done it.

There was a village pub in Birchlow, the Bird in Hand. But no shops. And no post office, of course. There was just a small car park behind the village hall, with a phone box and a parish notice board, and several cars parked up between the stone walls.

Looking for the farm whose land ran up the back of the churchyard, Cooper reflected that there were some characteristics that didn't endear you to people in villages like this. Being openly inquisitive was one. Knowing too much was another. Unfortunately, a police detective was likely to fall into both categories.

When he came to a sign for Rough Side Farm, he knew he was in the right place. Eyam was clearly visible from here, spread out on the opposite hillside. Some of the land here looked to be good pasture, so good that it ought to be supporting a dairy herd. But who wanted to run a dairy farm when prices for milk were so poor, and the bull calves worthless for meat?

Cooper found the farmer lurking in his workshop, surrounded by tractor parts and bits of oily machinery. He introduced himself, and learned the farmer's name was Peter Massey. He was a man in his late fifties, but lean and fit-looking, the way that the older generations of farmers often were. Physically, he was probably fitter than a lot of men half his age who did nothing but watch football and drink beer. He could certainly give Matt Cooper a fifty-yard start. No doubt all those hours spent out on the moors had done that for him. In a city, a man like Massey would probably credit his physical condition to tai chi or pilates.

Cooper commented on the quality of the land, usually a good ice breaker with a farmer who looked as though he'd been around for a while and could take the credit for it. Across the yard, he could see an empty cow shed, and the padlocked door to what must have been the milking parlour.

'Yes, it used to be all fields and cows round here,' said Massey, then paused for a moment. 'Now it's just fields.'

When Cooper explained that he wanted to see the route up to Birchlow that the old man had described, Massey wiped his hands on a rag and led him out of the yard. The farmhouse itself was a typical jumble of extensions and additions cluttering the outline of the original eighteenth-century building. A low profile against the Pennine winds, solid stone walls thick enough to keep out the cold.

'My father would have been upset that I gave up the dairy herd,' said the farmer as they passed through a gate and into the first field. 'He bred some nice Friesian crosses. Wonderful milkers, they were. But not good enough. No cows would have been good enough.'

'You inherited this farm from your father?' asked Cooper.

'Aye. And he took it over from *his* father. Lord, I was out in this yard helping with the morning milking by the time I was ten years old.'

'You must have a lot of memories, then.'

Massey's eyes clouded for a moment. He was gazing at the hillside, rather than at the house and buildings. Perhaps he felt he'd grown up out there in the fields, rather than indoors.

'You might say that. Yes, I've got a lot of my memories bound up in this land. Buried now, some of them.'

They followed the line of the dry-stone wall as it snaked across the contours of the hillside, following the dips and hollows. At a couple of points it was intersected by similar walls running at right angles to it, dividing the fields into long, sloping strips of land. Ahead of him, Cooper could see miles and miles of wall, an endless limestone tracery over-laying the landscape.

Massey stopped, removed his cap and scratched his head. His hair was wispy, and that distinctive sandy colour common among people whose distant ancestors had been Scandinavian settlers. Remarkable how that Viking blood had persisted through the generations.

'I reckon you must be talking about the bridlepath over there,' he said. 'We call it Badger's Way in these parts. It connects up with Black Harry Lane. You can get up to Black Harry Gate and way over to Longstone without going anywhere near a road, if you have a mind to.'

'A bridlepath. So it can be used by horse riders, not just walkers?'

'Aye. It would have been a packhorse road, I suppose, in the old days. It was made for horses. Trouble is, we tend to get motorbikes up here of a weekend. Those things muddy it up for everybody.'

Cooper looked down into the bridlepath, which was sunk a few feet between two grass embankments topped by stone walls. In many places, you could pass unnoticed by anyone in the adjoining fields, even if you were on horseback.

Up the hill, he could see the square Norman tower of the church at Birchlow. Along the edge of the moor, the land in front of him became even bumpier. One area seemed to be raised in a more regular shape, perhaps the site of an Iron Age hill fort or the capped shaft of an ancient lead mine. There were lots of those in the Peak District, archaeological sites that were the bane of farmers keen to plough up or improve their land, or to put up new buildings. This one seemed to share its location with a line of telephone poles, long since disused.

'Do you allow the Eden Valley Hunt to use your land, Mr Massey?' asked Cooper.

Massey hesitated, a habit he'd probably developed in the face of repeated questions about fox hunting during the campaign for a ban. He would be weighing up the answer, deciding whether it was wise to come down on one side or the other, or stay on the fence.

'They've got my permission,' he said finally. 'But they don't hunt this way often. We don't have the copses up here, see.'

'And perhaps no problem with foxes?'

The farmer straightened his cap. 'Funny, but the one place I've seen foxes regularly is here, in Badger's Way. They run up the lane at dusk sometimes. They've got it figured out, those buggers. They know they won't be spotted.'

'Yes, they're clever enough.'

Massey looked slyly at Cooper, perhaps remembering that he was a police officer.

'Besides, the Eden Valley don't hunt foxes any more, they just follow an artificial scent.'

'Yes, I know that.'

'So if I let the hunt come on to my land on that understanding, it's not my responsibility if they decide to go off and chase foxes. The landowner can't be prosecuted for it. That's the law.'

Cooper nodded. The hunt had made sure that farmers and landowners were reassured about their legal position after the hunting ban came in. Lots of them had been nervous that they would be targeted for prosecution if the hunt broke the law on their land by letting the pack kill a fox. It might be easier to prove whose land it had happened on, than who had been in charge of the hounds at the time.

But Peter Massey was right. The Hunting Act said that he was safe from prosecution if he had only agreed to allow legal activities on his land by the hunt.

As they walked back, Cooper asked Massey if he'd heard about the body found not a mile away from his farmhouse.

'Aye, I heard. That's not my land, though. It's farmed by someone over Housley way. He gets some crops out of the lower acreage, I believe. That's the only way to make money in farming these days.'

'He has some sheep, too.'

Massey sniffed. 'Ah, well. They keep the grass down, I suppose.'

'The dead man's name was Patrick Rawson. Does it mean anything to you?'

'Not a thing. He wasn't from around here, though, was he?'

'No.'

Before he left, Cooper gazed around the yard of Rough Side Farm. Not much money had been spent on maintaining the buildings in recent years. That was a common enough story. Matt was the same at Bridge End – he'd rather spend money on a new tractor than replace a shed roof. He said that if farm buildings were built properly in the first place, they ought to last for ever. In practice, the problem was just passed on to the next generation as part of their inheritance.

Cooper noticed a horseshoe nailed to the door of an old byre. But it was turned with the points up, to catch the luck, the way the old superstition said.

'Do you ride yourself, Mr Massey?' he asked.

'Ride what? A horse, do you mean?'

'Yes, sir.'

Massey shook his head. 'Never. That's for girls, isn't it?'

'Not necessarily.'

111

The farmer politely walked Cooper to his car, as if escorting an important visitor. He even removed his cap and held it in both hands as he watched Cooper negotiate the large, muddy puddles in the farm entrance.

'What about your family?' asked Cooper. 'Any sons ready to take over Rough Side Farm? Or daughters, perhaps?'

Massey shook his head. 'I've got two sons *and* a daughter, but they're not interested in farming. They work in computers, and logistics, and human resources. I don't think any of those things existed when I was at school. I have no idea what my children actually do all day. But I'm happy to live in ignorance.'

Cooper took one last look at the old farmhouse, and the acres of windswept White Peak landscape that Massey had to himself.

'What does ignorance of those things matter, when you've got the freedom of living out here?'

13

Back at the scene on Longstone Moor, Fry had found officers from the task force plodding wearily back to the rendezvous point in their boiler suits at the conclusion of their fingertip search. She gathered from their complaints about sore backs and wet knees that the search had produced precious little else.

SOCOs were still working at the old huts and on Patrick Rawson's Mitsubishi – she could see their van parked alongside the field barn, though the Mitsubishi itself was invisible from here. She ought to find a way over there to have a look at the car.

Now that the weather had cleared and the sun was out, there were flies everywhere, hovering over the sheep droppings, gathering in small clouds over the puddles of water under the hawthorn trees. Fry heard a whine near her ear, and swatted at it with a hand. Earlier, she'd opened her mouth and felt something tickle the back of her throat. She was pretty sure she'd swallowed a mosquito. They'd been everywhere during the previous summer and autumn, and some had even survived the winter.

Wayne Abbott was standing in front of her, a quizzical expression on his face.

'Yes, Wayne?'

'I wanted to update you.'

'Yes, I'm sorry. What have you got?'

'Well, first of all, there's no sign of anything that could have been used as a murder weapon – no bloodstained stones, or anything of that kind. But we've been working on the blood splatter, specifically traces of blood in the soil where the hoof marks are. The indications are that some of the impressions were made before the blood traces. You can see that the pattern of spatter is intact in those areas.'

As close as Fry peered at the ground beneath the evidence markers, she couldn't make out the tiny flecks of blood against the soil.

'I'll take your word for it.'

'Over here, however,' said Abbott, 'we can see that the hoof marks came after the injury. The pattern of spatter is completely broken up, some traces of blood have been pushed deep into the ground by the weight of the impressions.'

Fry straightened. 'So the horses were definitely here before *and* after the victim's injury. That would suggest they were present during the fatal attack.'

'It might be a reasonable conclusion,' said Abbott. 'Also . . .'

'Yes?'

'Assuming for a moment that your killer or killers did arrive on horseback, we think we've managed to identify their approach route. They came across the neighbouring field over there, lower down the hill. The hoof marks are still distinct. There's a crop of some kind planted in that field, so there's bare soil, rather than this coarse grass.'

'And what about the victim?' asked Fry.

'A little more difficult. But our best assessment is that he came direct from the location of his vehicle, which, as you know, was parked over by the old barn there. There's a stile he could have come over. We're examining that now, but it's about fifty yards from the car. He might actually have come over the wall. In any case, he then went into the derelict hut.'

'To try to get away from his assailants?'

'I couldn't say.'

'And from there . . .?'

'He came straight across this field. And he was running, which makes the shoe impressions smaller, but deeper. Because of the rain, not all the impressions are intact, but we've pieced together enough to be fairly confident.'

Fry was starting to form a picture in her mind now. The scenario was coming to life, the details filling themselves in. She could imagine Patrick Rawson easing the Mitsubishi slowly up the track to the field barn that morning and parking his car out of sight. Why had he done that? Because he was involved in a secret assignation? Or to surprise someone who didn't expect him to be there?

Whatever the reason, something had gone wrong for Mr Rawson. She didn't know yet how much time had passed between him arriving at the barn and the arrival of his killer or killers. Had there been an argument? Or had he been expecting someone quite different, and Rawson was the one who got a surprise? He must have been out of his car by that stage, or he would surely have got back in and driven away, if he felt under threat. She pictured him cut off from his vehicle, looking around for a means of escape.

And at some point, Mr Rawson had started to run. A businessman in early middle age, wearing a waxed coat and brown brogues, he'd scrambled over a stile and begun to run across an empty field in North Derbyshire. He would have been dashing through driving rain, slipping in the wet grass, covering his shoes in mud. Where had he been running to?

Fry turned and looked in the opposite direction, trying to imagine what Patrick Rawson would have been seeing as he ran. He had looked a reasonably fit man for his age, but he hadn't been dressed for sprinting. Could he have been hoping to make it to the stone mill, which was visible in the distance to the east?

'Anything else, Wayne?'

'Yes, there is. The office sent through a bit of digital video footage for you. Thought you might want to watch it in the van, rather than wait until you get back to West Street.'

Fry almost liked Abbott in that moment.

'Brilliant.'

'Apparently, this is from one of the protestors who were here yesterday,' said Abbott as he set up the screen.

'The hunt saboteurs.'

'Right. The quality is crap, of course. The Photographic Unit might be able to enhance it a bit, but the camera work is decidedly shaky, I'm afraid.'

An image came on the screen of a blurred road, then a section of dry-stone wall going past as the camera swung round rapidly. Splashes of rain hit the lens and ran sideways. Fry had almost forgotten about the rain. But anything filmed at the time Patrick Rawson met his death would have been shot pretty much underwater.

'This kid obviously spotted something, or one of his mates did,' said Abbott. 'It steadies down in a minute.'

The cameraman seemed to be running now, and the picture bounced up and down. Heavy breathing could be heard via the onboard microphone of his video camera, and somebody calling '*Over there!*'

Then, for a few seconds, there was absolute gold. Over the top of the wall, two horses could be seen being ridden across a field, kicking up a spray of water and dirt. There was almost no detail to the image, and before Fry could blink the horses had gone again, hidden by the slope of the land and an intrusive tree. Distant shouts could be made out, much too far away to be deciphered. But, listening as hard as she could, Fry thought she made out a name, shouted twice. Rosie?

The camera swung back again, wobbled, and focused on a group of young people standing in the road, their faces bright with excitement. Fry thought one of them could have been the girl she'd seen later with blood running down her face.

'Run it back to the horses,' she said.

Abbott replayed it and froze the image at the point where the two riders could be seen most clearly. Fry gazed at the picture for a long time. In truth, it told her very little. She could see the general colour of the horses. She could tell that the riders weren't wearing red coats, but tweed jackets and black helmets. But at least that was something.

At the bottom of the screen, the date stamp said it was zero-eight thirty-six, an hour before the first of the mounted hunt were supposed to have arrived for the meet. If she could discover where the cameraman was standing, she could work out whether the riders were going towards the location where Patrick Rawson had died, or coming away from it.

'So much for our Mrs Forbes and Mr Widdowson,' she said.

Cooper got a call from Fry as he left Birchlow, and decided to take the route across Longstone Edge itself. All along the edge were lay-bys, retired couples sitting in their little Smart cars to eat sandwiches and drink tea, enjoying the tranquillity of the Peak District before the Easter rush of tourists.

Driving along the edge was the closest thing to flying Cooper could think of, without having to queue at security and cram yourself into an economy-class cabin. Looking out of the passenger window of the car, he couldn't see any sign of the ground, just an open expanse way out into space, and a glimpse of the valley down below. Coasting down the Longstone Edge road was just like being in an aircraft coming in to land, watching the earth growing gradually closer.

It wasn't a good idea to take your eyes off the road and admire the scenery for too long, though. A while ago, a woman had driven her car off the edge somewhere about here, ending up lodged in the trees below the road. She'd stayed there for twenty-four hours, too, trapped in her car as motorists passed on the road without seeing her.

At the top, he heard the rumble of an engine, the whine of gears, the rattle of falling rock. Another quarry truck was labouring up the long track to the opencast workings. A scattering of sheep ambled along the roadside, where the dry-stone walls had fallen or vanished altogether. Their fleeces were thick and heavy after the winter, making their movements ungainly, like a bunch of walking armchairs. They didn't seem a bit concerned to be sharing their stretch of road with those massive haulage lorries.

When Cooper appeared at the scene to get the latest update, Fry described the video footage received from the hunt saboteur.

'A shout?' he said.

'Probably someone calling the dogs back. The hounds, I mean.'

He noted that she'd corrected herself on the use of 'hound'. Could it be that Fry was finally learning to fit in? She'd been in Derbyshire for a few years now, the big-city girl out of her depth in the country. For the whole of that time, she'd made it plain that she resented officers like Cooper for knowing better than she did. And Cooper felt that he'd made himself the prime target of her resentment, somehow. It was almost as if he'd done something much more personal that had caused permanent, unforgivable offence. It was a pity – he felt sure they would work better together if he could only get over this barrier.

'What did they shout?' he asked her. 'Could you tell?'

'The quality of the sound is terrible,' said Fry. 'But the name sounds like Rosie.'

'Rosie?'

That didn't sound right to Cooper. In his experience, hounds tended to be given names like Soldier, or Statesman, or Pirate. Rosie was far too twee for a foxhound. Fry wouldn't realize that, of course.

'It might tie in with what some of the hunt saboteurs told Inspector Redfearn about hearing the kill call,' said Fry. 'You know what that means?'

Cooper tried not to look too smug. 'Yes, I know what the kill call is.'

'So . . .?'

'These riders,' he said. 'Were they wearing hunting dress?'

'They were in tweed jackets.'

'Ratcatcher? But that's autumn hunting dress.'

Fry laughed. 'It doesn't matter what time of year it is, surely?'

This time, Cooper couldn't resist smiling at the awareness of his superior knowledge. 'I think you'll find it does, Diane. You don't wear ratcatcher in March.'

He saw Fry hesitate then. He had to say that for her, at least – if you sounded sure enough of yourself, it did make her stop and think twice.

'Anyway,' she said, 'what I really wanted you for was to come with me to the Forbes place. The woman there is joint master of the Eden Valley Hunt. There are three masters, apparently, but the other two live in Sheffield, and she's our local person. Do you know her, by any chance?'

'I know *of* her,' admitted Cooper. 'I don't think we've ever actually met.'

'Good. I spoke to her on Tuesday, during the hunt. But it wasn't a good time to get anything out of her. I want to corner her at home.'

'Corner her? You make her sound like a trapped rat.'

'Well, that's kind of what I'm hoping for. I'm sure the hunt people were closing ranks against me. Definitely covering something up.'

'So you said. But I wouldn't be too quick to jump to that conclusion,' said Cooper. 'When do you want to go?'

'This afternoon.'

'No problem.'

119

Feeling a sudden need to get a bit of distance from his colleague, Cooper walked as far as the dry-stone wall bordering the sheep pasture. The neighbouring field was much lower down the hill. Very unusually for this part of Derbyshire, the field was planted with an arable crop of some kind, its stalks already several inches tall and showing bright green. Some hopeful farmer praying for a break?

He shook his head. 'Diane, are you sure this is the way the riders came?'

'We think so. Why?'

'Well, on horseback, there would have been no way for them to get over the stile, or the wall. They must have come through the gate between the two fields.' Cooper pointed at the gate some yards away. 'Were there sheep in this top field when you first arrived?'

'Yes, we got the farmer to move them.'

'Well, the fact that the sheep were still in this field, and not raiding the crop next door, suggests to me that the riders closed the gate after them.'

'Fingerprints?' said Fry.

'Exactly. The gate is closed by a steel latch, and the underside of it is protected from the rain.'

'I'll get Wayne Abbott on to it.'

'Some of the prints will be the farmer's, of course. But you never know.'

'Here's hoping, then.'

Cooper thought even Diane Fry ought to have spotted something like that. It was pretty obvious, wasn't it? Gates were made to keep livestock in, so this one must have been closed by someone. *Ipso facto.*

But all she did was watch him in silence as he clambered over the gate, careful to avoid touching the latch, and studied the lower field. There was no mistaking those distinctive crescent shapes pressed into the soft ground, or the powerful odour lingering long after the horses had passed by. Brown, fibrous heaps lay on the soil, the weather too cold yet for the orange dung flies that would swarm around them in summer. But the hoof marks were in quite the wrong place.

'Look, they rode down the tramlines, too,' said Cooper.

'Tramlines?'

'The parallel tracks left by farm machinery through the crop. They're there for a reason – to guide accurate spraying and fertilizing – and they're easily damaged by horse riders, especially in wet weather.'

'So?'

Cooper felt himself bristle at her tone. He hated the way she said 'So?' like that. It seemed to sum up all her contempt for the way of life that he'd grown up with. She made that one word suggest that none of this could have any possible importance in the real world, the world that Diane Fry moved in. The implicit sneer made him so angry. He was glad that she couldn't see the expression on his face right now.

'Responsible riders don't ride down tramlines,' said Cooper, taking a deep breath to calm himself. 'If you did that on a hunt, you'd get sent home by the master. You're supposed to go round the outside of the field.'

'Do hunting people really have all these rules to follow?'

'Yes. And they stick to them rigidly.' Cooper turned back to face her. 'I don't care what your video shows, Diane. These weren't members of the hunt.'

14

Fry felt her determination harden as they drove to Watersaw House, where the Forbes lived. There was no way she was going to stand at her own crime scene and let someone like Ben Cooper tell her she was wrong. He wasn't even supposed to be here, for heaven's sake.

Yet Cooper seemed to be unavoidable. Trying to keep him at arm's length was as impractical as taking precautions against the plague.

'This Eyam place,' she said, as they passed the end of the village. 'The Plague Village. What's that all about, then? The Black Death as a form of entertainment? I know people are really stuck for things to do in these parts, but celebrating the plague is pretty weird, even for Derbyshire.'

'I think it's more a question of celebrating the village's survival,' said Cooper. 'That's what the story is all about.'

'If the place was a bit more civilized,' said Fry, 'they might not have got the plague in the first place.'

She heard Cooper sigh, and restrained a smile. He wasn't invulnerable. There were ways to wind *him* up, too.

'The plague came from London in a bundle of damp cloth,' said Cooper. 'Black rats had introduced the Black Death to England when they came off ships in the docks.'

'I didn't know you could catch bubonic plague from rats.'

'Not from the rats themselves. From their fleas.'

Fry shuddered, and began to regret that she'd mentioned Eyam at all. Rats and fleas were two of the things she hated most in the world.

'Watersaw,' said Cooper, when he saw the sign at the entrance to the Forbes' drive. 'There's a Watersaw Rake near here. One of the old opencast workings. Abandoned now, but it would be the nearest one to the crime scene, I think.'

There seemed to be horses everywhere at Watersaw House. As soon as Fry parked her car in the entrance to the stable yard, a huge black horse ran up to the post-and-rail fence and hung its head over to stare at her. She couldn't squeeze past the car door without brushing reluctantly against its inquisitive muzzle.

'It looks quite friendly,' said Cooper.

'Are you sure?'

The one other thing Fry knew about horses was that they were supposed to like sugar cubes. But who on earth used sugar cubes any more, let alone carried them around in their pockets in case they met a horse?

But she did have a packet of mints in her pocket, and she took it out. The horse nuzzled her jacket, as if searching the rest of her pockets, a quick frisk on suspicion of possession. When she unwrapped a mint and held it out on her palm, the horse went straight for it.

Fry was used to seeing horses, but usually at a safe distance – the mounted unit controlling a crowd at a football match, Up close, she was amazed by the way the animal's lips unfurled and grasped the mint. She had never realized horses had such prehensile mouths, almost like monkey's. She supposed it was a characteristic you had to develop when you had no hands to use.

'You seem to be bonding,' said Cooper, sounding quite impressed.

'Animals are all right, as long as they know who's the boss.'

But then the horse began waggling its ears, and showed its teeth. That was definitely a threat. She backed away, and turned to find the owner of Watersaw House regarding her with scarcely disguised contempt.

Today, Mrs Forbes had removed her riding boots and replaced them with a pair of green wellies. Definite working boots, a crack in the side, mud and straw stuck in the ridges of the soles. They seemed to be at least a size too big, because they flapped as she moved about the yard. To Fry's surprise, she was also wearing a head scarf. She didn't think non-Muslim women wore head scarves any more – well, except the Queen, and Tubbs off *The League of Gentlemen*.

'Mrs Forbes,' she said. 'Detective Sergeant Fry, Edendale Police. I spoke to you on Tuesday morning at the hunt, if you remember.'

'Oh, yes. What can I do for you?'

'We'd like you to assist us with our enquiries.'

'Good heavens, do you people really talk like that?'

Mrs Forbes laughed. Fry bristled.

'It's about the death of Mr Patrick Rawson,' she said. 'We're trying to gather as much information as we can about the circumstances of his death. Oh, this is my colleague, Detective Constable Cooper.'

Mrs Forbes examined Cooper with a critical eye, like a buyer weighing up a specimen of bloodstock. Fry wasn't sure whether she was imagining it, but the woman's expression actually seemed to soften a little. Mrs Forbes said nothing, but there was definitely a form of private communication going on that Fry wasn't party to.

'I see you run a livery stables, Mrs Forbes.'

The woman waved a hand around the yard. 'Yes, indeed. Twenty-eight stables, eighteen turn-out paddocks, purpose-built boxes, indoor and outdoor manèges . . . everything you

124

could want. We offer full-time or part-time livery. These girls you see here are some of our DIY-ers.'

Fry studied the youngsters brushing their horses and sorting out their tack. She could see straight away that these weren't the kind of kids who hung around in the alleys of housing estates in Edendale, drinking bottles of lager and passing round a joint. These girls smelled of saddle soap and horse manure instead of alcohol and cannabis. Yet there was something elusively similar in their manner, a total absorption in their own world, and a hostile stare for the outsider. And in both cases, as Fry well knew, the outsider meant her.

'We turn them out and bring them in, but the girls do their own feeding, grooming and mucking out,' said Mrs Forbes. 'I like to see young people who aren't afraid of a bit of hard work, don't you?'

A younger woman dismounted from a horse and came across the yard to join them, leading her mount by its reins. When she reached them, she took off her helmet and shook her hair free. Mid-twenties, probably. She wore an expensive-looking riding outfit. Nice leather boots. And those beige jodhpurs – they fit her rather well. Fry glanced at Cooper to see if he was noticing.

'This is my daughter, Alicia,' said Mrs Forbes. 'I started the yard about ten years ago, and Alicia has been helping me in the business full time for the past four, ever since she graduated. A BHS-qualified instructor, aren't you, darling?'

Fry blinked, but then realized the last comment had been addressed to Alicia, not to her or Cooper.

'And she's terribly interested in the use of complementary therapies,' said Mrs Forbes. 'Essential oils and all that, you know.'

Fry looked at the young girls again, sweating under the weight of rugs and saddles. Feeding, grooming, turning out, bringing in, mucking out . . . She didn't know what on earth it all was, but it sounded like an endless amount of work.

And for what? For nothing more than the chance to climb on the back of one of these monkey-lipped creatures and prance about the countryside in a pair of fancy leather boots.

'You appreciate we have to try to establish how Mr Rawson died, Mrs Forbes. You, and other members of the hunt, are potential witnesses. What we need from you is a list of who was present at the location of Tuesday's meet from about eight a.m.'

'Inspector Redfearn already asked us for that information.'

'Yes, he did. But so far as I'm aware –'

'Alicia?'

The younger woman produced an envelope from the pocket of her body warmer. 'This is the list you want. The hunt secretary drew it up for you. Names, addresses and phone numbers. The times that each person arrived, and what they were doing between eight o'clock and nine thirty.'

'You'll find it's a very short list, I'm afraid,' said Mrs Forbes. 'Largely the hunt servants, plus Alicia and I. And we were all much too busy to notice what was going on half a mile away from the meet, I can assure you.'

Fry could feel herself being pushed on to the back foot, and she didn't like it.

'Oh yes, of course,' she said. 'I suppose you all just happened to be in the wrong place at the wrong time.'

She had the satisfaction of seeing a pained reaction. 'Possibly.'

'We still need to talk to everyone. One of you might have seen something significant.'

'You'll do what you have to do, Sergeant. Personally, I can tell you right now that I didn't see anything out of the ordinary, or anyone who shouldn't have been there.' Mrs Forbes smiled. 'Apart from the antis, of course. But I don't need to tell you that, surely? Now, if you'll excuse me . . .'

The woman walked away towards the stables, and could be heard speaking to the girls. Fry turned her attention to Alicia.

'You're a member of the hunt, too?'

'Yes.'

'And you were out on Tuesday, I gather?'

'Of course. We all want to show our support. But we didn't see anything, really we didn't.'

As the daughter spoke, she moved a hand to stroke the inside of her horse's leg, where the skin looked smooth and soft. Fry found the gesture somehow disturbing.

'I've no idea who that man was who died, and I'm sure Mummy hasn't either,' said Alicia. 'We were just trying to get on with our own business, and avoid the antis. You'd be better talking to them, wouldn't you?'

'We have talked to them,' said Fry. 'But, you see, they weren't on horseback.'

Alicia looked away. 'I can't help you.'

The horse swung around restlessly, pointing its haunches at Fry. Out of the corner of her eye, she noticed Cooper moving away towards Alicia Forbes. But she was feeling more confident now, and she stood her ground, even when the rear end bumped gently against her.

'Do you happen to know the bridlepath called Badger's Way, Miss Forbes?' Cooper was asking.

'Yes, I've ridden there a few times. But everyone uses it – it's good to be able to get away from traffic for a while.'

'Yes, of course.'

'There have been several incidents of reckless driving near horse riders in this area. Perhaps you know.'

'Any motorists identified are being warned,' said Cooper. 'They could face prosecution for driving without due care and attention.'

Fry watched, feeling suddenly like a spare part, as Alicia Forbes looked Cooper up and down. She'd experienced this moment so often.

'Do you have any animals yourself?' she asked him.

'Just a cat,' he admitted, patting the horse's neck.

'Oh.' Then she looked at his hand. 'And you're not wearing a wedding ring.'

'No.'

'I just wondered – I know not all men wear them, even when they're married.'

'So I've heard.'

'So . . . are you? Married?'

'No.'

'You must be, what . . . thirty by now? Isn't it time to settle down?'

'Well, it's not quite so simple.'

'Mmm. I suppose not. Still – a single man, living alone with a cat. It could give the wrong impression.'

Just then, a powerful odour filled the yard. Not just the pervasive background smell, but something much more pungent and immediate.

'Diane, watch out,' said Cooper.

But he was too late. Fry felt the soft impact of warm, steaming lumps of fresh horse manure splattering on to her trousers and covering her shoes. For a second, she was so shocked that she couldn't move. And the plops just kept coming. How did one animal manage to produce so much at one go?

As if by magic, Mrs Forbes herself had re-appeared to witness the moment.

'Oh, I'm so terribly sorry,' she said. 'It appears you were standing in the wrong place at the wrong time.'

'These hunting people,' said Fry angrily as she got back into the Peugeot. 'Honestly, talking to them is like flogging a dead –'

She stopped, realizing the stupidity of what she'd been about to say. As she started up the engine, Cooper got into the passenger seat. Fastening his seat belt, he wafted a hand in an exaggerated gesture.

'Diane,' he said, 'I hope you don't mind if I open the window? Only, it's a bit –'

'Yes,' said Fry. 'I know.'

Back at the office, Cooper found a place to hang his damp coat and fetched himself a coffee from the vending machine. Hardly coffee, really – but it was hot.

He stood for a moment watching Irvine and Hurst busy at work in the CID room. He was remembering again his first ever visit to Eyam, with the school party. He recalled that he'd brought back a souvenir from the village museum. Cooper smiled when he pictured it. His mother had hated the thing, and didn't even want it in the house. She paid no attention to his explanation. Eyam was most famous as the Plague Village, right? So what else would you choose as a suitable souvenir to commemorate the Black Death? It was obvious, really. A black, plastic rat, with red eyes and a long, scaly tail.

The young Cooper had thought it was a fine example of *Rattus rattus*, the Black Rat – now one of the rarest mammals in the UK, thanks to its more successful cousin, the brown rat. The souvenir rat even came with its own information leaflet, explaining that this was the little beast that had spread from Asia to Europe in the Middle Ages, bringing its little gift of the bubonic plague. In dark corners of barns and warehouses it could be active at all hours, and ate almost anything it could find, its family groups organized on a hierarchical basis, dominated by one strong individual. They carried not only the plague, but typhus, rabies, salmonella, hantavirus, Weil's disease . . . oh, and trichinosis, the pork roundworm. Thank God the natural mortality rate of rats was ninety per cent.

Cooper recalled very clearly standing outside the Plague Cottage that first time, reading the names of the dead on the plaque. It was all very well for people like Diane Fry to scoff at Eyam's fame as the Plague Village, to laugh at the idea of souvenir rats and tableaux of people in night shirts with their necks covered in bubos. But for him, there was one fact which had made the whole story different, and much more personal. According to the well-documented history of Eyam's plague year, the very first family to fall victim to the Black Death had been Coopers.

Fry had been only a few minutes late for her appointment to see Detective Superintendent Branagh. Yet when she entered the superintendent's office, she felt a bit like the naughty child sent to see the head teacher for breaking wind in class.

The superintendent's office was on the upper floor of Divisional HQ, looking down on Gate C and the back of the East Stand at Edendale Football Club. That view seemed to have become a status symbol among the senior management team. It was also one of the few offices with air conditioning, but it wasn't in use today, and the room was a bit too warm. Branagh sniffed as she entered, like a disapproving matron.

After her visit to Mrs Forbes this afternoon, the first thing that struck Fry as she sat down was that Superintendent Branagh would make a good Master of the Hounds. She had a sudden image of Branagh, whip in hand, boots polished, riding britches specially tailored to accommodate her hips. The perfect companion for Lord Somebody or Other, whose portrait was in the National Gallery.

The superintendent flicked a file open impatiently, with no time to spare for the social niceties, making it plain that Fry had kept her waiting.

'As you know, DS Fry,' she said, 'I've been reviewing the files of all CID staff in this division. Some of the Personal Development Reviews make interesting reading. Very interesting.'

'I'm sure they've all been done properly, ma'am.'

'Indeed. I'll be talking to you about your team in due course.

130

But, in the first instance, I've been looking at your record, and your case histories, DS Fry,' she said. 'Would you accept that there have been some weaknesses in certain areas of your development during your time with E Division?'

'Well . . . I suppose I still have some experience to gain in a supervisory role.'

Branagh was watching her, waiting for more. But Fry wasn't about to give it to her. Why hand her superintendent ammunition by criticizing her own performance? It was an old managerial trick.

'Well, the fact is,' said Branagh, 'that you haven't really been getting results. At least, not the sort of results I would have hoped for from you, if I'd been here during the past couple of years. Would you agree with that assessment, DS Fry?'

No choice here. If Fry denied it, she would be forced to quote examples to support her argument. And right now, nothing came to mind.

'I suppose so, ma'am.'

Branagh nodded. 'I'm glad you agree. It's a shame, because your early reports suggest that you were once considered a potential high-flier.'

Fry's heart gave a lurch of shock. That was a real punch below the belt. All this time, she'd been considering herself a high-flier, on the surface at least. Deep down, she must have known that she wasn't, not any more. Still a Detective Sergeant at the age of thirty? For heaven's sake. It must have been obvious to everyone around her that she'd lost ground. She had been too busy with other concerns, taken up by so many distractions that she hadn't been focusing on the job. Not the way she should have done.

When had it all started to go wrong? Not when she first transferred to Derbyshire. Well, not immediately, anyway. She'd been given the promotion almost straight away. But maybe that had been on the strength of her previous record.

131

Somewhere, somehow, she had then taken her eye off the ball, had let her career get stagnant. She'd been drifting with the current, when she ought to have been swimming for land.

Damn it, Branagh was right. DS Diane Fry's career had been ruined. In this stinking backwater, she had become soft and lazy. She'd gone native. Jesus, if she wasn't careful, she could even end up like Ben Cooper.

Detective Superintendent Branagh was still talking, listing entries from her Personal Development Reviews. Targets and assessments, the occasions when guidance had been given, one instance when words of advice had been issued following a complaint of rudeness from a member of the public.

But Fry wasn't really listening. She was recalling her first week on the job in Derbyshire, meeting her DI, and Hitchens asking her what she was aiming to achieve. '*I'm good at my job,*' she'd said. '*I'll be looking for promotion. That's what's important to me.*'

And, of course, she'd soon become aware of the talk around the station. Everyone said the force was short of female officers in supervisory ranks, especially in CID. Provided she kept her nose clean and smiled nicely at the top brass, she would shoot up the promotion ladder without trying. And there *had* been a quick promotion, too – the step up to Detective Sergeant, which hadn't been popular with everyone.

But what had she done since then? Her brain searched for an answer that she could give Superintendent Branagh, some wonderful achievement that she could point to. But her mind was still coming up blank. That was the effect of shock tactics.

By a stroke of luck, the superintendent took her silence for absorption in some other subject than the one at hand.

'We can resume this conversation at another time,' she said. 'I appreciate that you're busy with the suspicious death case.'

'Yes, ma'am. That's true.'

'Very well, then. We'll resume tomorrow. That will give you a chance to think about what we've said so far.'

Reluctantly, Fry got up to leave. Then Branagh sniffed. 'What *is* that smell?'

Fry became aware of the aroma that she must have been carrying around with her all afternoon on her jacket, and on her hands. And maybe on her shoes, if she'd been really unlucky. She'd better check in a minute, as soon as she got out of the room – but not while Branagh was watching her.

'Horses, ma'am,' she said. 'It's the smell of horses.'

'I see,' said Superintendent Branagh. She said it in the tone of someone who didn't see at all, but considered it hardly worthwhile demanding an explanation.

15

As the temperature fell that evening, the moisture in the air began to form dense banks of fog on the higher ground. When Ben Cooper closed the front door of 8 Welbeck Street, he always looked up to see the hills. He found their presence reassuring, even in the dark, when they were black against the sky. But tonight, the hills above the town were masked by a grey blanket, and wisps of fog could be seen swirling above the streetlights.

Cooper's local in Edendale was the Hanging Gate, a pub sitting in its own little yard off the High Street. When he first moved into the flat at Welbeck Street, he'd taken some trouble in finding the right sort of pub. He wasn't a heavy drinker, not like some of his colleagues, who relied on alcohol to help them deal with the pressures of the job. A drink or two did help him relax. But most of all, a decent pub provided company, and a meal when you didn't feel like cooking for yourself – which, in his case, was quite often.

Like so many pubs in the area, the Hanging Gate had framed scenic Peak District views on the walls, and even a few hunting prints. But the beer was good, and the choice of rock classics on the juke box was familiar and reassuring.

As he and Liz Petty stepped through the door on to the

stone flags, Cooper nodded to a few acquaintances. He was pretty well known here now, but people left him alone. It wasn't the sort of place where you got bothered if they knew you were a police officer. Another plus for the Hanging Gate.

He and Liz had been going out for several months now. It was one of those relationships that had grown up gradually from a casual awareness of someone in a different department at work into something more than friendship. It was supposed to be the way the best relationships developed, if you believed what the women's magazines said.

They got their drinks, and found a table. Liz was a bit on edge, because she was due to meet Ben's sister for the first time. Claire was expected to arrive in another half an hour, though it would be par for the course if she was late. So he and Liz had some time together first.

'How did you get on at the vet's?' she asked.

Cooper looked at her over his bottle. 'Oh, that's nice. I like the way you're concerned about the cat, but you haven't bothered asking how I am.'

'I don't need to ask about you. I can see you're as always.' She studied him for a moment. 'It didn't go well, then?'

He shook his head. 'It's kidney failure. It seems old Rand must be more ancient than he looks. That, or he's led a riotous life.'

'Is there anything they can do?'

'Not without putting him through a lot of pain and discomfort.'

'I see.'

'So it's just a matter of time.'

She grasped his hand. 'I'm sorry.'

Cooper felt embarrassed. 'He's only a cat.'

'Yeah, right.'

There was a silence while they drank, each with their own thoughts. And then, in that inevitable way that it always happened, they began talking about work. No, not really work – office gossip.

135

After a few minutes, Liz looked away as she asked him another question.

'Do you think Diane Fry might be in need of some support?' she said.

Cooper put down his drink. 'What?'

'Support. You know what support is, Ben.'

'Right. But Diane –'

'Yes, Diane Fry. She's only human, you know. The talk is that she might be going through a bad time.'

Well, Cooper suspected that every week was a bad time for Diane Fry in one way or another, but he let it pass.

'Why particularly now?'

'The word around the station is that the new superintendent has it in for her. Doesn't think she fits in.'

'How is it that civilian staff always manage to gather far more information than detectives?' said Cooper. But he didn't really feel like joking. What Liz was saying matched his own feeling too closely.

He looked around the Hanging Gate. A thick brass rail and stools lined up at the bar. A trophy cabinet for the darts team. Rooms were separated by coloured glass panels. A florid-faced man with a bald head and a dark moustache came into the pub, and a young woman with unnaturally pale hair and sunglasses followed him. While he waited to be served at the bar, she walked past and found a seat near the back of the room. The bald man watched her all the way.

It was in this pub that Angie Fry had once tried to present him with a forged death certificate, expecting him to help her in a strategy to get her sister off her back. It recorded the death in Chapeltown, Sheffield, of Angela Jane Fry, aged thirty, and had been dated just over a year previously. It was the first time he'd ever sat at a table in a pub and talked to a dead person.

'*And presumably this isn't your real address,*' Cooper had said.

And Angie had laughed. '*That isn't even my name now. I changed it some time ago. The house was used as a squat, but the owners evicted everyone months ago.*'

And because of his refusal to be involved in that scheme to prevent Diane from finding her sister, the two women had finally been re-united and had ended up living together for months at Diane's place in Grosvenor Avenue. Cooper still had no idea whether Diane knew the full picture. Or ever would.

And the odd thing was, Diane Fry had been the bane of his life ever since her arrival in Derbyshire. She was the newcomer who had rejected his attempts at friendship, she was the woman who'd got the promotion he'd thought was his own. She was the supervisor who made him feel he never did anything right, who scoffed at his background and his way of life. She was the woman who looked at him as if he'd mortally offended her at some time, perhaps just by being who he was.

Yes, she was all of those things. He surely had every reason to hate her. Yet, when it came to the point, Cooper realized that he didn't want her to leave. Her departure would create a strange, inexplicable gap in his life that he couldn't imagine being able to fill in any other way.

'Yes, I'll speak to her,' he said.

Liz nodded. 'I think you should. You're the closest thing she has to a friend, you know, Ben.'

'You're kidding.'

But as soon as he said it, Cooper knew she was right. He couldn't think of a single person who was close to Diane Fry. Some had tried. In fact, he'd tried himself, for a while. But Fry was the sort of person who didn't want friendship. If asked, she would say she could manage without it. He could almost hear her saying it now.

He looked at Liz. 'I'll see what I can do.'

'Good.'

Liz had made a special effort tonight. Her hair was brushed back, and she'd applied touches of make-up that transformed her normal healthy bloom. Although Cooper was no judge, the glitter of her bracelet looked expensive.

He had a sudden feeling of panic that he hadn't been treating Liz well enough. And here he was, expecting her to sit in the bar of the Hanging Gate with him. She hadn't seemed to demand any more, but seeing her tonight, he had a nagging suspicion of a dangerous gulf between them that he'd been ignoring. What, after all, did he really know about her?

Liz's green eyes seemed to mock him, as if she was reading his thoughts. Was his face so transparent, that everyone could do that?

But then her eyes slipped past him, and Cooper turned. His sister had arrived.

'It's getting really foggy out there,' said Claire, shaking off her coat. 'Not so bad in town, but you can't see three feet in front of you on the hills.'

Introductions followed, and those few awkward moments before drinks were fetched and everyone settled down again. Liz clutched at his hand and held it firmly on the table, intertwining her fingers with his. To Cooper, it felt more like a proprietary gesture in the face of a rival than a need for reassurance. He saw Claire notice it, and felt oddly uncomfortable.

'It's lovely to meet you,' said Claire to Liz. 'I've heard such a lot about you.'

Cooper almost spilt his beer. He never talked about Liz to his family very much; in fact, he'd sometimes had to resist persistent cross-questioning from Claire. But Liz laughed, as if the idea of being gossiped about pleased her.

'I'm glad you spare the time,' she said. 'Ben always tells me you're really busy.'

'That's true.'

Claire Cooper often complained of being too busy for

anything. But that might change now that she was closing down her craft shop in Bold Lane. The 'To Let' signs were already up, and she was letting the stock run down. Last time Ben had called in to see her, there were almost no healing crystals or dream catchers to be seen anywhere, though the aroma of sandalwood remained, and would probably persist for ever. He wondered if Claire had ever sold citronella oil, which was used by hunt saboteurs to distract hounds, as well as being a perfume and natural insect repellent.

'So what are you going to do now, instead of running the shop?' he asked.

'Well, I'm getting a job,' said Claire.

'Oh, a New Age sort of job, I suppose?'

'Ben, the shop was never "New Age". It was just a little bit alternative, that's all.'

'Too alternative for the people of Edendale. It never made much money, did it?'

'Profit isn't everything.'

Ben laughed. 'Try telling that to Matt.'

Claire looked from Ben to Liz. 'You ought to go and visit Bridge End Farm. You haven't been for a long time, have you?'

'Well, a week or two, perhaps.'

'Longer than that, Ben. The girls are missing you.'

'Did they say so?'

'Yes, actually. Amy particularly. She asked if you were ever coming again.'

Cooper thought he'd always enjoyed a close relationship with his two nieces, Amy and Josie. He was shocked to hear they didn't think he was visiting them enough, that he might even have forgotten about them.

'I'll go this Friday,' he said.

Liz gripped his hand more tightly. 'Don't forget we're going out Friday night.'

'Oh, right.'

Cooper remembered Liz talking about what they should do

at the weekend. She wanted to go to the Dog and Parrot to see a band that was playing there this Friday, Midlife Krisis. Cooper had never heard of them.

'It doesn't matter, if you don't want to.'

'We'll talk about it,' he said.

Liz's phone buzzed, a text message coming through. There were times when she was on call-out for Scenes of Crime, and could disappear at any moment.

'Excuse me, I must take this. Besides, I've got to go to the loo, anyway.'

'No problem. See you in a minute,' said Cooper.

He smiled at his sister, taking a drink of his beer. But Claire looked at him steadily, waiting until Liz was out of earshot.

'I don't want to interfere, Ben . . .'

'It never stopped you in the past, Sis.'

'I'm sorry, but . . . I really don't think she's right for you.'

'We're only going out, you know. We're not about to walk up the aisle tomorrow.'

'I know that,' said Claire. 'But I know *you*, too. I don't want you to make a big mistake.'

Cooper leaned back in his chair, and rubbed a hand across his face. Why did everyone always want to tell him what to do? He wasn't a teenager any more, for goodness' sake. He hadn't been for a long time.

'So what's the problem, Claire? Is it because Liz is in the job? She's a civilian, you know, not a police officer.'

'What difference does that make?'

'They have an easier life,' said Cooper. 'But don't tell Liz I said that.'

'She gets called away, just the same way that you do. The job comes first, doesn't it? It came first for Dad, and it comes first for you. Another one like that, and –'

'We're all doomed?'

Claire sighed. 'It wouldn't work, Ben. What happened to that teacher you went out with for a while?'

140

'Helen? She just sort of disappeared.'

'Well, I thought she was all right. But this Liz Petty – well, she spends her life looking at crime scenes, picking up blood-stains and hairs, and goodness knows what. Besides . . .'

'What? There's more?'

'I think she's too possessive. I'm worried you'll get led into something you'll regret.'

'What do you mean?'

'Ben, you're the sort of man a certain type of woman could get obsessed with. Like a doctor – you know, someone depend-able, reassuring. Someone who actually wants to help you. There are women who would do anything to believe they had a relationship with a man like that. GPs know it well. It's called dependency syndrome.'

'She'd have to be an obsessive kind of woman.'

'Yes.'

Cooper put his drink down. 'Claire, I appreciate that you're concerned for me, but it *is* my life, you know.'

Claire sighed. 'Are you sure?'

'Sure?'

'I think you're missing Mum and Dad a lot more than you let on, Ben. And they do say that you're often looking for – Well, let's change the subject.'

He stared at her, puzzled by what she could mean. But before he could ask her, he saw Liz was making her way back through the crowds from the ladies. And then the moment had passed.

Watching the two of them in cautious conversation, Cooper tried to analyse his feelings. Sometimes he seriously doubted his ability to pick the right woman. He'd been going out with Liz Petty longer than anyone else he'd ever known. They'd even gone through a Christmas together, and he'd met her parents. Boxing Day lunch at their house in Bakewell. A subtle barrage of questions over the mince pies about his background, his family, his prospects in the police. Old-fashioned parents

141

who desperately wanted to feel that their approval was needed.

But he hadn't minded that. It would have been the same the other way round, if he'd been able to take Liz home to meet his father and mother. But that would have to have been years ago, before Dad was killed, before Mum became so ill. He tried to imagine Boxing Day lunch with all of his family there – Dad at the top of the table, upright and solemn like an Old Testament prophet as he carved the joint, Mum fussing about, backwards and forwards to the kitchen, until she'd crammed the huge table to capacity and plates of vegetables threatened to tip off the edge. And there would have been Matt and Kate, of course, and the girls. And maybe Claire, too – though she usually managed to avoid those huge meals and call at less demanding times, when only the sherry and chocolates were on offer.

Could he imagine introducing Liz into that gathering, subjecting her to the third degree, the iron-jawed inter-rogation by his father, the more discreet insinuations of his mother, the candid curiosity of Matt, and Kate's well meaning attempts at intimacy? Would he even have wanted to?

He couldn't really explain to himself why the question was important. But it had been preying on his mind ever since that Boxing Day visit. He thought he had probably passed the test with Mr and Mrs Petty. But would Liz have survived the same ordeal among the Coopers at Bridge End Farm?

And what was it that Claire had been about to tell him people said? Could it be that when you chose a partner in life, you were subconsciously looking for someone who was just like your mother?

Ben was used to being told that he was trying too hard to emulate his father, that he would be forever standing in the shadow of Sergeant Joe Cooper, the model copper who'd died in the course of his duty, kicked to death on the streets of

142

Edendale. The last thing he needed was a mother figure. That definitely wasn't what he was looking for in Liz.

It was a funny thing, though. It actually seemed to be Claire who was starting to turn into his mother.

That night, Claire had emailed copies of the photos she'd taken at the National Memorial Arboretum. While Cooper waited for them to download on to his PC, he spooned some tuna-flavoured Whiskas into a bowl for Randy, hoping the cat might be tempted by his favourite food.

He smiled to himself as he recalled the scene at Watersaw House stables, with the horse passing its opinion on Fry in a way that the owners had been a little too polite to do. He'd never seen Fry quite so angry before. Her nostrils had flared wider than the horse's.

Alicia Forbes had been all right, though, hadn't she? Well, for a pony girl. He wasn't sure what she'd meant about giving the wrong impression, though. Lots of men his age weren't married – either because they hadn't decided to settle down yet, or because marriage just wasn't regarded as the social obligation it once was. Perhaps it was different in the circles that the Forbes moved in. But what had owning a cat got to do with it?

Then Cooper looked at the cat, and the cat stared back at him in disgust. The wrong impression?

'Sorry, Randy,' he said. 'But I'm afraid she thinks you're gay.'

He went back to his computer screen, recalling another interesting fact about the black rat that he could have mentioned to Fry. The one group of people who had never been affected by bubonic plague were the nomadic tribes of central Asia, where the bacteria had first originated. Those nomads lived close to their companions, the wild horses of the arid Asian plains. And the one thing that rat fleas *really* hated was the smell of horses.

143

When the photos from Claire had finished downloading, Cooper clicked on the first attachment and opened the jpeg file with a strange feeling of reluctance.

He'd never really been keen on photos of himself, particularly in family snapshots. Now, they reminded him too much of his mother, who had always loved showing off the family albums, pages and pages recording the growth of her children from new-born horrors through the adolescent monster stage and into adulthood. Mum would have loved a snap of her sons together, treasured it as a testament of her crowning achievement in life. But without her being there to appreciate the photo, it was just one more embarrassment to suffer.

In this case, the picture was also too recent. It reminded him too much of the visit to the police memorial on Sunday. The comments made by Matt and Claire were fresh in his mind, and they weren't what he wanted to be thinking about right now. 'Persecuting law-abiding people instead of going after the real criminals.' 'Police officers standing around doing risk assessments while someone is dying.' Dad would never have done that. No, of course he wouldn't.

And when Ben saw the picture full-size on the screen of his laptop, he realized something he hadn't noticed at the time. He'd been too busy staring at the camera, wondering if he should try to hold a smile, or look serious because of the occasion. And wondering, too, whether he looked ridiculously windswept from being outside, those little bits of spiky hair sticking out like devil's horns. When someone pointed a camera at you, your attention was automatically focused on yourself and the lens, it was such a peculiar moment of intimacy. You forgot completely about what might be around and behind you. Even the photographer did that. It was an error that had caught a lot of people out.

But in this case, what he hadn't noticed was that he and Matt, gazing solemnly out of the screen, were standing right in front of the giant policeman in the main building of the

144

arboretum. The bobby loomed over them, vast and ominous, blocking out the light from the windows like a monstrous ghost.

He'd also been much too tall for the lens of Claire's digital camera. The head and helmet of the giant policeman were neatly sliced off.

Philip Worsley had finally admitted to himself that he was lost. The fog had come down so quickly on Longstone Moor that it had confused him totally.

When he'd set off to walk from Stoney Middleton, the weather had been clear, and he'd taken advantage of a spell without rain for his late afternoon walk. He couldn't believe that it was so different up here – so different that he could barely see his hand in front of his face. This didn't happen back home in Essex.

At one point, Philip thought he'd reached the path that led downwards to the crossroads. There was supposed to be a farmhouse not far from the junction, though he couldn't tell which direction it lay in. He'd been here before, years ago, and it was a pity that his memory wasn't clearer. He'd have to hope for a distant light visible when he got nearer.

He had a map in his rucksack, of course, but none of the landmarks seemed to fit. Nothing was where it was supposed to be. A slope where it should be flat, water where there should be land. It was as if he'd stepped out of the real world into some parallel universe.

He shivered in the damp fog. And for the first time, Philip started to feel concerned. Apart from his map, he had a waterproof, a bottle of water, a spare pair of socks in case he got his feet wet. But nothing to eat, except a roll of his favourite sweets, the perfumed Parma Violets that he'd remembered from his school days. There might be some sugar in them, but they wouldn't provide him with extra energy for long.

Philip kept walking, but without recognizing any signs or

gateways. Twenty minutes later, when his foot slipped into a hole and his ankle doubled up underneath him, he knew he wasn't on the path at all. For the last few hundred yards, the slope of the land had been tending upwards, not down. The ache in his calf muscles was enough to tell him that fact, but he'd been trying not to notice it.

As he nursed his painful ankle and wiped a bloodied scratch on his hand, he knew that he was now in difficulties. He had no idea what direction he'd been walking in, or whether he'd even set off from the place he thought he had twenty minutes ago. His ankle wasn't actually sprained, and he could still walk on it, if he was careful. But the fog was as thick as ever, and there were no lights visible, no sound of traffic from any direction. His senses detected nothing around him except muffled rustlings and coughs in the heather, sounds that he took for the presence of sheep.

Then he reached a point where the terrain sloped towards him on all sides, rough ground calloused with rocks and grimy with dead bracken. It seemed to him that the landscape had caught him up, and now held him in its grubby palm, like an insect it meant to crush.

On the ridge of the slope above him, a single hawthorn seemed to writhe in the fog drifting past its branches. For a few moments, Philip could do nothing but listen to the silence, his senses baffled by the absence of noise. It was as if he'd gone suddenly deaf, or someone had turned off the sound in the world around him.

Trying to make some contact with his senses, he held his hands up to his face. The smell of Parma Violets, and a single drop of blood.

He came to a low fence and decided to step over it, rather than casting backwards and forwards to find a gate or stile. A moment later, he was falling.

16

Living underground could have its advantages, I suppose. You're away from the wind and rain, which is something to be thankful for up here in the hills. But the drawbacks can be fairly serious.

I remember there was always a musty smell, as if something had died in there already. No matter what we tried, there wasn't a thing we could do about the smell. Well, the ventilation was bad – just this shutter thing in the end wall, and another in the toilet. Precious little air to breathe.

And the smell was all my fault, according to Les. Mister high-and-mighty Number One never took the damp as an excuse, or bad ventilation, or the fact I had nothing to use except what I could carry on my back.

It was my job to haul up the bucket, too, with bright blue Elsan slopping about over my head, terrified every second that the thing would tip in the shaft and come right down on top of me. Les wouldn't even let Jimmy help me with the bucket. He said there were three jobs, and the sanitary arrangements were my responsibility, since I was the youngest. 'Sanitary arrangements' – that's the way he talked. Jimmy and me, we called it something quite different.

Les had more important things to do, of course. He was saving the world, was Les. A big bloody hero in a hole in the ground.

Well, we were all fighting for freedom, in our own way. It was the age of liberation, after all. Or so we were told. There wasn't much liberation in our part of the world. Just the same old attitudes, the same instinct to condemn, the implacable willingness to destroy other people's lives. Whatever happened to 'He that is without sin . . .?'

I suppose those cold, damp walls were supposed to protect us. But really, they could just as easily have been a prison. And, you know what? If I'd been in prison, I might have had more luck with my cell mates.

Even now, I always see Jimmy's face. I see it as clear as my own reflection when I look in the mirror. There were the three of us, up on top in the daylight. And him, down there in the dark, alone. Just a single shaft of light, falling on his face, gleaming on his glasses.

And then the falling, falling . . . It seemed to take so long, yet it must have been over in a second. His skull cracked like an egg.

One down. Two to go.

17

Thursday

Diane Fry had never quite got used to stepping out of the real world, a world full of living, breathing people, into the cold, sterile environment of the mortuary. The postmortem room was all stainless steel and grey tiles, the smell of disinfectant barely even competing with the odour of carved flesh and exposed internal organs. Whenever she entered these doors, it was the smell that entered her soul.

The Home Office pathologist, Dr Juliana van Doon, was a cool customer herself. Fry supposed you had to be that way, to work in a place like this. For a while, there had been rumours that she was in a relationship with one of the senior CID officers in E Division, but the talk had died down. These days, Mrs van Doon was starting to look tired, perhaps slightly worn around the edges. The skin of her arms looked a little dry, the hair tucked behind her ears was in need of a colour rinse.

'We have here a well-nourished Caucasian male; physical condition matches the given age of forty-four,' said the pathologist briskly, when Fry called in on her way to West Street that morning. 'Height one hundred and eighty-nine centimetres. That's a fraction over six feet, for the metrically challenged.'

'Oh, thank you,' said Fry. 'That's a help.'

The pathologist's tone made her tense up. It sounded like a challenge, and there was nothing wrong with that to start the day, in Fry's book. For some reason, she and Mrs van Doon had never really hit it off. Maybe it was something Fry had done herself when she first arrived in E Division, but the hostility had never been far below the surface. Fine, if that was the way she wanted it.

'His weight is eighty-eight kilos.'

'Mmm. Fourteen stone?'

'Very good, DS Fry.'

'Actually, I was educated entirely in metres and kilograms. But I've learned to do the conversion the other way.'

'A triumph of our modern education system,' said the pathologist.

Fry gritted her teeth, but stayed calm. She tried to concentrate on the individual whose postmortem she was attending. The important person in all of this – the victim. A glance at the body on the stainless-steel table showed her that he was carrying a bit of surplus body fat, but his muscles were reasonably well toned. He had a fading tan that stopped at the waistband line. A holiday abroad not too long ago. His hair was dark, with hardly a speck of grey to be seen. Now that the area had been shaved and cleaned, the damage to the skull was very evident.

'Strictly speaking, eighty-eight kilos for a man measuring six feet in height is classed as overweight,' said the pathologist. 'But he didn't seem to have had any problems. The heart is sound. An active occupation, perhaps?'

'He was a businessman,' said Fry. 'A company director.'

Dr van Doon shrugged. 'A sport would have helped to keep him fit.'

Fry thought of how far Rawson had managed to sprint over rough ground when the need arose. It was said that fear gave you wings, but a lot of men of his age would have been doubled up with stomach cramp after fifty yards.

'I imagine he didn't smoke either,' said the pathologist. 'We can usually tell that pretty quickly when they arrive in here.'

'Do we have a cause of death?' asked Fry.

'Oh, that.' With a click of her fingers, Dr van Doon moved to the head of the table. 'For once, Detective Sergeant, your first guess is almost certainly the correct one.'

'His head was smashed in.'

'If you want to be technical. I've also heard it referred to as an open compound fracture of the skull. Also present are severe scalp lacerations, some loose bone fragments, and part of the skull has been depressed into the brain, causing a cerebral contusion and serious haemorrhaging.'

'There was quite a lot of blood at the scene,' said Fry.

The pathologist looked up. 'That would be the scalp. It bleeds like a swamp, even from a minor laceration. Lots of nice, thick blood vessels in the scalp. No, the fatal damage is internal.'

'How quickly would he have died?'

'Very quickly, if he was unlucky. But you can survive for a surprisingly long time with an injury of this kind. Prompt medical attention would have made a big difference.'

'It appears that he might have collapsed after the initial attack, then come round and run a few hundred yards across a field before he finally died.'

'Perfectly possible. Though I would imagine he was staggering rather than running. The human body does have a surprising capacity for physical activity when the brain is fatally damaged.'

Fry was starting to feel a need for fresh air.

'Can we get an idea of what caused the damage?'

'Well, we've pieced the shattered bone back together, and the area has been photographed under a range of lighting sources. I think you might have a chance of identifying the weapon from the pattern of the depression.'

'Excellent.'

151

'I hoped you might think so.'

Fry looked at the body again. She was still no nearer to knowing what Patrick Rawson had been doing at the barn on Longstone Moor when he met his killers.

'Is there any sign of sexual intercourse prior to death?'

The pathologist gave her a look of distaste. 'You have all the best ideas, don't you, Sergeant?'

Fry returned her stare. 'That's something we have in common, then.'

'Well, the answer is "no".'

'Thank you.'

Cooper sat at his desk in the CID room, watching Gavin Murfin studying himself in a hand mirror, rubbing his fingers over his cheeks.

'What are you doing, Gavin?' asked Cooper.

'Wondering whether I should grow a beard,' said Murfin. 'It's such a pain, shaving in the morning, and it's getting quite fashionable again. What do you think? Would it suit me?'

Cooper looked at him critically. He had some sympathy with the idea. His own electric shaver always seemed to leave a dark shadow that had turned into stubble by evening. If he left off shaving for a day, he looked like a dosser within twenty-four hours. Great for going undercover.

'Gavin, you'd look like Vincent van Gogh,' he said. 'Except your hair's the wrong colour and you've got too many ears.'

Murfin sighed and put the mirror away. 'Thanks for the advice.'

Fry came through the door briskly, like a woman who had already started the day with a series of minor triumphs.

'Morning, Gavin. Anything happening?'

'Yes, Deborah Rawson's brother has been on local TV news in the West Midlands this morning,' said Murfin, winking at Cooper.

'Doing what?' said Fry.

'Paying tribute to his brother-in-law. He says he was a dearly loved husband, highly respected by his friends and business colleagues alike, and he will be a great loss to the community in Sutton Coldfield – I quote.'

'The press will be chasing us for a statement on what progress we've made in the enquiry,' said Cooper.

Murfin nodded. 'They've been chasing already. Mr Hitchens has dealt with some requests from the press office this morning.'

'But we can't even confirm it's a murder enquiry until we get the postmortem report.'

'That won't bother the press. Anyway, West Midlands are sending us up a tape of the interview.'

Fry looked at the juniors, DCs Becky Hurst and Luke Irvine. They had been hanging on Murfin's words as if he was some kind of oracle. But, under Fry's glare, they became busy with their work.

'What is this thing about paying tribute to victims?' said Murfin. 'What did Patrick Rawson do that was so great, apart from getting himself killed? Which is something any idiot can do, if you ask me.'

'What do you mean, Gavin?' asked Cooper.

'Well, it beats me why people pop up on TV all the time paying tribute to their relatives just because they've died suddenly. Being a victim doesn't actually make you a more worthwhile person, does it? Not in any form. Getting attacked or killed doesn't make you brave, or good, or clever. Now, getting through life and *not* being a victim – that's something to crow about.'

'That's a damn cold way of looking at things.'

'Cold? It's reality, mate. Reality always was a bit on the cold side.'

'Speaking of which, I called by the mortuary this morning,' said Fry. 'That's about as cold as you get.'

'How is the lovely Dr van Doon?'

'Helpful as usual. The head injury was the cause of death, as we might have known for ourselves from the start.'

Fry found herself drawn to the list that lay on her desk – the one provided by Mrs Forbes, listing the names of members of the hunt and hunt staff who had been present in the area at the time of Patrick Rawson's death. She could almost smell the reek of horse manure rising from the sheet of paper. And that was despite the fact it wasn't even the original but a photocopy.

She ran her finger down to the hunt stewards, alert to any bells that the names might ring. There were six of them, led by chief steward Kevin Bell, also known as Kevin Delaney. Oh, that was a great sign for a start, having an alias. Then came Marcus Webb, Adrian Tarrant, Igoris Morinas . . . Nice to have a bit of cultural diversity in there, though she wasn't quite sure what culture Igoris came from. Steward number five was Rob Charlesworth, and finally there was Jake Gleeson.

Well, the Gleesons were very well known. A whole tribe of them lived around Edendale, and every single one had a criminal record by their seventeenth birthday, including the girls. They collected ASBOs the way other families collected tokens from cereal packets. But the Gleesons were inhabitants of the council estates. They were more likely to be driving hot-wired cars around the streets than hacking cross-country in a red jacket and breeches.

But then, maybe social origins didn't matter when it came to hired heavies.

'Any theories on who those horse riders were, Diane?' asked Cooper. 'Or are you still fixated on members of the Eden Valley Hunt?'

'I'm not fixated on anyone,' snapped Fry.

'Well, I just meant to say –'

'We'll have to pursue the usual lines. Don't forget that forensics show there was some kind of encounter at the field barn. And, most significantly of all, Mr Rawson was running away when he met his death. All of that seems to have been planned. The fatal outcome might have been planned, too.'

The room was silent as she spoke. Cooper was surprised how serious Fry was about this case. In fact, how could she be so sure that Rawson's death was planned? It wasn't like her to go out on a limb this way, unless she was desperate to create an impression. Well, Fry had been left in charge of the enquiry so far, and he supposed she was keen to make a success of it. At the moment, everyone seemed determined to make a good impression on the new detective superintendent.

'So we need to find out who Patrick Rawson was meeting. The appeals should go out today, asking the horse riders to come forward. And, of course, the man who made the 999 call.'

'Is it likely? He must have something to hide, if only the fact that he lifted Mr Rawson's phone. And, presumably, his wallet.'

'It's possible,' said Fry stubbornly. 'Also, anyone who stands to gain from Patrick Rawson's death becomes a potential suspect from now on. We have to make a start on looking into his financial affairs. First glance suggests they're going to be complicated. Mr Rawson seems to have had a finger in a lot of pies.'

'Not all murders are committed for financial gain, though,' pointed out Cooper.

'Well, it does account for quite a big chunk.'

'But there's jealousy, revenge . . . Probably a few others, more complicated.'

'Yes. In a way, I was hoping to find that he wasn't staying at Birch Hall on his own. If there had been a woman involved in his trip to Derbyshire, it would have made everything look a whole lot simpler.'

Fry looked around the team.

'Any other progress? Gavin?'

'We've still to analyse all his mobile phone records. There are an awful lot of calls over the last week, both in and out.'

'His wife said he did all his business on his mobile.'

'Yes, and his car seems to have been his office. We found a charger and a Bluetooth connection in the Mitsubishi. He was obviously the sort of man who liked to talk as he drove. Hands-free, though. He wouldn't have wanted to risk getting banned for using a hand-held mobile while he was driving. Anyway, we've identified a few of the numbers, which look like business contacts. R & G Enterprises in Staffordshire. C.J. Hawley and Sons in South Yorkshire. And a more local one, Morris Brothers – that's just a couple of miles away in Lowbridge. They describe themselves as general dealers.'

'Keep on it.'

Fry walked to the door, off to brief the DI. She paused, and turned.

'Are you with us again today, Ben?'

Cooper wasn't sure from her expression what answer she wanted to hear. He hesitated for a moment.

'Well, if you want me to be,' he said.

When Fry had left the room, Murfin leaned across to Cooper.

'At least that means no HOLMES,' he said.

'Not yet. Someone else will have to make that decision.'

Cooper knew that Fry would lose any influence in the investigation if HOLMES was activated. Once that happened, the Home Office protocols would dictate the direction of the enquiry. A collator would arrive from headquarters, and a specialist DS to task teams of detectives. But once you turned HOLMES loose, it could get out of control. It was liable to suck in anything that came within reach, like a basking shark feeding on plankton. Thousands of bits of information went into its jaws and were digested. Maybe they'd be spewed out later on, in some usable form. Cooper shrugged. That seemed to be the theory, anyway.

'You were in Eyam yesterday, Ben, weren't you?' said Murfin, sneaking his mirror out of a desk drawer again.

'That's right. And I didn't finish, so I'm back there again this morning. Do you know it, Gavin?'

Murfin nodded. 'Oh, yeah. All those lists of dead people by the cottage gates. I never liked that place – it's creepy.'

DI Hitchens had taken a call from the forensics lab as Fry entered his office. She listened carefully, trying to pick up a clue to the direction of the conversation.

'News?' she asked.

'Yes. The lab have enlarged the images of the hoofprints at the scene. It seems there *were* some shoe impressions present, after all. Human ones, I mean. Their position suggests that someone stood over the body, but their prints were overlaid and obliterated by the horses. The rain didn't help, either.'

'It makes sense,' said Fry. 'They wouldn't be able to take Patrick Rawson's wallet and mobile phone while they were still on horseback, would they?'

Hitchens nodded. 'At least we can be sure there was some element of intention. Even if Mr Rawson's death was an accident, they deliberately decided to rob him, or conceal his identity.'

'Yes, obviously.'

Fry was becoming exasperated at the DI's reluctance to upgrade the enquiry. But she had to admit that she hadn't yet found a single witness, or even any clue to explain Patrick Rawson's presence on Longstone Moor that morning.

'Could the lab get enough detail from the shoe impression for an identification?' she asked.

'Not a chance,' said Hitchens. 'They couldn't even testify to a size.'

'These would be riding boots anyway. Smooth soles, aren't they?'

'I wouldn't know.'

Hitchens spread his hands on the desk. They were strong, masculine hands, marked only by the small scar that crept across his fingers. Fry had never heard what caused that scar, and it probably wasn't the right time to ask. She wondered how the DI managed to stay so calm, when she herself was starting to feel the ground shift under her feet. She almost preferred the old Paul Hitchens, the man she'd first met when she transferred to Derbyshire, a young DI with a streak of irreverence and no great respect for authority. What had changed him?

Then it occurred to Fry that Hitchens must already have been through his own series of interviews with Superintendent Branagh. What had been said to him?

'Have your team come up with anything?' asked Hitchens, breaking the silence.

'Nothing substantial.'

Fry filled in the DI with what she had, and waited for him to ask for her assessment of the case. For her, it was simple. Nothing they had learned so far quite explained how Patrick Rawson had ended up lying on a mortuary trolley, with cotton wool stuffed in his ears to plug the trickle of cerebral fluids.

'Yes, I agree,' said Hitchens. 'So what is your next move?'

'What happened to Deborah Rawson?' asked Fry. 'Did she stay over in Edendale?'

'No, she went straight back down to Sutton Coldfield. We offered to find her overnight accommodation, but she wasn't interested. Her brother drove her home.'

'Did she show much interest in the direction of the enquiry?'

'In how her husband met his end? As much as you'd expect. Mrs Rawson didn't really ask many questions. She seemed to take it for granted that we'd keep her informed. Which we will, of course.'

'Yes, but that often isn't good enough for bereaved relatives. They demand answers.'

Hitchens shrugged. 'It takes different people in different

ways. There's often a period of shock, when they seem cold and lacking in any reaction. The questions might not come into her mind until later. You watch – another twenty-four hours, and we'll find we can't get rid of her.'

'So who's going to examine Rawson's house?'

'I thought you might like to do it. West Midlands have put a watch on the place for us.'

'I'll be looking for indications of what Mr Rawson's business was in Derbyshire, and who he was meeting.'

'Yes, that's what we want.'

'And another chat with Mrs Deborah Rawson, I think,' said Fry.

Hitchens nodded. 'I'll let West Midlands know you're coming.'

As Fry headed back to the CID room, Luke Irvine met her in the corridor. She found Irvine touchingly young and eager. She supposed she might have been like that herself once, when she first got a chance to take off the uniform and work as a detective, back in Birmingham. Uniformed officers thought CID got all the excitement and the glory. But when you'd worked behind a desk for a while with your groaning case-load and your stack of Narey files, you soon learned the truth.

'Sarge, you know we've been finding whatever we can on Patrick Rawson's background,' said Irvine.

'Yes, Luke?'

'Well, the PNC shows that he has no criminal record as an adult, but I checked intelligence, and his name was flagged up by another agency – Trading Standards.'

'Trading Standards? So, what? Has Mr Rawson been a bad boy in his business dealings? Sold something that breached the Trade Descriptions Act?'

'No, not exactly. He was entered in intelligence as a known associate of some dodgy characters Trading Standards got convictions for about two years ago. I rang the case officer,

159

by name of Dermot Walsh. He's coming in to talk to us about it this morning.'

'So soon?'

'He's very keen,' said Irvine. 'It's funny, but he sounded quite pleased to hear about what had happened to Mr Rawson.'

18

Dermot Walsh came in to West Street with a female colleague he introduced as Daksha Patel. They were an odd pair – Patel small and elegant, Walsh built like a prop forward, square and broad-shouldered, his neck padded with muscle.

As he was introduced to Walsh, Cooper thought he might actually have seen him playing against the Derbyshire Police first XV. He recalled a gap-toothed tight head with bandaged knees who'd tried to maim his opposing prop in the scrum every time the referee looked the other way. Even cleaned up and wearing a suit and tie, Walsh was still a bit scary.

The CID team had crowded into the small conference room to hear the Trading Standards officers. The room was nearly full and overly warm.

'So what exactly is Trading Standards' interest?' asked Hitchens, looking happy to be involved in co-operation with partner agencies. It was probably something he could add to his PDR. 'Can we help you? Or are you here to help us?'

'It's largely a question of background information which might be useful in your present enquiry,' said Walsh.

'The suspicious death of Mr Patrick Rawson.'

'Yes.'

'Please explain.'

161

'Well, two years ago, a series of prosecutions were brought by Trading Standards with the help of one of the national horse protection organizations. We achieved several convictions. One defendant was fined sixteen thousand pounds and ordered to pay six thousand pounds costs, when he was found guilty of breaching trading standards legislation, and certain other offences.'

'What other offences?' asked Fry.

'Selling a horse without a valid passport.'

There was a moment of silence. Some of the officers fidgeted uncomfortably, as if they thought they might have something more important to be doing. Cooper could see that Fry was one of them.

'I don't understand,' she said.

Walsh held up a hand. 'Please, let me explain. This all started when our animal health team launched an investigation on the back of a complaint from a first-time horse buyer, who said she wanted a mature, quiet horse for her children. She purchased an eight-year-old Irish cob mare for three thousand five hundred pounds over the internet, only to find the horse lame on delivery. The mare was returned, but the replacement, a gelding advertised as "four, rising five" and "quiet", bucked her off on the first ride. Her vet said the horse was obviously immature.'

'Do people really buy horses on the internet?' said Fry.

'People buy everything on the internet,' said Cooper, who had bid successfully for some Mike Scott CDs on eBay just the night before.

Fry looked amazed. 'Sight unseen?'

Walsh shrugged. 'If they think they're getting a bargain, buyers can be easily duped. It's always been the same way. The internet just makes it a bit simpler.'

'It's like buying a house or a car on the internet.'

'People do that, too.'

Patel was handing around a set of data sheets, listing the

details of complainants. Names and addresses, allegations of breaches of consumer protection legislation. And the names of companies and individuals the complaints had been made against.

Cooper scanned the list. The companies concerned weren't quite called 'Nags R Us', but they certainly had names designed to reassure customers that they were getting a docile mount, something suitable for a happy hack around the paddock.

'This was a full-scale investigation,' said Walsh. 'We raided the defendants' business premises. We followed up more than fifty complaints, dating back five years. As you'll see from the lists, horses had been advertised for sale under a variety of trading names, claiming they were suitable for novice riders or had perfect temperaments for children. Some of them even came with money-back guarantees.'

'And?'

'And, in reality, many of those animals were unsound, or unsafe to be ridden. Buyers alleged that horses were delivered lame, malnourished, or covered in bite or kick marks. Some of them had coughs, back problems – and, in one case, navicular disease diagnosed at a post-sale vet check. At least four of the horses had to be euthanased after purchase.'

'You can have a horse vetted *before* you buy it, though.'

Walsh looked up. 'Of course. But vets don't come cheap. If you're looking for an inexpensive horse, the vet's bill on top of the asking price can put it out of reach. Perhaps worse than all that, we turned up several personal injury cases involving children thrown from their horses – one suffered neck injuries, another a broken arm. Buyers who complained said that, instead of refunds, they got abuse and insults. These were members of the public who found themselves thousands of pounds out of pocket, and facing huge vets' bills.'

'Some of these purchases were face to face, though,' said Cooper, running his finger down the list. 'Not online.'

'The trouble with the equine trade is that face-to-face deals

163

are verbal, and payment is usually in cash,' said Walsh. 'There aren't many businesses where that's still true these days. As you know, anything that involves piles of cash and a minimum of paperwork is bound to attract a few rogue traders. There are lots more cases. Too many for me to mention.'

There were certainly plenty of them. Cooper could see an example of a couple who bought a horse for £1,500, which was described as being an Irish hunter, aged nine or ten, and in generally good condition. Vets who had examined the horse after purchase said he was nearer twenty years old and not fit to ride. He had a wound in his mouth that would have made the bit very painful.

'It's like a car dealer "clocking" his cars,' explained Walsh. 'People buy a horse thinking they're going to get x number of years out of it, but if the animal is ten years older than they've been told, then they won't get the same value out of it. It's always been a case of *caveat emptor* in this trade – "buyer beware". But buyers need to be very careful where they take their business. Very careful.'

'Was the website closed down?' asked Cooper.

'Yes. We managed to get an order under the Enterprise Act, plus the sellers took a hit on legal costs. That means contempt of court and possible imprisonment, if they commit any further breaches of the act.' Walsh looked around the table. 'This was a very lengthy investigation by the time it came to court. I was personally involved in the enquiry for nearly two years. I've got a file of paperwork on this a mile high – you wouldn't believe it.'

'Oh, I think we would,' said Fry, perhaps remembering the officers still processing the files from the E Division strike day.

Walsh smiled at her. Cooper noticed that he had a full set of teeth when he was off the rugby pitch. Presumably thanks to an NHS bridge or two, like many of the rugby players he knew.

'But I don't see Patrick Rawson's name on any of these allegations,' said Hitchens, who had been listening patiently.

'No. Sadly, Mr Rawson was never named in any of the charges. Our enquiries with Companies House revealed from the beginning that Patrick Rawson was listed as a director in several of the businesses that complaints had been made against. He was also a known associate of all the other named dealers, even where he wasn't a director. But so many of the arrangements were verbal that we were never able to build a strong enough case against him. Not enough to put him in court with the other defendants. The evidence just wouldn't stick.'

'He's either a very lucky man, or very clever,' said Hitchens.

Walsh nodded. 'Both. Believe me, we tried very hard to tie in Mr Rawson with these offences. We were convinced that he was personally responsible for many of the frauds, but Rawson seems to have avoided putting almost anything in writing that could have been incriminating. This is a very slippery customer indeed. I interviewed him myself on several occasions, and he was always extremely plausible. Charming, even.'

'What did Rawson have to say for himself?'

'He dismissed the allegations against him as scare-mongering by rival dealers,' said Walsh. 'Mr Rawson's solicitor said his client was disappointed that matters couldn't have been sorted out privately. If he'd been contacted with complaints, he would have responded, he said. But, as far as I'm concerned, Rawson showed all the typical signs of a dodgy trader.'

'It seems he was soon back in business,' said Fry.

'I'm not sure he ever went out of business completely. Just laid low for a while. The trade in misrepresented horses had probably become a bit too difficult for him. The horse passport legislation has helped a lot there, of course – most people know now that you don't buy a horse without a passport, because it's almost certainly stolen. Last I heard, Rawson was

165

expanding into some new areas of enterprise. We'd got him on our radar by then, though. So when your officers started making enquiries about him, it raised a flag.'

'Did you come across Michael Clay in the course of this investigation?' asked Fry.

Walsh frowned. 'Michael Clay? Is he an accountant?'

'Yes, that's right.'

'He's a peripheral figure. Our forensic accountancy people had to deal with him when they were going through the books. He was never in the frame for any charges, though. Is he involved in your enquiry?'

'We haven't interviewed him yet, but he's high on our list,' said Fry. 'He seems to have become Patrick Rawson's business partner.'

'Well, if that's the case, my view is that Rawson was probably using Michael Clay as a front man, for the appearance of respectability. Clay is just the sort of person he would be looking for, to protect his own reputation.'

'You mean someone to take the fall if things went wrong?'

'Yes, exactly.' Walsh began to gather his papers together. 'You know, that was always my biggest regret in this enquiry: that we could never close Patrick Rawson down.'

'And now –' said Hitchens, about to voice what everyone else was thinking.

But it was Dermot Walsh who got it in first.

'And now,' he said, 'someone has closed Rawson down for us.'

Sutton Coldfield had been in Warwickshire once. Now it was part of the huge West Midlands conurbation, centred on Birmingham.

Fry knew that Sutton people tended to see themselves as culturally very distinct from Birmingham, though they were only eight miles or so from the centre of the city. They hadn't forgotten that Sutton had been a municipal borough in its

166

own right for many years, boasting the title of 'Royal Town'. Here and there, street signs still recorded the fact. Fry had passed one as she drove into the town from the A38.

If this had been a working-class area, no one would have cared very much about its administrative status. But Sutton Coldfield was regarded as one of the most prestigious locations in Central England. Just a couple of years ago, a national property survey had placed two Sutton streets among the twenty most expensive in the UK.

Fry remembered this north-east corner of Birmingham only vaguely. She had never been stationed in this area, and had no friends who lived here. She did recall a shopping precinct known as the Gracechurch Centre, but now it seemed to be called simply The Mall. Other than that, during her time in the West Midlands she had known it mostly as the home town of a few TV actors: Arthur Lowe and Dennis Waterman among them. It was a sort of celebrity, she supposed.

The Rawsons' home was in the Mere Green district of Sutton. Fry drove around the northern edge of Sutton Park and found herself in pleasant, leafy streets typical of so many affluent outer suburbs.

'Nice,' said Gavin Murfin, who constituted the only assistance she'd found available for the trip. 'There's a bit of dosh tied up in these properties, I reckon.'

'Yes, Gavin. Can you see Hill Wood Road?'

'You should use a sat-nav like mine, Diane. Do you know, I've even got Sean Connery's voice on it now to do the directions? Brilliant.'

'Just check the *A to Z*: Hill Wood Road.'

'OK, got it.'

This was the semi-rural part of Sutton. Large houses set back from the road and sheltered by trees, with plenty of space between them to provide privacy. Perhaps no actual farming still went on, but it was certainly a place for people who could find a use for stables and paddocks, and large agricultural sheds with concrete hard standings big enough for a few lorries.

'Off to the right somewhere,' said Murfin.

They saw the M6 toll road in the distance and turned down a narrow lane for five hundred yards before they came to the entrance to the Rawsons' property.

'He did well for himself,' said Fry, drawing the Peugeot up in front of a triple garage, built in the same style and the same warm, brown brick of the house itself. They crunched across a gravel turning circle to the liveried police car standing near the front door. Fry introduced herself and Murfin to the two West Midlands officers.

'Good morning, Sergeant. We've been expecting you. How was the trip?'

'Fine,' said Fry.

'We should have taken the toll road,' suggested Murfin.

Fry sighed. 'Is Mrs Rawson at home?'

'Yes, we informed her you were coming.'

'How are we going to do this?' asked Murfin, as they walked to the door.

'According to the book,' said Fry. 'With courtesy and consideration.'

'I don't think I know that book.'

'They probably hadn't published it when you were in training, Gavin.'

'I don't go back to the Dark Ages, you know.'

'How come your eating habits are so medieval, then?' said Fry, as she rang the bell.

Deborah Rawson was sitting in a large conservatory watching a stable girl exercise a horse outside. Mrs Rawson wore a cream silk blouse that looked so expensive it was probably produced by some rare Buddhist silkworm in the foothills of the Himalayas. The atmosphere of the conservatory was thick with perfume. Mrs Rawson had prepared herself for her visitors.

168

'If you're married to a man like Patrick,' she said, 'you learn to expect that the worst will happen some time. Sooner or later.'

Fry's first question had actually been a polite one – an enquiry about Mrs Rawson's welfare. Now, as she studied the woman, she wondered whether Hitchens had been right about the effects of shock. She looked a little more upset than she had yesterday. Paler, more nervous in her gestures. Her eyes didn't seem to be able to settle on her visitors, but constantly darted back to the girl and the horse outside.

'Your husband had been in trouble on a few occasions, hadn't he?' said Fry.

Deborah lowered her head, tapping out a cigarette from a packet on the coffee table in front of her. 'He tended to sail a bit close to the wind, I suppose. Pat was just that sort of businessman, you know. I'm sure you've met the type before, Sergeant. He enjoyed the challenge, the adrenalin rush. Thrived on it, in fact.'

'The challenge of breaking the law?'

'No, not exactly. The challenge of seeing how much he could get away with. He's made quite a bit of money, at times.'

'But his main business was the buying and selling of horses. Is that right?'

'The equine trade. That's what he liked to call it, when he was talking to his friends down at the golf club. But I wouldn't say it was his main business. Not recently, anyway. He had a finger in lots of other pies.'

She lit the cigarette from a gold lighter. Smoke drifted up into the glass roof, and hung there, swirling slowly.

'I suppose you might say he was a born salesman,' said Deborah. 'Patrick had the charm to sell anything to anybody. Snow to Eskimos, isn't that the saying?'

'Something like that,' said Fry.

'He was selling cars when I first met him. Down in Digbeth, that was. A snappy suit and a dodgy hair cut.' Deborah laughed. 'But it was his smile that reeled me in. That, and the commission he told me he was earning.'

Yes, Fry could see Patrick Rawson as a used-car salesman. She reminded herself not to be taken in by a salesman's smile when she went to buy herself a new car. As if that was likely.

'What about the horses? Where did they come in?' she asked.

'From his father, Owen Rawson. It was in the family.'

Fry followed Mrs Rawson's gaze and watched the horse being trotted across the paddock. She had no idea what kind of horse it was. A brown one, that was all she could say. But even she could tell that it moved with eye-catching grace, muscles sliding smoothly over its shoulders, feet lifting high off the ground. For a large animal, its step was dainty, as if it was afraid of damaging the grass.

'I don't know a great deal about horses,' she said. 'But is there really much money to be made?'

'It's like anything else, Detective Sergeant. It depends whether you know what you're doing.'

'And your husband did?'

'Certainly. Patrick always knew what he was doing.'

Murfin had been gazing out of the conservatory windows, leaning to see the stable block to one side of the paddock. Fry wasn't sure he'd even been listening, but he threw her a glance, raised an eyebrow, and she nodded.

'And has business been good recently, Mrs Rawson?' he asked.

Deborah took the cigarette out of her mouth and looked at him, surprised. Until now, she had barely acknowledged him, probably regarded him as no more important than the stable girl, there only to rub down the horse when it got too sweaty. She seemed to have to think about his question.

'I really don't know,' she said at last.

'It's just that I notice the stables seem to be mostly empty.'

'Horses come and go. I couldn't even tell you what there

is out there, without Patrick being here. The girl might know, I suppose.'

'You don't even know how many horses there are?'

'As I told you yesterday, I've never had anything to do with the business. You'll have to talk to Michael Clay.'

'You told us your husband went up to Derbyshire for the horse sale. And you were right, there is one scheduled for this Saturday. But would he also have called on private individuals? Private sellers?'

'I suppose so, if it was worth his while. I think he had some regular dealings with stables and riding schools.'

'What sort of dealings?'

Deborah blew a cloud of smoke, narrowing her eyes. 'I think my answer is the same, Sergeant. You'll have to speak to Michael if you want to know more details.'

'Well, we're here to examine Mr Rawson's papers,' said Fry. 'You did say you would give permission for us to do that.'

'Yes, of course. You mean business papers, I imagine?'

'Particularly any appointments book, a diary. That sort of thing.'

'Yes, I see. But he was on a business trip – he might have had those with him.'

'If we could just check –'

Deborah Rawson rose. 'This way, then. Patrick does have a desk he uses when he's at home. Used, I mean.'

'Thank you.'

'"His friends down at the golf club"?' said Murfin when Deborah Rawson had left them alone in a sparse office.

'Yes, and the "equine trade". Mr Rawson seems to have had social aspirations.'

'He sounds as though he was just a dodgy horse dealer, though.'

'Not just that. A finger in a lot of pies, remember?'

171

Fry opened the first drawer. It rattled as she slid it out, and revealed only a few pens, a stapler, a scattering of jumbo paper clips.

'Besides, social aspirations happen to people a lot when they get some money, Gavin,' she said. 'It's never enough for them. They want respect as well.'

'Respect, maybe. Your average drug dealer on the street wants respect. But Rawson never seems to have worried too much about respectability, which is a different thing altogether.'

Fry nodded. 'Yes, that's an interesting bit of contradiction in his character there. Deborah was right – her husband seems to have had an urge to live dangerously, a need for a bit of risk in his life. I wonder what damage the Trading Standards investigation did to his standing in the club house.'

Murfin was rifling through a filing cabinet, tutting over dozens of empty suspension files and a half-full bottle of Laphroaig whisky.

'If I know anything about golf-club committees, any sniff of a court case could have been fatal,' he said.

'Fatal?'

'Just an expression, like. I meant fatal to his standing as a member.'

'Yes, you're right.'

Fry tapped her fingers on the desk. She was finding no diary or appointments book. No PDA or laptop either. Nothing where a schedule of meetings or the names of regular contacts might be listed.

'You know, if those two sides of Mr Rawson's personality clashed, he might have got very angry about it,' she said.

'Angry at who?'

Fry thought for a moment. 'Whoever landed him in court, I suppose.'

Murfin laughed as he banged the filing cabinet shut. 'Not Trading Standards.'

'No, I don't think so. They're a bit hard to get angry with, aren't they? I was thinking more of one of Mr Rawson's customers, someone who got stung when a deal went wrong. Or someone else in the same business, perhaps.'

'Dermot Walsh said that Rawson blamed jealous rivals when they first brought a case against him.'

'So he did. We should give Walsh a ring when we get back to the office, and ask him if Rawson mentioned any rivals in particular.'

'Right. You're thinking there might have been some kind of feud?'

'Yes, a feud that Patrick Rawson lost.'

'If that's so – and since Rawson seems to have come up to Derbyshire to meet him – the rival could well be someone local to us.'

'So he could, Gavin. So he could.'

Fry checked the desk for hidden drawers, ran a hand along a book shelf. Telephone directories, a road atlas, the *Official Form Book 2009*, with cover picture of jockeys straining hard for the wining post. Diaries, but filled only with dates of birthdays and dental appointments. She found the most recent diary and turned to the current week. Derby horse market was marked on Saturday, and the name of the Birch Hall Country Hotel on Monday night. But no names, no times of meetings he might have arranged. This really was a man who had learned not to put anything in writing.

'There's nothing here,' she said in disgust. 'Absolutely nothing of any use to us, Gavin.'

'Where to next, then?' said Murfin.

'We need to talk to Rawson's partner. Let's go and see Michael Clay.'

Michael Clay's home was further into the city, Birmingham proper. Well, after a fashion. Great Barr was a suburb on the outer edge of Brum, an ocean of pre-war red-brick semis bordering on Walsall and West Bromwich. The Clay home was easier to find than Rawson's, though. No need for a sat-nav here.

'No, I'm sorry, Mr Clay isn't at home.'

The door had been answered by a woman of about her own age, so tightly buttoned up in a woollen jacket that she appeared to have almost no shape. Her dark hair was pushed untidily behind her ears, and there was a faint sheen of sweat on her forehead, as if she'd been caught in some physical exertion. Moving furniture, or beating the carpets. Something she could take her feelings out on, judging from that sour expression.

'And you are . . .?' asked Fry.

'His daughter. Erin Lacey.'

The woman carried on looking at Fry blankly. Then she began to take a step back, as if to close the door firmly on an insurance salesman or a Jehovah's Witness. Fry held up a hand.

'Does your father have an office address, Mrs Lacey?'

'Well, he has an office in a business centre in Kingstanding. But he's not there, either. He's gone away for a few days.'

'Where?'

'He went up to Derbyshire.'

'But that's where we spoke to him yesterday. I thought he would have been back home today.'

Mrs Lacey threw out her hands helplessly. 'I'm sorry. If you had an appointment, he must have forgotten.'

'It wasn't exactly an appointment,' said Fry. 'But he did give me the impression he would be available. I need to talk to him about the death of his business partner, Patrick Rawson.'

'Oh, of course. How dreadful.' Her brow crinkled. But to Fry the frown seemed to suggest a concern at whether she'd left a piece of furniture in the wrong place, rather than sadness

174

at the death of Mr Rawson. 'All I know is that my father is away. I'm looking after the house for a while.'

'What about Mrs Clay? Your mother?'

'She died, five years ago.'

'I'm sorry.'

The woman seemed a little nervous. Fry would have loved to get inside the house to have a look around, but she had no warrant, no justification. Michael Clay wasn't a suspect, or even a material witness.

'I presume you can give us a contact number for him, though,' she said. 'A mobile? Mr Clay must have a mobile number we can reach him on?'

She raised an eyebrow, as the woman hesitated. 'I'll write it down for you.'

'Thank you.'

Fry took the number and exchanged it for her card. 'When your father returns, or if he gets in touch in the meantime, please ask him to contact us as soon as possible.'

'Is there trouble?'

'Not for Mr Clay. We just want to speak to him.'

'I'll tell him' she said, already closing the door.

Fry could see her shape moving behind the glass, long after they had walked down the drive to their car.

Standing on the pavement, she made a point of phoning the number she'd been given in full sight of the windows of the Clay house. She got a voicemail message, a man's voice claiming to be Michael Clay, but not available at the moment. At least it was a genuine number.

'Mr Clay, this is Detective Sergeant Fry of Derbyshire Police. We spoke yesterday. I'd be grateful if you could give me a call at your earliest convenience.'

'Not at home, then,' said Murfin, when she finished the call.

Fry glanced at the house again. 'I wonder . . .'

'What are you wondering?'

'I'm thinking about what Dermot Walsh said this morning, about Patrick Rawson using someone to take the fall if things went wrong. And I'm wondering whether Mr Clay discovered what his role was in Patrick Rawson's scheme of things.'

19

The barrel of the gun was held to the horse's forehead. There was just a brief moment when the only sounds were the nervous scuffling of the horse's hooves on the tiled floor, and the distant background of pop music, something bright and bouncy, probably Abba. Then a high-pitched *crack* echoed off the walls.

As Cooper watched, the horse's legs folded underneath it, collapsing as if someone had dropped the strings on a puppet. Its body hit the floor, and its head dropped lifelessly. As the animal rolled on to its side, the front legs went rigid, but the hind legs continued to kick furiously – that primal flight instinct still powering the muscles for long seconds after the brain had ceased working.

When the kicking had stopped, the operator put his gun down and began to secure the straps of a winch. A moment later, the dead mare was hoisted off the floor on two chains, its back legs high in the air, its head hanging downwards, swinging loose. A spiral of blood squirted on to the tiles.

'My God, it's like watching a snuff movie.' DI Hitchens stood behind Cooper, watching over his shoulder. 'Does this happen every day?'

'Well, every week, at least,' said Cooper.

They were watching a film that seemed to have been made secretly by an animal rights group. Somehow, they had managed to get a camera into the slaughterhouse in Yorkshire on the day they killed horses. The quality of the picture was poor, and the sound even worse. Also, the film had been shot from an odd angle. Cooper guessed at a small, hidden camera of some kind. Maybe even a mobile phone, though most people were wise to that now. It would need to have been left on a shelf or ledge high in a corner of the killing room, to get that angle.

'Where is this place?' asked Hitchens.

'C.J. Hawley and Sons. It's somewhere in West Yorkshire. North of Sheffield, anyway. I rang them a few minutes ago. They didn't used to take horses for slaughter, but there are only three other abattoirs in the equine business, and all of those are located further south. So Hawleys took up the spare demand. They slaughter horses one day a week now.'

'It looks as though the animal rights people were on to them pretty quick.'

'I suppose it looks bad when you watch like this,' said Cooper. 'It makes the whole thing look seedy and surreptitious. But the abattoir isn't doing anything illegal. They're inspected and supervised, just like any other operation.'

'So they're clean?'

'The protestors would probably argue a moral case.'

'Morality is beyond our remit,' said Hitchens.

'Hold on, sir. There's a bit here I want to listen to.'

The dead horse was disappearing through a doorway, being moved on some kind of overhead gantry. The carcass swung awkwardly as it entered the next room, its head bumping against a metal step. A caption to the film claimed that the horse looked pregnant, which it did. The slaughterman followed it, sliding the door shut behind him. That would be the butchering room, and it was probably as well that the camera wasn't able to follow.

After a few seconds, another *crack* could clearly be heard from behind the closed door. Cooper sat up straight. Surely the horse had been dead? It couldn't have recovered consciousness after the butchering had begun. But the caption didn't question that. Instead, it asked: '*Listen carefully for a second shot. Was it directed at an unborn foal?*'

More horses followed into the killing room. A large grey, a small black pony. The slaughterman was good. He shot each animal one-handed, smack in the middle of the forehead, and each one dropped instantly, dead but for the spasmodic twitching of their legs. The man even took time to chat to the horse handler as he manoeuvred a horse into the killing position: '*Did you watch the racing yesterday?*'

The strangest thing was the sound of Radio Two playing somewhere in the background. At one point, a door out of camera range must have been opened, releasing a louder blast of Abba. 'Money, Money, Money' or 'Gimme, Gimme, Gimme'. He half expected the slaughterman to burst into song himself, maybe to do a little dance in his white apron and cap. His work was almost choreographed, so it wouldn't have been totally unfitting.

The link to the film had been sent to him in an email. The sender's address was one of the free web-based email accounts, which could be set up without providing a postal address or a phone number, or even a real name. If you wanted to make sure you stayed anonymous, you could create an account specifically for sending one email. Then you sent it on a public access terminal in a library or internet café, and closed your account. He could attempt to get the sender traced, but it was probably futile.

He couldn't figure out why some of the footage had sound, but other sections didn't – even though they were obviously shot from the same place. At one point, a door partially blocked the view of the camera, resulting in a glimpse only of a horse's back legs thrashing on the floor, until they gradually came to a halt.

Cooper had grown up on a farm. He knew that animals had to be killed, for all kinds of reasons. As far as he was concerned, there should be no problem with that, so long as it was done properly. Quickly, efficiently and humanely. Those were the key words. He knew that most slaughtermen took pride in doing their job well, so that an animal didn't suffer unnecessarily. But it was a thankless role, one that the public at large would rather pretend didn't exist. That essential stage between the cute animal skipping around a field and the joint of lamb on a supermarket shelf was best left un-explored. What you didn't know, didn't hurt.

'C.J. Hawley and Sons,' said Hitchens. 'Do we know anything else about them?'

'Only that theirs was one of the numbers on Patrick Rawson's calls list,' said Cooper.

The rest of the film showed footage of a sick or injured horse lying in a yard outside the abattoir. Its head rolled, and it tried to sit up a couple of times, but gave up. Meanwhile, a man could be seen walking backwards and forwards past it, talking on a mobile phone. Eventually, he came back with a gun and shot the horse in the head. He was in ordinary casual clothes, a blue check shirt and a pair of worn denim jeans, and it was difficult to say whether this was the same man who'd been filmed in the killing room.

The caption pointed out that a sick or injured horse was supposed to be killed straight away, and suggested that the animal had been left to lie in the yard because it had arrived at the slaughterhouse outside normal operating hours when the butchering line wasn't running. Legislation said that for meat to be deemed fit for human consumption, an animal must be bled immediately after being shot or stunned. Therefore, it had to wait to be killed until the butchering line was ready. Yet the law also said that a seriously injured animal should be despatched without delay.

'Even if that's true,' said Hitchens, when Cooper pointed

it out, 'it's a matter for the licensing authorities. The RSPCA, maybe. Not us.'

'It's relevant to us if it suggests a motive,' said Cooper.

'The man in the film . . .?'

'Yes. The one in the yard with the injured horse. I'm pretty sure that was Patrick Rawson himself.'

Minutes after her return from Sutton Coldfield, Fry found herself sitting in the DI's office, warily eyeing a stack of papers he was extracting from a file. If Hitchens wanted to share something with her, it probably wasn't good news.

'No live investigations or outstanding offences for Patrick Rawson?' he said vaguely.

'None, sir. But that doesn't rule out the involvement of angry customers from earlier offences. Someone whose name might be on Dermot Walsh's list.'

'Good point. We'll have to speak to them all.'

'Given time, that might be possible. At the moment, I'm more concerned by the fact that I can't contact the partner, Michael Clay. Without him, we can't even start to analyse Mr Rawson's business affairs properly.'

'Yes, I heard. But he'll turn up, won't he?'

'I hope so.'

Hitchens frowned and looked up. 'Diane, have you ever heard of a disease called trichinosis?'

'What? No, I haven't. But it doesn't sound like something I'd want to be diagnosed with.'

'You're exactly right. Trichinosis is a parasitic disease caused by a nematode worm, whatever that is. I don't like the sound of it, personally. *Trichinella spiralis.*'

'Symptoms?'

'Initially, swelling of the eyes, diarrhoea, vomiting, and abdominal pain. Also fatigue, fever, headaches, shivering, coughing, aching joints, muscle pains. In severe infections, there may be heart and breathing problems, or difficulty co-ordinating movements. In extreme cases, death can occur.' Hitchens laughed drily. 'I like that – "death can occur". That should be our motto.'

'You don't look as though you have any of those,' said Fry. 'But I suppose it's difficult for me to tell unless you stand up and walk about a bit.'

Hitchens didn't seem to be listening as he ran his eye over a sheet filled with dense paragraphs of text.

'Trichinosis is actually quite rare in this country,' he said. 'Or it used to be.'

Fry felt a small shiver of unease. She wasn't a hypochondriac by any means, but even so, she didn't like the idea of this disease. What was that about a nematode worm? Just the name of it sounded disgusting.

'Are you saying we've got an epidemic, sir? Is this thing contagious?'

'Not exactly. Well, you don't catch it from other human beings.'

Reluctantly, Fry found her thoughts flicking back to the previous day. The smell of horses, the wet plop of something unspeakable hitting her shoes.

'I'm liking the sound of it even less now.'

'The infection is caused by eating raw or under-cooked meat, usually pork,' said Hitchens. 'The experts say cases have increased in recent years, generally blamed on Eastern Europe and the movement of migrant workers within the EU. There was a major outbreak in France, with more than four hundred people affected – traced to meat imported from Yugoslavia. Another case in Ireland, pork sausages brought in by Polish nationals. And the last outbreak of trichinosis here in the UK was in 1999 – eight Yugoslav immigrants. That was caused by salami from Serbia.'

Fry began to relax. 'Luckily, I'm not a big fan of pork. But I can't see the relevance of this to us, sir.'

'Well . . . there's been another outbreak here in the Midlands. The first in the UK for ten years. It's not widespread, and they don't want to cause panic. But the source of the infection might be relevant.'

'It's an Environmental Health job, surely? Them, or DEFRA. If somebody is selling infected pork meat they have the statutory powers to close businesses down and prosecute. They don't need us.'

'No, of course not. But some conscientious EHO must have been reading the bulletins. They made a connection to one of our current enquiries.'

'Which current enquiry?'

'Well, *you* put it together . . .' Hitchens slid the file across the desk to her. 'Historically, most outbreaks of trichinosis are caused by infected pork meat, but this one is different. The common factor among these victims is that they've been eating undercooked horse meat.'

Fry felt her stomach turn over. You didn't have to be a fan of horses to have doubts about eating one. Very big doubts.

'Horse meat? Isn't that illegal here?'

'Ah now, there you're wrong,' said Hitchens. 'It isn't illegal, just culturally unacceptable. I hear it's very popular among our friends in France and Italy, and no doubt other countries.'

'So what's the problem?'

'The problem,' said Hitchens, 'seems to be how this horse meat is sourced in the first place.'

'What?'

Hitchens sighed. 'This Rawson case gets more and more complicated. But let DC Cooper show you the film he was sent. The allegation seems to be that Patrick Rawson was obtaining horses to be sold for slaughter. When I say "obtaining", we have to be open to the idea that some of the horses were stolen, or obtained by deception, don't we?'

'Yes, given his history. But, by *slaughtered*, you mean . . .?'

'For human consumption.'

'Oh, god.'

'While you were in Sutton Coldfield,' said Hitchens, 'DC Irvine and DC Hurst came up with background on some of the contacts whose numbers were in Mr Rawson's phone book. One of those is a company we might be interested in: R & G Enterprises. They have a small distribution centre on an enterprise park near Buxton.'

'Distributing what?' asked Fry, with a sinking heart.

Hitchens smiled. 'Meat, of course.'

Down in the car park, a tow truck was bringing in Patrick Rawson's Mitsubishi for closer forensic examination. Fry found Cooper watching it arrive from the window of the CID room.

'Mr Rawson had hands-free mobile in the car, didn't he?' he said.

'Yes, why?' asked Fry.

Cooper shrugged. 'It's funny that he seems to have been more worried about getting caught using a mobile phone while driving than he was concerned about being convicted for fraud, or breaches of the Trade Descriptions Act.'

'That doesn't seem particularly odd to me.'

'Perhaps you're right,' said Cooper. 'So even Patrick Rawson had the feeling that he was more likely to be prosecuted if he was an easy target.'

He seemed to make the last comment to himself, so Fry ignored it.

'We're starting to get an angle on Mr Rawson's business interests, anyway,' she said. 'This is almost a local one: R & G Enterprises Limited, with a trading address in Buxton. Directors are listed as Patrick Thomas Rawson and Maurice Gains.'

'Mr Rawson, the man with his finger in lots of pies.'

'And how many of them are dodgy?' said Fry. 'If you want something really frightening, Ben, have a read of this briefing.'

'What's this?' Cooper took the file from her. 'Trichinosis?'

'It's the latest reason for turning vegetarian.'

'Oh, great.'

Cooper was silent as he read. Fry knew that the briefing was horribly specific about the progress of the disease. When any human being or animal ate meat that contained trichinella cysts, the acid in the stomach dissolved the hard covering, releasing larvae into the small intestine. Adults laid eggs, which developed into more larvae and travelled through the arteries to the muscles, where they curled into balls and became cysts again. And the cycle started over.

Most cases of trichinosis were mild, but if you didn't get treatment with anti-inflammatory steroids, you could die. Someone in Paris had done exactly that, during the last French epidemic from eating raw horsemeat that originated in Poland.

'This case in Paris,' said Cooper. 'Raw horse meat from Poland – It's . . .'

Words seemed to fail him.

'I know,' said Fry.

She had begun to feel even sicker when she read the details of that case. An infected horse head had entered the human food chain. Not just meat, but the head. The number of people infected was explained by a high concentration of larvae in the horse's carcass, and by the custom of mixing meat from several horses' heads, to be eaten as raw mince.

Worst of all, the originating farm entered on official documents did not exist. No one would ever know where that outbreak of trichinosis had come from.

Fry looked up at Cooper when he'd finished reading. He looked just about as sick as she felt.

'Will you take the abattoir, Ben?' she said.

'Oh, how did I guess? What about you?'

'I'll go where the meat is.'

The three men were on their weekly hike. They were three retired police officers, puffing a little as they reached the top of the track on the remaining unspoiled stretch of Longstone Moor.

Inquisitively, one of them diverted away from the path towards the deep gash of Watersaw Rake, the abandoned opencast quarry workings. There was a fence around the hole, but it was low enough to step over.

'Careful, Jack,' called one of his friends. 'We're not carrying you home if you break your leg.'

'You'd think they'd do something with this,' he said. 'Fill it in, or whatever.'

'They've certainly wrecked the hillside with their quarrying.'

'It employs local people, though. That's the important thing.'

His friends came to join him at the fence, pushing their way through the heather to find a rabbit track wide enough for their boots.

'Come on, Jack. What are you doing?'

'He still thinks he's on the job. Always wants to know what's going on.'

But the first man wasn't listening to them. He was over the fence and looking down into the rake. The sides were steep and lined with shattered rock. The bottom was fifty feet below, littered with debris from the quarrying.

'There's something down there,' he said. 'Right on the bottom of the rake.'

'Just rocks. Or a dead sheep.'

'No. That's not what it is.'

20

The Snake Pass had been closed between Glossop and Ladybower for several weeks after another landslip. The floods in January had also burst an old mining adit, the build-up of water cracking a hole the size of a railway tunnel in the side of Drake Hill.

It was proof, if anyone still needed it, that too much rain could change the landscape dramatically. If you watched the hills after a heavy downpour, you could see the smallest streams gushing into brown cascades as they tumbled into the valleys, washing down peat from the moors and loose stones from the hillsides.

But Cooper was driving eastwards from Ladybower, heading in towards Sheffield on the A57, now clear of the previous night's fog. From Sheffield, he had to find his way north, skirting Howden Moors, to enter the tangle of former mill towns on the Yorkshire side of the Pennines.

DC Luke Irvine had declared himself free enough of the backlog of file preparation work to accompany Cooper on the trip to Yorkshire. Fry had looked a bit sceptical at first, but had given him the nod. Cooper was glad to have Luke with him. It made such a difference being in the car with the younger DC instead of travelling with Diane Fry and having to watch every word he said.

'My family are from West Yorkshire,' said Irvine as they came in sight of the wind farm near Penistone.

'I didn't know that,' said Cooper, who had assumed Irvine was of Scottish origin, what with his surname and the blue eyes, and the sandy hair.

'Denby Dale, between Huddersfield and Barnsley. My Dad used to work in the mining-equipment industry, but his job went when all the pits closed down. So he got a job at Rolls-Royce in Derby. And the family moved down. I was only five at the time, so I don't remember much about Denby Dale, except visiting my grandma.'

'You never thought of going into engineering like your dad?' asked Cooper.

'No.'

Irvine said it so abruptly that Cooper wondered what the story was behind his decision to join the police. There was a long history of conflict between the police and men working in the coal industry, going back to the 1984–85 miners' strike. Communities had been split, families divided, and the resulting bad blood had lingered for twenty-five years in some areas. He decided it might be better not to ask – until he knew Luke better, anyway.

'I think we need to get on to the A636,' said Irvine.

'Sure.'

A few minutes later, Cooper steered the Toyota down a bumpy lane, following directions taken from a local. Sheltered behind a line of dense conifers, the slaughterhouse was almost invisible to a casual passer-by. Even if he'd been a rambler out on a stroll, he might not have seen it. The approach was via a long, winding lane that would have been difficult to find in itself without directions. At the end of the track was a collection of grubby stone buildings, devoid of any signs to indicate what they were. In the yard stood a row of steel-sided wagons that had brought animals for slaughter.

But once you reached it, and got out of the car, there was

no mistaking what this place was. A distinctive smell filled the air. Blood, urine and dead flesh.

Cooper was no vegetarian. He liked a good steak as much as the next man. But the smell of meat in large quantities was cloying and sickly. It made him think of an old-fashioned butcher's shop his mother used to take him to in town when he was a child. There had always been joints of meat hung all around the shop, and some had probably been there for days. It was one of those childhood impressions that could be brought back instantly by a smell like this.

The butcher's was long gone now, of course. If his mother was still alive, she would be buying her meat shrink-wrapped from a chill cabinet at the supermarket, just like everyone else. That, or she would have found her own private source, which was still possible if you knew where to ask.

'I hope we get masks,' said Irvine. 'I don't think I can hold my breath until we get back to the car.'

'You'll get used to it.'

But this was more than just the smell of meat. There was an underlying odour of putrefaction that no amount of cleaning and disinfectant could alleviate. It was obvious to anyone with a functioning sense of smell. With one sniff, you could tell whether meat was fresh or had gone off.

Cooper glanced around the site. Somewhere, there would be skips where the waste and offal were discarded to await incineration. He pictured hoppers full of skins from butchered animals, drains where rivulets of blood soaked away.

There used to be a small, privately owned abattoir in Lowbridge, near Edendale, which he'd visited once with Diane Fry. But it had gone out of business, like many local operations, unable to bear the cost of regulations and new equipment. Now Hawleys was the sort of place that animals went to, travelling longer distances to meet their fate.

'Slaughterhouses like ours aren't doing anything wrong or inhumane, you know,' said Melvyn Hawley, who introduced himself as one of the sons in C.J. Hawley and Sons. 'These animal rights people are talking out of their arses.'

'Really?'

'Oh, there might be a bit of ill treatment in the industry, here and there. But the level of welfare abuse is nothing compared to what would go on if there was no abattoir trade. Abattoirs like ours are regulated and inspected to the nth degree. If you were to take away that commercial structure, and the professionalism that goes with it, you would lose control of the whole process.'

'I suppose so.'

Melvyn Hawley was a tall, thin man, and so pale that he looked as though he'd never eaten meat in his life. Did working in a place like this put you off? If he was one of the sons, Hawley must have grown up with the idea of what went on in an abattoir. Killing as a means of earning a living. It was enough to make anyone a little awkward in normal company.

When they arrived, Cooper and Irvine had been taken into a small office. Bright, white-painted walls, the smell of disinfectant. Just enough room for three or four chairs, and a row of filing cabinets.

'Besides,' said Hawley, eyeing Cooper cautiously, 'when it comes to the slaughter of horses, we're just clearing up the mess left by the racing industry. That's what I always say.'

'How is that, sir?'

'Well, they have massive breeding programmes, you know. Far too many horses are produced, and only the best survive. It's a dirty little secret the racing industry would rather no one knew. I dare say horse lovers fondly imagine that all those unwanted racehorses live out their days grazing happily in some sunlit meadow. Some nice, kind person is looking after them somewhere in their old age? Yeah, right.' He laughed bitterly. 'Well, that nice person would need to have very deep pockets. It costs thousands to feed and look after just one retired race horse.'

190

'So you're saying that the racing industry has to cut its losses and make something on the carcasses?'

'That's it. Horses can live to more than thirty years on average, but most are killed before their fifth birthday. There are a few specialist slaughterhouses around the country, like us, who deal with the surplus.'

'What happens to the carcasses?' asked Irvine.

'After the horses are slaughtered, they're shipped abroad in quarters. Overseas buyers bone them out and cut them up. Some of the meat goes into pet food, but there's quite a demand for human consumption, you know.'

'And what size of surplus are we talking about?'

'Up to ten thousand horses a year. Mainly to France.'

Cooper watched Hawley carefully as he answered Irvine's questions. 'I take it you're aware of the outbreak of trichinosis, sir?' he said.

Hawley winced visibly. He couldn't have gone any paler, but the pain was clear in his face.

'Have they traced the origin of the meat yet?' he asked.

'Not so far as I'm aware.'

'It will have come in from overseas. Someone has imported it illegally, you can bet.'

'Have you been affected by the investigation?'

'Have we! They've been all over this place with a microscope. We got a clean bill of health.'

'You must have been relieved,' said Cooper.

'Oh, we knew we were clean. The trouble is, packaging indicates the location of slaughter, not the source of the animal. We had to produce documentation on where all our horses came from. It's a real hassle. But we're properly regulated in this country, like I said. There's very little enforcement of the regulations in some other EU member states. Everyone knows that.'

Hawley led them into a viewing area overlooking the slaughter line. Blood could be seen seeping under the edges of plastic doors. Four men were working in the butchering room, their white overalls spattered with blood. Above them, three horse carcasses hung from metal shackles fastened to their hind legs. Their hooves had been cut off, and their heads removed. One man was using a set of knives to skin a dead animal.

'I'm afraid we can't allow anyone into the killing room,' said Hawley. 'It's too dangerous.'

'You still use live bullets?'

'Yes. It's quicker and more efficient – provided you have an experienced operative.'

Outside were holding pens, full of more horses waiting their turn. As they walked through the pens, a gunshot went off. Two young horses jumped and began biting each other's necks.

Hawley looked from Cooper to Irvine. The younger detective had gone pale, almost as pale as Hawley himself. He gulped the fresh air eagerly.

'I know it's a tough fact to face,' said Hawley, sounding a little more apologetic. 'But there are thousands of British thoroughbreds that are too old, too slow, or just not good enough jumpers. A lot of them never even make it to the starting gate.'

Cooper nodded. For the unwanted, the end was pretty brutal. If not a bullet, then a steel bolt into the side of the brain. Then their butchered carcasses loaded on to refrigerated lorries and driven to France.

'Why thoroughbreds, though?'

'It's what the trade wants. Thoroughbreds make good, lean meat. You might think the shire types would be better, but they have too much bone, and too much fat in the carcass. And those overweight ponies that some child has ruined – they're no good, either.'

'There must be dealers who find the horses to send to the abattoirs,' said Cooper.

'Yes, of course. The animals that come here are sourced in a variety of ways.'

192

'Horse auctions?'

'That would be one way.'

'You take horses from dealers like Patrick Rawson, don't you?'

'I knew Rawson,' said Hawley. 'He died, didn't he? It was on the TV news. I thought that must be what you came about. You being from Derbyshire Police.'

'Your number was one of the last that Mr Rawson called before he died,' said Cooper. 'Did you speak to him yourself?'

'Yes, I talked to him on Monday.'

'What time?'

'Oh, during the afternoon some time. He sounded as though he was in his car. But then, he was almost always in his car when he called. That was the way that Patrick did business.'

'On the move, yes.'

'Exactly.'

'And this *was* a business call?'

'Oh, yes. I wouldn't say I was on social terms with him exactly.'

'What was the reason for his call?'

'The usual,' said Hawley. 'He expected to have some stock to bring in. He was calling to make sure we could take them.'

'Stock?' said Irvine.

Hawley turned to him. 'Horses. Horses for slaughter.'

'Did he say how many?'

'Up to a dozen. He wasn't sure on the number.'

'Which suggests that he hadn't actually bought them at that stage,' said Cooper.

'I suppose so.'

Hawley walked with them towards the car park, away from the nervous horses and the smell of blood.

'Mr Hawley, if a buyer went to a horse auction, what would he be bidding on?'

'Horses from riding stables, some from private punters.'

193

Cooper thought about Patrick Rawson's Mitsubishi 4x4 parked by the field barn near Longstone Moor. He recalled that it had a tow bar, but there was no sign of a trailer, let alone anything that would be big enough to accommodate a dozen horses.

'How would Mr Rawson have transported the animals that he wanted to bring to you?' he asked. 'Would he bring them himself?'

'Sometimes, if it was just one or two. But if there were bigger numbers involved, he would use a local haulier. He had contacts in every area.'

'You would keep records of each delivery, I suppose?'

'Are you kidding? There are mountains of paperwork. The drivers hate it.'

Cooper produced his card. 'Would you do something for me? Check your records for hauliers that Mr Rawson has previously used in the North Derbyshire area. Then give me a call with their names.'

'I can do that, certainly,' said Hawley. 'But, if you're thinking of the Eden Valley, I think I know the one you want. Senior Brothers in Lowbridge.'

21

Leaning back in his office chair, Maurice Gains shook his head at Diane Fry and wagged a long finger. 'We don't call it horse meat, as a rule, Sergeant. We prefer "cheval".'

'Oh?' said Fry. 'Why not call a spade a spade?'

'Because of the sensitivities of the British consumer.'

Fry didn't think Maurice Gains looked the sensitive type. Sensitive to the size of his own bank account, maybe. And that was about it. He was the type of businessman she hated most. Supercilious, complacent, obsessed with his own success.

'We don't eat cow, do we?' he said. 'We eat beef. We don't eat pig – we eat pork, or ham. You see, it protects the housewife from having to picture the actual living creature when she's doing her shopping in the supermarket. If we give it a different name, it becomes just another product on the shelf. It's all about the image.'

Well, it would have to be. The unit occupied by R & G Enterprises was all about image, too. Money had been spent on the entrance and signage, a smart logo that must have been professionally designed. The carpets in reception and in the manager's office were deeper and more luxurious than anything ever dreamed of at E Division headquarters. Fry had been ushered to a low, modernist lounge chair that Gavin

Murfin would have had difficulty getting out of again, if he'd been with her. But this was one interview she'd felt might be better done alone.

'Who eats this product of yours?' she said.

'Well, cheval has always been popular among the French and Belgian working classes, usually in urban areas. You may have seen the specialist butchers' shops in Paris, the *boucheries chevalines*, with those wonderful gilded horse-head advertising signs?'

'I can't say that I have,' said Fry. 'I must be promenading on the wrong boulevards.'

Gains smiled, a condescending smile which got right on her nerves. 'Well, in recent years, horse meat has become more popular in the fashionable *arrondissements*. A lot of French consumers began switching from beef to horse when mad cow disease appeared. Cheval is marketed as a healthy, low-fat alternative to British beef.'

'They started eating horse instead of our beef?'

'Yes. Ironically, it's often *our* horses they're eating,' said Gains. 'And even young people in France have taken to horse meat. I'm told there's a horse meat dining society known as Le Pony Club. But Italy and Eastern Europe are big markets, too, and parts of Japan and China.'

'We don't eat horse meat in this country, though.'

'Historically, that's true. Though, actually, people have been eating horse meat for some time, without being aware of it. There was a Food Standards Agency investigation a few years ago which found salami on sale in the UK containing horse and donkey meat, without it being mentioned on the food label. No one died of shock. And times change, you know. We're living in a much more multi-cultural country.'

'So I've heard.'

Gains had a habit of stroking his hand along the smooth grain of his desk. A possessive, self-satisfied gesture, Fry thought.

'I'm not just talking about ethnic minorities,' he said, 'but the large numbers of our fellow EU citizens who now live and work in the UK. Many of them are from countries where horse meat is perfectly acceptable. Indeed, the meat is highly regarded by some communities. And quite rightly, given its low fat content and excellent flavour.'

'You think you can make horse meat part of the British diet?'

'We acknowledge that we have a bit of a PR challenge on our hands. But it's not an insurmountable problem. In fact, there's a precedent. Thanks to the Asian and Caribbean communities, goat meat has become more common in the UK market during the last couple of decades. Now we just want to widen the food experience a little. The time is absolutely right, when you consider the increasingly health-conscious environment, the public awareness of the risks of eating too much fat. Horse meat is splendidly healthy, with half the fat of beef and ten times the Omega Threes to reduce your cholesterol. It's free from bird 'flu, mad cow disease, tuberculosis, Foot and Mouth, and tape worm – all the scourges of our traditional meat industries. There's a huge opportunity for a dynamic, enterprising company to break new ground.'

'And that's you?'

He smiled smugly. 'Absolutely. R & G Enterprises are ideally positioned in the market place, Sergeant. We saw an opportunity, and we're taking it. That's what enterprise is all about. One day, we'll expand into Europe and take on the French and Belgians at their own game. A shame we can't establish a market in the USA. But the Americans are most against eating horse meat.'

Fry looked at the company logo, etched into the window of the manager's office.

'I take it Patrick Rawson is the "R" in R & G Enterprises, Mr Gains?'

'Yes, poor Patrick. Do you know how it happened?'

197

'Not yet.'

'I spoke to Deborah yesterday. She said it was a robbery. Unusual place for it to happen.'

'We can't be sure of the circumstances,' said Fry stiffly.

'Pity. I was hoping you might have some news.'

'How did you and Mr Rawson happen to go into business together?'

'Well, it didn't just "happen",' said Gains. 'We had talked about the possibility for some time. Years, I suppose. We met through Hawley and Sons, the abattoir owners. I used to work for the Meat and Livestock Commission. Then, about a year ago, we agreed that the time had come, and we put the package together.'

'Mr Rawson put up some of his own money?'

'Yes. I was fortunate – I had an inheritance from my father, a few thousand I had put away for just such an eventuality. Patrick, I believe, raised some equity from his property in Sutton Coldfield.'

'He used his house as security?'

'That's right. But the majority of the finance came from our business loan. That has to be serviced, and paid back first. But we're building the enterprise well. Everyone will be happy with the outcome, I believe.'

Fry tried to ignore the complacent smile. 'Do you know Michael Clay, Mr Gains?'

'Oh, Clay? I gather he's worked with Patrick on some other projects. But I've never met him.'

'He's not involved with R & G?'

'No, that's just the two of us. Me and Patrick.'

Fry was vaguely disappointed. At the moment, Michael Clay could only be counted as an elusive witness. But ever since she'd spoken to Erin Lacey in Great Barr this morning, she'd been bothered by a nagging feeling that he would soon turn out to be something more than that.

'I see. And, Mr Gains, I have to ask you – were you aware

that Patrick Rawson was the subject of a Trading Standards investigation?'

Gains hesitated, for the first time. 'Yes, I was. It was quite well known in the trade. But no charges were ever brought against him, so I couldn't see any problem. Innocent until proven guilty, eh, Sergeant?'

'So they say.'

'Patrick is in regular touch – sorry, *was* in regular touch. He phoned on Monday, in fact. Just for a chat, nothing specific.'

'He was in his car when he phoned, I suppose?'

'Yes, I believe he was.'

Fry was interested that Maurice Gains had volunteered the information about Rawson's phone call before she asked the question. Clearly, this man wasn't stupid.

'Was that the last time you spoke?'

'Yes.'

'And he was happy with how things were going?' said Fry. 'No problems?'

'None at all. Between you and me, we talked about future expansion. We're modelling ourselves on a well-established Belgian company, which does the whole job – buys the horses, slaughters them, carries out the butchering, then packages and distributes the meat. But that's for the future. We're only just getting a toe-hold on the market at the moment.'

'You'd be looking to buy a slaughterhouse, then? Like Hawleys, for example?'

'Yes, that would be ideal,' said Gains. 'We've already had talks with Hawleys. Of course, the equine side of their business is a drop in the ocean. The countries supplying the most horse meat in Europe are Poland and Romania. And we do need certain types of horse. The optimum age for slaughter is between ten and fifteen years, the minimum about seven. Funnily enough, the older the horse, the more tender the meat. It's the opposite of other meats.'

'No young horses?'

'Well, foal is OK up to fifteen months, but it's a special-ized market. Italy likes white meat from very young horses, but the French prefer red. We think the UK market will favour red meat, too.'

Through a window, Fry could see into the packing room, where women dressed head to toe in white plastic aprons, hats and hair nets, were processing the meat. The steaks she could see going through the line were enormous – big slabs of purplish-black meat, thickly marbled with fat.

Gains had followed her gaze. 'The taste is a bit sweet, compared to beef,' he admitted. 'Traditionally, it was thought that it would never suit the British palate, even if we didn't have a cultural problem to overcome. But the taste can easily be improved with seasoning and spices. Like lamb, it goes rather well with herbs such as rosemary or sage. You really should try it.'

Fry wished there was some way she could shake Maurice Gains' complacency, make that hand stop stroking the smooth wood of his desk, just for a moment.

'Mr Gains, an outbreak of trichinosis from eating infected horse meat isn't very good news for you, is it?' she said.

'No connection with us,' snapped Gains, losing his compos-ure for just a moment. 'I made a call this morning, and I'm told the suspect meat came from Poland. Brought in by some Polish workers living in a multi-occupancy property in Birmingham. That's up to the Polish authorities to deal with, if they're the country of origin.'

'But, Mr Gains, don't you think you might have something more serious to deal with than a PR challenge?' she said.

'We'll take all the steps that are necessary to protect our brand.'

'"Protect your brand"? That wasn't what I meant.'

'I don't know what you do mean, then.'

'I mean animal rights activists,' said Fry. 'Some of the protest groups out there can be pretty extreme in their actions. You must have taken that into account?'

'We considered it, naturally,' said Gains. 'It was a factor that our business partners raised at the planning stage.'

'Business partners?'

'Our financial backers. Banks, I mean. They don't play any active role in the business, but we needed finance to meet our start-up costs. So we had to put together a business proposal for them, and the public reaction was factored into that. But we're not dealing with live animals here, you see. Currently, all our meat comes from Italy. It's boned, cut and packaged in a plant near Turin, then shipped back to the UK in refrigerated lorries. You won't find any ponies gambolling around in paddocks waiting to go on to the slaughter line. Not here. There's nothing for the animal rights fanatics to get steamed up about.'

'You think not?'

'Look, we're only distributing to specialist shops at the moment, and a few restaurants where the owners are willing to be innovative. But wait until we get our products into Tesco and Waitrose. Then public acceptance will soon follow.'

'I'm glad you're so confident.'

'I suppose it might just be me, Sergeant, but I don't understand where these animal lovers are coming from,' said Gains. 'Why do people who eat cows and sheep get so upset at the idea of eating a horse?'

'They think of them as companions, not food.'

'That's the way most of us think about dogs, isn't it? Yet the Chinese and Koreans eat dog meat, even consider it a delicacy. One man's pet is another man's protein.' Gains smiled. 'Isn't that right, Sergeant?'

Fry was relieved to get out of the R & G distribution centre. Though the smell had been clean, and maybe even overly hygienic, there had been a strange contradiction in the sight of those purple slabs of meat being handled and shipped out. By the time she got back to her car, she was very glad that Gavin Murfin wasn't with her. She couldn't have stood it if he'd produced something to eat right at this moment.

A message from Murfin was waiting on her phone. There must have been no signal while she was inside R & G Enterprises.

'Thought you might like to know,' said Murfin when she called him back. 'SOCOs lifted some latent prints from that gate on Longstone Moor. They've visited the farmer and printed him for comparison, but some of the latents don't match. Could be you were right, Diane.'

'Well, actually, Ben Cooper was right.'

'I'll tell him that.'

Fry sighed. 'Yes, do.'

'Are you OK, Diane?'

'Yes, I'm fine. I've just escaped from a vision of the future – R & G Enterprises.'

She told Murfin about her visit, not leaving out the slabs of meat.

'I know you said Patrick Rawson had a finger in a lot of pies,' said Murfin when she'd finished, 'but I didn't realize some of the pies were made of horse meat.'

Fry winced. 'Don't, Gavin.'

'Oh, got to go,' said Murfin. 'There's something happening.'

'What?'

But he'd gone. And Fry had to sit tapping her fingers on the steering wheel while she waited for him to phone back.

'What's going on?'

'We're just picking up a suspect,' said Murfin breathlessly. 'The DI's taking the lead, and we're on the way there now.'

'Who, Gavin? Who is it?'

'It seems we've got information on some youth who has Patrick Rawson's wallet and credit cards in his possession.

His mum saw the appeals on TV and shopped him. Good news, eh?'

Fry looked at the frontage of R & G Enterprises, with its smoked glass and its designer logo. Had she just wasted a precious hour of her life being patronized by Maurice Gains while all the action was happening elsewhere? And on *her* case, too?

'Yeah. That's great news, Gavin.'

'Oh, yes,' said Murfin. 'And one more thing: we've got another body.'

22

Cooper and Irvine were the first to arrive back in the area from their trip to Hawleys. They diverted off the A57 to Longstone Moor, where the body that had been spotted by a walker was being carefully recovered from Watersaw Rake. Mountain rescue had lowered a stretcher and rigged up the ropes to get it safely clear of the broken rocks.

'We've identified him,' said the officer in charge of the recovery team, as Cooper and Irvine reached the scene. 'He was overdue to return to his B&B. Chap went for a walk right before the weather came down. Just bad timing.'

'A tourist?' said Cooper.

'Yes, and a keen walker. Fit for his age, too. But he was walking on his own, and he seems to have stumbled into the rake in the fog.'

'There's a fence, though.'

'He climbed over it – you can see his boot prints are right there. He must not have realized what was on the other side, poor sod.'

Cooper looked down at a damp blue object lying on the ground at the officer's feet.

'Is that his rucksack?'

'Yes. He wasn't heading far, but he came well equipped.'

'Where was he staying?'

'Middleton Dale. He told the owner of the B&B that he was going to walk up to Wardlow and back.' The officer shook his head. 'I know it was really foggy. But all he had to do was keep going in a straight line, and he would have reached the road, no problem.'

'In fog, the loss of visual clues destroys your sense of direction,' said Cooper. 'In open ground like this, the tendency is to go round and round in circles. I reckon that's what he must have done.'

'At least the weather has kept most of the public away. No casual passers-by to disturb the scene. All you need with an incident like this is fifty members of the Healthy Life Rambling Club trampling through the scene with their fell boots and hiking sticks.'

'But he was found by walkers?'

'Three nosy retired bobbies.'

Cooper drew a damp wad of paper out of the pocket of the rucksack and carefully unfolded it on the ground.

'What's that?' asked Irvine.

'An Ordnance Survey map, Luke. Outdoor Leisure series, White Peak area.'

'He should have been able to find his way with that, shouldn't he? They're incredibly detailed. Every slope and contour line is on them. Every field boundary.'

'Yes, two and a half inches to the mile. You'd think it would have helped him, even in dense fog.'

When Cooper unfolded the wet mass, he discovered a cover picture of Dove Dale, one of the Peak District's most popular limestone valleys, photographed in the summer, of course, with a few strollers by the riverside. And the cover of the map bore a price: £2.95.

'This is an old edition of the OS map,' he said. 'Yes, look – last revised in 1979. It's thirty years out of date.'

'Does that make a difference?'

'Well, compare it to mine.' Cooper drew his own map from a pocket of his coat. 'I've got the most recent edition, reprinted in 2006. There's Middleton Dale, just the same. And Black Harry Lane going up across the moor to Black Harry Gate. But then, see – in this big hollow –'

'Blimey,' said Irvine. 'There's a lake.'

'A flash. Flooded quarry workings. On the old map it shows "Brandy Bottle Mine (Disused)". But the mine has gone from the new map. The workings filled up with water, and the OS took it into account when they did their revisions.'

'But our tourist wouldn't have seen a stretch of water on *his* map. It wasn't there, because his map was out of date.'

Cooper nodded. 'When he reached water, he must have thought he was completely lost. He ended up disorientated, trying to work out where he was on the map.'

'The poor bloke,' said Irvine, looking at the map. 'He was never more than a few hundred yards from a road.'

'Which doesn't help at all. Not if you're walking round in circles.'

Cooper took a call from Diane Fry. She was still in her car somewhere, stuck in a bottleneck near Glossop.

'This body,' she said. 'I suppose you're at the scene, Ben?'

'Looking at it right now.'

'It isn't Michael Clay, is it?'

'Why would you think it's him?' asked Cooper.

'Because he's too elusive. I'm starting to think I'll never get the chance to interview him. So please tell me this body isn't Michael Clay.'

Cooper watched the body slowly being lifted to ground level, and an officer passing up something else that he'd found in the bottom of the rake. He leaned closer to take a look, and could see the manufacturer's name and model quite clearly.

'It isn't Michael Clay, Diane.'

'Thank God.'

'But,' said Cooper, 'we do seem to have found Patrick Rawson's phone.'

Fry drove back to West Street as fast as she could, bearing in mind the speed cameras on the approach to Edendale. But Sean Crabbe had already been processed through the custody suite by the time she arrived. His fingerprints had been taken in Live Scan, a sample of his DNA had been obtained on a buccal swab, and his personal possessions had been logged by the custody sergeant. Now he was waiting for the duty solicitor before being questioned.

DI Hitchens explained that a call had been put through after the young man's mother had responded to the public appeal on the local TV news. She hadn't called straight away, but had waited a couple of hours.

'Otherwise, you would have been here for the arrest, Diane,' he said. 'It was just one of those things.'

'It doesn't matter,' said Fry, though they both knew she was lying. 'What made the connection for her?'

'The mention of the old agricultural research centre. The TV people took some footage of it for background to the piece. You know – crime-scene tape, bobby fidgeting in front of the camera. She recognized the place. And she knew perfectly well that young Sean goes up there regularly when he bunks off from college. It turns out she's been worried about him for a while, thinks he's been going off the rails a bit.'

'And he was up there on Tuesday morning?'

'Mum didn't know that for certain,' said Hitchens. 'But she remembers him coming home early that day and behaving oddly. She says he tried to make out he had 'flu, but she wasn't fooled. Mothers rarely are, no matter what they tell us to our faces.'

'If you say so.'

'Anyway, young Sean is going to get a shock when he realizes his mum knew what he was up to all along.'

'But why didn't she call as soon as she saw the appeals?' asked Fry.

'Well, being of a suspicious nature but not wanting to think the worst of her beloved son without proof, she waited until he was out of the house and took a gander in his room. And she turned up the wallet in his underwear drawer.'

Fry looked at the plastic evidence bag. 'Patrick Rawson's wallet?'

'Yes. And here are his credit and debit cards. Golf club membership. A pocket full of business cards – there might be some useful contacts there that we haven't spoken to yet. Oh, and just under five hundred pounds in cash.'

'Five hundred?'

'For those last-minute cash deals, I suppose.'

'I wonder if Crabbe spent any?'

'Impossible to tell. We'll have to ask him. We can't find any record of him attempting to use the cards, so maybe he had the sense to hang on to the cash until things died down.'

'If he had that amount of sense, why didn't he get rid of the wallet?' said Fry.

Hitchens shook his head. 'No idea. We've seized the clothes Sean was wearing on Tuesday morning, and they've gone for forensics. Mum says he changed as soon as he came home that day, and showered. If we find Patrick Rawson's blood on his clothes, it will look very bad for him.'

'Does he have any previous?'

'No, he's clean. Not even a bit of juvenile on his record. Actually, he doesn't seem the type from what I saw of him. Long hair, and a bit dreamy looking. I wouldn't be surprised if he wrote poetry. You know the sort of kid.'

'An emo?'

'Is that what they call them?'

'Emos are more likely to kill themselves than anybody else,' said Fry. 'Did Mrs Crabbe understand what she was implicating him in?'

'She must have done, surely?' said Hitchens. 'Here's his custody record anyway, Diane. The name is Sean Crabbe, aged twenty, student. He's local, too – so his voice could well match the 999 call.'

Fry sat up straighter. 'You want me to do the interview, sir?'

'Well, why not?'

Sean Crabbe sat in Interview Room One, a desperately hangdog expression on his face. He was staring down at his hands, which gripped the edge of the table. His knuckles were white, a sign of the tension he was under.

If he'd been in any doubt about the seriousness of the charges he might face, he had been enlightened by his brief, who looked almost as anxious as Crabbe.

'It wasn't me who killed him,' was the young man's first sentence when Fry sat down opposite him and started the tapes.

'Killed who, Sean?' asked Fry, hoping this was going to be an easy one.

'The man in the hut. The dead man.'

Fry reminded herself that the 999 call had reported a dead body in the abandoned hut. That was despite the fact that Patrick Rawson had clearly not been dead at the time, since he'd recovered sufficiently to run a few hundred yards across the adjoining fields. Of course, that didn't preclude Sean Crabbe from being responsible for his death.

'You'd better tell us about it, Sean. From the start.'

He glanced at his solicitor, and Fry could sense that they'd agreed what Sean would say – and perhaps what he wouldn't. But she'd encountered this brief before, he was pretty straight. Besides, Sean Crabbe seemed more than ready to tell his story.

'It was the sight of the phone, just lying there. That was what did it. I couldn't resist picking it up. It was really smart, you see – a Sony Ericsson.' He leaned forward and stared at

Fry to see if she understood. 'It happens all the time, people nicking phones. I've had two nicked in the last year. All my mates have, too. I thought it would be all right, just to – you know, take one back.'

'Sean, I don't think you've started from the beginning, like I asked you,' said Fry.

'What?'

'Let's begin with why you went up to the old agricultural research centre on Longstone Moor on Tuesday morning. I need to know what you were doing there in the first place.'

Sean hesitated. 'The old huts are just somewhere I go, to be on my own. There was no other reason.'

'Were you going there to meet someone?'

'No. It was like I just said.'

'But someone else *was* there,' insisted Fry.

'Just . . . well, just the dead man.'

'His name is Patrick Rawson. And he was alive when you first saw him, Sean.'

'He was dying, though. He was practically dead. And I wasn't responsible for that.'

'Oh, come on.'

'I'm telling you the truth.'

Fry sat back in surprise. He almost looked as though he was going to cry. Twenty years old, and he was upset by somebody speaking to him a bit sharply. What was it the DI had said? He didn't look the type. Sean Crabbe was the kind of boy who ought to be writing poetry somewhere. The kind who wanted to be on his own, and wouldn't like an intrusion into his little hideaway. She decided to try a different tack.

'You said the old huts are just somewhere you go, Sean. So you go up there often, do you?'

He ran a hand across his face, though there weren't actually any tears that Fry could see.

'Quite often. Whenever I get the chance.'

'Because it's somewhere you can be on your own?'

'Yes.'

'Don't you ever meet anyone up there?'

'No, never. No one goes there, except me.'

Fry nodded. 'So you must have been annoyed when you saw Mr Rawson arrive.'

Sean looked confused. 'I told you.'

'No, you didn't, Sean.'

'I told you, I didn't see him arrive. He was already nearly dead when I saw him.'

The duty solicitor was starting to get restless. The same question asked in a different way could often get a result. But not with Sean Crabbe.

'Sean, you were in possession of Mr Rawson's wallet. So we know you robbed him. Didn't you also hit him over the head?'

Now he was really anxious.

'No. I would never do that. He was just lying there in the hut. I never even heard anything. I didn't know anyone else was around until I smelled something. And it was his after-shave. He was wearing a really strong aftershave. He was lying near the back door of the big hut, and he had blood coming from his head.'

'And what did you do, Sean?'

'I took his phone. It was on the floor, as if he'd been trying to use it.' He glanced at the solicitor, who nodded. 'And then I took his wallet.'

Sean looked so ashamed when he got out the last part of his admission that Fry didn't know what to say for a moment.

'Go on. What next?'

'I got out of there, scarpered. I was scared of getting caught.'

'Oh, were you? What did you do with the phone?'

His shoulders slumped with embarrassment. 'I realized after a minute or two that it was stupid to have taken it. They can trace you by a phone, can't they?'

'Right. But you made a call on it, didn't you. Sean?'

'I dialled 999 and told them there was a body.'

'Why did you do that?' asked Fry. Despite the conclusion she was gradually arriving at, this was a question she really wanted to know the answer to.

Sean sighed. 'I had this horrible thought. Like I said, no one else ever goes up there. Not ever. And I had this awful idea that the next time I went up to the huts, that man would still be there, lying dead on the floor. Rotting. Because no one had found him.'

'And that would ruin your little sanctuary,' said Fry.

He hung his head again. 'And then I got rid of the phone.'

'By throwing it into Watersaw Rake.'

'Yes. It made it all seem so pointless, but I knew I had to do it, or I'd get caught.'

'But you got caught anyway,' said Fry, 'thanks to your mother.'

'Yeah.'

'She seems to know everything you've been up to, Sean.'

'It really pisses me off. Not having any privacy, no life of my own.'

Fry looked at him for a moment, considering the irony of what he'd just said. It was an irony that was lost on Sean Crabbe.

'Sean,' she said, 'what made you think Mr Rawson was dead when you first found him?'

'What made – ? Oh, I get it. Well, I've seen a dead man before. There was an old homeless bloke who died there months ago, some down and out. I thought . . . well, I thought it would be the same this time. Except I got a new phone.'

23

DI Hitchens was waiting for Fry expectantly when she came out of the interview room. She felt faintly grubby, and depressed by what Sean Crabbe had done with his life.

'So, Diane. Can I tell the Super we've got a result?' said Hitchens with a grin.

Fry wished for all the world that she could say 'yes'. She very much wanted Superintendent Branagh to hear that DS Fry had brought the Rawson case to a successful conclusion. And she knew that her DI wanted to give her that opportunity.

'No, I'm sorry,' she said.

'But we've finally got a suspect in custody,' protested Hitchens.

'Yes, sir. The trouble is, I believe he's telling the truth.'

A file would have to be prepared on Sean Crabbe for the Crown Prosecution Service before a decision was made on any charges he'd face. Fry supposed that theft would be on the list, given the confession. And perhaps perverting the course of justice, which was a CPS favourite.

Meanwhile, Becky Hurst and Luke Irvine had been doing their research, and the extent of the picture they were building up was alarming. Listening to them give their reports, DI

Hitchens looked as though he might be starting to feel out of his depth.

'It's back to square one, then,' he said. 'If Sean Crabbe is telling the truth, the answer must lie in Patrick Rawson's business activities. Someone he got the wrong side of.'

'And there must be plenty of those.'

The DI listened carefully to the results of the visits to Hawley's abattoir and the meat distributors.

'So we could be talking seriously big money here,' he said.

'The value of the horse industry has been estimated at three and a half billion pounds,' said DC Hurst, reading eagerly from her notebook. 'Bookmakers alone generate an annual profit of more than a billion from horse racing. Owners of leading stallions can charge hundreds of thousands for a single mating, and a stallion can cover two hundred mares in a season. Big money, all right.'

'Given all those vested interests, who's going to be bothered in the least about what happens to the failures?' said Hitchens. 'Let the French and Belgians eat them, if they want to. Why not?'

'It's not just the French and Belgians any more,' said Fry, remembering all too clearly the packing line at R & G Enterprises.

'Did you know horses have the intelligence and sensitivity of a seven-year-old child?' asked Hurst.

But Fry wasn't impressed by that. Seven-year-old children could be obnoxious, certainly – but they didn't usually shit on your shoes for no good reason.

'We were told at the abattoir that they pay as much as eight hundred pounds for a large thoroughbred,' added Cooper. 'That's an attractive proposition for an owner faced with the expense of disposal by some other means. It can cost anything from a hundred and fifty pounds for collection and processing by a renderer, to seven hundred and fifty or more for euthanasia by a vet. And there aren't many animal sanctuaries for racehorses. It's way beyond the pockets of most animal charities.'

'And, much though they claim to love horses, the British public are far more concerned about the welfare of stray cats and dogs.'

'Oh, yes. Try slaughtering those for meat, and see what sort of outcry you'd get.'

'Live export of horses for slaughter isn't actually illegal,' said Hurst. 'But there haven't been any exports for several years. The government put a mandatory minimum value on any horse exported abroad. It's intended to be an amount more than any horse slaughterer would be willing to pay. In effect, it allows the export of racehorses, but blocks the live trade in food animals.'

'But horses of higher value must be exported for competitions and breeding.'

'Yes. And no doubt some of them end up joining the slaughter trail somewhere else in Europe.'

'What about horse passports?' asked Hitchens.

'Just a minute, I asked that,' said Hurst. 'Since March 2006, any horses sent to abattoirs in England must have a passport before they can be slaughtered. They contain details of any medications given to the animal, to ensure certain drugs don't enter the human food chain. There's a section in the passport where the owner can declare whether a horse is intended for human consumption or not.'

'So if you don't want your dobbin turned into horse steaks or salami, you can say so.'

'In Section Nine of your horse passport, yes. The rules are pretty strict on identification and so on. The valuation certificate has to be issued by someone on the DEFRA list, and is only valid for a month.'

'Are these rules working?'

'Yes. Apparently, European Union legislation could over-turn the regulations at any time. If the restriction were

215

removed, the main market would be the horse abattoirs in southern Italy. Live animals would be on the road for days before slaughter.'

'When you think of that, Hawleys and those UK horse-meat distributors start to look like a godsend,' said Cooper.

'So,' said Hitchens. 'What's the outcome of all this? Are horses being stolen to be sold for meat? What do we think?'

'We don't actually have any evidence of that.'

'But it must be a suspicion, given all the links in the chain.'

'You know, Horse Watch have an entire list of stolen equines that have never turned up anywhere,' said Cooper.

'Yes, I do know that.'

'Well, chances are, those animals have gone through someone like Rawson. The dealer will either sell them on to a new owner, or he'll make a few hundred pounds on the carcass at the horse slaughterer's. Patrick Rawson is at the centre of this somehow. He has connections with the abattoir, he's a partner in R & G Enterprises. We know he has a history as a dodgy horse dealer. The number of people who might have wanted to kill him is beginning to look endless.'

'Yes, just about every horse owner or animal lover in the country,' said Fry. 'But if Trading Standards couldn't get enough solid evidence against him to put him in court after a five-year investigation, how would some animal rights group find out enough to target him?'

'I don't know.'

'Have we traced the source of the video footage you were sent, Ben?' asked Hitchens. 'That would give us a line on the animal rights people.'

'Becky has been helping me on that,' said Cooper. 'But at the moment, it looks as though it could have been almost anyone. The video is available on the internet, for members of the public to download and distribute.'

Hitchens shook his head. 'The internet makes things so

damn difficult. Well, we must at least have identified all the calls on Rawson's mobile phone?'

'Yes,' said Fry. 'Apart from Hawleys, and Mr Gains at R & G Enterprises, there were three calls to the number of Michael Clay, one to Senior Brothers at Lowbridge. And two calls each way to an unregistered pay-as-you-go mobile.'

'This was on Monday evening?'

'Right. There were no calls logged on Tuesday morning.'

'Do you think there could have been a woman involved?'

'It might have been anyone – a customer, a seller . . . who knows?'

Hitchens looked thoughtful. 'I'm still not clear how the operation works. How do horses end up as meat when they're not supposed to?'

'It's not clear to me, either. I suppose we could mount an undercover operation.'

'How?'

'We send someone in as a horse owner with an animal to sell.'

'Who could we use for that?'

'I'd be willing to give it a go, sir,' said Fry.

But Hitchens shook his head. 'We have specially trained officers for undercover work, Diane. Operational Support will provide someone, if necessary.'

'I hope they've got someone who can pass as an expert on livestock.'

'I doubt it.'

They looked at each other for a moment, then they both looked at Cooper. Oh, yes. The officer everyone thought of when there was an expert needed. Fry could have kicked herself for the reaction.

But Cooper didn't respond. And it wasn't like him to be reluctant to jump forward and volunteer.

'We'll think about it,' said Hitchens after a moment. 'There's no rush. Let's check out the horse market first. See if we can pick up any useful leads.'

'By the way,' said Cooper, 'this restaurant . . .'

'Which restaurant?'

'Le Chien Noir.'

'Oh, yes. I had hopes that the head waiter would remember more about Patrick Rawson's visit, but he's never called me.'

'A French restaurant, is it?'

'In principle,' said Fry. 'I doubt any of the staff are actually French.'

'Did you happen to get a copy of the menu?'

'No. Why? Are you thinking of taking your girlfriend there?'

'Well . . . we know France is one of the biggest markets for horse meat. And the guy at R & G Enterprises told you they were trying to introduce horse meat to the British market gradually –'

'– through a small number of select restaurants. You think Le Chien Noir could be one of them?'

'It might just be a coincidence. But if Patrick Rawson was known there . . .'

'The manager said not.'

'And did he seem reliable?'

'He was very helpful,' said Fry. Then she thought back to her conversation with Connelly. 'Well, up to a point.'

'Let me guess. He clammed up about Rawson?'

'No, about the man Rawson was with. Mr Connelly said he was much too ordinary a middle-aged businessman for anybody to be expected to remember what he even looked like.'

'That's a good one.'

'Yes. Yet he was so good on his impressions of Rawson.' Fry sighed. 'Never mind. We should find out who Le Chien Noir is actually owned by.'

'Good idea.'

Fry looked at him. 'You really think horse meat might be on the menu?'

'I've never heard of anything like it in Edendale,' he said.

'But it could be presented as something else. Is the menu in French?'

Fry sighed. 'I didn't even look.'

When he got back to Welbeck Street, the first thing Cooper always did was check his answering machine. Nothing, of course. He thought Liz might have called, but perhaps she was waiting for him to do it. Besides, she would have called his mobile. Hardly anybody used the answering machine any more, if they had his mobile number.

The second thing he did was feed the cat. But Randy had no appetite tonight. Cooper sat with him for a while, stroking his fur until he got the familiar deep purr, willing the cat not to give up just yet.

When he straightened up, his back twinged slightly from being in the same position for too long. He got himself a beer from the fridge – some Czech brand that had been on special offer at Somerfield's.

Last night, before he went to bed, he'd been reading a novel, a fantasy epic. It still lay on the table – closed, but with a bookmark stuck into the pages to show where he'd got up to. About a third of the way through, he judged.

But wait. It wasn't really a bookmark at all. When he'd closed the book last night, too tired to keep the lines of text from blurring in front of his eyes, he'd picked up the first thing that came to hand. It was a habit he'd developed as a child, and had never got rid of. In fact, he didn't think he'd ever owned a proper bookmark – not one with leather fringes and gold-blocked lettering, the sort that other people had. He just used anything that would fit between the pages.

Cooper opened the book. He saw that last night he'd used the postcard he brought back from Eyam. Plague Cottage and the memorial plaque to the Cooper boys. Like most of the other plague victims, their graves had never been found, but their names still lived on.

He drank only half the beer and put it down reluctantly, remembering that he was driving tonight. He thought about what Gavin Murfin had said about Eyam. Personally, he couldn't see why the village should be considered creepy. In spite of the tourists, it seemed a peaceful kind of place. Perhaps that was because its memories weren't locked away in the dark, as they were in other places. In Eyam, they were out on display, for everyone to see.

Fry had watched Ben Cooper leave the office. It had been another bad day, and Cooper always seemed to be involved somehow. Perhaps he didn't actually intend to show up her failings. But he did it so effortlessly.

She so hated to admit that Cooper was right. That he was *ever* right. In retrospect, she much preferred the old Ben Cooper, the one who'd been careful not to say anything, had tried not to rub it in, even when he'd turned out to be right in the end. These days, he seemed to be proving that he knew better at every turn. The bastard.

When she got into her car to leave West Street, Fry sat for a moment in a kind of dull apathy. She didn't really want to go home to her flat in Grosvenor Avenue. But she couldn't think of anywhere she did want to go. It wasn't as if there was anything to look forward to, except more bad days.

Half an hour later, Cooper drove down the track to Bridge End Farm. At one time, his nieces would have run out to meet him when they heard his car coming down the lane. Now, there was no sign of them. Busy doing their homework? Well, perhaps. More likely, they couldn't even hear his engine above the music playing on their iPods.

He pulled up in the farm yard, and got out of the car. Then he stood for a moment, doing nothing. Just listening to the familiar sounds, and smelling the familiar smells. And he realized Claire was right – he'd stayed away from home far too long.

24

Journal of 1968

Well, it was quite a year, 1968. It was all Dr Strangelove and the Prague Spring – Soviet tanks crushing Czechoslovakia, the USA getting a kick up the arse by the Viet Cong, and Enoch Powell making his Rivers of Blood speech. In Londonderry, it was the start of The Troubles. In Paris, students thought they were starting a revolution. That summer, the two best-known people in the world were Sirhan Sirhan and James Earl Ray. Famous because they'd killed the right people.

But most of the time, we were too busy listening to the Beatles' *White Album*, and watching *Hawaii Five-O* on TV. Trying to shut out reality, some might say. And that wasn't the same after 1968, either.

Some people talk about the sixties as if it was nothing but sex and drugs, and love and peace, the decade of liberation. Well, that's a pretty bad joke. It might have been all free love and Carnaby Street down there in London, but things take a bit longer to change in these parts. Here, we still had narrow minds and twitching curtains. There was no Technicolor in Birchlow back then, just the same old black-and-white grimness, the dyed-in-the-wool, stuck-in-a-rut, holier-than-thou hypocrites whose disapproval ruined people's lives. If you took one wrong step, then everyone knew it. The Swinging Sixties? Here, it was still the fifties. In some ways, it was still the Dark Ages.

But if you were young in 1968, you could sense the world changing. Every day, you felt things shifting under your feet, as if the whole of existence could tip in one direction or the other at any moment. We might shake off the old ways, or we might all be destroyed. It was hard to tell. We didn't know what the future looked like, but we knew it would be different.

It's strange how the mind works. For me, bits of music used to pop into my head all the time, as if every thought and feeling I had was connected to a tune playing somewhere, like a soundtrack of my life. In 1968, you never knew where you stood with pop music. One week it was the Rolling Stones at the top of the charts, the next week it was bloody Des O'Connor.

Just thinking about threes reminded me of the Three Degrees, even though I never really liked them. They would have been one of Jimmy's favourite groups, if he'd lived a bit longer. He was mad on the Supremes and the Four Tops, all that Tamla stuff. I thought of him often in the months after it happened, the fact that he never heard the Supremes sing 'Love Child', and completely missed 'I Heard it through the Grapevine'. He died too young. We heard that a lot, in those days.

No, me and Jimmy saw eye to eye on a lot of things, but I never got into Motown myself. Give me the Stones any day of the week. 'Jumpin' Jack Flash' had come out just about then. Now, *that* was music. With half a chance, I'd like to have turned it up loud in that hole, let it bounce off those bloody concrete walls until my ears ached. *It's a gas, gas, gas.*

But not down there, not while the mad people ran the world. And Les would never have let me do it, anyway. Because Les was number one.

For hours on end, it seemed my world revolved around the

pee pot and the pump. Bloody strange way to save the world, I always thought. The stink of Elsan and Glitto, the bad air you had to breathe until you got back up into the daylight. Why some blokes put up with it, I couldn't tell you.

Me, I just reckoned I was doing something for my family, and for my village. But, you know what? I was never too sure what I would have done, if the call had ever come for real.

And I was never sure – not *really* sure – whether I was capable of killing a man.

25

Friday

When she arrived at West Street next morning, Fry found
Murfin motionless at his desk, staring into space.

'Watch it, Gavin. If you're not careful, they'll replace you
with one of those cardboard policemen.'

'Sorry.'

'And it might even be an improvement.'

Fry knew she didn't need to explain what she meant. A
few months ago, life-size cardboard police officers had been
placed at businesses across the division in a bid to deter
shoplifters. Ten cardboard cut-outs of a beat officer. According
to the subsequent press releases, the cut-outs had reduced the
number of reported thefts from stores, thieves thinking at first
glance that the image was a real officer. It had become part
of office lore that it was so easy to be confused.

Cooper laughed. 'I think you're safe, Gavin. You know the
Chief Super said cardboard cut-outs can never replace real
officers.'

'Well, that's what he told the press.'

Fry recalled that the senior management team were in a
meeting again this morning. She imagined them talking about
optimizing performance outcomes at the point of delivery.

There must be something about becoming a senior manager that destroyed your sense of irony. That was the only reason Gavin Murfin got away with what he did.

She turned to the files on her desk. Still no news of Michael Clay's whereabouts. He certainly hadn't returned her calls, but that would have been too much to hope for. It was probably time to step up the efforts to find him. Her elusive witness was starting to look downright suspicious.

So what else was there? Horse Watch had sent a list of the latest horse thefts in their area. The thefts went back a few weeks, but there weren't too many of them. Lucky, because all the owners would have to be spoken to.

Fry surveyed her team. Come to think of it, Murfin had some of the characteristics of a horse, like falling asleep standing up.

And then there was the envelope full of enhanced photographs from the lab. These should be the shots of the depressed fracture to Patrick Rawson's head.

Fry took the photographs out of their envelope and glanced at the first one. Patrick Rawson's skull, shaved and cleaned under bright laboratory lighting. The flash had cast just the right amount of shadow and perspective on the head injury, outlining the depression in the bone as if it had been a crater on the Moon.

Apart from one obliterated and smashed end, the bloodied sides of the depression formed a distinct pattern, an almost perfectly preserved shape. There was no medical knowledge necessary. Fry recognized it immediately.

'It's a horseshoe,' she said. 'His skull was crushed by a horseshoe.'

Fry called Dermot Walsh at Trading Standards, and was struck by how different he sounded on the phone. She would never have pictured him the way he actually looked.

'Thank you for the briefing yesterday,' she said.

'I was glad to share what we have. I hope it was useful. There are a lot of upset victims out there who never got justice. Not against Patrick Rawson, anyway.'

'We're particularly sensitive to crimes involving animals in this country aren't we?'

'Well, I don't know,' said Joyce. 'We learn a lot of things from the USA. Horse thefts have been rising dramatically in the States. There are substantial dollars to be made in the legitimate market, and virtually nothing to lose in the black market. A horse can be stolen, slaughtered, packaged, shipped to Europe, and served up on a plate before a ranch owner realizes the animal is missing. That's fast cash. And any method of earning fast money makes its way here sooner or later.'

'Are the Americans as fond of their horses as we are?'

'A few years ago there was a scandal involving a group of individuals running a charity that was supposed to be "adopting" horses rescued from inhumane conditions. It turned out they were then shipping the horses off to Japan to be slaughtered for food. A lot of people were horrified that they'd contributed money to a charity fighting animal abuse, only for the animals to be sent off to be killed. Cue much outcry, little girls walking in protest lines and so on. Fines and prison sentences for the perps. That hasn't happened here yet, so far as we know.'

'I wanted to ask you – can any horse be sold for human consumption?'

'No, it depends whether the owner has made a Section Nine declaration.'

'In the horse passport?'

'That's right. The trouble is, once you've signed "not intended for human consumption", a Section Nine declaration can't be changed. Of course, what I mean is – it can't be changed *legally*.'

'And if a horse doesn't have a passport?'

'It's stolen. You should treat a horse passport like the log

226

book of a car. Never buy a horse without one and always check it's in order before you pay.'

'Frankly, I'm amazed that people can still be duped when all these regulations are in place,' said Fry.

'Oh, you'd be surprised how many people don't bother to check in the excitement of the moment. You want to look at your new horse, not at boring old paperwork. Just like you want to get in your new car and take it for a drive. You're more interested in what's under the bonnet than what's in the log book. It's the same with a horse.'

'What's the penalty for not having a passport?'

'A maximum five thousand pounds fine,' said Walsh, 'or imprisonment for up to three months, or both.'

Had she heard that right? Five thousand pounds? It was more than many thieves and other petty criminals were fined, even after repeated appearances in Edendale magistrates' court. Fry wrote it down just to be sure that she remembered it properly.

'I wanted to ask you about something you said yesterday,' she said.

'Yes.'

'You mentioned that Patrick Rawson had tried to blame the allegations against him on rival dealers.'

'That's right, he did.'

'I'm wondering if there were any particular rivals who might have had a grudge against him.'

'Of course you are,' said Walsh. 'That makes sense. Well, I'm sure there must have been a few over the years. We didn't really go into that as a serious possibility, you know. It was just Rawson trying to weasel his way out.'

'I understand that. But if there was any chance . . .?'

'I'll have a trawl through the intelligence, and send you any names I come up with.'

'Thanks. It's appreciated.'

'Can I ask how Patrick Rawson died?' said Walsh.

'It seems his head was kicked in by a horse.'

'That's the rumour I heard. Poetic justice, if you ask me.'

'So the results from the postmortem suggest that Patrick Rawson's head injury was caused by a blow from a horse's hoof. The impression of the steel shoe is quite clear in his skull.'

'He was kicked in the head by a horse?'

'Or trodden on, while he was already on the ground.'

'An accident, then,' said Cooper. 'An accident, after all.'

But Fry didn't look too sure. 'We can't assume that. We won't know for certain until we've established the sequence of events. And that means tracing the people who were present when he was killed. I'd be very interested to hear their account of the incident. And their explanation of why they rode off and left him to die, if it really was an accident. Even if there was no intention to kill, they could still find themselves facing manslaughter charges.'

Cooper was flicking through the list provided by Horse Watch. Brief details of missing and stolen horses, with phone numbers for the owners. No names, which was a pain. It made you look inefficient from the start when you had to ask an IP's name.

A 14.2 hh chestnut mare of unknown breed, fifteen years old, suffers from arthritis. Very friendly. Taken from a farm near Buxton.

Dutch Warmblood mare, grey, 15.2 hh, thoroughbred in appearance, very well mannered and friendly. Stolen from a field in Derbyshire.

They all represented someone's valued animal, often a friend. These were animals that had never been recovered. Who knew what might have happened to them?

There was another list circulating in the office, too. The

complainants against Patrick Rawson and his associates in the Trading Standards investigation. There were even more of those, and they all had to be spoken to. But at least Dermot Walsh had supplied full names and addresses.

'Which one of those is the most local?' asked Fry, looking at Walsh's list of aggrieved horse owners.

'Just a second,' said Cooper. 'Yes, this one. Naomi Widdowson, Long Acres Farm.'

'Widdowson?'

'That's right.' Cooper looked up at the tone of Fry's voice. 'And an address near Eyam, too. Is there something in particular we should ask her, Diane?'

'No,' said Fry. 'I'll take that one myself.'

Cooper shrugged and passed her the details, then went back to his list from Horse Watch.

Piebald gelding, only owned by IP for six weeks, therefore no photos. Black and white, 15.3 hh, five years old. Stolen while on loan as companion horse.

Irish Draught gelding, grey, 16.1 hh, eleven years old, suffers from navicular and coffin joint arthritis. Stolen while on loan.

Stolen while on loan? Why did that crop up more than once? Was it common?

He sighed, anticipating the emotion and anger he was about to encounter, and began to make some phone calls.

Long Acres Farm wasn't really in Eyam at all. It was a nominal address for an out-of-the-way holding that looked to be a lot closer to Birchlow than to Eyam. But Fry wasn't surprised. That was typical of the eccentric way the parish boundaries were drawn in this part of the world.

Fry was certainly no expert on farming, but she thought Long Acres looked too small to be a farm. There were stables

229

and a few paddocks, certainly. But nowhere near as much land as the Forbes owned at Watersaw House. This was on a much smaller scale, more run down, the surroundings much less pristine and tidy. Fry could see that she and Murfin would have to cross a makeshift drainage channel and a yard that had yet to be brushed out and washed down since the horses had passed through. She guessed there must be a shortage of willing stable girls on the Widdowsons' payroll.

Jackdaws shouted and chattered in the trees as they stood by the car and looked at Long Acres. Large, muddy puddles lay between them and the house.

'Come on, Gavin,' said Fry.

'Oh, shit.'

Naomi Widdowson had blonde hair tied back in a ragged ponytail. Dyed blonde, of course. Fry couldn't often be fooled about that, but even someone like Gavin Murfin must have been able to see those roots. Naomi struck Fry as a bit hard-faced, her skin a bit too weathered. That was probably due to spending too much time outdoors.

'Mrs Widdowson, is it?' said Fry, showing her ID.

'Miss. What do you lot want? I don't like you being here.'

Fry tried to ignore the belligerent reception. It was some-thing you got used to after a while, even from people you were trying to help. She looked around the yard, with the stone house to one side and the stables on the other, a row of horses' heads peering out at her from around their hay racks.

'Nice place. Do you live here alone?'

'No. It's my mum's house really. My boyfriend Ade helps me with the horses. And there's my little brother, Rick. But you knew that, didn't you?'

'No. That's why I asked.'

'It isn't Rick you're looking for, then?'

'No – you, Miss Widdowson. We had your name from Dermot Walsh, of Trading Standards. You were interviewed some time ago as part of their investigation into fraudulent trading in horses.'

'Oh, that,' said Naomi, with a shrug.

'You can't have forgotten it.'

'No. She was a mare that a woman had on loan from me. When the passport scheme came in, this person forged my consent on the application and got a passport for my horse, in her name. And then she sold the mare on. In foal, too. But it's all over and done with. Someone got a rap on the knuckles. And then they were free to go off to rob some other poor sod.'

'You weren't satisfied with the outcome?'

Naomi laughed bitterly. 'That doesn't even deserve an answer. There are still a lot of con merchants out there,' she said.

'Speaking of which – did you ever come across Mr Patrick Rawson?'

'No,' said Naomi.

'You never met him?'

'No. But he's one that people talk about a lot.'

'People?'

'Horse people. Whenever a few of us get together, at a meeting or an auction, or something. His is a name that comes up. There used to be a piece on a website, warning against him. But he got a lawyer to make us take it down. Threatened to sue for slander.'

'Libel,' said Fry.

'What?'

'That would be libel, not slander. A published form of defamation.'

'Oh, thank you for the legal nit-picking. How is trying to protect other people from a con man a crime? That's what I want to know.'

'It depends how it's done,' said Fry.

Naomi sneered. 'You lot are bloody useless. You and those

231

Trading Standards people. You never did anything to Rawson. He got away scot free.'

Fry tried to stay calm. 'We're trying to help, you know.'

'Oh, yeah? It's not the first time we've had trouble, and I don't suppose it will be the last. Sometimes, it makes you feel like giving up.'

'You still have horses, though.'

Naomi's face softened when she looked at the heads hanging over the loose-box doors.

'Yes, three. We had a bit of luck, actually. We bought a nice piebald filly, about thirteen hands. Halter broken and completely adorable. The owners said they were having to sell Bonny because they'd lost their land to flooding. We paid twelve hundred pounds for her.'

Murfin whistled quietly. But Fry still wasn't surprised. These horse people were so far out of her orbit that nothing they did was going to make sense. She might as well just accept it.

'Where did you buy him?' asked Fry.

Naomi looked at her contemptuously. 'I just said she was a filly.'

'Oh. *She*, then?'

'At Derby. We got her at the horse sales.'

Fry looked along the line of loose boxes. She remembered Gavin Murfin doing that in Sutton Coldfield. Here, she wasn't sure what it was supposed to tell her, except that horses ate hay, which she thought she probably knew already.

'I see you have one empty stall.'

'We had a nice old gelding, but he got bad with arthritis. I really cried when he was PTS.'

'PTS?'

The woman sneered again. Fry was getting tired of that expression now.

'Put to sleep,' said Naomi.

'Oh, you mean killed.'

Her face froze. 'We have our horses put to sleep humanely, when it has to be done at all.'

'I'm not suggesting you don't do it humanely, Miss Widdowson. But, let's face it – whatever way you do it, they're still dead, not asleep.'

Somewhere, a tune started up. A loud, irritating noise, high-pitched and tinny. It was a familiar tune, but it seemed to be coming from one of the stables, and it took Fry a moment to recognize it. Then the noise stopped just before the zap of laser guns came in. The *Star Wars* theme. It conjured up images of Han Solo and that big, hairy Wookiee – what was his name?

'Yes, that's my brother,' said Naomi, as a heavily muscled young man peered over the half-door, clutching his mobile phone to his ear. 'That's Rick.'

'Good morning, sir,' said Fry.

Rick Widdowson merely nodded, and went back to what-ever he'd been doing in the depths of the stable. Perhaps it was uncharitable to think that he'd only been keeping his head down until it became clear he wasn't the subject of the visit.

Murfin had walked over towards the horses and was clicking his tongue at them. The animals stared at him as if he was mad. He clearly wasn't carrying anything edible. Or was he?

'What are their names?' he called.

Fry winced. It was the way you'd ask a doting mother the names of her triplets. These were just animals, after all, weren't they? Yet Naomi Widdowson didn't bat an eyelid.

'That's Bonny at the end. Baby is the one in the middle. And the gelding is called Monty.'

'Thank you.'

Taking the cue that Murfin had given her, Fry looked at Naomi again.

'Does the name Rosie mean anything to you?'

'No.'

'I mean a horse, not a person.'

'Still no.'

'What about the horse that was fraudulently traded?'

Naomi shook her head empathically. 'She was called Star. What is this about, anyway? Is there a reason for you being here, or did the police just have some time to spare in between harassing motorists?'

Fry smiled. 'How would you describe Patrick Rawson? Was he a plausible sort of man? What did he look like?'

Naomi opened her mouth, then shut it again. She glowered at Fry, angry now. 'I told you, I never met him. What sort of trick are you trying to pull?'

'Are you a member of the Eden Valley Hunt?'

'Me? Are you kidding?'

'Could you tell me where you were on Tuesday morning, then?' asked Fry.

'What are you saying?'

'It was a simple question.'

'If it's any of your business, I was here, on my own. I work part-time at the Devonshire Hotel in Edendale, but Tuesday was my day off this week.'

She said it in the tone of somebody accustomed to being asked for an alibi. If you told the police you were on your own at the time, then nobody could be asked to back up your story and get the details wrong. It was difficult to prove a negative.

'And I think I've heard enough now,' said Naomi. 'If that's all you have to say, I'd like you to go.'

Fry turned to leave. Then she stopped, as if to ask one more question.

'Widdowson is quite an unusual name. Are you related to the huntsman of the Eden Valley Hunt?'

'John? He's my cousin.'

'I see.'

'What?' said Naomi. 'Is that a crime as well?'

* * *

Murfin sniffed dismissively as they got back to the car. 'If you ask me, that woman has spent far too much time talking to her horses, and not enough time learning how to make conversation with other human beings.'

'She was certainly a bit lacking in social graces,' said Fry.

'She smelled, too,' said Murfin bluntly.

'I've got so used to that smell in the last few days that I didn't really notice, Gavin.'

'Well, don't forget to check the soles of your shoes before you go back into the office.'

'Oh, God,' said Fry, recalling her interview with Superintendent Branagh. 'You're right.'

'And did you notice her fingernails?'

That was something Fry *had* noticed. Black, every one of them. That was due to too much mucking out, or too much time spent running her fingers lovingly through the coats of horses.

'Gavin, did we ever get results from forensics on the prints from that gate on Longstone Moor?'

'No, we didn't. I'll give the lab a nudge.'

'Yes, with a cattle prod.'

26

Meanwhile, Cooper had found himself working backwards and forwards between calls to the horse owners on his list, and the conversation going on around him in the office. They were two worlds, existing alongside each other in the same place. The voices of strangers in his ear, speaking of their anger and loss. And the background sound of his colleagues in the CID team, familiar and somehow prosaic, just doing their day to day job.

'. . . I thought those wretched horse passports we all had to buy at great expense were supposed to stop this sort of thing. Mind you, have you seen some of those passports? Mine looks like an A4 school project. It would only take a photo-copier and a cheap binding machine, and a small child could forge one.'

'Did you know the penalty for not having a horse passport is a maximum five thousand pounds fine, or imprisonment for up to three months, or both?' said Becky Hurst.

'Prison? For not having the right bit of paperwork for your horse?'

'You offend the bureaucrats at your peril.'

'God, I'm beginning to think Matt and Claire were right about easy targets,' said Cooper, dialling his next call.

'What, Ben?'

'Oh, nothing.'

'. . . I guarantee, if the gypsies have your horse and you don't have a passport for it, the police will not take it off the gypsies. Possession is nine-tenths of the law. So off to Appleby they go. I tell people to get the feet post-coded if they breed their own.'

'What's a flesh mark?' asked Luke Irvine, in between calls of his own.

'A patch of pink skin on the horse's face. It's hairless in summer, so it shows up as a distinctive mark.'

'Thanks.'

'. . . I suppose she's gone for pet food, or glue.'

'And what the heck's a Prophet's Thumb?'

'A small indentation on the neck. Like a thumb mark in putty.'

'Really?'

'If you ask me, that wasn't really the purpose of horse passports. They were actually for the benefit of the pharma-ceutical industry, and the vets. To make sure medicines like Bute don't have to be withdrawn from market.'

'Why?'

'They haven't been tested to see how long they take to with-draw. So the only way of being certain they don't enter the human food chain is by not slaughtering any horses that have been treated with them. It's overkill, almost certainly. But that's the way our authorities like to do it in this country.'

Then Cooper found one case where a horse had been sent out on loan, but was slaughtered without the owner's knowledge. How on earth could that happen? He was about to find out.

'Yes, Starlight was a fourteen-year-old gelding. He'd been with us for about six years, but he was suffering from arthritis, and I decided he'd have to be retired. I browsed some of the local papers, and I came across an advert. It said something *like:* Wanted. Horse or pony as a companion. Need not be sound. Small fee paid. Knowledgeable home.'

'*Do you still have a copy of the advert?*'

'*Yes, I'll find it for you.*'

'*So you contacted the advertiser?*'

'*Yes, and arranged to visit her farm to see the facilities. To be honest, I was quite impressed with the set-up. Her idea was that Starlight would be a companion to an in-foal Arab mare she had. I saw the mare, and she was in beautiful condition. The stables were better than mine, and the paddocks were bigger. It didn't occur to me that I could have anything to worry about. I delivered Starlight on the understanding that he'd be there for a two-month trial period. From the start, I thought it had been made clear that this was a loan arrangement and didn't involve a change of ownership. I got on well with the woman, and we agreed not to bother with a fee. We kept in touch. I fact, I phoned her a couple of weeks before . . . well, before it all went wrong. She told me Starlight was fine.*'

'*How did you know something was wrong?*'

'*I was reading that same newspaper, and I saw a "for sale" advert for the Arab mare. Since Starlight was supposed to be the mare's companion, alarm bells started to ring. I went straight to the farm, but there was no sign of Starlight. I reported him stolen to the police. They didn't seem very interested when I explained the circumstances. But it was theft, wasn't it?*'

From the sound of her voice, Cooper could tell that the tears had begun falling as soon as she started talking, and she made no attempt to disguise her distress over the fate of her animal.

'*I kept going back to the farm until I found the woman in, and confronted her. I know I should have got a proper loan agreement drawn up from the start. I realize that now. But she seemed so nice, and the place was just perfect. I only wanted the best for Starlight. It was theft, pure and simple. The destruction of someone else's property for financial gain. I'm right, aren't I? I can't believe that anyone could be so evil.*

238

There are just no words to describe what she did. It's barbaric. If she didn't want him any more, she could have called me and I would have gladly taken him home.'

When Fry got back to the office, Cooper broke his calls off to give her the details of his last victim.

'I've just phoned the local police in Staffordshire about this one,' he said. 'The woman who took the horse was called Annette Wood, and she never denied that she sent Starlight to the abattoir. But she claimed the horse wasn't on loan to her but was hers to do with as she saw fit. Without any evidence to the contrary, it came down to a question of one person's word against another's. And you know how hopeless that is in court.'

'What about the abattoir?' asked Fry.

'They confirmed that a skewbald gelding arrived in a batch of horses delivered to them a week before Christmas. They were brought in by a man who said he was Annette Wood's brother-in-law.'

'Patrick Rawson?'

'Correct. They'd dealt with him before, so they had no reason to be particularly suspicious. In fact, they claimed ignorance in the whole matter. All the police could establish was that the abattoir gave Rawson between four and five hundred pounds for each horse. The correct paperwork was filled out and, as far as the abattoir knew, the horses were signed over by their owner or the owner's agent. They co-operated with the investigation. There's no allegation against the abattoir, and no suggestion that the horses were maltreated at any stage.'

'And no charge against Rawson?'

'The problem was establishing a chain of events. Without that, it wasn't even possible to consider pressing charges. Of course, it was mad not to have had a proper loan agreement in writing from the start. It should have specified whose authority was needed before the horse could be destroyed. A verbal agreement is worthless in evidence.'

'So Rawson did the deal.'

'That was his speciality – dealing. He would buy and sell, always to his own advantage. He worked with the abattoirs all the time, places like Hawleys.'

So that was at least one woman who had been taken advantage of. All she'd wanted was a good retirement home for her beloved horse in the last years of his life. How many more owners were there who'd had similar experiences? The list of people who had reason to hate Patrick Rawson was growing rapidly.

'Couldn't uniforms help with some of this?' asked Murfin.

'They're more used to looking for stolen cars.'

'In some ways, finding a missing horse ought to be a lot easier than locating a stolen car,' said Cooper.

'Why?'

'Look at this – each horse now has its own passport containing a full description – silhouettes from front, back and both sides, showing the colour and all the animal's markings. Whether it has a stripe, a blaze or star. Exact placing of whorls and feathers. Its microchip number, freeze brand, its height, age, the colour of its hooves. That should help, surely? You don't get that level of description for any car.'

'And you can't exactly give a horse a re-spray and change its number plates.'

'Also, it's possible to consult NED for information on the identity of horses in the UK.'

'NED? For goodness sake.'

'The National Equine Database. You can get microchip numbers and freeze brand information.'

'We'd have to find someone who knows the difference between a skewbald and a piebald.'

Fry was gathering her phone and car keys, pulling on her jacket.

'Where are you going, Diane?'

'I've still got a call to do on my own list. One of Patrick Rawson's business contacts: Senior Brothers in Lowbridge.'

Fry couldn't quite believe Rodney Senior's appearance. No one still had sideburns like that, surely? They must be a joke. He was probably wearing false ones for a fancy-dress party later that day. Some event with a Dickensian theme. He was going as Mr Micawber, or Bumble the Beadle.

To find him, Fry had picked her way carefully across a muddy concrete yard where several livestock transporters were parked, following the sound of hissing water. Then she saw a cloud of spray rising from one of the vehicles, and found a man in boots and blue overalls at work. She had to call his name twice over the noise to get his attention.

'Aye, Rawson rang on Monday and said he might need some stock transporting later in the week,' said Senior, turning off a power hose he'd been using to wash out a wagon. 'I never heard from him again.'

He had broad, rough hands, which dangled aimlessly at his sides when they had nothing to do. The backs of those hands were astonishingly hairy, and a thatch of hair burst from the top of his open-necked shirt, like the down from an over-stuffed mattress. Of course, the sideboards were real, too. Fry had no doubt about it when she got a bit closer to him.

'Did you think that was odd?' she asked.

'Odd? No.'

'Didn't you hear that he got killed?'

'It was on the news.'

'So?'

Senior just looked at her, as if she was speaking a different language. He didn't bother to ask what she meant.

'So you still didn't think it was odd?'

'I just thought that whatever deal he was doing must have fallen through. It happens.'

'But what about the timing? You lost some business through his death, Mr Senior.'

Streams of filthy water ran out of the sides of the transporter and down a steel ramp. Senior gestured at Fry with a yard brush.

'We've had business from Rawson for years, but I wasn't sorry to hear we won't be doing his transporting again. I never liked the bloke myself, and I don't mind admitting it.'

Well, that was some form of communication, at least.

'What did you object to about him?' asked Fry.

'He was a bit too smooth for my liking. Fancy talker, always trying to get one over on you, if you know what I mean. I prefer plain speaking, myself. I gave him a bit of plain speaking once or twice, too.'

'You had disagreements? Why?'

'Disagreements? That's a big word for it. I told him to bugger off a couple of times. He was forever trying to knock us down on price, or put off paying for a few months. That's no good for a business like ours. If he'd tried it again, I would have told him where to stick it.'

Senior loped up the ramp with his brush, moving in a stooped kind of way as his feet pushed against the ridges in the ramp. Fry supposed they were designed for the hooves of livestock to grip on, but Senior seemed equally at home in his work boots.

'When he phoned on Monday, he must have told you what he wanted transported?' said Fry.

'Oh, aye. Horses. It was always horses with Rawson.'

'Did he say where you were to pick them up from?'

Senior thought for a moment. She had obviously asked him a tough one, because his brow wrinkled ferociously. With his hairiness, large dangling hands and that slight stoop as he walked, there was a simian look about him. Fry was reminded of an illustration from a textbook on the theory of human evolution. Senior came from somewhere halfway along the scale, just after *Homo erectus* had stood upright for the first time and lost the sloping forehead.

'Now then,' he said, as if that was somehow an answer.

'Perhaps you wrote it down,' prompted Fry impatiently.

But Senior shook his head. 'Nay. I'll remember. He didn't give an exact address, just said it was Eyam way. He was supposed to give us the details when he called back. But he never did, you see.'

'And the horses were supposed to go to . . .?'

'Hawleys. Like always.'

'Thank you.'

'Now, if you don't mind, I've got this next wagon to do.'

As she watched him lope away, Fry recalled that *Homo erectus* had borne a fair resemblance to a modern human. The main difference was, its brain was only about three-quarters the size.

As Fry left Senior Brothers' yard, she wondered what the other brother was like. Probably Rodney was the brains of the outfit.

Though she was picking up bits and pieces about Patrick Rawson's business activities, she needed to know much more. And she felt sure the man who could give her the information she needed was Michael Clay. A man who was rivalling the Scarlet Pimpernel for elusiveness.

Before she got into her car, she tried his number again. Still on voicemail. What a surprise.

Then, as soon as she ended the call, her phone rang. It was Gavin Murfin, of course. Fry hesitated before she answered it. Lately, Murfin had started to develop the habit of delivering bad news every time he called. It was getting so that she hardly dared to leave the office.

'Yes, Gavin?'

'Hey up, boss. Having a good time at Lowbridge?'

'No,' said Fry. 'What have you called me about?'

'Michael Clay.'

243

'Excellent. He's the man we most need to speak to right now.'

'Oh. Well, I'm sorry, but it seems that Erin Lacey has changed her mind about her father's whereabouts.'

'His what?'

'His whereabouts. Remember she told us Michael Clay was away on a business trip? Well, she's telling a different story now. Mr Clay has officially been reported MFH.'

'Missing From Home?' Fry sighed. 'He's done a runner. That's a very stupid thing for him to do.'

'And strange, too, when there's no evidence against him.'

'No evidence that we've found yet, Gavin.'

'It could just be a clever ploy,' suggested Murfin.

'Oh, right. A clever ploy to cast suspicion on himself.'

'What do you want to do, Diane?'

'We'll talk about it when I get back.'

On her way back to Edendale, news came in that a horse had been badly injured in an RTC somewhere outside the town. Fry had barely managed to calculate that it was directly on her route, before she saw the flashing lights ahead. That was going to mean another hold-up, unless she could find a way round.

Like dogs and sheep, horses came within the definition of 'animal' in the Road Traffic Act. That meant you had to report it to the police, if you ran over one. If it was a cat, a badger or a fox, you didn't. It was strange how some laws stuck in your mind, while more recent legislation had to be looked up and puzzled over for a sensible interpretation every time it came up.

Fry caught a glimpse of the body in the roadway. A dead horse must be an incredible weight. This one looked to weigh as much as a small car, and there was no way it was going to be shifted easily. They'd need a flatbed truck and a winch to get it off the road.

She reversed the Peugeot into a field entrance, and turned round. Then she began to search for a way to get back on track.

27

The machinery was soon swinging into action. A stop on Michael Clay's Mercedes, a description issued of the man they were looking for. But it was always the same in these cases. The moment a man's description was circulated, people would start to see him everywhere.

'So Michael Clay has suddenly become our number one suspect?' asked Cooper. 'Because he's gone to ground?'

'Well, perhaps he wasn't directly involved,' said Fry. 'He doesn't seem to have been in Derbyshire at the time that Patrick Rawson was killed.'

'Well, no . . .'

'I think there must be something in their business affairs that will cast a light on the motive for Rawson's death, though. The trouble is, that could take time for us to figure out now.'

'You know we were looking for a rival dealer who might have had a feud with Patrick Rawson?' said Cooper.

'Yes?'

'What about the relationship between Patrick Rawson and Michael Clay? Partnerships like that can easily go wrong, especially where there's criminality involved.'

'You're right, Ben. And even more so if it's just one of the partners who happens to have criminal tendencies. I can imagine Rawson filling his own pockets, and Clay catching him out.'

'Do you think it could it have been Clay who shopped his partner to Trading Standards?' said Cooper.

'He might not have gone that far in the first instance. But it's possible he provided evidence against Rawson when the investigation started.'

'To save his own skin?'

'Yes.'

'Trading Standards never mentioned that, though, did they?' said Cooper.

'No. They might have been able to put a case together without Michael Clay, once they'd got the information they needed. That would have allowed Clay to look clean.'

Cooper eased back in his chair, teasing out the theory. 'But perhaps Rawson found out what he'd done, that Clay was the informant. That would cause a problem between them, all right. But then it would have been Rawson who came after Clay. What do you think?'

'Well, it's a possibility,' said Fry. 'What have you got on at the moment, Ben?'

'Still a few calls on the Horse Watch file,' said Cooper, looking at the items checked off his list. 'I couldn't get a reply from the owner of the Dutch Warmblood.'

'Leave it for now. This is more important.'

'OK.'

They spent the rest of the afternoon concentrating on trying to piece together Michael Clay's movements since he left his home in Great Barr. If his daughter was telling the truth now, he had set off on Tuesday afternoon, and must have arrived in Derbyshire early in the evening. Did Patrick Rawson's death prompt the journey? But how could Clay possibly have known about it by then?

A quick phone call established that he hadn't booked in at the Birch Hall Country Hotel, where Patrick Rawson had stayed. Why was that? Well, maybe Clay was more careful with the company's money, and had found somewhere less expensive. Perhaps he just wasn't interested in golf.

That raised the question of Michael Clay's relationship with Deborah Rawson. Fry thought back to the one occasion she'd seen them together, in the reception area downstairs. Had there been any hint of a closer liaison between them than was suggested on the surface? Could she have read a suggestion in their body language that they were having an affair?

Fry set Beck Hurst and Luke Irvine to phoning other hotels in the area. There were plenty of them, but at least it wasn't the height of the tourist season in the Peak District, when strangers passing through for a night or two were so common that they might hardly be noticed.

'And once you've covered the hotels, start on the B&Bs,' she said.

Unlike Patrick Rawson, Clay hadn't used his credit card everywhere, or his movements would have been traced by now. Here was a man who had learned the lesson about dropping out of sight, then.

Normally, Fry would have had hopes of tracking his movements by his mobile phone. When a mobile phone was turned on, it was constantly transmitting its position to the nearest tower, identifying itself to the network by its electronic serial number. Phone companies were required to keep records to assist criminal investigations. But in a rural area like the Peak District, the region covered by a tower could be pretty large. Another bit of technology that was more useful for catching criminals in a city.

In this case, the disappearance of Patrick Rawson's phone, and the fact that Clay's had already been turned off when she'd tried to call him herself that morning, convinced her that she was dealing with someone who was aware of the technology.

'Have we got anything from the mobile phone company yet?' she called. 'When did Clay's phone log off the network?'

'Wednesday afternoon, about two thirty. But they say they can't narrow down the position of the handset better than a radius of a mile or two. And since then he could have gone anywhere, with his phone switched off.'

'It's Friday now,' said Fry. 'He could have reached Australia since Wednesday afternoon, for heaven's sake. Erin Lacey has a bit of explaining to do, when I get to speak to her.'

'I wonder what she thought her father was up to,' said Murfin.

'Well, what's the betting she suspected that he was involved in Patrick Rawson's death?'

'And she was giving him a chance to get away?'

'That, or a chance to come home and give an account of himself.'

Fry felt sure that Michael Clay was no longer in Derbyshire. Why should he be? If Clay *was* involved in Patrick Rawson's death in some way, he'd had at least one accomplice. Someone local, too, with access to horses.

Clay hadn't been in Derbyshire for very long, but long enough to make his mark. No one had yet been found who admitted seeing him, which was predictable at this stage. Even his own daughter had been reluctant to talk. Yet someone must certainly have crossed his path. They needed to get more public appeals out in the media, but that was a slow process. Time lost again. It was so frustrating.

'What sort of area are we looking at from the mobile phone signal?'

'Let's work it out.'

They pored over the map. Even with masts sited at Sir William Hill and Calver Peak, the potential area for Michael Clay's last-known location covered the whole of Eyam, Birchlow and Foolow, as well as Longstone Moor and east-wards towards Calver.

'We're looking for a car again, aren't we?' said Hurst. 'Mr Clay drives a blue Mercedes.'

248

'The details have already been circulated.'

'Just a minute,' said Cooper. 'Does this mean that Michael Clay wasn't the second man having dinner at Le Chien Noir on Monday night?'

Fry shook her head. 'He can't have been, if the daughter is telling the truth now. Erin Lacey says he drove up to Derbyshire on Tuesday.'

'Didn't the description fit?'

'The manager at the restaurant was very vague in his description of the second man. Very vague. It could have been almost anyone – one of the other contacts in Patrick Rawson's phone book, perhaps.'

Murfin put the phone down from a call to Clay's bank.

'Well, that could explain why Mr Clay wasn't registered at any of the hotels. It seems he's been paying rent on another property. Right here on our patch, too.'

'Well, well. Have you got the address, Gavin?'

'Yes.'

'Let's go, then.'

'Wait just a second.' Cooper held up a hand. 'Diane, I can see you're convinced that Michael Clay is implicated in Rawson's death somehow. And you think you're going to go chasing off and arrest him. But stop for a minute. Isn't it also possible that we have *two* victims now? Two victims, but only one body.'

Eden View was a nice double-fronted stone property on the edge of Birchlow, with farmland to the rear and views over the village itself to the front. 'For Sale' signs stood outside the house, and an estate agent arrived, breathless and worried, to let them in.

'The property belongs to a local farmer, who had it built for his son,' he explained. 'But the son has left the area. He moved to Leeds to try a career as a teacher.'

'So you found a tenant for him while the house was empty?' said Fry. 'Isn't that unusual?'

The agent fiddled with a set of keys to find the right one for the front door.

'We knew the property would be vacant for a long period,' he said. 'It's been on the market for two years already.'

'Why haven't you been able to sell it?'

'It has an occupancy restriction.'

Cooper nodded. 'Oh, the five-year permanent residence rule?'

'That, or a strong local connection and essential need. You know the way it goes.'

'Yes, that must make it difficult.'

In some areas, the national park planning authority had taken steps to prevent villages from being taken over by incomers and second-home owners, restricting ownership of new properties to people with a minimum of five years permanent residence in the parish or adjoining parishes living in unsatisfactory accommodation or setting up a household for the first time. The only exceptions were those who had an essential need to live close to their work, or to care for an elderly or sick relative.

'It reduces the market value by a vast amount,' said the agent. 'Unrestricted, this property might have fetched the best part of three hundred thousand, but we're marketing Eden View for just below two hundred. Even so, it's going to be difficult finding the right buyer.'

Cooper looked at the house. That seemed a shame. But then, there were lots of people who were having difficulty selling their houses. He remembered Fry telling him once about the young migrant workers who had been replacing the students in her part of town. Poles, Czechs, Romanians. It was odd that the country should be so open to European migrants on the one hand, while here in some of the villages, properties could only be bought by someone from the very same parish, by a person who *belonged* here, in the old-fashioned, traditional sense. They were two distinct worlds, existing alongside each other.

250

Finally the agent let them into the house. The interior seemed incongruous, hardly fitting for a house worth half a million pounds on the open market. No one was taking much care about cleaning and maintenance. That might be common for a rented property, but the feeling of the place didn't fit the image of Michael Clay, the businessman and certified accountant.

In the sitting room, a pile of celebrity gossip magazines lay on the table by an armchair. They all seemed to have headlines like *Chanelle spills the beanz*. Not what he would have imagined as Mr Clay's choice of reading.

'Perhaps I was right about there being a woman involved,' said Fry. 'But I just had the wrong man.'

'You think Michael Clay might have been the one having an affair?'

'This looks like a kind of love nest to me, Ben.'

'A love nest on the cheap, though.'

'Well, yes.'

'Clay's wife died five years ago,' said Cooper. 'Why would he go to such lengths to conceal a relationship? Who was he hiding it from?'

Fry shrugged. 'His children? I bet Erin Lacey doesn't know about this place. Or maybe his business colleagues? Perhaps he was ashamed of his relationship. Ashamed of *her*, whoever she is.'

The kitchen seemed to contain a microwave and not much else. Cooper opened a cupboard. No, he was wrong. Half a jar of coffee and a tin of powdered milk.

'I can't imagine that Michael Clay spent much time here himself.'

In a corner were black plastic bin liners bursting with rubbish. Amazing how often he saw that. As if it was too much trouble to put the stuff out for the binmen once a week. Or maybe the household had got on the wrong side of the garbage police and been penalized for putting the wrong stuff in their recycling bin. You could get your collections suspended for failing to distinguish between tin foil and plastic these days. Some authorities were really cracking down on bin crime.

One wall of the main bedroom was decorated with a poster containing the famous peace symbol, a circle surrounding a cross with its horizontal arms inclined downwards. Cooper had once read that the designer of that symbol had based it on the representation of an individual with palms stretched outwards and downwards. The gesture of despair, associated with the death of Man. And the circle, an unborn child. But the symbol was also said to incorporate the semaphore letters 'N' and 'D' for 'nuclear disarmament'. It was best known as the official logo of the CND.

'Did Michael Clay strike you as an old hippie?' he called to Fry.

'No. But how can you tell? Lots of hippies turn into accountants and bank managers when they grow up, don't they?'

'I've heard there are even some in the police.'

One of the top drawers of the dressing table was very stiff. At first, Cooper thought it was locked, but with a good tug it moved slightly, and he realized it was just jammed. Probably the wood had warped over the years, so that the drawer no longer slid straight on its runners.

With a bit of manoeuvring, he managed to get the drawer straight, and it finally squealed open. Inside was just one item – an old-fashioned, velvet-covered jewellery box with metal clasps. Quite a large box, too. It had filled the drawer completely. When Cooper gently prised the box open, it was like looking down at a miniature dragon's hoard. A tangled mass of silver chains lay on the velvet, with the occasional glint of a solid band or the glitter of a gemstone. Blue stones, translucent stones like diamonds – and one that was jet black. Was that onyx? He couldn't quite remember.

Then Cooper smiled. He should have been thinking gold and

252

silver-coloured. Because surely these items were all imitation. They would have been worth a fortune otherwise.

Something at the bottom of the heap caught Cooper's eye. A glint of gold, but an unusual shape. He pushed the chains aside and drew it out. He found himself holding a small badge. A crown and a wreath around a curious little figure he couldn't quite make out. The left hand seemed to be raised to the eyes, and the right hand was holding a flaming torch. And the figure was wearing – what? A breast plate? Armour? The only help was the motto etched on a scroll at the bottom of the badge. It said: *Forewarned is forearmed.*

'What the heck does that mean?'

At that moment, Fry called him to join her in the other bedroom. She had opened a case containing a laptop computer and some papers.

'Michael Clay's?' asked Cooper.

'Yes, it seems to be. He must have been here at some time since he left home on Tuesday. Unfortunately, the laptop is password protected, so we'll have to hand it over to the experts if we want to get anything off it. Did you notice that both bedrooms have been occupied?'

'Yes. That's interesting.'

'And what do you make of this?'

Fry shook out the contents of a large buff envelope on to the bed. Cooper saw an old colour photograph of about a dozen men and one woman, all dressed in identical outfits, a sort of blue tunic and trousers, with berets worn at various rakish angles. They looked cheerful, a group of mates enjoying their work. He guessed their ages must have ranged from about seventy down to seventeen or so. A motley bunch, definitely.

But when was it taken? Most snaps had been in black and white until the early sixties, if the Cooper family album was a typical example. The earliest colour photo he could remember was of his parents on holiday in Wales with some friends, back before they were married – 1962, or around that time. In this photo, the subjects were standing in front of a small brick tower with a set of steps leading up the outside wall. There appeared to be no roof to the tower – he could see the sky through a doorway at the top of the steps. There also seemed to be an old-fashioned striped canvas deckchair leaning against the wall up there.

Automatically, Cooper turned the print over. Many people did what his mother had always done, and recorded all kinds of information on the back of a photograph. Date, place, the names of everyone shown in the picture. You never knew your luck.

But this one was infuriatingly sparse in its caption. It said simply *4 Romeo.*

He pointed out the inscription to Fry.

'Which one is Romeo, then?' she said.

'Number four? The fourth one from the left?'

They both looked closely at the line-up faces. The fourth man from the left was a fat character with a jowly chin. An unlikely Romeo. Cooper counted four from the right instead, and came up with a weedy-looking youth peering at the camera through round, wire-rimmed glasses. TinTin maybe, but not Romeo.

Fry placed a finger on another face. 'I think this one could be Michael Clay, though,' she said. 'A lot younger, of course. But there's something about the shape of the face that's very distinctive.'

'What else is in the envelope, Diane?'

'Just these –'

Fry held out a tie with a small logo on it, and a badge identical to the one Cooper had seen in the drawer in the other bedroom.

'"Forewarned is forearmed" – but what does it mean?'

Before Fry could reply, the front door of the house opened cautiously. They heard a nervous voice downstairs.

'Who are you? What are you doing here?'

*   *   *

254

Her name was Pauline Outram, and she seemed to be permanently on the verge of bursting into laughter. What Fry had
at first taken for a nervous cough was actually a sort of
constant half-snigger, as if she didn't want to be considered
lacking in a sense of humour if someone made a joke that
she didn't understand. Fry wanted to tell her to stop it, that
she wasn't about to make any jokes.

'We're here because we're looking for Michael Clay,' said
Fry.

'That's funny, because so am I.'

'You don't know where he is?'

'He should be here. But I guess . . .'

'You know who we are,' said Fry, after identification had
been shown. 'Now explain to us who exactly you are.'

Fry was genuinely curious to know. She didn't think
Pauline Outram looked much like a secret mistress. Not
even the right age, really. A fifty-one-year-old man going
through a mid-life crisis was likely to go for someone about
half his age. Or so she'd heard. But Pauline must be in her
late thirties, and there was nothing sexy or glamorous about
her. Nothing about Pauline Outram suggested she'd come
here to meet a lover.

But the question didn't seem easy for Pauline to answer.
She looked from one detective to the other, struggling for
words.

'We won't be shocked,' said Fry. 'You can tell us the truth.
We only want to locate Mr Clay. It doesn't matter what your
relationship was, as long as it helps us to find him.'

And then it dawned on Pauline what Fry was suggesting.

'Oh no, you've got it wrong,' she said, shaking her head,
that nervous half-laugh setting Fry's nerves on edge.

'Are you not having an affair with Michael Clay?'

'No, no. You don't understand. I'm not his lover. That's
not why he leased this house for me.'

'Who are you, then?'

255

Pauline Outram looked her in the eye, her face calm and serious for the first time. And it was only then that Fry saw the faint family resemblance to Michael Clay.

'I'm Michael's niece. His brother Stuart's daughter.'

28

Back at the office half an hour later, Cooper went to his PC and Googled the motto on the badge he'd found in Eden View. *Forewarned is forearmed*. It was a common enough phrase, an old adage that he must have heard his parents use time and again.

Google presented several sources for definitions. '*Praemonitus, praemunitus*. Knowledge of imminent danger can prepare us to overcome it.' There was even a link to George W. Bush using the phrase in a speech about Iran. Corporate intelligence, cancer research, travel tips on avoiding pickpockets . . . Not much use.

Cooper clicked through three or four pages of links without success, and was about to give up looking when he saw a different reference. It was a book title, advertised by a seller on ABE, the second-hand book dealers' site. He clicked on the link and found himself reading a description of the book being offered. A history of the Royal Observer Corps, evidently some branch of the British armed forces. Could that be right?

A fresh search and a few more clicks found a picture of the ROC logo. The figure on the badge was apparently based on an Elizabethan beacon lighter, who used to watch the coast and warn of approaching Spanish ships. And, yes, that was the Corps motto: *Forewarned is forearmed.*

So there had been a Royal Observer Corps cap badge in Michael Clay's briefcase, along with the tie and the photograph. Had Clay served in the ROC? And what about the identical badge in Pauline Outram's jewellery box? Sentimental value, presumably. A former boyfriend? Or had there been women in the ROC? Did it still exist, in fact? Too many questions. But Cooper had an idea there was someone he could ask, who might know those things.

There was obviously more of a local connection to be explored in this case than at first appeared. Patrick Rawson might be Birmingham Irish, but it was only thanks to Pauline Outram that they'd discovered Michael Clay's origins.

Cooper had almost smiled as Fry had confronted Pauline in that rented house and discovered a fact that might have taken another twenty-four hours for them to turn up.

'My name is Outram because my mother never got married,' Pauline had said. 'Not to Stuart Clay, or anyone else. She died when I was very young.'

'And you're from a local family?' Fry asked, trying to piece together an entirely new angle.

'Yes.'

'So how did your mother meet Stuart Clay?'

'They were neighbours.'

'What?'

'Oh, didn't you know?' said Pauline. 'The Clays are from Birchlow originally. But they moved away from the area, and it was only recently I was able to get in touch. Michael didn't even know of my existence. I was brought up in the name of my adopted parents, and changed it back to Outram when I came of age.'

Remembering it, Cooper really did smile. He felt sure that Fry wasn't going to like all this.

*   *   *

Fry studied Erin Lacey with a critical eye. They were sitting in the DI's office, Mrs Lacey being regarded as the distressed relative of a missing person, even if she had been unnecessarily evasive about her father's movements earlier in the week.

'Yes, I'm aware of the existence of Pauline Outram,' she said. 'I've never met her, and I don't want to. I didn't realize Dad had gone so far as to provide her with a house.'

'It's only leased,' said Fry.

'Well, that hardly makes it any better. She has no right to financial support from Dad.'

DI Hitchens straightened his tie, a signal that he wanted to come in on the money issue. That was his thing, financial problems. The word was like a bell to one of Pavlov's dogs.

'Is there a problem with money, Mrs Lacey?' said Hitchens.

'No. But . . . well, it's our inheritance he's squandering on her. Mine, and my children's.'

'I see. You're worried that your father has been diverting too much money to help Miss Outram.'

'Far too much. She's not worth a tenth of it.'

Fry shifted in her chair to get a better view of Erin Lacey's eyes. She was sitting to one side, so that she could observe her profile and her posture, the little nervous mannerisms that could be such a giveaway. But the eyes were often just as revealing.

'You say you've never met Pauline Outram, yet you seem to have a strong degree of animosity towards her,' she said.

'From what I've heard, she's wasted her life. She's, what . . . in her late thirties? Dad says she's never married, never had any children, and never been able to hold down a proper job. I dread to think how she's been spending her life until now. She was brought up in foster homes, you know.'

Fry instantly felt her attitude to Erin Lacey freezing. In her heart was an iciness deeper than the Arctic Ocean. Professionalism and training barely held her back.

'That doesn't', she said, 'make her a worthless person.'

In other circumstances, she would have had taken Lacey apart verbally, lain her own history in front of the woman and confronted her with her own prejudices. But that wasn't what she was here for. Right now, she had to suppress her own feelings, try not to alienate an important witness too much. She felt Hitchens watching her, and tried not to meet his eye.

'She's had relationships with all kinds of men,' said Lacey. 'And none of them has ever hung around very long. That has to tell you something, doesn't it?'

Something about the lack of commitment from men, perhaps, thought Fry. But she held her tongue and didn't say it.

'Anyway, I don't think she was a fit person for Dad to be spending money on. She's not really a member of the family. She was illegitimate.'

'Do you know what happened to her mother?' asked Hitchens.

'I heard that she killed herself.'

'That's correct. According to Pauline Outram, she drowned herself in Birch Reservoir. Pauline was only a few months old at the time.'

'That's hardly my fault. It doesn't justify Pauline Outram selling some sob-story to my father when she found out that we had money and she didn't.'

'But Miss Outram told us that her father and yours were very close,' said Fry.

'Well, that's true, at least. They were almost inseparable, even though Dad was a few years younger. He told me that's how they were right back to when they were boys here in Derbyshire. I think that's probably quite unusual for brothers, isn't it? Normally they tend to fight a lot – well, I know my two do. But when Uncle Stuart died of pancreatic cancer last year, it broke Dad up. You could see then how close they were. It took Dad ages to get round to sorting out Uncle

Stuart's things, because he just couldn't face the memories. He found that job very difficult, stayed shut away with his brother's papers for hours. And this thing with the illegitimate daughter – well, I think this is Dad's way of trying to express his feelings towards his brother. He can be so naïve about people sometimes. So easily taken in.'

'You think Pauline Outram has conned him in some way? Do you think she's not really who she says she is?'

'No. I know Dad did a few checks on her.'

'Not so naïve, then?'

'I made him do it.'

'Which means Pauline Outram is your cousin,' said Fry.

'I suppose so. But you don't have to be tied to your cousins, do you?'

Fry sat back, feeling suddenly tired. Erin Lacey's version of events fit quite closely with the story told by Pauline Outram earlier, though with a different spin, of course. Strange that the two women should feel so diametrically opposed to each other when their fathers had been so close. But then, perhaps that closeness was the sole reason they hated each other.

'Before I forget, I brought these photos that you asked for, of my Dad,' said Erin Lacey. 'I think there's one here of him and Uncle Stuart together. They're so alike, Uncle Stuart was like an older version of Dad.'

'Thank you.'

Fry looked at the photos, remembering the man she'd met earlier in the week, with the strange grey eyes and the wide jaw line. And here were the two brothers, at a much younger age. Michael had probably been in his late teens, Stuart mid-twenties. And Michael Clay did indeed look like a junior version of his brother. But there was a certain amount of contrivance about the similarity. The younger brother had tried to tease his hair into the same style, had adopted the same casual, slouching pose, hands thrust into his pockets. A hero-worshipping younger brother, if ever she saw one.

'You know, it's one of Deborah Rawson's problems, too,'
said Erin.

'What is?'

'The fact that Dad has been sensible with his money. She
and Patrick have a huge mortgage on that place out at Mere
Green. It was rather out of their range when they bought it,
if you ask me. They're desperate to keep up, both of them.'

'To keep up with the Clays?'

'Well, they're not really the same class. Patrick is basically
a horse dealer from a family of Irish tinkers in County Offaly.
Deborah is the daughter of a garage owner in Handsworth.'

'You know a lot about them.'

'They've always been keen to socialize with us.'

'So you had to check them out, too?'

Erin didn't answer. But Fry was getting signals from
Hitchens, and she didn't press any further. She'd heard enough
to form a picture, anyway. It seemed it wasn't just a question
of golf-club syndrome. Deborah Rawson was just as enthu-
siastic a social climber as her husband, if Erin Lacey was to
be believed. And that, as far as Fry was concerned, was quite
a big 'if'.

'Mrs Lacey,' said Hitchens, 'can you give us any other information that might help us to find your father? No matter
how insignificant a detail, it could prove useful.'

Lacey shook her head. 'I don't think there's anything I
haven't told you.'

Fry felt her eyebrows rise at that. She didn't believe it for
a moment.

'If you could try to think back to when you last spoke to
him,' she said. 'Didn't he say anything about where he was
going, what he was planning to do?'

'No. Well, I knew that he was coming up to Derbyshire,
so he would have been visiting that woman. That's why he
didn't mention it.'

'Because he knew you would have disapproved?'

'I think I have the right to.'

Hitchens leaned across his desk. 'Mrs Lacey, we have to ask you these questions. Was your father his normal self? Or did he appear depressed, or worried about anything?'

'Not when he left home, no,' said Lacey. 'When I spoke to him on the phone on Wednesday, he was upset about Patrick Rawson's death, obviously. But I think there was also an element of relief, though he would never have said so. I knew him so well that I could practically read his thoughts. I think Dad was already starting to work out in his mind what Patrick's death would mean from a business point of view. He was beginning to think about the paperwork, make calls to lawyers, all that sort of thing.'

'He was planning ahead, then?'

'Definitely. He's that sort of man. Conscientious, methodical, always thinking about his work. He was almost itching to get his teeth into the business formalities.'

Hitchens glanced at Fry. People who were busy planning ahead rarely committed suicide, as they both knew.

'And one final question, Mrs Lacey: Is there anyone you can think of who might have wished your father harm?'

Lacey shook her head again. 'No. Except –'

'Yes?'

'Well, I thank God that Dad never changed his will in favour of the Outram woman. For a gold digger, that would have been a big temptation put in her way, wouldn't it?'

Before Cooper could explore the Royal Observer Corps any further, Fry came back into the CID room with a disgusted look on her face. That didn't bode well. He'd seen that look too often, and it had usually ended badly. These days, though, it didn't seem to matter quite so much. He could survive whatever Fry threw at him.

'Uh-oh,' said Murfin, looking up and noticing the same thing. 'What's wrong now, I wonder?'

'I don't know.'

'You could ask her, if you're feeling suicidal.'

Cooper got up to follow Fry to her desk.

'Ben?' said Murfin, in horror. 'I didn't think you really *were* that tired of life.'

'So,' said Cooper, when he faced Fry, 'what's the next move?'

She raised an eyebrow, then looked uncertain when it seemed to have no effect on him.

'Back to square one,' she said. 'Back to Longstone Moor, and the two people on horseback caught on the hunt saboteurs' camera. Back to the hunt themselves.'

'You can't still be obsessed with the hunt, Diane?'

'I am not –' began Fry. Then she seemed to calm herself. 'I'm not obsessed with the hunt. But we're going to start again from first base, we're going to identify the people Patrick Rawson met. Those riders were either members of the hunt, or they were seen by them.'

'You're sure of that?'

'Ben, as far as I'm concerned, the hunt is all about violence. Even if the violent instincts are dressed up in red coats and following an artificial scent, it's still about violence. Basic principle.'

'There must be some way I can change your mind.'

'I doubt it.'

Cooper realized it was probably true that her mind wouldn't be changed. But it was no reason for him to stop trying.

'What about Michael Clay?' he said.

'Well, now that we know his family is local, it puts a different complexion on his possible involvement.'

'Just because he was born in Birchlow?'

'He must know people in the area,' said Fry. 'People must know him. I don't have to tell you how it works, Ben.'

'He would have been a young man when his family moved away to Birmingham.'

'It makes no difference. His roots are here.'

'I suppose you're right.'

'I am right,' said Fry.

Cooper knew she was right, but it was interesting to hear her argue the significance of someone's roots. Fry had always seemed to him to be a totally rootless person. She'd been taken away from her parents when she was very young, moved from foster home to foster home, separated from her sister, then finally washed up here in the Peak District, a hundred miles from anywhere that she knew.

'Some connections might emerge from the family history,' he said. 'Did you happen to ask Pauline Outram about the jewellery box?'

'Yes. She said it was her mother's. The only thing Pauline inherited from her.'

'And her uncle's briefcase?'

'She has no idea.'

'So how do you fit the Eden Valley Hunt into this picture?' asked Cooper.

'Patrick Rawson was staying at the Birch Hall Country Hotel, and had arranged to meet someone near Birchlow. During that encounter, he was killed, and the hunt were right in the middle of it. Given Michael Clay's origins in Birchlow, you can't tell me that's a coincidence.'

'No. So, what? Some kind of old family feud that Rawson stumbled into by accident? Could Clay have been the real target?'

'That,' said Fry, 'is what we should be trying to find out.'

Hesitantly, Cooper continued to hang around Fry's desk until there was no one within earshot. After a moment, Fry looked up at him again. She seemed uneasy, probably because she wasn't sure what Cooper wanted, or what he was going to say. Silence unsettled her, he'd noticed.

But Fry had no reason to be uneasy. As soon as he'd seen her enter the room, Cooper had been overwhelmed by an impression that she was going through a difficult time. She'd looked so alone and vulnerable.

'Was there something else you wanted to say, Ben?' she asked.

Cooper took a deep breath. 'Just that . . . I'm concerned about you, Diane. I know it's difficult going through a stressful time without any support . . .'

She stared at him. 'Is that it? Is that what you felt you had to say?'

'You can feel very isolated. If it were me, I'd be glad of all the support I could get.'

Fry was lost for words for a few moments. 'Support? From you? What kind of support do you think you can give me?'

Cooper was deterred only for a second. He glanced around the room, made sure there was no one near, moved in front of Fry as she seemed to be about to get up and walk away. There were times for walking away, and this wasn't one of them.

'Just talk to me, Diane.'

'Talk to you?' she said. 'Ben, we're different people, you and me. You have support from your family, you've been surrounded by it all your life. I'm sure that's lovely and warm and fuzzy, and all that. But some of us have grown up without the need for support. We're strong enough to look after ourselves. So your concern isn't necessary.'

'You know, if we're going to get a forced shake-up in this department, we should stick together.'

'Are you the shop steward all of a sudden, Ben? I didn't even know we'd got a trade union.'

'I'm not suggesting we work to rule or anything. Just – you know, support each other.'

Fry hissed, a sound low enough that no one else in the office would hear it, but piercing enough for Cooper to get the message loud and clear.

'Ben, I don't *need* your support, OK? I'll be just fine. Go and give your support to someone else.'

'Think you'll get support from Superintendent Branagh? It would be like Dracula becoming a vegetarian.'

266

Fry stood up and began to stack the files back together.

'I'll do that, if you like,' said Cooper.

'I can do it myself.'

She grabbed her phone off the desk, flicking it open as if to check whether she had any messages, though they both knew it would have rung if she had. He was perfectly familiar with her ring tone. No downloaded pop tunes for Fry, just a few unobtrusive electronic notes like something from the opening of *The X Files*. Nothing to upset a bereaved relative.

In fact, a strange silence had descended on the CID room. Cooper turned, and saw Detective Superintendent Branagh standing in the doorway. She said nothing, but looked at Fry and raised one eyebrow.

'Coming, ma'am,' said Fry.

She went almost eagerly, and Cooper began to wonder whether he was completely wrong, and everyone else was wrong too, about Fry going through a bad time. Maybe it was something else entirely. Perhaps it was quite the opposite.

Before they left, Cooper looked at Superintendent Branagh again. Who would want to hitch their wagon to that kind of horse?

29

'So,' said Branagh when Fry had settled in a chair in her office. 'DS Fry, do you think you have the full support of your team?'

Fry felt herself grow tense. She'd tried to prepare herself before she came into the superintendent's office, but this wasn't the question she'd been expecting. Branagh might look like a bruiser, but this was surely fighting dirty.

'Has someone said –'

Branagh shook her head. 'Whatever discussions might have gone on with other members of staff, they're confidential. Just as our discussion is this afternoon.'

'Of course.'

'DS Fry, I know you came here after a distressing incident in Birmingham, when you were with the West Midlands force.'

Fry swallowed. 'Yes, ma'am.'

'The management team here were impressed with you. Hence the quick promotion. But since then . . .'

'I've worked very hard for this division,' said Fry. 'I hope my work has been appreciated.'

'Indeed. But to go back a few steps . . . After the incident, you began the standard counselling process. But there's a note here that you abandoned the counselling sessions before they were complete. A personal matter.'

'That's right.'

'Yet the earliest reports on you said that you were suffering no ill effects from the incident. Your supervisor even suggested that the experience might have made you a stronger person. "Baptism of fire" was a phrase used. He described you as "solid as a rock".'

'Yes.'

'Of course, that report was written by a man,' said Branagh.

'I'm sorry, ma'am. I don't understand.'

'My own view,' said Branagh, 'is that no one is strengthened by an experience like the one you went through.'

And then the superintendent did something even worse. She leaned forward and smiled. A friendly, understanding smile that made Fry's heart sink.

'Diane, I do appreciate that it must have been very traumatic. Impossible just to put it behind you and forget all about it.'

And suddenly it was first-name terms. Fry steeled herself. There was no doubt about it now. Something horrible was about to happen.

Liz Petty phoned Cooper on his mobile in the office. He glanced around, but there was no one near enough to overhear.

'How did it go with Diane Fry?'

'Not good. In fact, she told me to keep my nose out of her business and stop trying to interfere in her life.'

'She was a bit cool on the idea, then?'

'You might say that.'

'Mmm,' said Liz doubtfully.

Cooper wondered what that sound meant. 'She doesn't really have a private life, you know. She talks about work all the time.'

'Does she really never talk about anything properly? Anything that matters?'

'No. Well, not to me.'

'What happened to that sister?'

'Angie? She was here for a few months, then she disappeared again. Besides, Angie was always bad news.'

'Diane must need to talk to someone, some time.'

'Maybe it's just me, then.'

'Yes, Ben.'

He sighed. 'I really thought we were starting to get on a bit better, too. When she first transferred to E Division, I made an effort to be her friend. But something went wrong, and I'm not quite sure what. Now she only seems to see me as a threat.'

'It's all about control,' said Petty.

'Control?'

'For some people, control is very important. More important than anything else. They'd rather give things up than feel they've let somebody else take control from them. It makes people very defensive.'

'Well, it's too much for me. How do I get myself into these situations?'

'By being you, I guess, Ben.'

'Who'd be me, then?'

'You have to get her out of the office,' said Liz. 'She can't relax while she's at work. You can see it in her face, all the time. What does she do when she's off duty?'

'I don't really know,' admitted Cooper.

He heard an exasperated sigh on the other end of the phone. 'Why not? What do you talk about in the office, apart from the job?'

'Well, it's usually Gavin doing the talking,' said Cooper. 'So – football, telly, the problems with teenage children . . . Food.'

'Does Diane never mention what she's done the night before, or at the weekend?'

'No.'

'I despair.'

'It's not my fault.'

'You have to show an interest, Ben.'

Cooper thought back to when Fry had first arrived in Edendale as the new girl. He'd done his best. One game of squash, which had gone OK – except that he'd won, which hadn't pleased Fry. And one visit to the dojo, which had gone very badly indeed.

Since Fry's promotion, there had never been any question of them socializing. He'd always assumed that she didn't want it, that she deliberately kept a distance between herself and the rest of the officers in CID. But what if there was a different reason?

He could see it was true that she was having a hard time. If it had been him, if he was going through a really bad week at work, he would have taken a long walk on the moors, whatever the weather. There was nothing like a good blow to clear the mind and make you feel better. There wasn't any point in suggesting it to Diane Fry, though. Or was there?

'So what do I do?' he asked.

'I told you, Ben. Get her out of the office.'

'I'd better go now. She's back.'

When Fry came out of her interview, she found herself looking at her colleagues differently. Who had said what to Superintendent Branagh? Where did the disloyalty come from?

First, she eyed Gavin Murfin. Murfin grumbled, but would never stick his head above the parapet. DC Becky Hurst and DC Luke Irvine were young, they hadn't been here too long, but they might be intimidated by Branagh into blurting out whatever she wanted them to say.

Of course, it might have been another DS on the division. Rivalry wasn't unknown in E Division, though she couldn't think who she'd offended. Not recently, anyway.

She looked further down the room. Cooper was the man who'd actually offered her his support, made quite a point of it, in fact. Had he been feeling guilty, trying to deflect suspicion? Or was he actually biding his time, waiting for her to slip up, looking for a chance to take the credit for himself? She knew he resented the fact that she'd gained promotion ahead of him. Maybe he'd never got over it, and had been seething ever since. Fry wondered if Cooper was really that devious. When he offered support to her face, was he stabbing her in the back at the same time?

She drew in a deep breath. A bit of extra oxygen could make the brain sharper, keep her alert. And she needed to be alert right now, more than ever. Fry had never felt so isolated. And she didn't know where the threat might come from.

Perhaps she was being left to handle this suspicious death on the assumption that she'd mess up and strike another black mark on her PDR. But responsibility didn't work like that in the police service – she was supposed to be supervised by more senior officers, and if things went monumentally wrong, they would be expected to take a share of the blame. The best thing she could do would be to refer upwards as often as she could, ask advice, consult her DI on the most minor decision, make sure he was fully informed at every stage. And record it. That was important. Keep a log of every action, and who she'd discussed it with.

But wait. Was that what they wanted her to do? Were they hoping that she would lose confidence, that she would prove herself incapable of taking responsibility, devoid of initiative, unable to take the smallest decision on her own? Hitchens couldn't have planned that, it was too clever for him, too devious. But Branagh . . .

On the other hand, she could just be getting paranoid. And, if she was, did that mean that they weren't all out to get her?

Fry sat at her desk, watching everyone else leave the office to go home, back to their families, off to meet their girlfriends, get drunk, or watch TV. They all sounded like alien activities that she was excluded from.

What the hell was going on? Right now, her week couldn't get any worse than it already was.

When Fry finally got back to her flat in Grosvenor Road later that evening, her answering machine was blinking. When she pressed the 'play' button, there was the briefest of messages. And from that moment, things did get worse, after all.

'Di – call me as soon as you can. It's important.'

The caller didn't need to leave a name. It was Angie.

There was no mistaking death when you saw it. Cooper had seen two dead bodies already this week, but it was so much worse when it was personal.

The cat had curled up in his usual spot by the central heating boiler in the conservatory. He looked so relaxed and peaceful that he could have been asleep, at first glance. But the stillness was too unnatural, the lack of even the slightest stirring of the fur as he breathed.

And, of course, Cooper had never arrived home before without Randy running to greet him. He didn't even need to go to the conservatory to know that something was badly wrong.

He knelt and stroked the long black fur. The cat was stiff. He'd died some time during the day, while Cooper was at work. He'd died alone, which was the worst thing he could imagine. It was what he dreaded for himself, dying alone and in the dark.

'Sorry, Randy,' he said, barely able to get out the words as a rush of guilt overcame him. He should have been here.

Though the light had gone, Cooper found a spade and dug a hole in the garden behind the conservatory, underneath a beech tree. Randy had spent a lot of time here. Not hunting much lately, just sitting and watching the birds, enjoying the sun. Giving him a permanent place here was the least he could do.

Somewhere in the darkness, among the beeches, a male tawny owl called. It was the eerie full-volume hoot, *hu . . . hu-hooooo*, made only by the male. The owl must be establishing a territory here, at the start of the new breeding season.

As he straightened up from the grave and knocked the last of the soil off his spade, Cooper thought he glimpsed a dim shape, winging silently into the trees.

Fry was discovering that there were some things you couldn't keep buried. Her sister had been a sort of talisman in her life, a symbol of the high points and low points. Well, no. Mostly the low points, it had to be said.

Since Angie had walked out of their foster home in the Black Country as a teenager, Diane had spent years trying to track her down. It had been her reason for coming to Derbyshire in the first place. Yet when they had finally been reunited, the taste of success had been a sour one. Diane had found that her sister was no longer a person she could trust.

'You must have realized that I got mixed up in some things that I didn't mean to,' said Angie on the phone that night.

'Obviously. The drugs –'

'I don't mean the drugs. Well, not the drugs on their own. There's a whole world that heroin gets you into. You've no idea, Diane.'

And Diane had to accept that she really didn't have any idea. She'd never thought of herself as naïve. How could she be? But there were things about her sister that she didn't understand. She supposed that she never had understood them, really. It was probably that mystery, the constant hint of wickedness and the unknown, that had led her to worship Angie as a teenager. Not just sisterly love, after all. She had been drawn to the scent of danger like a moth to a flame. And Angie had, too. In that way, they were the same.

For a moment, Diane wondered whether her sister was involved in some gigantic conspiracy against her. Had she been seething with jealousy and hatred all these years? Was she determined to bring Diane down, one way or another? If she was, she was doing a damned good job, and Diane felt helpless to fight her intentions.

'I was recruited,' said Angie. 'First by the bad guys, then by the good guys. It's not always easy to tell the difference, though. Funny, that.'

'You've been working for the drugs squad?' said Diane. 'As an informant.'

She realized it had been a suspicion that she'd been suppressing. She could easily have believed anything of her sister, but not that. The evidence had been there, in front of her nose, but she'd refused to believe it, had never even tried to confront it.

'SOCA,' said Angie. 'The Serious and Organized Crime Agency.'

'I know who SOCA are.'

'You were very slow, Di. Your nice Constable Cooper figured it out long ago.'

Diane gritted her teeth. She was realizing another truth that she ought to have accepted a long time ago. Not only was her sister someone she couldn't trust; worse, Angie had become someone she no longer knew.

'How did Ben Cooper come into it? I never understood that.'

'Oh, don't take it out on him,' said Angie, sounding faintly less sardonic. 'He was only trying to help. It's what he does. You must have noticed.'

Fry was within a second of putting the phone down. But she knew that she couldn't leave a question hanging. It would torment her for days.

'Angie, what is it you want?' she said.

'I want you to come back, Diane.'

'Back? Back where?'

'To Birmingham, of course. You know it's where you belong.'

275

'Damn it, Angie, you know perfectly well why I left Birmingham.'

''Course I do. But that doesn't stop it being the place where you belong.'

That night, Fry couldn't sleep. It wasn't the first night it had happened, and it wouldn't be the last. But tonight, as soon as she was alone in her bedroom, the darkness began to close in around her. That darkness was full of her memories. It moved in on her from every side, dropping like a heavy blanket, pressing against her body and smothering her with its warm, sticky embrace. Around her, the night murmured and her flesh squirmed.

She'd always known the old memories were still powerful and raw, ready to rise up and grab at her mind from the darkness. Tonight, once again, dark forms seemed to loom around her, mere smudges of silhouettes that crept ever nearer, reaching out towards her.

And then she seemed to hear a voice in the darkness. A familiar voice, coarse and slurring in a Birmingham accent. 'It's a copper,' it said. Taunting laughter moving in the shadows. 'A copper. She's a copper.'

The reality of the horror was years behind her now, and the only wounds still raw were those in her mind, where they were exposed to the cold winds of memory.

She breathed deeply, forcing her heartbeat to slow down. Control and concentration. Yet she could feel the sweat break out on her forehead. She cursed silently, knowing what was about to come.

These were memories too powerful to be buried completely, too deeply etched into her soul to be forgotten. They merely writhed in the depths, waiting for the chance to re-emerge.

Bodies could be sensed, further back in the darkness, watching, laughing, waiting eagerly for what they knew would happen next. Voices murmured and coughed. 'It's a copper,' the voices said. 'She's a copper.'

She remembered movements that crept and rustled closer, fragmented glimpses of figures carved into segments by the streetlights, the reek of booze and violence. And then she seemed to hear the one particular voice – that rough, slurring Brummie voice that slithered out of the darkness. 'How do you like *this*, copper?' And the taunting laughter moving in the shadows.

Then she was falling, flailing forward into the darkness. Nothing could stop the flood of remembered sensations now. 'How do you like *this*, copper?'

Then suddenly it was all over. Until the next time.

30

Journal of 1968

And that's the thing about memories. They come back to you in the darkness or in the daylight. They arrive like strangers at night, they appear out of the shadows in the heat of the sun. Or they walk up to you, smiling, in the rain.

No matter how guilty you feel, you know the truth when you come face to face with it. You know it by its eyes, and its voice. You know it so well that you don't need to ask its name.

And then what do you do? What would *you* do? No one knows until it happens, until the call comes and you do whatever is needed.

1968. A year of revolution? Well, maybe. But every spasm of rebellion was ruthlessly crushed. Russian tanks rolling into Prague, students facing riot squads outside the Sorbonne, Boss Daley's police clubbing hippies on the streets of Chicago.

But that was the 1960s to me. The world on a knife edge. It was the U2 incident, the Bay of Pigs, the Six Days War, the building of the Berlin Wall. American B-52s circling constantly just outside Soviet airspace, ready for the first strike.

But the one thing I remember most about events in the outside world is something that everyone else seems to have forgotten. That January, a B-52 Stratofortress crashed in

278

Greenland, spilling its load of nuclear warheads across the snowy wastes. When I read about that, I imagined the aircraft coming down a few miles to the east, in Soviet territory. US bombs falling on Kamchatka. And it could have happened so easily. Across the world, fingers were on the button, and World War Three hung on a hair trigger.

Often, when I was out there in the fields, I could feel Jimmy alongside me, walking in the midst of a shadow, even on the sunniest day. And we'd talk about this subject a lot, the way that things worked out. I'd tell him about the feeling of guilt. The guilt of being the one who survived.

Of course, a lot of people have died since Jimmy. But it's different when you've seen them die, when you know their last sight of the world was your own face, that your reflection was caught in their eyes as they took their last breath.

And worse, when you wonder every day if they believed it was you that killed them.

You know, it took me a while to be sure that it wasn't me. But I remember the exact moment. It was the night I saw them on the street, the two of them, just leaving the Bird in Hand. I could see straight away that they'd forgotten Jimmy. They'd managed to put his death in the past, the way I never did.

Arm in arm, they were. A laugh, a kiss, and something more than that. There was a terrible anger that came up inside me then. It burned like a flame, and it never went out. It blazed inside me like a nuclear core, scorching through my heart and my blood, contaminating a part of my brain with its fallout.

They had made me guilty. I could never forgive them for that. They had made me feel responsible for Jimmy's death, and they made me tell lies. Why had I listened to Les, just because he was number one? Why had I thought that life was too short, that we could all die tomorrow, so none of it mattered?

That was the moment I changed. In that one, bright, devastating flash, I realized what I had to do. No matter how long I had to wait, I knew who the person was that I needed to kill.

31

Saturday

A series of gritstone buildings stood at the end of a long drive, guarded by a locked gate. Fry could see nothing grand about any of the buildings, nothing to justify their secluded position. This was hardly Chatsworth House, or any other stately home.

'Take a closer look,' said Cooper, passing her the binoculars.

'What is this place?'

'The hunt kennels.'

'The Eden Valley Hunt?'

'Right,' said Cooper. 'This is where the hounds are kennelled.'

Many of the structures were single storey, their slate roofs darkened by rain. A couple of vans with muddy wheel arches stood in the yard. Fry could hear the distant sound of barking dogs.

'The huntsman and kennel man live on the premises,' said Cooper. 'The building to the right is the flesh house.'

'The *what*?'

'Well, you know about the flesh run?'

'Jesus, do I want to?'

'Like a lot of hunts, the Eden Valley provides a service for farmers,' said Cooper. 'It collects fallen stock – dead and sick animals, or ones that just don't happen to have any value. They pick the dead ones up from the farm, or put live animals down humanely, if necessary. It's a real boon for farmers. Fallen stock would cost them the earth to dispose of, otherwise. The regulations make incineration expensive, and you can't bury animals on your own property, the way a lot of farmers used to.'

'But what do the hunt want with dead livestock?' asked Fry. She turned her head to listen to the sound of high-pitched barking drifting from the kennels – a wild, haunting sound that must have struck terror into the heart of many a fox. 'Oh God, I think I know already.'

'You do?'

'There are about forty damn big dogs in there.'

'Hounds. Eden Valley Hunt have sixteen and a half couple – thirty-three hounds.'

'And big dogs take a lot of feeding, don't they?'

'Yes, you're right,' said Cooper.

Fry felt sick to her stomach. She couldn't bear to look at the innocuous grey stone buildings any more, couldn't stand to hear the barking any longer. The images in her mind were too vivid, and too bloody.

'Can we get away from here, please?'

She knew what Cooper was doing – he was trying to make her see the hunt differently, to convey a picture of some kind of essential cog in rural life, regrettable but necessary. So far, it wasn't working.

But Cooper hadn't finished yet.

'The kennel man does the flesh run, collects the fallen stock from farms all across the hunt's area. He uses a captive bolt pistol to kill any animals that need putting down. Then he skins them, guts them, and feeds the carcasses to the hounds. A pack like the Eden Valley's can get through a lot of raw meat in a day.'

'This place is no better than the abattoir,' said Fry.

'Well, they're serving a similar purpose.'

'If you say so.'

Fry lowered the binoculars. The hunt was gathering again for the second time this week. Something called a lawn meet, she was told. It sounded ridiculous, and created images in her mind of people playing croquet on horseback.

'Let's get this straight,' said Cooper. 'The Eden Valley Hunt aren't doing anything illegal. Neither are the owners of the abattoir where horses are slaughtered. So anyone who tries to interfere with their legal activities by obstruction or intimidation is committing a crime, and is liable to be arrested. Right, Diane?'

Fry could feel her jaw tighten. Strange, but she'd thought this would be a safe subject, a way of keeping Cooper off more personal topics. So why was it that he seemed able to make any subject unsettling?

'Of course,' she said. 'We could never condone vigilantism, by animal rights activists or anyone else.'

'I'm glad about that.'

'But it's still disgusting.'

Cooper looked at her, but she couldn't meet his eye.

'Everything ends the same way, Diane,' he said. 'Animals don't live for ever. Farm livestock are there for a purpose.'

Everything ends the same way. She supposed that was right – for humans, as well as animals. It was just a question of how much pain you had to go through first.

Cooper suddenly seemed to lose interest in the direction of the conversation. He pointed beyond the kennels.

'See down there, on the road?' he said. 'About a hundred yards short of the gate to the kennel drive.'

'Yes. There's an old Bedford van parked up on the verge.'

'That's the sabs' van. They're on kennel watch. They're waiting for the hounds to leave, so they can follow them to this morning's meet. Sometimes, if the hunt expects to be sabbed, they try to change the location at the last minute from the one listed on the meet card.'

'If the van is there, that means the animal rights activists are due back in the area today.'

'Right,' said Cooper. 'Well, it's the last hunt of the season. They'll want to go out on a high note.'

'Speaking of which,' said Fry, 'I'd really like to follow up the hunt saboteurs' claim to have heard the kill call before the hunt on Tuesday morning.'

'You think the kill call was real, Diane?'

'Yes,' said Fry. 'I believe in the kill call.'

They went back to the car, and Cooper drove up the road two miles from the kennels to where the hunt was gathering at the home of a member.

Cooper surveyed a scene that he had once thought would be a vanishing tradition, no more than a memory in the British countryside. Everyone was in correct hunting dress this morning, of course – gentlemen in three-button red coats with brass buttons, white breeches, and top boots. The traditional bowlers and top hats had disappeared now, though, in favour of protective hunting caps to meet safety standards.

'See, no one in tweed jackets, except for the small child there,' he said. 'It's not acceptable dress. And there are the hunt staff – the huntsman and kennel man. The joint masters, and then the mounted hunt followers. Plus all the foot and car supporters. It's quite a crowd, isn't it?'

They had found a spot in a small stretch of woodland overlooking the meet. A dense cover of brambles and dead bracken, trees still bare but for the thick, strangling snakes of ivy wrapped round their trunks.

'Are you actually a member of the hunt, Ben?' asked Fry.

'Of course not. But my brother Matt is.'

'Really? I've seen your brother. What's he like on a horse?'

'He doesn't ride.'

'So how come farmers are members of the hunt? I thought they were all supposed to be poor. I heard the subscription is more than a thousand pounds a year.'

'Farmers get a reduced rate. Masters have to keep them on side, or they'd have nowhere left to hunt.'

As Peter Massey had said at Rough Side Farm, farmers committed no offence as long as they didn't knowingly allow illegal hunting on their land. As they watched, a terrier man was letting his dog scent along the hedgerow. But that meant nothing, either.

'This is the end of the hunting season?' asked Fry.

'Mid-March, yes. There's Flagg Races on Easter Tuesday, and that's it.'

'What races?'

'Flagg. You've never heard of it?'

'Is there a reason I should have?'

'Well, it's on our patch.'

'Ben, there are all kinds of little out-of-the-way hobbit burrows on this patch that I've never heard of. Half of them haven't seen a human being for years. Some of them are so small you can't see them for the nearest telegraph pole. Why would I have heard of this one in particular?'

'Because it's where the races are held.'

'For God's sake —'

Cooper looked at her. 'Are you all right, Diane?'

'I wish people would *stop* asking me if I'm all right.'

Cooper shrugged. He'd thought Flagg's point-to-point races were pretty famous, in their own way.

'The protestors are gathering in the lane,' said Fry. 'Discussing tactics, you think?'

'More than likely. They're usually well organized.'

Once, when Cooper had been on hunt policing duty as a uniformed officer, one group of saboteurs had turned up with something called a 'gizmo', a sort of modified loud-hailer which played tapes of hounds in cry to distract the pack away from the quarry. He'd watched them drive along a dirt track in their van, playing their gizmo, with the hounds running towards them from a field away and loping along behind their wheels. And then there were the ubiquitous sprays – cans of Anti-mate, or a home-made brew concocted from citronella or garlic – anything that would mask the scent of a fox.

These days, of course, the hunt only followed a fox-based scent mixed with vegetable oil, laid by followers.

'Tarmac and concrete won't hold scent for long,' said Cooper. 'Wet ground provides good scenting conditions, but not in heavy rain – the scent gets washed away.'

'Just like our DNA and trace evidence.'

'Yes.'

Of course, it wasn't always a scent that attracted the hounds. The hunt wasn't riding through local villages to exercise the pack any more, not since someone's pet cat had been killed by them early one morning. You'd think the sight and sound of a few dozen hunting dogs would be enough of a warning to a cat, let alone the scent. Cooper could smell these hounds himself.

'Now, if we get among the horses, Diane, remember that a red ribbon on the tail of a horse means it's liable to kick, so avoid passing behind it.'

'Don't worry. I have no intention of getting behind a horse ever again.'

'Oh, I heard.'

Fry changed the subject rapidly.

'Hunts are always policed, whether there are protestors or not. And we do make arrests sometimes, don't we?'

'The hunts expect it.'

'How do you mean?'

'You'll find every hunt supporter carries a Countryside Alliance membership card. If they get arrested, they'll use their right to a telephone call to phone the CA legal team. So they get expert legal advice from the word "go".'

'There's the huntsman now,' said Fry.

'You recognize him?'

'Yes, I've spoken to him. John Widdowson.'

'Widdowson?' said Cooper. 'That reminds me, Diane – there was something I meant to mention to you.'

'What?'

'There was a Naomi Widdowson on Walsh's list of complainants in the Trading Standards investigation. But she was also one of the IPs on the Horse Watch list. I know you told me those calls weren't so important any more, but I didn't like to leave the job half finished, so I tried again. It turned out she was the owner of the Dutch Warmblood mare. Miss Widdowson. She sounded a bit annoyed when I told her who I was.'

'When did you speak to her?' asked Fry.

'Yesterday morning, while you were out with Gavin.'

'I see. Well, she was annoyed because we'd just visited her and got her back up.'

'Oh, of course.'

'Just a minute,' said Fry, 'This Dutch –'

'Warmblood.'

'What was its name?'

Cooper hesitated. He was always nervous when faced with that tense, expectant expression from Fry. Every time, he felt as though he might be going to let her down.

'Its name?' he said. 'I didn't ask.'

Fry groaned. 'Who's on duty this morning? Luke Irvine or Becky Hurst? Whoever it is, give them a call and get them to check. Right now, Ben.'

'I'll have to get out of these woods,' said Cooper. 'There's no signal here. I'll walk back down to the car.'

Almost as soon as Cooper had left her alone, Fry became aware of several figures in balaclavas appearing silently through the trees. They were carrying pickaxe handles and baseball bats. She stood facing them, hand on her extendable baton, ready to fight if necessary, but knowing there were too many of them.

Motion attracts, she kept telling herself. If you stay completely still, they don't see you, even if you're right out in the open. It's movement that the eyes notice. The instincts of an animal. *Motion attracts*.

For two minutes, nothing seemed to happen. Fry tried to take in as many details as she could. Four men, she counted. Camouflage jackets, black balaclavas, only their eyes showing, like bank robbers anxious to avoid security cameras. But there were no cameras out here, no witnesses to identify them later. Only her.

Though it was broad daylight, and the woods couldn't be more different from the back streets of Birmingham, her mind overlaid the scene with memories of a dark night. She felt as though she could sense other bodies, further back in the woods, watching, laughing, waiting eagerly for what would happen next. Voices murmuring and coughing in the darkness.

Something had stirred up the images that she always tried to keep buried. Today, once again, those dark forms seemed to loom around her, smudges of silhouettes that crept ever nearer, reaching out towards her. They merged with the trees, like creatures that had risen from the undergrowth.

She remembered the movements that crept and rustled closer, the reek of booze and violence. She was waiting for the taunting laughter, for that familiar voice to break into her mind, coarse and slurring in its Birmingham accent. 'She's a copper.'

Some form of communication seemed to take place between the men around her. One of them stared at her keenly, as if he knew her, or would know her again if he saw her.

And then they slipped away through the trees as quickly as they'd come. Fry breathed a sigh of relief, and realized that her hand was starting to cramp where it had been gripping the handle of her ASP.

287

She thought of calling in the incident. The group had been armed with baseball bats and pickaxe handles, after all. But her reluctance stemmed from her fear of being a bad witness, a dread of expending her colleagues' time and effort for no worthwhile result.

She also knew she'd recognized the first man, just as he'd recognized her. She felt sure he was the same hunt steward who had stared at her on Tuesday as she'd waited for the hunt to go by.

But there was a difference. On Tuesday, she hadn't been able to recall where she knew him from. Her powers of recognition had failed her.

This time, she knew who exactly he was.

'Diane?' The voice was Cooper's, instantly reassuring.

'I'm here.'

'Are you all right?'

'Did you see them?' she said. 'The hunt stewards?'

'No,' said Cooper.

She stared at him, not sure whether she could believe him. Whose side was he on, after all? The realization that she had no one she could trust made her suddenly, irrationally angry.

'Why did I come to this place? Why do I put up with these people?' She gestured at the people down on the road, at the hunt kennels, at the whole world in general. 'Horse-eating, fox-hunting, baseball-bat-wielding Neanderthals.'

Cooper gazed after her in amazement as she strode off. 'That's a bit unfair.'

'I don't care.'

'Diane,' called Cooper, 'don't you want to know? Becky Hurst has come up with some information for us.'

Fry stopped. 'And?'

'We have to get moving, if we want to make a quick arrest.'

288

32

The A52 into Derby had been re-named Brian Clough Way some years ago, creating a fume-laden memorial to a legendary manager of Derby County Football Club. At the mere mention of his name, many people around here still shook their heads and said he should have been the England boss, if there'd been any justice in the world. But what a pity about the drink problem.

In light traffic, Cooper made the Pentagon roundabout in a few minutes, and turned off past a Mercedes dealer, following signs into the Meadows industrial estate. Beyond a large car park stood a range of single-storey brick buildings with flat roofs – a plant centre, an equestrian supplies company, two firms of auctioneers, and the Meadows pub. The market was somewhere behind these buildings, occupying a stretch of ground between the railway sidings and the gravel pits.

'Is this what I was called in for?' said Gavin Murfin grumpily.

'You were rostered on call, Gavin,' said Cooper.

'I know, but blimey – a horse auction?'

'Diane has gone to the house herself. But the mother says they'll be here. Don't worry, we'll get back-up if we need it.'

Chequers Road was a strange place for a cattle market. It stood in the middle of this industrial estate, surrounded by car showrooms. Horse owners had to reach it by battling through the Saturday traffic jams. Outside the Meadows pub, someone had put up posters warning of GM crop trials taking place in a secret location in Derbyshire. There was no date on the posters, but they were starting to fray at the edges. Cooper was pretty sure those trials had been abandoned a couple of years ago. Too much of a risk, even for the bravest farmer.

'It's a bit public for an arrest,' said Murfin, as they entered the market itself, mingling with the crowds of buyers and sellers.

'If we see them, we'll wait until they're back in the car park,' said Cooper.

'OK.'

Cooper walked along a line of tubular steel pens, glancing at the details attached to the front of each one: *15.2hh seven-year-old bay gelding Welsh cross, owner gone to college and has no time to ride.* Labels with red numbers were gummed to the hindquarters of the horses. Some of the smaller ponies were dwarfed by the cattle pens. He reached through the bars to touch a soft nose, sensing the animal's apprehension.

The typical cattle-mart smell of animal dung had begun to fill the air. Handfuls of horse hair lay in clumps on the concrete floors, combed out by owners wanting their animals to look their best in the sale ring. Some of the horses stood resignedly in a corner of a pen, others were clearly nervous, swinging restlessly from side to side as far as their halters would let them, scraping their hooves on the concrete as they shied away from potential buyers. An elegant yearling colt was tugging at his halter and whinnying.

'No sign of them.'

In the pig building, an auctioneer in a white coat was selling saddles and tack, standing on a metal walkway over the pens. Another had begun to work his way through the farm implements lined up outside. Stalls were selling horse vitamins, hoof picks and blankets. From the back of a lorry, a youth was unloading nets of stock-feed carrots.

'There's plenty of intelligence on the Widdowsons in the system,' said Cooper, 'not to mention a few convictions for Rick Widdowson, Naomi's brother.'

'And they should be here?'

'According to their mother.'

But the first market worker they spoke to just shook his head. 'The Widdowsons? No, not today. They're practically gippos, aren't they? You're more likely to see them at Appleby horse fair.'

The second person they asked was no more help than the first.

'No. But if I do see them, I'll act normal, shall I?'

'Yes, that might be helpful, sir,' said Cooper.

Fry was standing outside Long Acres Farm, listening to the mocking chatter of the jackdaws. A liveried police vehicle was drawn across the entrance to prevent anyone leaving, though she feared it might be too late.

Only the elderly mother was in the house, a cantankerous old woman in carpet slippers who could barely move across the room on her sticks. But a white Fiat was parked in the yard, which the PNC confirmed was registered to Naomi Widdowson. And beyond it, under the cover of a Dutch barn, was an old blue Land Rover belonging to the brother, Rick Widdowson.

Rick had quite a record. A series of minor assaults and convictions for criminal damage dating back to his early teens, and later public order offences and petty thefts that had barely let him stay out of prison. If the jails weren't so full, he might not have had such luck, with a sheet of previous like that. As it was, Rick Widdowson was currently on probation, with a set of conditions. No wonder Naomi had assumed that the police had come looking for her brother.

291

Fry looked at the stables, with two horses' heads hanging over the loose-box doors to see what was going on. And she corrected herself. In the circumstances, Naomi couldn't possibly have assumed automatically that they'd come for Rick. It must have been a ploy on her part, a diversion to give an impression of her own innocence. Interesting that she'd drawn attention to her own brother to protect herself.

'Are we going to search the outside premises, Sergeant?' asked one of the uniformed officers from the response team.

'Not until we have a few more bodies,' said Fry. 'There are too many outbuildings. Too many nooks and crannies. The three of us couldn't possibly cover it.'

'We might be here a while. It's Saturday.'

'I know.'

Fry wondered how Cooper and Murfin were getting on at the horse market. Last she'd heard, they were just waiting, as she was.

Then she looked at the stables again. She was trying to remember the details of her visit here yesterday with Gavin Murfin. She had a clear picture of Murfin standing in front of the loose boxes, clicking his tongue like an idiot, and asking the names of the horses. *'That's Bonny at the end. Baby is the one in the middle. And the gelding is called Monty.'*

Bonny, Baby, Monty. But there were only two heads watching her, with no sign of the gelding. Where was the third horse?

After half an hour, Ben Cooper and Gavin Murfin were still sitting in their car at the cattle market in Derby. People passed them clutching bags of carrots, bits of leather tack and hoof oil.

'Hello, do we know them?'

Cooper jerked his head around at Murfin's question, thinking he must be missing something. But he saw only a couple of women in denim jeans and body warmers who had stopped to stare at them.

'You're going to miss the Rams today, Gavin,' said Cooper, relaxing again. 'Aren't they playing at home?'

'I don't care any more,' said Murfin. 'I'd rather support Nottingham Forest.'

'Really? But you were always such a big Derby County fan.'

'Until last season.'

'Relegation from the Premiership? Or the new American owners?'

'Both. And the team has been crap, too. Since the Americans came in, everyone calls them the Derby Doughnuts – because there's always a hole through the middle.'

'Is that what's making you restless?' said Cooper. 'You haven't been yourself for days.'

Murfin pulled a face. 'Jean has made me go on a diet.'

Now that he thought about it, Cooper hadn't seen Murfin snacking anything like so much as he used to. It must be the reason for Murfin's strange behaviour all week.

'And how do you feel?' asked Cooper.

'Terrible. I've got no energy. Nothing seems to matter any more. I really don't want to go into the office on Monday.'

'I suppose you could phone in sick.'

'I've used up all my sick days. I'd have to phone in dead.'

Cooper dialled Fry's number. 'They're still not here, Diane,' he said. 'We've been all round the cattle market. No sign of them. How long do you want us to wait?'

'I think the mother has pulled a fast one on us,' said Fry. 'Head back and meet me at Long Acres Farm, soon as you can.'

If this had been Watersaw House, there would have been stable girls around to give Fry information, instead of just one bad-tempered old woman glaring at her from a side window of the house. And there might not have been quite so many muddy puddles for her to negotiate as she crossed the yard towards the stables, avoiding the drainage channel where dirty water swirled among little dams of straw.

She recalled thinking that Naomi Widdowson spent too much time outdoors, that her skin was weathered, her fingernails black. Fry had to remind herself sometimes that the people she dealt with often did things she would never consider doing herself. She'd met more than a few of them already in the present enquiry. Eating those huge, purple steaks of horse meat, dressing up to pursue the artificial scent of a fox – it took all sorts.

Fry looked around the yard, with the stone house to one side and the stables on the other, the horses peering out at her from around their hay racks. Bonny and Baby, but no sign of Monty. She could picture the three of them practically mugging Gavin Murfin for some kind of tidbit. It was obviously what they had come to expect from visitors. So what could be of more interest to a horse than a stranger walking up to their stables?

Stepping carefully, Fry came nearer to the end loose box and edged along the wall. The top half of the door stood open, like all the others. If it hadn't, she would have noticed something out of place sooner. She could hear faint stirrings from inside now, the sounds of an animal breathing noisily and pawing at the straw.

That was when Fry made her mistake. She flicked up the latch and flung the door open, bursting into the stable, her mouth open to start shouting the commands. For a second, she heard the two uniformed officers running towards her. But then the whole of her world was suddenly taken up by the huge, rearing animal in front of her, its eyes rolling in alarm, its nostrils flaring, its steel-shod hooves lashing out at the intruder. How could she have forgotten how big these animals were, how easily the impact of a steel shoe could crush a man's skull?

Frantically, Fry tried to dive clear of the flying hooves. The

294

last two things she remembered for a while were the thud of those hooves hitting the concrete wall, and the overpowering smell of wet horse.

Cooper and Murfin were on the A6 approaching Bakewell. As they passed Haddon Hall, still closed to visitors for the winter, they were held up at the turning to the huge car park for the agricultural business centre. Bakewell was always busy on a Saturday, no matter what the time of year.

Cooper tapped his fingers impatiently on the steering wheel as a coach manoeuvred off Haddon Road, splashing through the water that sometimes closed the access to the car park completely in bad weather.

'It's frustrating not knowing what's going on,' he said.

'Me, I never know what's going on,' said Murfin. 'It's the best way to be.'

They were already in the centre of the small town, waiting for traffic to clear on the roundabout in front of the Rutland Arms, when they got the first indication of what was happening at Long Acres Farm.

'We've got Naomi Widdowson in custody,' Fry told Cooper when she called.

'Great. What about –'

'Her brother Rick? No, he got away.'

She sounded so disgusted that Cooper didn't ask her how it had happened. If it was her own fault somehow, she would be blaming herself enough by now.

'He made it to his Land Rover while we were dealing with his sister,' said Fry. 'There was a horse that proved a bit of a distraction.'

'Didn't you have the entrance sealed off?' asked Cooper, though he knew it was too obvious.

Fry sighed. 'Yes, of course. But there was another way out: a track across the fields. His Land Rover made it, but there was no way we could follow.'

'Which way is he heading?'

'He should come out near the stone mill. Who knows which direction he'll take when he gets back on the road, though. Too many tracks and unmade roads in this area.'

Cooper mentally pictured the map. 'We're not far away. We'll take a chance and head up through Great Longstone on to the Longstone Edge road.'

'Thanks, Ben. I'll catch up with you somewhere.'

Her voice sounded a little shaky. No way to conceal that, except by not saying very much. Cooper wondered what had frightened her.

'Diane, are you – ?'

'Just don't,' said Fry. 'Just don't ask me if I'm all right.'

With his foot down on the Toyota's accelerator, Cooper left Bakewell behind on the A6 and turned up the hill in Ashford in the Water. He slowed through Great Longstone, watching for Rick Widdowson's blue Land Rover as they passed the two pubs, the White Lion and the Crispin, but in Great Longstone, you were more likely to see a well-known former cabinet minister walking his equally well-known dog.

Moor Lane took them up to the Edge. It was quiet up here today. Saturday was the day for shopping in Bakewell, and tomorrow would be the time for enjoying the view. A sharp left-hand bend marked the point where the haulage road from High Rake and Black Harry Lane both met the public road.

Cooper stopped the car for a moment, surveying the landscape for a cloud of dust, or a flock of sheep scattering across a field. The Toyota had four-wheel drive, but he was reluctant to find himself drawn in to a pursuit across open country.

'What's that up ahead in the road?' said Murfin, pointing straight on.

Cooper let in the clutch again, and drove on slowly.

'It's a dead sheep.'

'And look, in the ditch – a blue Land Rover.'

They were on the edge of the last surviving stretch of genuine moorland on Longstone Moor. To the east, Cooper could see the glint of the flash, the water-filled quarry workings, edged by a screen of trees. To the west, the moor itself was a sea of heather, black in the rain, a dark ocean stirred fitfully by the wind.

He drew the car into the side of the road, and parked on the rough grass verge. They peered into the Land Rover to make sure Rick Widdowson wasn't lying injured inside it. But the driver's door stood open, and it was clear what had happened.

As Cooper straightened up, he saw Fry's black Peugeot coming the other way. She pulled a face at the sight of the dead sheep lying bloodied in the middle of the carriageway.

'Better help me drag this out of the way, Gavin,' said Cooper. 'It's a bit of a hazard.'

'Oh, shit,' said Murfin. 'What a great day this is turning into.'

Fry got out of her car and pulled up the collar of her coat as the wind across the moor caught her hair.

'He's abandoned his vehicle and legged it, then,' she said.

'Yes. But we can only have been a few minutes behind him. So where is he?'

In this landscape, there was only one answer. Widdowson must have gone to ground somewhere on the moor, and was lying flat to the earth in the heather. As long as he remained still, they would need an awful lot of time and luck to stumble across him.

Cooper walked as far as the first turn in a track that snaked across the moor towards the distant opencast rakes. Nothing moved anywhere, not even a rabbit.

'We'll need to get the helicopter unit to guide us in with their infra-red camera,' he said.

'I'll put in the request.'

Then a noise broke the silence of the moor. A tuneless

warble, no skylark or curlew. Cooper turned his head to listen and focused in on the noise before it stopped. He fixed his eye on a patch of heather close to one of the capped mine shafts.

'No need for the helicopter, after all,' said Fry.

'What was that?'

'The *Star Wars* theme, I believe. Mobile phones are a great way of locating people, even out there.'

Rick Widdowson heard them coming, and stood up from the heather, clutching his phone in his hand as if about to hurl it from him in a fit of anger. But it was far too late for that.

'You should remember to switch it to vibrate next time,' said Fry, as she read him his rights.

33

Most suspects who ended up in an interview room weren't bright enough to maintain a consistent lie. Their stories were easily undermined by the use of logic, their memories too short to survive a few hours' wait in the cells between interviews. And a change of interviewers usually seemed to unsettle them.

It was always a source of amazement to Fry that anyone thought they could get away with telling a different story to a different interviewer. Did they think that no one compared notes? Did they not notice the tapes running? Yet it was true what they taught you about interviewing techniques: Suspects seemed to feel they had to try harder to impress one or the other.

In Interview Room One, Naomi Widdowson had been waiting for a while. She was pacing restlessly, muttering to herself, fidgeting like a junkie suffering from withdrawal symptoms.

'Get close enough to smell her breath, to see if she's been drinking,' suggested Hitchens, before Fry went in.

'You think she might be drunk?'

'That, or mad. But when they're mad, you can usually tell it from their eyes.'

Fry entered the interview room and persuaded Naomi to sit down. The woman kept flicking her fingers, and shuddering as if she was cold.

'Yes, Rosie was my horse,' she said. 'I never denied that.'

'When I asked you, you said the name meant nothing to you,' said Fry.

Naomi looked at Fry as if she couldn't really see her, the way someone might look at a ghost, not quite able to focus properly on the figure in front of them.

'She was stolen and went for meat, I'm sure of it. Rosie died the same way as all those other horses. It was horrible to think about – I've never been able to get it out of my mind since. Patrick Rawson did that to me. He did the same to so many people. He deserved to be punished.'

'He didn't deserve to be murdered.'

'You know what? A lot of people would consider Patrick Rawson to be guilty of murder. But we never meant to kill him.'

'Who made the arrangement to meet on Longstone Moor?' asked Fry.

'I did. I phoned him and set up the appointment. Told him we had a lot of horses for sale. Thoroughbreds, for meat. He fell for it completely. Greedy people always do.'

'You deliberately used an unregistered pay-as-you-go mobile to make this call to Mr Rawson, didn't you?'

Naomi frowned. 'A what? Yes, my phone is pay-as-you-go. What does that have to do with it?'

Fry looked at her, registering her puzzlement. So Naomi Widdowson hadn't planned that, didn't know that a call from an unregistered phone would be almost impossible to trace. Her phone just happened to be pay-as-you-go. This wasn't turning out to be a clever criminal mind at work, was it?

'Is this your mobile number?' asked Fry, showing her a copy of the phone record.

'Yes.'

'You went to the meeting on horseback, Miss Widdowson. Why did you do that?'

'It was the easiest way to get there, and get away again quickly. We pulled scarves over our faces, so he couldn't identify us. He might have remembered a car. Besides . . .'

'Yes?'

'It just seemed, well . . . right. In the circumstances.'

Fry nodded. It was just what Dermot Walsh had said: poetic justice. But there hadn't really been anything poetic in the crushed skull, in the fatally injured man trying desperately to run from his attackers, even as his blood drained away into the ground and his brain swelled against the shattered bone.

'And your brother went with you on this meeting, didn't he?'

Naomi pushed herself up on to her feet, her fingers tense and trembling on the edge of the table.

'No. You can't fix any of this on Rick.'

'Please sit down, Miss Widdowson.'

'I need to make you understand that it had nothing to do with Rick.'

'He does have a record. Several previous offences of violence.'

Naomi slowly sank into the chair again, as if deflated. 'What does that have to do with it? You're all the same, once a person gets into trouble. Isn't it supposed to be innocent until proved guilty?'

'And you still say you didn't intend to kill Patrick Rawson?' asked Fry.

'No. It was an accident.'

Her tone carried a hint of regret. And it was probably that which finally convinced Fry she was telling the truth.

Rick Widdowson had recovered from the humiliation of his arrest very quickly. He walked into Interview Room Two with a strut, swinging his shoulders, his head tilted to spread a smirk around the room.

301

'Have you been informed of your rights?' asked Fry. 'Offered facilities and refreshments while you've been waiting?'

'Good cop, bad cop – never goes out of fashion, does it?' he said.

'This is good cop, good cop. You haven't even seen the bad one yet.'

'You don't have anything on me,' said Widdowson, sitting confidently at the table opposite Fry. 'If you did, there'd be a solicitor here, and the tape recorders running.'

That was the trouble with regular customers – they knew too much. Rick was right, of course. She had no evidence to implicate him in the death of Patrick Rawson. Not yet.

'So why did you try to escape when we visited your home?' said Fry.

He smiled. 'I was going for help. I thought we had burglars.'

Fry sighed. 'You know your sister is in trouble. Wouldn't you like to help her?'

''Course I would. Only too keen to help.'

If that was so, his loyalty might only be one way, thought Fry.

'You can start by telling me where you were on Tuesday morning.'

'I don't have anything to say.'

'You might as well go, then.'

Widdowson made a move to get up, then froze. Fry could see the calculation going through his mind, and she guessed what he was thinking.

'Yes, you're free to leave at any time, Mr Widdowson. You can get up and walk out. But that would be a strange thing to do if, as you claim, you want to help your sister. "Only too keen to help" – wasn't that your phrase? And I believe you, of course.'

Widdowson continued to hesitate, glancing at the door instead of at Fry.

'But if you walk out now, sir, I'd probably have to stop believing you.'

With a deep sigh, Widdowson sat back down and stared at his hands.

'I *do* want to help her.' He paused, seeming to realize that what he'd said didn't sound enough. 'I'm her brother, after all.'

'That's good. I was starting to get the opposite impression.'

'It's just ... Well, I know what you lot are like. If you haven't got anyone else in your sights, you'll fix it on the nearest person you can find.'

Fry raised an eyebrow. A little too dramatically, perhaps. But an interview room was a stage of a kind. You had to make your gestures understood by the dimmest suspect sitting at the back of the intellectual stalls.

'You're suggesting that we were going to accuse you of being involved in Patrick Rawson's death? Where did you get that idea from, Mr Widdowson? I'm sure I didn't say anything to give you that impression, did I?'

'Well, not exactly.'

'Was it something one of my colleagues said? Did they give you that impression?'

Widdowson frowned. 'I don't know what made me think that,' he said. 'It was nothing.'

'Oh, well.' Fry gave a hint of a shrug, and smiled. 'Perhaps it was just something in your own mind, sir? It happens sometimes, doesn't it? We hear what we're expecting to hear, rather than what someone actually says.'

With an effort, Widdowson squared his shoulders and met Fry's stare. 'I'm here to help. Like I said. If you tell me what you want from me, I'll do my best. Otherwise, we're all wasting our time, aren't we?'

Fry looked down at her notes. Her scrawl was illegible, even to her. To Widdowson, it must have looked like an indecipherable code.

'It would be helpful, sir, if you could just go over the events of Tuesday morning. Who knows what it might produce?'

'Like what?'

'It could be something really useful,' said Fry. 'Something that might help us —'

'Yes, I know: Help you to catch the killer.'

'Right. I'm glad we're all singing from the same hymn sheet at last, Mr Widdowson.'

He looked at her with a puzzled frown. 'Tuesday morning, I was at home doing a bit of rip and burn on some CDs I'd borrowed.'

'Any witnesses who can confirm that?'

'Not unless Bill Gates has managed to sneak some spyware into Windows Media Player.'

'You didn't make or receive any phone calls?'

'No. Besides, how would that tell you where I was? I use my mobile all the time. I don't even have a land-line at home.'

Fry shrugged. She wasn't going to get drawn into a discussion on that one. The less that certain members of the public knew about what was possible and not possible, the better. The cleverer ones already knew too much about fingerprints and DNA from watching re-runs of *CSI*.

'You didn't watch any daytime TV?'

'Nah. I don't watch much these days, except the football. There's too much else to do.'

'So no one else was at home with you?' said Fry.

Widdowson hesitated, suspecting that he might have detected a trap. 'Mum, of course. She's practically housebound.'

'Your sister was out, then.'

'I suppose she must have been.'

'You help her with the horses, don't you?'

He didn't like the change of subject. But that was fine. 'Yes, sometimes.'

'So you must ride, too. Which horse is yours? Bonny or Baby?'

He laughed scornfully. 'No way. You wouldn't get me

on one of those things. I do a bit of work to help out, that's all.'

'So your sister must have been out riding on her own that morning.'

Widdowson stared at her.

'I don't have anything else to say.'

'Thank you,' said Fry. 'That's all I wanted to know.'

DI Hitchens listened to Fry's theory carefully. She could tell that he wanted to believe her, and didn't want to see some huge hole in her case.

'So Patrick Rawson and Michael Clay were drawn to Derbyshire deliberately, for the purpose of revenge,' he said, knitting his fingers together, which in him was a gesture of satisfaction.

'Patrick Rawson, certainly,' said Fry.

Hitchens looked at her, surprised. 'These Widdowson people carried out their own sting operation. Having got Mr Rawson into the area, they then intended to kill him. Isn't that what you mean?'

'No, I don't think so.'

'You think Naomi Widdowson is telling the truth? It was an accident?'

'I don't think Miss Widdowson intended to kill Patrick Rawson,' said Fry carefully.

Hitchens unlocked his fingers. 'Let me get this straight. She admits that she made a phone call to Mr Rawson, arranging to meet him at the field barn on Longstone Moor that morning at eight thirty.'

'Yes.'

'She gave a false name, and claimed to have a number of horses for sale. Unfit horses, unsuitable for riding. But Thoroughbreds, to tempt him.'

'Thoroughbreds that had clean passports. No Section Nine declaration.'

'So they could go for human consumption.'

'Yes.'

Hitchens looked at her interview notes, as if he thought he might be missing something. 'And her story is that she went to the meeting alone, on horseback.'

'Because it was more anonymous, and easier to make a getaway.'

'Right. And all she intended was to give Mr Rawson a scare. In her own words, "to teach him a lesson". But when she galloped her horse at him, Mr Rawson tripped and fell. The horse spooked and reared, and he got kicked in the head. That's it?'

'Pretty much,' agreed Fry.

'In her account, there were no witnesses.'

'No.'

'And without a witness, it would be difficult to prove that it happened any differently. It could have been an accident.'

Fry nodded. 'It's funny,' she said. 'We started off with the assumption that Patrick Rawson's killing was the result of some human relationship that had gone wrong.'

'Well, that's usually the case, Diane.'

'Yes. But, in the end, it turns out that Rawson died because of the nature of someone's relationship with an animal. That's a new one on me.'

'And me.'

'The trouble is,' said Fry, 'Naomi Widdowson obviously knows nothing at all about what happened to Michael Clay.'

'So are we accepting Miss Widdowson's account?' asked Hitchens.

'No, we're not,' said Fry. 'Because we know that she wasn't on her own.'

'She's shielding someone, then. Her brother?'

'I don't think so.'

Fry took the postmortem photos of Patrick Rawson's head injury from her case file and lay them on Hitchens' desk.

'Mrs van Doon has completed her analysis of the injury pattern,' she said. 'As we can see, the depression in the skull is basically the shape of a horseshoe, which would substantiate Naomi Widdowson's story. But this area here, where the pattern has been obliterated – that was caused by a later injury. Mrs van Doon thinks a blunt-ended weapon.'

Hitchens examined the photos closely. 'Interesting. So someone finished Patrick Rawson off.'

'That's our murderer,' said Fry. 'It's whoever the second person was who went to that meeting with Naomi Widdowson. It's the person she's shielding. And it's someone who had a reason for making sure that Patrick Rawson was dead.'

Cooper knew only too well how an overnight resolve could dissipate completely by morning. You went to bed with your mind full of determination, and by the time you got up your willpower was as mushy as the muesli in your breakfast bowl. Things seemed so much less important in the cold light of day. Easier, surely, to let it all go by and get on with life.

But that morning, a couple of hours before dawn, he had already been wide awake and planning how he would carry out his intention.

'You're getting really good at these interviews,' said Cooper in the CID room.

'I always was good,' said Fry.

'No, I mean – you really knew how to handle the Widdowsons. They're going to give more away about what happened at any moment.'

'If they have anything more to give away.'

Cooper turned. 'What? Do you think they might be genuine?'

'I've no idea, Ben.'

'Oh.'

Cooper wasn't quite sure how Fry had managed to make

307

him feel in the wrong when all he had tried to do was pay her a professional compliment.

'You know,' he said, 'if something's bothering you, you should talk about it.'

Fry looked at him, a cool expression on her face that he couldn't read. Sometimes, it seemed to be an expression that she put on entirely for his benefit, a mask that he wasn't supposed to penetrate.

'Ben,' she said, 'if I was going to talk to someone about what's bothering me – it certainly wouldn't be you.'

Cooper sat back, feeling the physical force of her rebuff.

'OK. It's up to you.'

'Yes, it is.'

'I'm being serious, Diane.'

'No, you're being ludicrous. There's a difference.'

'I'm sorry you feel like that,' said Cooper. 'Because I wanted to ask you something.'

Just then, Gavin Murfin came into the office with a report in his hand.

'Fingerprint section have got their, er . . . fingers out at last,' he said, with a grin. 'They've got us a result on the prints lifted from the gate in that field where Patrick Rawson died.'

'And . . .?' said Fry, completely forgetting Cooper.

Murfin scanned the report. 'Adrian Tarrant, aged thirty-two. HGV driver, with an address in Eyam.'

'He has a record? If his prints were on file, they should have made the match long before now. Days ago.'

Murfin shook his head. 'They weren't on file until today,' he said. 'He was arrested this morning, during a meeting of the Eden Valley Hunt.'

'What?' said Cooper. 'We were there.'

'Well, you must have missed it. It seems Mr Tarrant was identified by a female hunt saboteur as the person who assaulted her during an incident on Tuesday. He was arrested and brought here for processing. DNA sample and finger-prints taken, as per routine.'

'And when they put his prints into the system, they got a match.'

'Bingo,' smiled Murfin.

'Adrian Tarrant,' said Fry. 'I knew it was him.'

Adrian Tarrant had been employed by one of the haulage companies whose lorries rumbled constantly backwards and forwards to the opencast quarries on Longstone Edge. Fry reflected that he might well have seen her as he passed along the haulage road in a cloud of dust. But she wondered whether his job might not give an alibi for eight thirty on Tuesday morning, when Patrick Rawson was killed.

That was, until she discovered Tarrant had been sacked by his employers the previous week, for turning up over the alcohol limit once too often.

The house in Eyam was already guarded by uniformed officers standing at the gate. It was a small, stone-faced council house, not much more than a two-up, two-down, with a tiny kitchen and bathroom. According to the neighbours, Adrian Tarrant shared the house with another man, possibly a cousin, who worked as a long-distance lorry driver and was currently away on a job.

Fry could see from the state of the house that this was likely to be true. A couple of days' washing-up stood on the kitchen drainer, newspapers and empty beer cans decorated the carpet in the sitting room. The TV remote looked much better used than the vacuum cleaner.

The team moved through the house systematically, not entirely sure what they were looking for, so looking that bit more carefully.

'Apparently, it was Tarrant's fellow hunt stewards who pointed the finger initially,' said Cooper. 'Then, when he was pulled in, the girl he injured made a positive identification. So it just shows –'

'Not all hunting people are bad, I know,' said Fry.

'They can't risk someone like him giving them a bad reputation. Not any more.'

In the sitting room, Fry began to open the drawers of a small dresser, her gloved fingers moving through the contents. Some CDs, spare batteries, a pair of gloves. Luke Irvine was examining a desktop PC on a table in the corner. Was Tarrant the type to send a lot of emails? She doubted it, but you had to check. Just as Cooper came into the room from the kitchen, she touched something solid in the drawer. Her fingers closed around an unusual shape.

'That's odd.'

Cooper came over to her. 'What have you found, Diane?'

'I'm not sure.'

Fry showed him the object she'd found in the drawer – a small, flared brass and copper tube, no more than nine inches long.

'Those things aren't easy to use,' said Cooper. 'It takes a lot of practice to get it right.'

'What is it?'

'A hunting horn, of course.'

Carefully, Fry bagged the horn for evidence.

'Adrian Tarrant must have had it,' she said. 'So it looks as though the kill call was real, after all – and Tarrant was the one who blew it. For a while, I thought the sabs were making it up.'

'Rather a theatrical gesture, wasn't it?' said Cooper.

'Theatrical?' Fry thought of all the gleaming horses and red coats, the panting hounds and glossy boots, all the centuries of ritual and tradition. 'Well, that's what it's all about, isn't it? A bit of theatre.'

'The kill call?' said Irvine, straightening up from the PC when he overheard their conversation.

'It's a hunting term,' explained Cooper. 'Three long notes, calling the hounds in to kill the fox.'

'Oh, I see. It has another meaning, too.'

'Of course. Something to do with computer programming, isn't it?'

'Yes, it's used in multi-tasking. The kill call lets one process terminate another.'

Fry looked around Adrian Tarrant's home, sniffing at the beer cans and unwashed plates. 'Well, let's see if we've found enough to terminate Mr Tarrant's activities.'

That afternoon, Fry spent a long time sitting across the table from Adrian Tarrant in an interview room, watching him as if he was an animal at the zoo. She wasn't sure what sort of animal he would be. He might as well have been a hibernating bear, for all the communication that was going on between them.

Tarrant was silent, stubbornly so. He didn't even need the presence of the duty solicitor to encourage him to go 'no comment'. But now and then he raised his head and stared back at her. Fry remembered his eyes – those eyes that had stared at her as he ran past her near Birchlow on Tuesday, and again in the woods on Saturday.

'Why did you kill Patrick Rawson?' she asked. 'Was it for money? We know you lost your job. Or perhaps you've got yourself into some kind of trouble? Do you owe a lot of cash? Is it for drugs?'

He remained silent, denying the tapes any response. These were facts that might come out some other way, and other members of the team were already at work in the CID room, phoning his ex-employers, former colleagues, members of his family. SOCOs and a search team were about to pull apart his house. But Tarrant wasn't going to help. Why should he save the police time?

'What did you use to finish Patrick Rawson off when the horse didn't kill him?'

311

Fry really wanted to know the answer to that one. Her money was on the pickaxe handle that he'd been carrying when she saw him in the woods. She hoped the search would turn it up. Bloodstains were preserved well on a wooden handle. Patrick Rawson's DNA would clinch it, even if Adrian Tarrant stayed permanently dumb.

'How well do you ride a horse? Not well, I bet. You're not the type.'

He didn't rise to it. She hadn't expected him to. In a way, he had only been doing what everyone else did, making a living by exploiting his natural talents. In Tarrant's case, his talent was a capacity for violence.

After interviewing the other hunt stewards, Fry had two witnesses to the fact that Tarrant had been absent from steward duty until later, around the time that she'd seen him on the road. She thought of the protestor who had been injured during the hunt and had identified Adrian Tarrant as her assailant. Tarrant had come fresh from killing Patrick Rawson, and the assault had probably come all too easily to him.

Now Fry knew what sort of animal Adrian Tarrant was. The sort whose instinct was to kill. Once the scent of blood was in their nostrils, they were likely to attack anything that crossed their path.

'He's saying nothing,' said Hitchens, when she took a break. 'And I'd anticipate that he doesn't intend to.'

'I agree,' said Fry.

'No explanation for how his prints came to be on the gate?'

'None offered.'

'I'm not surprised.'

Fry did at least have a clearer picture now of what had happened to Patrick Rawson. Earlier, she'd imagined him running across the field in his waxed coat and brown brogues, and had wondered where he'd been running to. But it had been more a question of what he was running away from.

Sean Crabbe had just been the final element in deciding Mr Rawson's fate.

And that reminded her it was Sean's turn to face his fate now. The CPS would be making a decision early next week on what charges to bring against him. Fry found herself hoping that he'd avoid a custodial sentence. Of all the people prison would do no good for, Sean Crabbe had to be top of the list.

'So what are we going to do now, sir?' asked Fry. 'We don't have any other evidence against Adrian Tarrant.'

'I suggest you have another go at Naomi Widdowson,' said Hitchens.

'Why?'

Hitchens smiled. 'Because, according to Tarrant's colleagues at the haulage company, Naomi is his girlfriend.'

34

That evening, David Headon needed to take only one glance at the badge found during the search at Eden View.

'The ROC,' he said. 'Where did you get that?'

'The Royal Observer Corps, right?' said Cooper.

'That's it. Did you know I was a member?'

'No, I didn't. You're just the sort of person I'd expect to know about these things.'

Headon was an old friend of his father's, a man of about the same age as Joe Cooper. He'd visited Bridge End Farm a few times when Ben was a teenager, and he could remember Headon talking endlessly about annual camps at RAF stations around the country.

'All the ROC posts were closed in 1991, and we were stood down completely a few years later,' said Headon. 'There were quite a few of us, you know. Eighteen thousand observers, until the cutbacks started in the sixties. The Corps did a brilliant job during the Second World War, tracking German air raids. Then, when the Cold War started, the observers were needed again. We had posts all over the country. There was even one at Windsor Castle, in the coal cellar.'

'What did the ROC do, exactly?' asked Cooper.

'What do you think?'

'Observe, I suppose.'

'That's right. Observe and report.'

'I thought I recognized the logo. I was at the National Arboretum the other day.'

'Ah, you saw the ROC grove. So how were the trees doing? Still waterlogged?'

'No. They're small, but alive.'

'I'm glad.'

'The trees had labels with this logo. They said "7 Group Bedford, 8 Group Coventry". For some reason, the labels stuck in my mind. It's the emblem, I think. It's quite distinctive, and not immediately obvious what it's supposed to be.'

Headon stroked the emblem on the ROC badge. 'He's an Elizabethan beacon lighter, who used to warn of Spanish ships approaching the coast.'

'Yes, I found that on Google.'

'Well, that's pretty much the role the observers carried on, though during the Second World War it was German planes they were tracking. A series of observer posts could follow an aircraft's flight path right across Britain, the way they did when Rudolf Hess flew to Scotland in 1941.'

'Aircraft recognition, then,' said Cooper.

'That was it, for long time. It was what a lot of the blokes that I knew came into the Corps for. But that job went out when aircraft got too fast for us. By the 1960s, it was becoming a bit impractical. A low-flying enemy aircraft could have entered UK airspace, flown to London, dropped its bombs and been on the way home again, all while the observers were still trying to make their minds up whether it was friend or foe. The ROC would have been wound up right then, if it hadn't been for the Bomb.'

Cooper could tell that Headon pronounced the word 'bomb' with a capital 'B' this time, and he knew immediately what he meant.

'The atomic bomb.'

'That's the baby. Believe it or not, Ben, when you were a child, me and my mates in the Royal Observer Corps were your first line of defence against a nuclear holocaust. That was the time we went underground.'

Fry knocked on the door of the DI's office. She was feeling very pleased with herself. Almost smug, some might have said.

'Get any more out of Naomi Widdowson?' asked Hitchens.

'No,' said Fry. 'She's gone "no comment", like her boyfriend.'

The DI looked at her. 'But there's something else. I can tell from your face, Diane.'

'I decided to get the calls record from the phone network,' she said.

'But we already did that. Irvine and Hurst went through all the calls on both of Patrick Rawson's phones, didn't they?'

'Yes.'

'The only calls we couldn't identify were to a pay-as-you-go mobile. And that was the one Naomi Widdowson used to set up the false deal.'

'That's right.'

'So?'

Fry shook her head. 'I didn't mean Patrick Rawson's phone records, sir. I meant Deborah's.'

'What – Deborah Rawson's?'

And Fry finally allowed herself to smile. 'Luckily for us, some people have no idea how to cover up a crime.'

On the edge of the hill, Cooper was able to look back at the town of Edendale, constrained in its hollow by the hills to the north and the sharp cliffs of the edges to the east. The pressure of housing demand might force Edendale to expand some time, if national park planning regulations allowed it. He could foresee a day when those houses would gradually push southwards into the limestone of the White Peak.

'It wasn't a popular idea, going underground.'

'I can imagine.'

'But it was inevitable. There's not much point finding yourself standing on a brick tower with a pair of binoculars in
your hand when a nuclear bomb goes off.'

Cooper nodded, keeping his eyes on the road. He had David
Headon and his friend Keith Falconer in his car, and they
were heading out of Edendale, driving west until they'd left
the houses behind and there were only the cat's-eyes in the
road and the light rain that drifted across his bonnet.

'That's what we were reduced to by then,' said Headon.
'Modern aircraft had developed until they were much too fast
for us. So it became a question of reporting the size and direction of a blast, monitoring the fallout, observing a nuclear
attack without putting yourself in harm's way. That could
only be done underground. It was all very different.'

To Cooper, that sounded like a massive understatement.
Watching your world destroyed around you was different from
anything he could imagine. But Headon and Falconer talked
about it all so calmly, in such a matter-of-fact tone, that they
might have been discussing a new type of lawnmower, or the
arrival of wheelie bins.

'In the old days, the main job was to watch out for rats,'
said Headon. 'That was the code word for hostile aircraft. A
lot of men liked that part of the job, distinguishing friend
from foe, a bomber from a fighter. Losing that aircraft recognition role was very disappointing. Quite a few observers left
the ROC then. But we were still serving our country, weren't
we? Well, that's what we thought.'

Two miles out of town they turned and headed uphill.

'Some people didn't want underground bunkers on their
land,' said Headon. 'It was usually the bigger landowners who
refused. Farmers were a bit more co-operative. There was a
little bit of money to be made out of it, but not much.'

'And Edendale?'

317

'Edendale was a master post. It had the radio set.'

Cooper knew that Headon and Falconer were both enthusiasts, the kind who wanted to talk about their obsession. The trick was to filter out the information from the mass of reminiscence. But he was glad of the excuse to get out of the way, to interest himself in something else and let Diane Fry bring her case to a conclusion back at West Street. She didn't need him getting under her feet. In fact, she didn't need him at all. She'd said so herself.

'The ROC was stood down in 1991, you said, David?'

'That's when the last posts were closed.'

'They thought they didn't need the Observer Corps quite so much by then?'

'Right.'

Following Headon's directions, Cooper swung the Toyota on to a narrow single-track lane that ran uphill between high dry-stone walls. Throughout the area, wallers were hard at work repairing the ravages of the Peak District winter. They passed one waller who had an old DAF towing a small caravan. If you had a long job to do, it was easier if you could live on site, he supposed.

'But do you all still keep in touch?'

'Some of us,' said Headon. 'There's an association, you see. We have a newsletter, a benevolent fund, social get-togethers occasionally. I think there's even a forum on the internet.'

'So what are these underground posts like?'

'Pretty basic. There's a twenty-foot vertical ladder leading down to an underground chamber, seven feet wide and sixteen feet long. That housed the observers, their bunk beds, generators, the operations desk, other equipment. Conditions were very primitive.'

'No running water, or mains electricity,' chipped in Falconer.

'Yes, and the only communication with the outside world was a Tele-Talk device connected to Group HQ, and of course the warning receiver. You needed dedicated people, prepared to lock themselves away in those conditions.'

'Let's be honest. We were a bit out of the ordinary,' said Falconer. 'The general public reaction was "If the bomb drops, we're all going to die anyway, so why bother?"'

Cooper looked at him through his rear-view mirror. He was about the same age as David Headon. They were two old men, living on their memories. The further in your past a period was, the more it started to seem like the best days of your life.

'There was a Peter Cook sketch once,' said Cooper. 'From the Footlights, maybe: "*When the four-minute warning sounds . . .*"'

'"*. . . hold your breath and jump into a paper bag.*" Yes, I remember.'

'The Government's preparations for nuclear war were ridiculed, weren't they?'

'Well, I blame the media for that,' said Headon. 'The public got the idea that if there was a nuclear attack, everyone would be wiped out and there'd be nothing left except some kind of radioactive wasteland. That's why the advice sounded ludicrous. But if people took sensible precautions, most of the population would have survived an attack. You just had to make sure you stayed indoors until the fallout dispersed.'

'If you say so.'

'It's true.'

Cooper had grown up accustomed to the idea that history was all around him – many thousands of years of history, right there, visible in the Peak District landscape. Stone circles and Iron Age hill forts were curiosities to be explored, the bumps and hollows of ancient lead mining added an intriguing feature to many parts of the county. Tudor manor houses and the vast mansion of the Dukes of Devonshire at Chatsworth were obvious historical landmarks. Eyam itself was a monument to a seventeenth century disaster.

But more recent history was sometimes overlooked. Apart from the Dambusters museum at Derwent Reservoir, there was precious little to remind people of the events of the Second World War. And the Cold War, even less.

Perhaps it was because those events were still within living memory for so many people. The years when the world was on the brink of extinction didn't need a museum or visitor centre, because they were still clear and vivid in the minds of those who'd lived through them, and survived. Well, it was only true of the older generation now. Cooper couldn't recall being taught many details about the Cold War when he was at school.

But then he thought about the dates again. Of course, the Cold War had still been going on when he was a child, with the likes of Reagan and Thatcher rattling their sabres at the Soviets. All through the nineties, new Trident submarines were still being rolled out. What were they called? *Vanguard, Victorious, Vigilant*. They sounded much like the names of foxhounds, really.

In 1991, John Major had been in his first year as prime minister, and George Bush Senior was still president of the USA. The pre-Blair, pre-Clinton years. It seemed like a millennium ago.

'So, 1991 . . .' said Cooper. 'The Soviet Union collapsed. The Berlin Wall had come down . . .'

'Yes, and a suddenly there was a big hole in the nation's defences,' said Headon. 'That September, our Chief Observer had a letter asking him to arrange the clearance of the post, and return the equipment and keys. It was adding insult to injury. Frankly, we told them "sod that". They could collect the stuff themselves. And that was the last we heard from the ROC.'

Diane Fry took Deborah Rawson into a vacant interview room. The woman looked more nervous today, which was what she'd been hoping for. Nervous people were more likely to tell the truth. They found it difficult to concentrate on maintaining a lie. All she needed was one slip, one flaw in Deborah's story.

'Mrs Rawson, you said earlier in the week that you didn't get involved in your husband's business, you didn't even know exactly who he dealt with.'

'That's right.'

'Well, I have to tell you, I don't believe that's entirely true.'

'Oh, don't you? Well, I'm not lying.'

'Why should we believe you, when you lied to us before?'

Deborah smiled. 'I only tell lies when I've got something to gain by it.'

Fry studied her thoughtfully. She still didn't trust Deborah Rawson, but her last answer sounded pretty much like the truth.

'You must know that your husband was supplying horses to an abattoir, for meat.'

'Meat.' She pulled an expression of disgust. 'Do people really eat horses?'

'Yes, lots of them.'

'Not in this country, though, I bet. It would be the French.'

'Did your husband sometimes travel abroad on business?'

'Yes, sometimes.'

'To France?'

She hesitated. 'Yes. He flew to Paris from East Midlands Airport three or four times a year. Brussels, too, now and then. So he said.'

Fry looked at her curiously, detecting a change of tone in her last comment. Watching Deborah Rawson's face, she saw a faraway look in her eyes, as if at a memory or a recurrent, familiar thought.

'Mrs Rawson, did you have any reason to think that your husband might be having an affair?'

The woman's eyes focused sharply on her again as she tried

to rearrange her expression. 'What makes you say that? I've been following your logic so far – that Patrick went up to Derbyshire to meet either a seller or buyer, and they had an argument of some kind, and Patrick got hurt. I can understand that. I can live with it. But why are you asking me this question about him having an affair? What has that got to do with anything?'

It was the longest speech Deborah Rawson had made during Fry's visit, by quite a long way. In relative terms, it amounted to an emotional outburst.

'We have to keep our minds open to all the possibilities,' said Fry. 'In this case, it might not have been a business contact he was meeting. The Derby horse sale isn't until Saturday, yet he went up a few days early. What he was planning to do, we don't know. You never asked your husband who he was meeting, and he never felt the need to tell you, did he?'

'No.'

Deborah regarded her stonily as she waited for Fry to explain further.

'So the possibility is there. He definitely had the opportunity. In fact, you practically gave him free rein, if you showed so little interest in his movements. Are you really telling me that you never once had the slightest suspicion about those days away here and there, the trips he took to Paris . . .?'

'I wouldn't be human if it hadn't crossed my mind.'

'Of course. And I imagine you must have checked up on him at some time?'

The woman sighed and stubbed out her cigarette. 'I can't deny it, I suppose.'

'What made you think your husband might be in trouble?'

'Patrick? Anyone with such a short fuse was bound to end up in trouble one day.'

'And he did.'

'It seems so.'

Fry let a few moments pass in silence as she read her notes,

322

allowing Deborah Rawson to wonder what question was coming next.

'As a matter of fact,' she said, 'we've talked to Naomi Widdowson and Adrian Tarrant this afternoon. They've told us about the arrangement you had with them.'

Now it was Deborah's turn to be silent. Fry could see the mental calculation going on. It was written all over her face. Deborah was running a few scenarios through her head, deciding how much Fry knew, what the best response would be, deciding on the least incriminating thing to say. The woman wasn't a very good actress.

'They were only supposed to give Patrick a scare,' she said finally. 'To teach him a lesson. There was never any intention of hurting him.'

But Fry shook her head at that. 'No, Mrs Rawson, that won't do. I know all about the payment you made to Adrian Tarrant. Three thousand pounds. That wasn't just to teach your husband a lesson. That money was to make sure he died.'

35

The Edendale ROC post had been located in a field off a back lane running between Edendale and Calver. It didn't look much on the surface. A square concrete structure about three feet high, green paint flaking from its surface. A few feet away stood a smaller ventilation turret with a louvred opening. And there were a few smaller protrusions here and there, whose purpose wasn't clear. Cooper staggered as his foot hit something like a green steel mushroom lurking in the rough grass.

'That's the top of the blast pipe for the bomb power indicator,' said Headon. 'A lot of people trip over that.'

'Thanks.'

'These bunkers are still quite common – there were over fifteen hundred of them originally, all over the country, built in the late fifties and early sixties. When we were stood down in 1991, most of them were just abandoned, and a lot have been demolished. You'd never know some of them were there. Often, the only evidence you'll see of an underground post is a couple of redundant telegraph poles on a field boundary.'

'I never knew *any* of them were there,' said Cooper. 'Do people visit them?'

'Sometimes. There are a few enthusiasts, or old observers.

324

You have to be careful, though. You should always go with someone.'

Headon pointed to a fenced section of ground with a small gate. There certainly wasn't much to see.

'On the surface, there's the shaft, of course,' he said. 'That's where the ground-zero indicator was mounted. Over there is the ventilator turret, and the mounting point for the fixed survey meter, with the top of the blast pipe near it.'

'What's left inside the bunker?'

'This one still contains the bunk beds, mattresses, chairs, kettles, a few other odds and ends. We had to be self-sufficient, you know. If fallout did occur near a post, the observers could hardly pack up and go home. It could have taken a couple of weeks for the air outside to clear enough for the crew to be relieved. These posts were designed to close hatches to the outside world until the danger passed.'

Headon stood by the hatch at the entrance to the shaft and patted the concrete with a gesture of fondness.

'I was number three observer,' he said. 'It was one of my jobs to climb up through the hatch and sound the siren when Attack Warning Red was received.'

'Attack Warning Red?'

'The warning of an imminent nuclear attack. Attack Warning Black was the fallout alert. Strike command would pass a warning to the carrier control points in police stations, then it was transmitted across the network to activate the sirens.'

'If the receiver hadn't been accidentally left on and flattened the battery,' said Falconer.

'Yes, provided the circuits hadn't been knocked out by a thunderstorm. There was absolutely no EMP protection.'

They both laughed, sharing their hilarious memories of British incompetence in the face of a nuclear holocaust.

'As number three, I also had to look after the ground-zero indicator,' said Headon, 'which was a sort of bread bin with four pinhole cameras. That meant coming upstairs. It would have been the most dangerous job of all, if the balloon had ever gone up.'

'Upstairs?'

'On to the surface.'

'We were part of 8 Group, based in Coventry,' added Falconer. 'But posts were organized in clusters. Edendale was post 8/A5. We had Buxton to the west, but the other two posts in 'A' cluster were out at Beauchief and Wickersley.'

'Those are in South Yorkshire,' said Cooper. 'So each cluster covered a pretty big area, then.'

'Yes.'

Cooper thought he detected a momentary exchange of glances between the two men. But it was very brief, and he didn't have a clue what it could mean. He'd probably imagined it, anyway.

'Were there other local clusters?'

'Of course. B-Cluster covered the Derbyshire and Nottinghamshire border – Ashover, Whitwell, Farnsfield. There were two more clusters in the south of the county.'

Cooper located the places mentioned on his map. Each of those other clusters had a post not too far away, but their coverage spread outwards to the east, west and south. A-Cluster looked odd, though – the three posts were pretty much in a straight line from Buxton across the southern outskirts of Sheffield and Rotherham. The line ran right through Eyam.

'Just four posts in A-Cluster?' he asked.

'Oh, yes.'

'Was there anyone called Clay in your post crew?'

They both shook their heads. 'No, not here,' said Headon.

'Or Outram?'

'No, sorry.'

Finally, Cooper showed them a copy of the photograph taken from Michael Clay's laptop case.

'Not our crew,' said Headon.

'No,' agreed Falconer. 'The big chap looks familiar, though.' But then he shook his head. 'I probably saw him at an annual camp somewhere.'

'You don't recognize the building?' asked Cooper.

'Those Orlit posts are long gone. They were for aircraft recognition.'

Disappointed, Cooper looked down at the green-painted hatch cover on top of the shaft, and the ventilator turret close beside it.

'Is it possible to take a look inside the bunker?'

There was that glance again. He was sure of it this time. Something they didn't want him to see down there? A locked underground bunker in the middle of nowhere presented all kinds of opportunities. He was just starting to run through them in his head when Falconer nodded.

'Yes, OK.'

'I can?'

'There's no light down there, though. We only ever had a battery for power.'

'That's all right. I've got a good torch in my car.'

Falconer produced a set of keys and opened the padlocks on the hatch. Then he inserted a narrow rod like an Allen key into a slot on the cover and twisted it. The iron cover lifted on its levered hinge much more easily than Cooper had expected.

'There's a counterweight,' said Headon.

'So I see.'

The mechanism looked old, and rust was showing through the green paint in patches. But it worked easily enough, so someone must have done a bit of maintenance on the post in the last eighteen years.

Cooper mounted the step and looked into the shaft. A metal ladder ran vertically down for about twenty feet, and in the light from the open hatch he could see oily water glimmering at the bottom through the mesh of an iron grille set into the floor.

'There isn't too much water,' said Falconer, peering over his shoulder. 'This was always a dry post – not like some of the others. They could flood right up to the shaft if you didn't pump them out regularly. That's the sump you can see there. You won't get your feet too wet.'

'I'm not bothered.'

He clambered gingerly over the edge and found a rung of the ladder with his foot. There wasn't much room in the shaft, and anyone overweight might have had a bit of trouble. When he'd climbed down a few feet, he looked up again at the sky, only for something heavy to hit him hard on the back of the head, making him see stars for a few seconds.

'Oh, sh—!'

'Sorry!' called Headon. 'We should have warned you to watch your head on the counterweight. If you go down in a crouch, it catches your back, and if you straighten up it gives you a crack on the skull. Are you OK?'

'Yes, I'm fine,' said Cooper, though he felt anything but. There'd be a lump on the back of his head tomorrow morning.

He landed at the bottom of the shaft with a small splash. Falconer was right, there was only about an inch of water, not enough even to wet more than the soles of his boots.

'Are you coming down?'

'One of us should stay up on top, for safety,' said Falconer. 'We don't want the hatch blowing shut, do we?'

There was just a moment then, as Cooper looked up at the two faces silhouetted against the sky twenty feet above him, when a small spurt of panic ran through his chest. He couldn't make out the faces of the two men well enough to see what their expressions were, or whether they were exchanging that secretive little glance.

'I'll come down with you,' said Headon. 'I'm more appropriately dressed.'

Cooper waited at the bottom of the shaft while Headon joined him. There wasn't much room for two people standing on the grille of the sump. The handle of a pump protruded from the wall, and Cooper shone his torch on it.

'That hasn't worked for years,' said Headon. 'None of them do, now. They always seemed to be the first thing to seize up.'

'It worked the sump?'

'That's right. You filled the priming point there and pumped the handle. My God, you had to pump hard, though, if you had a wet post. There might have been three or four hours of pumping to be done on a full exercise. One of the lads reckoned once that each stroke of the pump shifted about half an egg cup of water.'

'Well, the exercise kept you warm on a cold night,' said Headon with a laugh over their heads.

'Some posts suffered so much from water that their crews had to bail them out with a bucket lowered down the shaft on a rope. You can imagine how comfortable those places were.'

In a cupboard was an Elsan toilet, like a big green metal can with a plastic seat, still permeated with that distinctive odour of the thick, blue chemical. On a shelf stood a brush and a tub of Glitto – whatever that was. A ventilation louvre stood partly open over the toilet.

Headon opened a door still labelled with a 'no smoking' sign.

'This is the monitoring room. And that's it, really. A full tour of the facilities.'

The room was so low that Cooper felt he ought to duck to avoid banging his head on the ceiling. A table and some drawers stood against the side wall, with a couple of folding chairs. Cabling ran along the wall and vanished upwards, through crumbling polystyrene tiles.

'Seven feet wide and sixteen feet long. Like a giant coffin, we used to say.'

When Cooper pointed his torch at the far wall, he saw two

bunk beds, their mattresses still wrapped in damp plastic, with a second sliding ventilation panel over them. And Headon was right. That was pretty much it. Except for a smell of abandonment and neglect.

'All the operational equipment was taken out, of course,' said Headon. 'On the wall there, you can see the fitting for the bomb-power indicator. The blast pipe was attached to a baffle assembly upstairs. And that hole in the table is where we had the fixed survey meter. That was the fallout radiation sensor, which measured the level of gamma radiation outside. The only other measuring equipment we had was the ground-zero indicator, and that was up top, too.'

'What was that supposed to do?'

'The GZI? It recorded the height and direction of a nuclear detonation, so we could report exactly where a bomb had gone off, and whether it was airburst or groundburst, which made a difference to the fallout.'

'And that's all you could do?'

'It was a simple idea. The only trouble was, someone had to go outside to get the readings off it.'

Cooper realized there was some rubber sheeting on the floor, squelching as his weight squeezed out the water.

'That's conveyor-belt rubber. It was donated by the National Coal Board some time in the eighties. That's all the insulation we had, apart from the polystyrene ceiling tiles.'

After only a few minutes, Cooper was glad to get back up into the daylight. He couldn't imagine staying down there all night, with the hatch closed and nothing more than a dim six-watt bulb to see by. Let alone being trapped down there for the duration. Trapped inside for – what was it? – fourteen days, until it was considered safe to come out? You could go mad down there in fourteen days.

'Seen enough?' asked Falconer.

'Yes, thanks.'

He got clear and watched Falconer re-fix the padlocks and turn the Allen key in its slot.

But even when the hatch was shut and locked again, Cooper still had the feeling that there was something he was missing.

'Well, you finally meet a decent bloke, and he turns out to be a murderer,' said Naomi Widdowson.

Fry looked at her. 'There's something wrong with the logic of that sentence.'

'Well, what I mean is . . . he seemed all right, anyway.'

Naomi was being transferred from the custody suite at West Street to a cell on remand. Magistrates' court would decide whether to bail her on Monday. She had been issued with her personal belongings at the desk and was waiting for the van to pull up in the yard.

'He hasn't been convicted yet,' pointed out Fry. 'In fact, he hasn't even been charged.'

'Yes, but you must be sure that he did it, right?'

'We can't comment on that,' said Fry.

'Like I said in my statement, Adrian went back to the huts when I left. I argued, but I couldn't stop him. So if someone did Rawson in, then it must have been him, mustn't it?'

'It will be for a jury to decide.'

Naomi shrugged. 'I'm cutting my losses, anyway. Time to forget about him and move on, I think. Don't you?'

'Aren't you going to make even the least effort to argue that he's innocent?'

'What? You expect me to stand by him? Act the loyal girl-friend for the newspapers? No way. Absolutely no bloody way. He took some money to do this, didn't he? And he never even told me. Bastard.'

'Did you want a share?'

'It's got nothing to do with me, do you hear? As far as I was concerned, it was all an accident.'

'An accident?'

331

'I had no idea what he meant to do. He let me think he was just going along with the plan. In fact, he seemed to be really into it. Like that thing with the hunting horn. He said it would be a laugh.' Naomi shook her head. 'He was pretty useless at it, though. He'd only learned the one call.'

'The kill call,' said Fry.

'If that's what it was. I wouldn't know.'

Fry and Murfin watched in amazement as Naomi Widdowson walked away towards the van, accompanied by a prison escort officer.

'Well, I've heard about women who care more for their horses than they do for people,' said Murfin. 'And I've just seen one.'

'I'm not a big fan of horses,' said Fry. 'But, even so, I know how she feels.'

That evening, in the CID room, Fry stood by the window. It was only a few minutes after six, but darkness was falling rapidly. Heavy clouds gathered in the sky to the west. More rain was on the way.

She had been watching the pedestrians passing by on the pavement. There was nothing unusual about any of them. They were perfectly ordinary members of the public. A young woman in a smart grey business suit, talking on her mobile; a young couple carrying rucksacks, probably early tourists; a man with a dark beard and stained jeans; two girls with magenta hair and nose studs. Ordinary, innocent passers-by.

But were they all so innocent? How many potential murderers were out there, walking the streets of Edendale? Well, wasn't everyone a potential murderer, in the right circumstances? Or the wrong circumstances. Push any average person into a corner and most of them would cross the line, wouldn't they?

Fry thought so. The vast majority of these people hurrying

by her now probably couldn't imagine what those circumstances would be. But some of them would. A few might have a specific victim in mind right now. Who knew what fantasies were going on in their heads; violent scenarios playing out, involving a partner, a boss, or a motorist who had just given them the V-sign. Only a tiny minority of them would ever follow through on their fantasies, or act out a violent thought. But there was no way of telling who those individuals were. It might be the man with the beard. But it could just as easily be the young businesswoman, who might be plotting bloody vengeance as she chatted on her phone.

Naomi Widdowson might, or might not, have intended Patrick Rawson to die. But she certainly had no regrets that it had happened. She had badly wanted a person's death. Deborah Rawson had gone further than that.

Fry knew there were individuals in prison right now, serving life sentences for murder, who were every bit as ordinary as these passers-by on the streets of Edendale. She'd met some of them, and talked with them. They were people who had found themselves in the wrong circumstances, people who had crossed the line.

She thought about what Angie had told her last night. In a smaller way, her sister had crossed a line at some time, too. But was it ever possible to cross back again?

Cooper dropped David Headon and Keith Falconer back at the pub and bought them a drink for their time. He knew they'd enjoyed themselves, because it had been impossible to stop them talking all the way back to Edendale.

When he left them, Cooper drove home in the dark, remembering that there would be no Randy to welcome him, and never would be again. Was that why he had subconsciously been seeking something to distract himself, an excuse to avoid going home? It was the sort of thing that he suspected of Diane Fry. But it was definitely disheartening to think that the flat would be so dark and silent, with Randy lying in his grave.

He'd heard nothing from Fry since he left West Street, but he hoped for her sake that her interviews had led to a successful conclusion. His own interest in the Rawson enquiry had waned, and he wasn't sure why. It was something to do with the ROC badge he'd found at Eden View, and with Michael Clay's local connection. If Clay hadn't been a member of the Edendale ROC post's crew, why did he have the badge?

As he crossed the lights and turned into Welbeck Street, Cooper thought about the stories Headon and Falconer had been telling him about the 1960s and the start of the Cold War. It was hard for him to imagine what people had gone through in those strange times. The 1960s weren't so far in the past, yet they might as well be a chapter in a history book, for all he could understand of the world those young ROC observers had lived in.

Come to think of it, he didn't think it had even been covered in his Modern History lessons at school. The Cold War did get a mention, the Cuban Missile Crisis, the Vietnam War. But the preparations in Britain for life after a nuclear apocalypse? That had gone unremarked.

Yet for many thousands of ordinary people it had been something right at the forefront of their lives. Any day, any night, they could have heard that rising and falling wail of the siren, following an Attack Warning Red, and know that they had only four minutes. Four minutes – to do what? To find some way to live, and to decide the way they wanted to die.

When he thought about the present enquiry, Cooper felt as though they'd all been drawn off on a false trail, misled by a powerfully laid artificial scent. It seemed as though he and Fry had almost physically been following a trail of meat across the country, their noses close to the ground, sniffing the scent like a pack of hounds. But, like all hounds, they were easily mis-directed by a clever and experienced saboteur.

For a moment, Cooper wondered what those big, purple steaks of horse meat that Fry had described actually smelled like.

But he knew, of course. Like all meat, they would smell of blood.

In their underground bunkers, the ROC observers would have been able to lock down the hatch and protect themselves against nuclear blasts and radioactive fallout. But there were some things you couldn't close your door against. Time, death, the plague.

The people of Eyam had done much the same thing when the Black Death hit their village, hadn't they? Battened down the hatches, stayed indoors waiting out the storm, until the fallout cleared, emerging only to bury their dead. He imagined Mompesson's parishioners peering out of their cottage windows, praying that it was safe, that the holocaust was finally over. But wondering, all the same, whose turn it was to die today.

36

Journal of 1968

Well, then came the time for Les to die. He might have been number one, but he had to take his turn. Nature stepped in, struck him down with a heart attack. And I couldn't say I was sorry.

Since then, there have been some days when I would just go down there and think. For a while, we still had the folding chairs, the wooden cupboard, a set of drawers that came out of Les's kitchen. Now and then, I would light one of the tommy cookers at the bottom of the shaft, though it would take twenty minutes to boil a kettle, the way it always did.

For a few minutes, I'd sit and remember the foul air, the cold of the concrete that crept into flesh and bone. We wore two of everything back then, because once the cold got into your bones, you would never get warm again. There was always an icy draught across your feet as you sat there waiting for the messages, filling in the log, baling out the sump. The only thing you could do was go for a walk or run round upstairs. We were pretty numb by the end of the night.

Of course, the pit was long since derelict and overgrown. When we were active, we were given an allowance to keep it tidy. Twenty-five pounds a year, I think it was. The grass wasn't allowed to grow then, not a single weed or thistle was allowed.

In the real old days, we spent our time watching the sky for rats. But it was all different when the 1960s came round. Instead of the sky, we had a concrete ceiling and a pair of metal-framed bunk beds. Some blokes sneaked in a comfy chair or two, curtains, or an office desk. Once we took down some carpet pieces. Years afterwards, they still lay there, half-rotted.

I don't know what would have happened if it had really all kicked off one time. I reckon it would have been a bit like musical chairs, a matter of luck who found themselves down below. We talked a lot about what would happen to our families. You wanted to be sure they were looked after, if you were one of the crew underground.

But some of us never knew, were never entirely sure, whether we'd leave our wives and children when it came to it. Once you were down there, you might have to stay for a fortnight. Imagine waiting for the message to come – those three fatal words: Attack Warning Red. Then measuring the fireball over your own county, taking the elevation and bearing, waiting for the radioactive dust cloud to arrive. Attack Warning Black.

And that meant the maroons. Three of them, of course. According to regulations, we were supposed to fire them, one after the other, to warn against nuclear fallout. Two bangs meant nothing; it was the third one that counted.

So what about Jimmy and Les? Did they mean nothing? Was Shirley's death the one that really mattered, the final thump and scream that changed the whole world? There are some situations where we have no regulations to follow, some questions that can only be answered from the heart.

And here we are, forty years later . . . Did there have to be so many deaths to restore the balance? I thought there was just one, but I was wrong. There had to be another, and another.

It's funny, really funny, how everything happens in threes.

37

Sunday

It had rained heavily again during the night. Below ground, the limestone caves of the White Peak would be flooding dangerously, water roaring through fissures and cracks like thunder, scouring another half a centimetre from the rock.

Yet when the sun came out after heavy rain, the amount of colour in the landscape was stunning. On the main street of Eyam that Sunday morning, Cooper could detect a real feeling of spring in the air. He could smell it, and taste it, and even sense its warmth on his skin.

Each year, it was becoming more difficult to judge when to expect this feeling. It seemed to come anywhere between the middle of January and April. That was climate change, he supposed. Hawthorns were in blossom in February instead of May, blackthorns had been flowering since the end of January. Once again, there had been no real winter.

Cooper had passed an ancient lock-up garage with a collapsing roof. And here on the village green were the stocks, still intact – a reminder of the days when justice was not only harsh, but had to be publicly seen to be done.

In this part of Eyam, there were no pavements or foot-paths, doors opened directly on to the road. He could never resist peeking into the front windows that were so temptingly available to the passers-by. Didn't other people do that?

He looked up at the sound of a car, but it passed him by, and he walked back down the road. He found himself standing in front of Plague Cottage again, where the Black Death had first arrived in Eyam. A massive stone lintel sat over the door of the cottage, pressing down on the frame, as if representing the great weight of history.

'So this is Eyam. Sorry – Eem.'

Fry was standing on the pavement a few feet away, not looking at him but at the houses. She was regarding them as if they were exhibits in a museum – which, in a way, they were.

'I didn't think you would come,' he said.

'It was touch and go. The washing and ironing nearly won.'

Cooper smiled. He had been amazed when Fry agreed to come. He'd been expecting the usual rejection, the sharp response of someone who had far better things to do with her time than socialize with her colleagues, thank you very much. He didn't know what had changed in her, to make her accept. But now she was here, he realized he had no proper plan. He'd only suggested Eyam because it seemed to have some relevance, a link to the one aspect of life they had in common.

'And this is the Plague Cottage.'

Fry looked at the green plaque with its gold lettering.

Edward Cooper, aged four, died on the 22nd
September 1665
Jonathan Cooper, aged twelve, died on the 2nd
October 1665
Mary alone survived, but lost thirteen relatives.

'Two brothers, who died within days of each other,' said Fry.

'They told us in school that the arrival of the Black Death was blamed on a miasma,' said Cooper. '"Evil humours" drifting in the air. Women carried scented posies around to ward off the poisonous fumes, and men smoked pipes, hoping to protect themselves with tobacco smoke.'

He felt no need of maps or tourist guides to find his way around Eyam now. It had a familiar feel to it already. As they walked, they passed interesting little alleyways, passages into back yards and stone-flagged ginnels. At one point an enormous stone water trough stood by the side of the lane, a trickle of water still issuing from a pipe in the wall, as it must have done for centuries.

For a few minutes, they ploughed through the usual small talk. Cooper had wanted to prise Fry away from the office, disentangle her from any of her crime scenes, and get her on neutral ground where they could talk about something other than work. Eyam had been the best place he could think of, without sounding too unlikely.

But he was finding it hard going. Fry constantly steered the conversation back to a safe topic. Of course, the murder of Patrick Rawson had absorbed her attention for the past week. It had opened her eyes to subjects she hadn't been aware of before, too. It was bound to be in her mind.

'So what about the wife?' said Cooper, finally giving in to the inevitable. 'Deborah Rawson?'

'She'll be charged with conspiracy to murder. She didn't kill her husband herself, but she arranged it, at least.'

'And it was well planned, too.'

'She's a woman,' said Fry. 'She would have worked it all out in her mind, run through the scenario over and over, imagined what it would be like, and how she would feel afterwards. It wouldn't have been some spontaneous impulse to violence, with no thought or emotion behind it. That's a man's type of crime.'

'You think anyone is capable of murder, don't you?' said Cooper.

'Yes.'

Cooper had parked the Toyota near St Lawrence's Church, and they strolled through the churchyard as Fry told him the story. St Lawrence's boasted a large sundial over the chancel door, and a small group of visitors stood in front of it, checking the time and trying to figure out the Roman numerals. At some time, a motto had been inscribed in Latin on the supporting stones. It was almost worn away, but Cooper could just make out in the right light: *Ut umbra sic vita* – 'As the shadow passes, so does life'.

'So Deborah Rawson contacted Naomi Widdowson and told her when her husband would be visiting Derbyshire?' he said.

Fry nodded. 'Yes. Naomi had been phoning Sutton Coldfield, trying to get hold of Patrick Rawson to give him a piece of her mind. Deborah got talking to her, and decided to use her. It's all backed up by the phone records. She gave Miss Widdowson her husband's mobile phone number, so she could arrange to meet him. It seems Naomi told him she had some horses for sale.'

'Thoroughbreds, ideal for their meat?'

'Exactly.'

Cooper looked at Fry's face to read her expression. She sounded almost approving of the attention to detail that had gone into Deborah Rawson's planning. But the satisfaction in her eyes might just have been her contentment at being able to discuss work, when she'd feared some kind of social occasion.

'It all hangs together,' said Fry. 'Rawson had told Melvyn Senior that he'd have some horses that would need transporting later in the week, and he'd also phoned Hawley's abattoir to book them in for slaughter. As far as Rawson was concerned, the deal was all set up.'

When the tourists had moved on, the only sound in the churchyard was the wind stirring the branches of the trees.

341

Cooper still thought it was strange that the only plague victim buried here was the rector's wife. The dead bodies were hardly likely to be infectious – they would already have been abandoned by plague-carrying fleas in favour of living hosts. The same sort of thing had gone on everywhere in the Middle Ages, though no amount of corpse-dumping would have saved a doomed town when the plague swept through Europe.

He realized that Fry was looking at him oddly, a faintly derisive smile suggesting that he was behaving in exactly the way she expected. Cooper wondered if this idea was going to work, or whether she would lose patience with him and walk away. The situation seemed so fragile.

'I don't understand why Rawson went back to horse dealing when he had his other enterprises,' he said, desperate to regain her attention.

'Well, he was getting himself into financial difficulties with the new ventures,' said Fry. 'He'd stretched himself too far, that was his problem. The house in Sutton Coldfield was fully mortgaged to raise capital for the meat-distribution business. But with the way the housing market has been, the property was worth less and less, and interest rates were going up. That outbreak of trichinosis would have ruined R & G Enterprises. Their hopes of public acceptance of horse meat would have been wiped out in a stroke.'

'I can just imagine the headlines,' said Cooper. 'So Rawson was going back to his old living?'

'It had done well for him in the past, and he'd managed to keep just the right side of the law, despite everything. Patrick Rawson was a man confident of his own abilities. And Naomi Widdowson came forward and offered him the perfect deal at exactly the right time. The psychology of it was very clever.'

'That doesn't sound like something Naomi would figure out.'

'No, of course she didn't.' Fry sounded exasperated, as if

she thought he wasn't really listening. 'It was all planned by Deborah Rawson.'

'Oh, right,' said Cooper.

They were passing a corner by the Riley Graves, one of Eyam's macabre little tourist attractions. The majority of plague victims were buried in unknown graves, but here was a memorial to John Hancock, who'd died at the height of the plague. The inscription was just about legible, despite some cracking to the gravestone.

As I doe now, So must thou lye.
Remember, man, That thou shalt die.

'But why would Rawson's wife set him up like that?' said Cooper.

'She'd convinced herself that her husband was having an affair. She overheard some argument between him and Michael Clay over payments that were going out through one of their business accounts.'

'Rent for the house? Eden View?'

'Yes. Deborah put two and two together, and came up with the conclusion that her husband had a love nest in Derbyshire, and that explained why he was in the habit of spending longer away from home than seemed necessary for business purposes.'

'I see.'

Cooper saw that many of the names on adjacent gravestones to John Hancock's were members of the Hancock family. The plague had taken old and young, grandparents and children. None had escaped. As a result, John Hancock's wife Elizabeth had buried almost her whole family here in the course of a week, struggling through the fields every day with a diseased corpse for the protection of the village. Self-sacrifice and the acceptance of suffering weren't fashionable ideals any more, were they?

343

'I think that was the first sign I had that she was lying,' said Fry, breaking into his thoughts again.

'What was?'

'Aren't you listening, Ben? When Deborah insisted she'd never had any suspicions about Patrick. It didn't fit with the picture of the man I'd built up.'

'A charming rogue, with a smooth tongue and a casual disregard for the truth.'

'Exactly. Deborah Rawson would have been mad not to wonder occasionally whether she could trust him. But when I asked her, she exaggerated the lie too much. She would have been better telling me a small part of the truth.'

'You're getting very cynical about people, Diane,' said Cooper, as they walked on.

'I always was,' said Fry. 'Always.'

She was right that he was having difficulty listening to her. This wasn't what he'd come to talk about, and her manner was making him nervous. She was freezing up minute by minute.

'The trouble was, Deborah had it completely wrong,' said Fry. 'It was Michael Clay who was making the payments, supporting his brother's illegitimate daughter. That's the poison of suspicion. Anything you hear can seem like evidence.'

Cooper nodded as they headed back to the village square. A powerful smell of cooking food hit him. Food. That would make a difference.

'So Patrick Rawson's death only happened on our turf because of the existence of Eden View and Michael Clay's niece?' he said.

'Yes.'

'But Naomi Widdowson insisted in interview that Rawson's death was an accident, didn't she?' said Cooper. 'She said they just wanted to scare him, to pay him back for all the distress he'd caused to her, and scores of people like her.'

'That might have been what Naomi thought,' said Fry. 'Her boyfriend Adrian Tarrant is quite a different matter. I knew

344

I recognized him at the hunt meeting, when he was acting as a steward. Just the sort of person the hunting fraternity don't need if they want to improve their image, Ben.'

'Fair enough.'

'And Deborah Rawson made quite a separate deal with him. She paid him three thousand pounds.'

'Three thousand pounds? It's not much, really.'

'It is, if you think you're going to get away with it. And Adrian Tarrant thought he would.'

'Just as Patrick Rawson always did.'

'I suppose so.'

Cooper thought back to the hunt saboteurs' report of hearing the kill call on the morning of the hunt. Earlier, there had been the phone call from Naomi Widdowson to Patrick Rawson, the call that had brought him to his death. That was a kind of kill call in its own way. And there had been the call from Deborah Rawson to Adrian Tarrant, too.

'The argument Mr Wakeley heard . . .' said Cooper.

'Yes?'

'I was assuming he'd heard Naomi Widdowson shouting at Patrick Rawson, and perhaps Rawson arguing back. That doesn't fit with the story, though, does it?'

'Not quite,' said Fry. 'Naomi must certainly have shouted at him about Rosie. But Rawson didn't stand there and argue with her. He ran.'

'Yes. So the rest of the argument must have been between Naomi and Adrian, mustn't it?'

Fry nodded. 'Of course. She didn't want Tarrant to go back to the hut, she was trying to make him come away with her. I think Naomi was telling the truth on this point – that she only wanted to give Patrick Rawson a scare. But Adrian had another job to do.'

'He wasn't much of a hit man, though. Too fond of un-necessary showiness – I mean, the business with the hunting horn and all that. The kill call.'

'Well, he enjoyed the work too much,' said Fry. 'That was his problem. It doesn't do to get emotionally involved.'

'So I've heard.'

Then Cooper remembered David Headon's almost casual reference to Attack Warning Red, the recognized alert to an imminent nuclear attack during the 1960s. Attack Warning Red? That would have been the kill call on a massive scale.

They had lunch at the Miners' Arms, a pub boasting that it was old enough to be pre-plague. Fry ate bacon-wrapped chicken breast stuffed with leeks and mushrooms, while Cooper had the home-made venison and orange pie.

As they ate, Cooper tried to close his ears to the voice of a man at a nearby table, boasting to two women that he kept a loaded pistol on his bedside table, in case of burglars. *'If I caught a burglar in my house, I'd shoot him. It's the way I was trained.'*

'I heard your cat died,' said Fry, draining half a glass of the house white.

As small talk, it wasn't a brilliant opening. Cooper looked at the rapidly disappearing wine and wondered if Fry could really be as nervous as she seemed, so unaccustomed to a purely social situation.

'How did you hear that?' asked Cooper, genuinely curious about her sources of information.

'Oh, it was mentioned around the office,' said Fry vaguely. 'Becky Hurst said something, I think.'

Office gossip, then? He didn't think she ever noticed it, let alone paid any attention to it.

'Yes, it's true. Though I'm not entirely sure he was mine. He kind of came with the flat, and adopted me.'

'Shame, though.'

'You're not a cat person, are you?' said Cooper. 'I'm sure you can't be.'

'Why shouldn't I be?'

'Well . . . no, you're just not, Diane.'

Fry swallowed some more wine. 'Can't stand 'em,' she admitted. 'Aren't you going to get a new one?'

'I'm going to look this afternoon.'

'From a sanctuary?'

'Yes.'

'I thought it would be.'

Despite his best intentions, Cooper felt himself bridle at her tone. 'What do you mean?'

'Human or animal, it has to be a lost cause with you. You have to be able to ride in like a knight in shining armour and perform the noble rescue. It's what you get off on. I've seen it often enough.'

Her accusation was so unfair that Cooper didn't know what to say. How had she known that he would choose a sanctuary? He'd been thinking only the other day of Cats Protection, who had a centre somewhere near Ashbourne. But there was a sanctuary closer than that, just outside Edendale, and he'd decided to give them a try first. That wasn't wrong, was it? Anyone would do the same, rather than leave all those animals abandoned in cages.

Fry put down her glass for a moment.

'Can I ask you something?'

Cooper could feel the mood change, like a cold draught blowing through the bar. He almost looked round to see who'd left the door open.

'Go ahead.'

'Did you ever really understand why I came to Derbyshire from Birmingham?'

'Well, there was your sister,' said Cooper cautiously, remembering a particularly difficult period between them, and reluctant to open up any old wounds. 'You thought she was living in this part of the world. Sheffield, right?'

'Yes. And?'

Fry gazed at him challengingly, waiting for a reply. It made

Cooper feel as though he was a suspect in an interview room, forced to fill that uncomfortable silence with some confession of his own.

'Well, I heard you had a bad time in Birmingham,' he said.

'A bad time?' Fry tossed back the rest of her wine and looked around for another. 'What does that mean?'

'There was the assault case.'

'Oh, you heard about that? Who told you?'

Cooper shifted nervously. He recalled mentioning it himself, to Liz Petty.

'I don't know, Diane. It was a story that went around the office, not long after you arrived.'

'I'd like to know who spread the story.'

'I honestly don't know. Are you saying it isn't true?'

'No, it's quite true.'

'I appreciate it's something you might not want to talk about.'

Fry stared at her empty glass. For a moment, Cooper thought she was going to start talking to him about it, that she wanted to tell him about the rape that had blighted her career in the West Midlands and had followed her to Derbyshire, like a shadow.

But if the thought had crossed her mind, she decided against it. Cooper realized that she wasn't going to say more. Though he'd barely touched his own drink, he fetched her another glass of wine, and after a while the conversation moved on.

'Lies,' said Fry. 'Casual disregard for the truth. Why do people always feel the need to lie, even about the smallest things?'

'It's an occupational hazard in our business,' said Cooper, watching her attack her full glass.

Fry nodded. 'My sister called me this week.'

Cooper froze. Not only at the unexpected turn of the conversation, but at Fry's sudden change of tone. Just when he thought she was about to thaw a little, she produced a knife to stab into his guts.

'Angie?' he said, knowing that he sounded completely feeble.

'I don't have any other sisters.'

'Is she . . .?' Cooper didn't know what he meant to ask.

'Much the same as the last time you talked to her,' said Fry. 'Probably much the same as the first time, too.'

'Diane, I know we never talked about that –'

'You're damn right we didn't.'

'Is there anything I can say that would help?'

'You can tell me why you went to all that trouble to find my sister and plot with her behind my back. It's something you should have explained to me a long time ago, Ben. A long time.'

'I didn't,' said Cooper.

'What?'

'I didn't find her. She found me.'

He was starting to feel a bit more confident now. None of it had been his fault, really. He knew that. But Diane was right – he'd never explained it to her. He'd been afraid to.

Fry stared at him. 'Are you saying it was all Angie's idea?'

'Yes.'

That didn't make her look any happier. Cooper searched for the right words to use that would get him past this moment. But Fry was too impatient, and she couldn't wait for him to make his mind up.

'More lies,' she said. 'It gets depressing.'

'Diane –'

She held up a hand. 'No, that's enough. I shouldn't have asked. I ought to have known better.'

There was an awkward silence. Cooper fidgeted, wishing for an excuse to get up and move away. He exchanged glances with the people at the other table, who'd been staring at Fry. They turned away in embarrassment.

To his immense relief, it was Fry who broke the silence.

349

She seemed to have two distinct halves to her brain, the way she could switch from one to the other so easily. But there was no doubt about it, thought Cooper – the professional part of her brain was the one that assumed dominance most easily.

'Lies,' she said again, and took a long breath, as if inhaling the fumes from her wine. 'You know, the first person to deceive us in the Rawson enquiry was the manager at Le Chien Noir,' she said.

'How is that?' said Cooper, eager to encourage this time.

'He was so vague about the man that Patrick Rawson was having dinner with that Monday night. He couldn't give a completely misleading description, in case we asked anyone else and their version contradicted his. So he was deliberately vague. He knew perfectly well who the other man was – Maurice Gains, Rawson's partner in R & G Enterprises.'

'Oh. They were trying to find restaurants to serve their horse meat, weren't they?'

'Of course,' said Fry. She took another long gulp of her drink. 'But they already had wind of the trichinosis outbreak. The restaurant must have been desperate to avoid any suggestion they were serving horse meat. Reputation is every-thing in that business. Neil Connelly was already trying to distance Le Chien Noir from the bad publicity.'

'What are you going to do?'

'Suggest that Environmental Health pay a visit to Le Chien Noir.'

Cooper noticed that she was having a bit of difficulty saying the name of the restaurant. The third time it had definitely come out wrong.

'Diane, are you all right?'

'Why does everyone keep asking me if I'm all right?'

'Well . . . I don't know why everyone else does,' said Cooper. 'But I just noticed you seemed to be drinking quite fast.

For a lunchtime, anyway. I didn't know you were a day-time drinker.'

'I'm not.'

'OK.'

'Except in exceptional circumstances.'

Cooper laughed uneasily. 'You almost managed to say that without slurring.'

'I don't slur. I've never slurred in my life. I'm a positively slur-free zone.'

Overwhelmed with relief that the moment had passed, Cooper began to feel giddy with the idea that had come into his head.

'You know what?' he said. 'I think we should go for a walk. A bit of fresh air will do us good. Did you bring your boots?'

'It's raining,' protested Fry.

'No, it's stopped. It's nice and fresh out there.'

38

They crossed the road at Middleton Dale, then walked up through the Tarmac site at Darlton Quarry, its sides terraced like a huge amphitheatre. Excavators were loading dumper trucks in the bottom of the quarry. A hydraulic drill probed at the rubble, splitting the larger stones. Nearer by, a giant shovel sculpted the edges of the worked-out areas.

Black Harry Lane was marked with wooden sign posts etched with horseshoe symbols. A bridlepath, then. Fields would be separated by gates, not stiles. But Cooper could see that this wouldn't be easy going for a horse. One section of bridleway was so split and crevassed that it looked as though it had been involved in the same earthquake that had left those giant gashes on Longstone Edge.

It struck Cooper that Naomi Widdowson and her boyfriend had been almost a modern equivalent to Black Harry as they waylaid the unsuspecting Patrick Rawson, though the actual robbery had been left to Sean Crabbe.

Along the edge of the lane were a few skeletal hawthorn trees shattered by the wind, their branches broken, their buds blotched with leprous patches of lichen. They passed a dried-up watering hole, where sheep had stepped into the mud in search of the last inch of water. The concrete lining must have cracked, so that no amount of rain would ever fill it up again.

'Deborah Rawson says she believed her husband was having an affair,' said Fry, 'and that might be true. But I think Patrick Rawson did something quite unforgivable in Deborah's eyes, and it wasn't to do with another woman.'

'What?'

'He proved that Erin Lacey was right about him. At heart, he was just a dodgy Irish horse dealer. That must have been the killer for Deborah Rawson.'

'What – the fact that he'd gone back to horse dealing when she thought he was becoming a respectable businessman? Or the fact that Erin Lacey had been proved right?'

Fry nodded. 'Both. There was certainly no love lost between those two women. So it was a double whammy. Can't you just hear Mrs Lacey's reaction?'

'"*Blood will out*" – that sort of thing.'

'Exactly.'

'So if he hadn't been tempted by the call that Naomi Widdowson made . . .'

'He might still be alive now. Yes, that was what sealed his fate, I'm sure of it.'

'But Deborah would rather let people think that he was having an affair, betraying her with another woman.'

'Image,' said Fry breathlessly. 'It's all about image.'

From Black Harry Gate, a path ran eastwards through a steep-sided dale that squirmed its way towards Calver. But Cooper continued to lead the way towards the rakes on Longstone Moor, where the sheep were still playing chicken with the quarry lorries. Who would be the last to get out of the way? From the stubborn expressions on their faces, these sheep didn't realize how unequal the confrontation was.

Finally, he stopped to allow Fry to get her breath, and looked out over the patchwork of fields. The sun was breaking sporadically through the clouds, highlighting one field and then another, changing the colours in the landscape as it went, catching a white-painted farmhouse, casting faint shadows from a copse of trees.

The tracery of white limestone walls was spread out before him like a map laid over the landscape. Cooper sometimes thought that if you just followed the right lines in that map, you could discover any story you were looking for, find the right clues to any mystery. All the answers seemed to lie in this gleaming web, so painstakingly constructed that they almost held the countryside together.

And there was still a question to be answered. The charges against Naomi Widdowson and Adrian Tarrant ought to feel like a conclusion. But instead, it was quite the opposite. The death of Patrick Rawson now felt like a distraction. The real mystery was what had happened to his partner.

Officers in blue boiler suits were still working their way along the edge of Longstone Moor, trying to pick up traces of Michael Clay.

'Hey, look,' said Cooper. 'It's Sitz, Platz, Holen and Bissen.'

He looked at Fry, to see if she'd heard the joke around the office. Derbyshire Constabulary had recently been buying German-speaking police dogs, which meant that dog handlers had to learn the German commands to make their dogs work properly. Some wag had named the dog handlers after the German commands for sit, stay, fetch and bite: *Sitz, Platz, Holen* and *Bissen*.

'Somewhere there ought to be an "Aus",' said Fry. 'Let go.'

'Yes,' said Cooper, searching for clues to whether he should be laughing or not. He marvelled at the change that had taken place in her. For a short while this afternoon, he thought he'd got close to the real Diane Fry. But she'd slipped away from him and he'd lost the scent. And that was wrong, because this was his territory, not hers.

Cooper gazed around. You could see Longstone Moor quite clearly from here. On these moors there were still traces of the old packhorse ways that had once been used by travellers such as pedlars, tinkers and badgers. The inhabitants of one valley often knew nothing of the neighbouring dale, because they were separated by inhospitable moorland. For directions, they had only rock formations with descriptive names, or ancient man-made features. *Head for the Eagle Stone, turn left at Hob Hurst's House.*

And the biggest problem was the weather, which changed so suddenly on the moors. Low cloud, heavy rain, fog, snow – they could all reduce visibility so much that travellers often lost their way during the winter, and that meant losing their lives. Just as Philip Worsley had on Wednesday.

The landscape was scattered with the small white dots of sheep, a typical White Peak sight. But here and there among them, like alien giants, were much larger objects, bright yellow, their long necks swinging as they hunted backwards and forwards, the scream of their alarms reaching him on the wind. Quarrying machines, hacking out more limestone to fill the dumper trucks. Soon, this landscape would be gone for ever.

'And what about Michael Clay?' asked Cooper. 'Is there a woman involved there, too?'

Fry frowned. 'Well, not his niece, Pauline Outram. And not his daughter, either.'

'Could there be some other local connection then, apart from Pauline? What if there's a real significance in the Royal Observer Corps stuff?'

'But Michael Clay didn't serve in the Observer Corps,' said Fry.

'No.'

Cooper recalled the photo of the ROC members. Their blue battledress tunics, their berets at rakish and unflattering angles, their cap badges glinting. It had been a colour photo, so he'd guessed the date to have been the sixties. In the photo, the ROC crew were standing in front of a small brick tower with no roof and a set of steps up the outside wall. An aircraft-monitoring post. According to David Headon, the last overground structures had been abandoned when the RAF no longer required the ROC for that purpose.

Then he realized what he'd been missing. When he'd first spoken to Headon about the ROC, he'd mentioned cutbacks in the Corps. But he hadn't been talking about the final stand down in 1991. That was Cooper's own mistake, a wrong assumption.

So what was it that David Headon had said, exactly? *'There were thousands of us, until the cutbacks started in the sixties.'*

The sixties, of course. But if there had been a big reduction in the number of observers four decades ago, then there must also have been a cut in the number of posts. Cooper pictured the map again, with that imaginary line running across Derbyshire and South Yorkshire. It was a big area for a cluster of observation posts to cover. And it wouldn't be the way you planned it, if you were creating the network from scratch. It was more the sort of arrangement you'd end up with if some of your posts had been closed. The result of cutbacks.

The other clusters in the county all formed triangles. That made sense. So why wasn't it the case in the north of the county? Well, he suspected it had been, once. A trio of posts – one at Buxton, and a couple of others around, say, Hope and Eyam.

So, if he was right, where was that closed post?

Cooper found himself standing above Birchlow, looking down on some of the land belonging to Rough Side Farm. Near the top of the slope was that strange hump that he'd taken for the remains of an Iron Age hill fort, or the capped shaft of an ancient lead mine.

Then he saw the line of truncated telegraph poles next to the site, and realized he'd been wrong. History was all around him in this area, yes. Thousands of years of it, dating all the

356

way from the Romans and the Neolithic stone circle builders. But not all of its history went back quite so far.

He looked round for Fry. 'Diane, will you come with me to see an old friend?' he asked.

She automatically looked at her watch. 'Well . . .'

'Unless you've got something better to do, of course.'

David Headon nodded over his glass of beer in the pub. 'Yes, a lot of ROC posts closed in 1968. Late in the year, it was. October. The cutbacks, like I said. It *was* 1968, after all. A Labour government, Harold Wilson – you remember?'

'Well, no, I don't.'

Headon squinted at him. 'You can't remember what the sixties were like. You're not old enough. I forget that you young people weren't even around then. You missed something, you know.'

'Music, drugs and sex, right? The Beatles, LSD and mini-skirts.'

'Bollocks. That's just the PR. The sixties always had a lot of good public relations men, I'll say that for them. They have a much better image than the fifties or seventies. Well, it wasn't like that.'

'That's a bit disappointing.'

'Look at this place,' said Headon. 'Do you think it was all sex and drugs and rock'n'roll here in the sixties?'

'Well –'

'Was it buggery. If you wanted all that stuff, you had to go to London. The Clappergate bus shelter wasn't exactly Carnaby Street.'

'The Clappergate – ?'

'That's where we kids used to hang about. It had a shelter, you see – so it was the only place to get out of the rain, if you didn't fancy the youth club. And the only drug we ever saw in that bus shelter was the nub end of a Woodbine.'

'I bet your dad had a Ford Anglia, too,' said Fry.

Headon glowered at her. 'No, he had a brand-new Mark II Cortina. But it was about more than that, a lot more. And not all of it was good. Not everything about the sixties was swinging.'

'What do you mean?' asked Cooper.

'It's hard to explain if you didn't experience it. But some of us who were youngsters at the time grew up with the idea that we could die at any moment. Blown to bits in a fireball and a mushroom cloud. We genuinely believed that World War Three could start at any time. It was worst around the time of the Cuban Missile Crisis, of course, a few years earlier. That was when –'

'Yes, I did study a bit of Modern History at school. The Cold War, and all that.'

'History? Well, I suppose it is history, now. No, the sixties were the Berlin Wall, John F. Kennedy's assassination, the Six-Day War in the Middle East. The Soviet Union and China were both testing atomic bombs. And everyone talked about the four-minute warning we'd get of a nuclear attack. At school, we didn't discuss whether there'd be a nuclear war but what we'd do in those last four minutes.'

Fry laughed. 'Among schoolboys? I bet there was a reasonable consensus.'

'So what happened to the ROC when the cuts happened?' insisted Cooper.

'About half the Derbyshire posts were closed. We lost Baslow, Chinley, Hope, and several others. The strength was reduced by fifty per cent in 1968, each post was limited to a maximum of ten observers.'

Cooper nodded. When you came to think about the events of the 1960s, the world must have seemed a pretty unstable place. Student revolutionaries on the streets. Civil rights, women's lib. A time when anything seemed possible. And, if you'd asked his mother at the time, the biggest sign that the world was coming to an end would have been the introduction of decimal coins, those strange new ten-pence pieces that were making their way into her purse.

'Yes, it was a very weird time,' said Headon. 'All around us, people spent their time talking about pop music and fashion, as if they were the only things that were important. But we knew the apocalypse was a real possibility. You know the nuclear strategy of the super powers was called MAD – Mutually Assured Destruction? It was commonplace to fear the end of the world. Now no one knows what an air-raid siren sounds like, or a fallout warning. I've even heard sirens going off by mistake, and no one takes a blind bit of notice.'

'So the posts must have been re-organized. Including 8 Group?'

'Of course. In fact, it was only after the re-organization that we became part of 8 Group. Until 1968, we were 18 Group here. Based in Leeds, that was.'

'Really?'

Headon laughed. 'It's a long way from Leeds, I know – but that's just the way they divided the country. Edendale was Post 18/R5 back then. We were part of the 18 Group R-Cluster, along with Buxton and Baslow, and Hope. And Birchlow, too.'

Fry and Cooper looked at each other. 'Birchlow?'

'Yes, Post 4. That was one they closed. The clusters became bigger, and this area was moved into Coventry district instead of Leeds. Those earlier posts were just handed back to the landowners. And you know how much care some farmers take of historic sites on their land.'

'Why didn't you mention the Birchlow post before?' said Cooper.

'Because of its history. It's best to let sleeping dogs lie, isn't it? People in Birchlow don't like anyone poking their noses into old trouble.'

Cooper sighed. The old man with the clock, Mr Wakeley, had almost told him this when Cooper visited his home in

Eyam on Wednesday. *Skeletons in the cupboard*, that was what he'd said. Was there some kind of family feud here that went back over the decades? The sort of story that everyone knew about, and no one ever mentioned. In a small community, people who hated each other had no chance of avoiding contact, as they might in a city. So they did the next best thing, and kept their mouth shut. He should have pushed Mr Wakeley to explain what he meant, but at the time he'd put it down to an old man just wanting someone to talk to.

'I think you'd better tell us about it, David,' said Cooper. 'We're going to find out now, one way or another.'

Headon stared into his glass. 'Someone died. A boy got killed.'

39

'I don't really understand this, Ben,' said Fry. 'But we need to know more about these deaths. You're right – there is some connection, isn't there?'

'I think so, Diane. But I just can't see why, or what the link is.'

'I'll make a few calls. It should all be on record.'

'What about Pauline Outram? Do you think she knows more than she told us?'

Fry thought for a moment. 'No. She was genuine. Don't forget, she never knew her mother, or her father either. She has no memories of her own from that time, and none that have been passed down to her, either.'

'And everyone else in Birchlow seems to have decided not to talk about it.'

'We'll see.'

The archives took a lot of tracking down on a Sunday. Without the internet and digital archiving, they would have had to wait another day. But, over the course of the afternoon, they dug out newspaper reports of the original incident, an inquest report, photographs of some of the individuals involved. Bit by bit, they managed to piece together the story. The story of the Birchlow observer post.

'June 1968,' said Cooper. 'They were dismantling at the end of an exercise. Three observers on a shift, as usual. The young man who died was Jimmy Hind.'

Fry had brought a drink of water to her desk. Archives made her mouth feel dry, even when they were digital. She could practically feel the dust on the back of her throat. But it was such a relief to be back at work properly. She felt much more at ease now, restored to her own environment, with Cooper back in his chair, head bent over a file. Enough socializing for now.

'The other two people involved were . . .?' she said.

'The first was Leslie Michael Clay – he was leading observer, the number one in charge of the post during the shift.'

'Leslie Michael Clay? But that can't be the same Clay we're looking for. He'd be well into his eighties by now.'

'Our Michael Clay is fifty-one. He would have been too young in 1968.'

'This was probably his father then, do you think?'

'Could be,' said Cooper. 'Then there was the number two observer. Jimmy Hind's friend, Peter Massey.'

'Your farmer at Rough Side Farm. Go on.'

'At the end of an exercise, the crew had to take down and dismantle all the equipment. The smaller items they took home with them for safe-keeping, but the larger bits of equipment were stored inside the post. When the accident happened, Clay and Massey were lowering the siren down the shaft, and it seems they hadn't tied a very good knot. Hind was underneath it, waiting to position it at the bottom of the shaft.'

For a moment, they both studied the photograph of the post crew. Jimmy Hind was identifiable from the newspaper pictures. A slight young man in round, wire-rimmed glasses, with long hair sticking out from under his beret.

'It was reported at the inquest that Clay was a lot bigger

and stronger than Massey, so maybe there wasn't an equal strain on the rope, but they could never be sure exactly what went wrong. Anyway, when it was halfway down, the siren bumped off the side of the shaft, and a knot slipped loose. Hind might have tried to dodge – there was a sort of toilet cubicle just behind him. But he didn't make it. The siren hit Hind on the head, cracked his skull open. He went down, and the siren broke both his legs when it fell on him.'

'And he was killed outright?'

'Not outright. He lived on for a couple of weeks, before they turned off his life support.'

'How old was Jimmy Hind again?' asked Fry.

'Seventeen.'

'All his life ahead of him.'

Cooper nodded. 'That's what the coroner said, too.'

Fry looked at the printouts Cooper had gathered. She had the impression that he, too, was glad to be back at work. Since they'd both returned from Longstone Moor, their eyes had hardly met – the reports they'd unearthed had taken all their attention. With luck, some of the things they'd talked about today would never be mentioned again.

'You've got another inquest there,' she said.

'I looked up Shirley Outram, too.'

'Pauline's mother?'

'Yes. Shirley Outram died in 1970. Inquest verdict: took her own life while the balance of her mind was disturbed.'

'Pauline said her mother killed herself. That's why she was brought up in foster homes.'

'I wonder why she wasn't actually adopted?' said Cooper.

'Some children aren't. They just never find the right home.'

'I suppose so.'

'How did Shirley do it?' asked Fry. 'A drowning, wasn't it?'

'Yes. They found her floating in Birch Reservoir.'

'Floating. So she must have been dead a few days. And no one else was involved?'

'Not that was ever shown,' said Cooper. 'There was plenty of evidence that she was depressed. The coroner heard witness statements from Shirley Outram's parents, her GP, and one of her friends.'

'Oh? Which friend?'

'Peter Massey again. He seems to have been close to both Hind and Outram.'

'What did he have to say?'

'According to Massey's statement, Shirley Outram had been having a bad time after the birth of the child. The child was illegitimate, as you know.'

'Yes, the father was Stuart Clay.'

'That wasn't mentioned at the inquest,' said Cooper, frowning. 'It probably never came out at the time.'

'Well, it was 1968 – that's the way it was back then.'

'Yes, you're right. It was something that people didn't talk about. It was still the 1950s, in some ways.'

Fry tapped the file irritably. 'That was the trouble with public inquests then, too. In suicide cases, the coroner would fall over backwards to make the whole process more tolerable for the victim's family. That meant being, well . . . sparing with the details.'

'They suppressed evidence, you mean?'

'If it was considered potentially distressing for the family, yes.'

'It ought to have been covered in the initial police enquiry, though.'

'Possibly.'

But Fry didn't feel entirely convinced of that. The tacit agreement not to talk about things had probably included the police in these parts. She was sure that old-school officers like Cooper's father would have been perfectly willing to leave embarrassing details out of their reports.

She felt the familiar surge of satisfaction running through her veins now, the feeling of an enquiry that was finally starting to come together.

'Massey and Hind were about the same age,' she said. 'And this ROC post was on the Masseys' land, wasn't it?'

'Yes.'

'So does it still exist? Or was it demolished?'

'I couldn't tell you,' said Cooper.

Fry raised an eyebrow. 'I'm disappointed in you, Ben.'

The windscreen wipers on the Toyota were struggling to clear the rain sweeping across Longstone Moor as Cooper drove back towards Rough Side Farm.

He remembered his assumptions about Birchlow. The natural instinct to distrust the unfamiliar. Politeness on the surface, suspicion underneath. He wouldn't have endeared himself to these people by asking questions, or by seeming to know too much. His worst crime was probably sticking his nose into something that no one ever talked about.

The pastures of Rough Side Farm were wet, their acres of deep browns and greens stretching along the hillside. Peter Massey met him near the gate, as if he'd been expecting a visitor. Rain dripped from the peak of his cap, but Massey seemed oblivious. He screwed up his blue eyes to examine Cooper as he got out of the Toyota.

'Mr Massey, I've been hearing about Jimmy Hind,' said Cooper. 'How he was killed, in the accident.'

'The accident. Oh yes, that.'

'It must have been terrible for you.'

Massey's face remained impassive. 'What would you know?'

'Jimmy Hind was your friend, wasn't he?'

The farmer turned away, and Cooper followed him as he walked towards the field gate. Cooper had his leather jacket on, but the rain was wetting his face and hair. It wouldn't do to go back for a waterproof. That would mean showing weakness.

'You were there, Mr Massey. You must remember it. I bet you remember it very clearly.'

'Of course I do.'

'The siren fell when you were dismantling the equipment. It was an accident.'

'So they say.'

Cooper had to walk more quickly to get in front of him, to see Massey's face. The farmer stopped, his way blocked.

'What is it you want?' he said.

'To hear it from you. How did it happen?'

Massey's face contorted then. 'Jimmy never uttered a word when he saw it falling. None of us did. When something like that happens, when you know it's inevitable and there's nothing you can do to stop it, you just freeze. That's the way we all reacted. Just in those few seconds, you know.'

'I understand.'

'Jimmy wore these thick lenses in his glasses. When he looked up at us, they made his eyes look all distorted and out of proportion. Like smooth stones lying in deep water.'

He leaned against the dry-stone wall, looking towards the tower of the church at Birchlow, square on the horizon. Cooper had a sudden recollection of the stained-glass window, depicting the death of a saint. He had an image of a pale face, turned up to the sky as the saint died. A calm, wordless appeal, addressed to the clouds.

'I didn't know for certain,' said Massey. 'I didn't know for certain which one of us failed to tie the knot properly.'

'Tell me about that knot.'

'It was on the rope that we were using to haul the siren out of the shaft. One of the knots came loose, and that was why the siren fell. I thought it might have been me. But we told it all to the inquest, and they said we weren't to blame. Well, that's what they said. The official verdict.'

'And what did Jimmy do? Did he try to avoid it?'

'Not really. He didn't panic or anything when he saw the siren falling. He was dead calm. Calm as a freshly dropped calf.'

He took off his cap, a gesture that came close to an expression of emotion. His sandy, Viking hair gleamed briefly in the rain. Then he began to walk on, and Cooper was obliged to follow.

'What was Jimmy Hind like?' he asked.

'He was a good lad. Clever. And dead keen.'

'Keen on . . .?'

'The job. The ROC, you know.'

'Yes, I know about the ROC and the observation posts.'

Massey grunted. 'You know, you couldn't sign up for the ROC until your fifteenth birthday. But Jimmy was mad on aircraft spotting and modelling, and he joined up the minute he could. It was one of the great things about the ROC – you were among people who talked about planes. There was a monthly magazine that was full of planes, too. So, yes, Jimmy was keen. He was the sort who was desperate to take the master test on a Sunday to get some badges on his uniform. Trouble was, his age. He was only seventeen when he was killed.'

'Why was his age a problem? He was old enough to join, wasn't he?'

'I just said, you could join when you were fifteen. No, it wasn't that.'

'What, then?'

'We used to have post meetings every week. Ours were on a Wednesday evening, seven thirty until nine thirty. In the summer, we met at the post, but during the winter we went to the pub.'

'The Bird in Hand?'

'Of course. It was the only one in the village, even then.'

'And Jimmy wasn't old enough.'

'The landlord wouldn't let him in until he was eighteen.'

'So he missed some meetings.'

'He hated that. But there was another problem.'

Massey speeded up his pace, as if to leave Cooper behind. Cooper slithered on the wet grass as he tried to keep up.

'Mr Massey?'

'Shirley,' he said.

Cooper thought he'd misheard. 'What?'

'It was Shirley. Shirley Outram.'

'What was?'

'The problem.'

Cooper ran and put his hand on the next gate to prevent him opening the latch.

'Tell me, Mr Massey. Please.'

Massey looked at him, with a searching gaze. Cooper seemed to pass some kind of test, because Massey dropped his hand.

'Shirley was our only female observer. Yes, we just had the one in our section, and that was quite an innovation at the time, I can tell you. Somehow, she managed to make the uniform look good. A tight mini-skirt and kinky boots. I don't know how she got away with it. Most of the observers were middle-aged men, you see, and she was a real breath of fresh air. There was quite a social life in the Corps – as well as the pub, there were parties, dances, and so on. You can imagine she was in demand.'

'Yes.'

'Well, that was something else Jimmy was mad keen on – Shirley Outram.' Massey sighed. 'It could get pretty tedious on a long exercise. We took radios down, cards, dominoes. But a lot of the time, we just sat around and chatted. You found out a lot about people, sitting down there all night. When you're frozen solid at two o'clock in the morning on an all-night exercise, on the graveyard shift, it makes a differ-ence who you're stuck down there with.'

'You had Jimmy. And you had Leslie Clay.'

He nodded. 'Les Clay worked in the engine shed at Rowsley until it shut in '66. He was made redundant in the October, transferred to Bakewell as a porter and got made redundant again five months later, when the line closed. Dr Beeching – there's a man whose name lives on.'

Cooper recalled that there was a little woodland station

not far from here, at Great Longstone. The last stop before the crossing of Monsal Dale viaduct. Now the station was passed only by walkers and cyclists.

'What age are you?' asked Massey. 'I suppose you think this was all a different century?'

'Well, strictly speaking, sir . . .'

Massey laughed sourly. 'Yes, all right. The twentieth century, damn it. Consigned to the history books now.'

'I heard about the closures,' said Cooper.

'The 1968 reorganization came as a jolt. We thought the ROC was safe. It ought to have gone on for ever. But we were called to a special meeting at Group HQ in Coventry, and we went like lambs to the slaughter. The commandant got up and read out a list of posts that would close. Alpha One, Bravo Two . . . we were devastated. There was a lot of antagonism and bad feeling. They asked the older ones to retire, said they couldn't go up and down the shaft any more. Some they wanted to transfer to other posts miles away, but that wasn't the same at all.'

Cooper was glad to see they were walking back towards the house now. His hair was sticking to his head, and the water was running down his neck.

'Do you know Michael Clay, Mr Massey?' he asked.

'Who?'

'Les Clay's son.'

Massey shook his head. 'I've heard his name mentioned. I never met him.'

Cooper watched him for a moment. It sounded like the truth. And Peter Massey just didn't seem like a man who could tell a lie so convincingly.

'What about Patrick Rawson? Do you know him?'

'Who's he?'

'Michael Clay's business partner.'

'Wasn't that the man who died up the way there? You asked me about him before.'

369

'So I did.'

Cooper showed him the photograph of Rawson. But Massey shook his head. 'I've never seen him.'

'You've never done anything with the old bunker.'

'It was lucky there was no aircraft recognition post here. Some of them were snapped up by mobile telephone people, so they could put masts up. This one wasn't of interest to anybody, so they just gave the site back to the landowner.'

'Your father?'

'Yes. It's been abandoned since 1968, you know. It always flooded badly, and my dad said it was too dangerous to go down. So we locked it up and let the cows graze over it. When we had cows, that is.' Massey gave him an odd look, curiously hopeful, almost plaintive. 'Why? Did you want to have a look what it's like inside an ROC post?'

'No, thanks,' said Cooper. 'I've seen one.'

'And you're sure that Mr Massey was telling the truth when he said he'd never met Michael Clay?' asked Fry when he phoned her.

'Yes. I'm certain of it. He never batted an eyelid. Besides . . .'

'What?'

'Well, if there's a family feud involved here, I'm just not seeing it, Diane. Les Clay and Peter Massey were the two men who might have been considered responsible for Jimmy Hind's death in 1968. But Clay died years ago, leaving Massey as the last man standing, so to speak. And Jimmy Hind doesn't have any family still around to worry about it.'

'Yes, I see what you mean. There's no logic in it. No logic that would make Michael Clay either an obvious target as a victim, or a man looking for revenge either. Neither scenario fits.'

'And yet . . .' said Cooper. 'There's still something I'm missing.'

'So what next?' asked Fry.

370

Now it was Cooper's turn to look at his watch. 'I've got to get myself a new cat.'

Cooper had never actually had to choose a cat for himself before. There had been plenty of them around the farm over the years, of course, but they'd just sort of appeared under their own initiative, and the main problem had been controlling their numbers.

At Welbeck Street, he'd inherited Randy with the flat, courtesy of Mrs Shelley, who encouraged strays without any favour or distinction. Judging from Randy's battered looks, there certainly hadn't been any selection process based on cuteness, or the potential for posing as a cover model for calendars and birthday cards.

There were all kinds of animals at the Fox Lane Sanctuary – dogs and cats, of course, a few horses and donkeys, even a pig and a couple of sheep. He was surprised to find an injured owl in an aviary, its feathers ruffled miserably, a broken wing hanging at an unnatural angle. It was a tawny, just like the one he'd heard calling again last night. It had woken him in the early hours of the morning with its hunting cry, a sound that would strike fear into some helpless prey.

Cooper stopped in front of a loose box, eyeing an old horse who stared straight back at him unblinkingly.

'Hello. What's your name?'

He glanced aside to look at a notice on the wall next to the loose box. It said: '*This horse has been ill-treated. Watch her – she bites.*'

Cooper had been warned just in time. Out of the corner of his eye, he saw an enormous set of teeth flashing towards him. He jerked his head back instinctively. What had happened to the animal in the past that it would lunge at a complete stranger the moment his attention was distracted?

Ah, well. That wasn't what he was here for. He made his

371

way to the cattery, which was at the back of the sanctuary: a couple of low buildings with concrete walkways.

When he got there, Cooper hesitated. So how, exactly, did you go about choosing a cat? How on earth did you make a judgement when you were faced with rows and rows of felines in mesh cages? All of them were animals who'd been abandoned or mistreated in some way. All of them deserving of a good home.

It wasn't like buying a car, when you could look at the mileage, check under the bonnet, sit in the driving seat and try out the controls. He hadn't even thought about what colour of cat he'd like, which was the first question that Claire had asked him when he told her. Did it matter whether it was a tabby, a tortoiseshell or a ginger tom? It was the personality that mattered, the question of whether you were compatible. And you wouldn't discover that with a cat until you'd worked on the relationship for a while.

So standing here in the animal rescue centre, being asked to make a choice, seemed suddenly too daunting. It was an impossible challenge, surely?

But, in the end, it proved to be very simple. The question was resolved for Cooper beyond doubt by the time he got halfway down the first row of cages. There, he found a small, furry bundle clinging to the mesh, two bright green eyes fixed determinedly on his, and a tiny paw reaching desperately for his sleeve until claws hooked in and drew him closer. He barely noticed the colour of the fur in the intensity of the moment of communication. A pink mouth opened in an almost silent cry as the young cat spoke to him.

And somehow, Cooper knew exactly what he was being told. He didn't have to choose a cat, after all. His cat had chosen him.

Dorothy Shelley was waiting for him when he arrived home in Welbeck Street. Cooper never really understood how his

372

landlady knew everything that was going on. But he certainly wasn't going to be able to keep a new cat secret from her. He could see her grey-haired figure in a faded blue cardigan, hovering by the window of number 6 as he pulled his Toyota towards the kerb.

'She's lovely,' said Mrs Shelley, peering into the pet carrier before Cooper even got to the door of his flat. 'She is a "she", isn't she?'

'Yes, this time,' said Cooper, with a laugh. He remembered that his landlady had not been too expert at assessing the gender of a cat in the past.

'Have you decided what you're going to call her?'

He looked at the bright green eyes, huge and anxious, set in a face marked with perfect tabby tiger stripes.

'Not yet. It's going to take some thinking about.'

As he went inside his flat, Cooper reflected that he might have to take some time over that decision. It wasn't something to be rushed into. A name had to match a personality. And you didn't really understand another person's character until you'd got to know them properly. Sometimes, you could know a person for quite a while, and never understand them at all.

40

Monday

Fry didn't know why she had such a bad feeling as she walked up to Superintendent Branagh's office first thing on Monday morning. Often, an urgent summons meant you were in trouble, but she was confident that she hadn't put a foot wrong this week. She had obtained a good result, hadn't she?

So it ought to be good news – a commendation, or a bit of praise, at least. It had been known, even from Branagh. Perhaps she was going to apologize for having been wrong about Fry's record. That would be a turn-up for the books, all right. Like Count Dracula turning vegetarian.

Fry entered the corridor from the top of the stairs and saw the superintendent's office door ahead. Actually, praise from Branagh was definitely her due. She should go in expecting it as her right, not nervously approaching the feet of an angry god.

But, no matter how she rationalized it, she still had a bad feeling.

'Come in,' called Branagh at her knock.

Fry entered cautiously, and glanced around the room. She realized straight away that she'd been right to be uneasy. The atmosphere in the superintendent's office was tense, the silence that met her arrival too unnatural. Branagh's two visitors were immediately recognizable as police officers, though they wore civilian clothes. Detectives, then? Were they from another division, or headquarters staff? Strange that they didn't look familiar, either the man or the younger woman who now stood to greet her.

'DS Fry. Thank you for coming up to see us.'

'Sir.'

Fry held out her hand automatically to take his, feeling in no doubt from the start that she was addressing a more senior officer. He wasn't much above her own age, his hair just starting to recede a little from his forehead, grey eyes observing her sharply from behind tiny, frameless glasses.

Then he smiled, and Fry hesitated, wanting to let her hand drop, but feeling it still clutched awkwardly in his.

'It's been a long time, Diane,' he said.

And then she recognized him. They'd been in uniform on the same shift years ago, but he'd got his stripes really early. Too early, some had said. But he'd been ambitious, with the right mix of ambition and ability that got you noticed in the force. Blake – that was his name. Gareth Blake. He'd matured now, dressed better and went to a decent hairdresser. He still reeked of ambition, though.

Fry realized that he was staring at her, that smile still lingering on his face, a bit uncertainly now. She looked from Blake to the woman, and back again.

'So,' said Fry, 'I don't suppose this is a social call. What exactly can I do to help Birmingham CID?'

Blake introduced the woman with him as Rachel Murchison. She was smartly dressed in a black suit and a white blouse, dark hair tied neatly back, all businesslike and self-confident. Fry cautiously shook hands, wondering why the woman was studying her so closely. She could sense that Branagh was watching her too, from behind her desk. She couldn't still smell of horse shit, surely? She'd showered three or four times since then, and thrown everything into the wash.

'Rachel is a specialist counsellor who works with us sometimes,' said Blake.

So she'd been wrong, then. Not a police officer. Too smartly dressed, perhaps – that should have been the giveaway. The woman was a professional, though. It was that guarded watchfulness that had given Fry a misleading impression.

'What sort of counsellor?' she asked.

Blake and Murchison exchanged glances. 'We can go into that shortly, Diane. There's a bit of explanation to do first.'

'So what section are you working in these days, Gareth?'

Fry could hear her voice rising, already developing that strident tone she tried so hard to avoid. Blake raised a placatory hand.

'Let's take things one step at a time.'

But Fry shook her head. 'Tell me what section you're working in.'

Branagh looked about to interrupt, but changed her mind. Fry waited, her face set in a grim line.

Blake sighed. 'Cold case rape enquiries.'

Gavin Murfin dipped his fingers into a paper bag for an Eccles cake he'd bought on the way into work. At least some things were back to normal, thought Cooper. Murfin had explained that he couldn't keep the diet up. Not even with all the talk about horse-meat pies.

'You know what?' said Murfin, after he'd listened to Cooper talk about 1968 and the Royal Observer Corps. 'We've still got one of those here.'

'One of what?'

'One of those . . . what did you call them? Carrier control points. This is where the four-minute warning came through. I remember my old sergeant showing me the equipment when I was a probationer here.'

'And it's still here?'

'Right here, in the station. It's up in the store rooms some-where. There's a siren up there, too. Nobody has even tested it for a long time, so far as I know.'

'I had no idea, Gavin. Do you think we'll get a look at it?'

'Leave it to me.'

Murfin wandered off and came back a few minutes later with a key he'd obtained from an admin office somewhere in the building. Used his charm, presumably. He waved the key at Cooper.

'Security clearance.'

In the base of the receiver was a small drawer containing instructions on testing, battery replacement and fault reporting, as well as how to respond to the types of message that might come through. Attack Warning Red, imminent danger of an attack. Fallout Warning Black, danger of fallout. And Attack Message White, the all-clear.

'I don't suppose it was ever used, except for testing.'

'They had exercises regularly,' said Cooper. 'Everyone felt they had to be prepared. Or so I'm told. The ROC posts weren't closed until 1991, after the collapse of the Soviet Union.' He looked at Murfin. 'Do you remember that, Gavin? You're older than me.'

'Are you kidding? Well, I suppose I was around in 1991, but I was more interested in *Silence of the Lambs* and *Terminator II*.'

'I was into *Sonic the Hedgehog*.'

'You're such a baby.'

Cooper tried to imagine the awful piercing wail of the siren. The sound that had never been heard for real in the Cold War.

'So what would *you* do, then?' said Murfin suddenly.

'What? Do when?'

'In those last few minutes. If you knew that you had just four minutes to live, like.'

377

'Blimey, I don't know. It isn't much time to do anything really, is it?'

'No, you're right. Nothing worthwhile.' Murfin laughed. 'It makes a joke out of all those "fifty things to do before you die" features in the papers, doesn't it?'

'Yes.'

Murfin thought for a moment. 'You could pray, I suppose,' he said.

'I didn't know you were religious, Gavin.'

'Well, of course I'm not *now*. But if I knew I only had four minutes left to live, I might want to . . . you know, cover my options.'

'I see.'

'You could get quite a few "Our Fathers" in, couldn't you? In four minutes.'

Cooper laughed. 'I'm sure you could. But just one might be better, Gavin, if you could get the right amount of sincerity into it.'

'Right.'

'Or, instead of praying,' said Murfin, 'you could just do something you'd always really, really wanted to do, all your life, and never got the chance.'

'Ye-es.'

They were both silent for a moment, Murfin chewing the last half of his Eccles cake, Cooper wondering how long he could resist asking the obvious question. It wasn't long.

'So what would that be, Gavin? The thing you've always really, really wanted to do, all your life?'

But Murfin shook his head. 'I can't tell you.'

'Oh, go on.'

'No way. You'd take the piss out of me, and I'd never hear the end of it back at the office.'

Cooper gazed at Murfin, watching him lick a few crumbs off his fingers and wipe them on his tie. He was wondering whether his colleague had some hidden psychological depths that he'd never suspected. What was this deep, seething urge that he daren't even speak about?

'I tell you what would be embarrassing,' said Murfin. 'If you just *thought* you had four minutes left to live, and you did . . . well, whatever it was you really, really wanted to do. And then you found out it was a false alarm.'

'Well, it would depend on what it was,' said Cooper. 'I mean, if what you did in that time was something *really* awful, Gavin.'

Then it was Murfin's turn to laugh. 'Yeah. It could be *so* bad, you might have to kill yourself.'

'No, really.'

'Well,' said Murfin, seeing that he was serious. 'It would be the ideal opportunity to take the revenge you'd always wanted.'

'Yes,' said Cooper. 'So it would.'

Fry could feel the sweat forming on her skin, the prickling at the back of her neck. She shifted uncomfortably in her chair, wanting desperately to get up and walk out of the room. There was something intolerable about sitting here, under the scrutiny of her superintendent and these two people from Birmingham, discussing something that for her was too deep and intimate to be spoken about, yet for them was just another case.

Gareth Blake was watching her carefully, trying to assess her reaction. And so was the woman, of course – Rachel Murchison, the counsellor, there to judge her psychological state.

'When we get a cold case hit, we consult the CPS before we consider intruding into a victim's life,' said Blake. 'The public interest consideration isn't in doubt, because of the seriousness of the offence, but we have to take a close look at how strong a case we've got, and whether we can do something to strengthen it.'

'With the help of the victim,' said Fry.

'Of course. And in this case . . .'

'In *my* case. This is personal, DI Blake. Don't try to pretend it isn't. It's very personal for me.'

Blake held up his hand again, a defensive gesture, as if trying to fend off an attacker.

'In your case, we had a very credible witness report from the victim. From you, Diane. Force policy has changed since the 1990s, when we only kept files on unsolved rape cases for five years. Everything is on file for this one. We have an e-fit record in the imaging unit, and a copy of everything has been kept by the FSS. But the bottom line is, we got a DNA match.'

'And you have to consult a counsellor before you approach the victim. Between you, you will have developed an approach strategy before you even came here.'

'You know exactly how it works, Diane.'

'So Rachel here – ?'

'She's a trained rape counsellor and support worker. She accompanies any of us when we interview a victim.'

'I'm just here to help,' said Murchison. 'There's no pressure. It's all about support.'

Support. It was such an over-used word. Fry had already heard it too often during the past week. At least when Ben Cooper used the word, it was with some sincerity. Here, in this overheated room, looking out over the back of the football ground, it had the dead sound of a curse.

'Diane, we'll understand if you say you've moved on and you don't want to testify,' added Blake. 'But there are things we can do. A victim can agree to interview without any commitment to give evidence.'

'Don't keep calling me the victim.'

'I'm sorry, I'm sorry. Look, you might not be sure about this until you re-read your own statement. That's often what we find. A woman has tried to forget the incident, put the trauma behind her – of course. But then she goes back and reads the statement she made at the time, and she changes her mind. She agrees to go ahead and give evidence in court.'

Blake was starting to look a bit flustered at her lack of reaction. He glanced at Superintendent Branagh, as if appealing for support. But Branagh's face was impassive. For once, she wasn't weighing in to put pressure on Fry.

And there must be a reason for that. Fry knew that everything Branagh did had a reason. There might be even more going on in this room than it seemed.

Fry wiped her palms on the edge of her jacket, then tried to disguise the gesture. Too much of a giveaway.

'In court, you can have a screen, if you want,' said Blake, leaning forward earnestly. 'So that the accused can't see you and you can't see him. We often take victims into court to show them where they'll give evidence from, and where everyone sits. We might not need to do that for you, obviously. But you understand what I'm saying? We bend over backwards to make it easier.'

'Easier?'

'Less difficult, then.'

Rachel Murchison would be from a sexual assault referral centre. Fry knew the police would already have examined the stored exhibits for blood, saliva or semen traces, with the help of the Forensic Science Service. They might have found the tiniest speck of sperm on a tape lift from her clothing. Without statements from independent eye witnesses, the police were reliant on forensic science.

But in rape cases, juries were the problem. They were notoriously sceptical of a rape victim's behaviour if she didn't put up a struggle, didn't make her refusal absolutely clear, didn't rush straight to the police, didn't tell the full story straight away.

The research said that rape trauma syndrome could make a victim seem unmoved by the experience as she gave evidence

381

in the witness box. But the general public had never read the research. They had expectations of a rape victim – that she should resist physically, make non-consent very plain, that she should rush off to the police station, give a full and consistent account of everything that happened. Without expert witnesses, juries sometimes weren't deciding cases on the facts, but on preconceived notions.

'In every case I've dealt with since joining the unit,' said Blake, 'victims have been delighted to be approached. They say that a conviction brings closure, often after many years of torment.'

'But you do need consent to go ahead.'

He hesitated. 'In almost one hundred per cent of cases.'

Fry nodded. DNA techniques had advanced significantly over the last twenty years in terms of sensitivity, reliability, and speed of results. They had become really important in revisiting old cases, reviewing the evidence recovered at the time. Preservation must have been good in Birmingham, because DNA deteriorated over time if it wasn't kept cold and dry.

'We had the element of luck,' said Blake. 'Our suspect had a DNA sample taken when he was arrested for robbery and possession of a firearm. Criminals don't just commit sexual offences, but other offences too.

'We firmly believe that murderers and rapists who think they've got away with it should no longer sleep easily, but should be looking over their shoulder.'

Out of the corner of her eye, Fry could see that Superintendent Branagh was nodding. It was a sentiment that no one with any sense could disagree with.

'How was he arrested?' asked Fry. It hardly mattered, but she felt a need to know every little detail, to make the picture come together in her mind. Perhaps it was just that the more detail she asked for, the longer it put off the moment when she would have to make a decision.

'We had intelligence,' said Blake.

'Intelligence?'

'Information from a member of the public.'

'You mean one of the gang?'

'No.'

Fry stared at him. She couldn't imagine what other member of the public he could mean. There had been no witnesses to the assault, at least none that she could remember, and certainly none had come forward at the time. There had been plenty of appeals, of course. Lots of trawling from house to house in the area, hours spent stopping cars that used the nearby roads, and talking to motorists, lots of effort put into leaning on informants who might have heard a murmur on the streets. All to no avail. It was an offence with no witnesses other than the perpetrators and the victim.

Apart from her own statement, the only evidence she had of the attack were bruises and abrasions. And those faded with time, leaving only the crime-scene photographer's prints to pass around a jury. As for the psychological scars . . . well, they didn't show up too well in court.

'Do I get to find out who the member of the public is?'

Blake pursed his lips. 'Sorry. They're on witness protection. You know how this works, Diane.'

'Yes. They're putting themselves at serious risk to testify. You must have done some pretty smooth talking, sir.'

'You know, I don't like to hear you call me "sir", Diane. It was always "Gareth", wasn't it?'

'It was, but . . .'

Fry stopped, realizing that she didn't quite know how to put into words what she was feeling at this moment. Blake was trying to be friendly, of course. But his insistence on his first name was the way he would talk to a nervous defendant he wanted to put at ease.

It was a clear signal that their relationship wasn't going to be a professional one. They weren't to be considered a DS and a DI working together, no longer colleagues who could safely share information fully with each other. From this moment, from the second she called him 'Gareth', she wouldn't be a police officer any more. She'd be the victim.

Now Blake changed tack, thinking that she was on side. Hit her with the bad news.

'I'm afraid the conviction rate in rape cases is still very low in this country.'

'Yes, I know that.'

Blake tilted his head in acknowledgement. 'Of course you do. And I'm sure you're aware, too, that there's a lot of pressure to improve conviction rates.'

'Absolutely. The inference from the poor figures being that the police don't take rape allegations seriously enough.'

'Well, that's a perception the public might take away from the statistics. We know it isn't true, though, don't we? Generally speaking. There are lots of other factors that make convictions difficult to achieve, especially in cases where the defendant is known to the victim.'

'Like the fact that it's impossible to provide objective evidence on whether consent was given.'

'Exactly. It always comes down to one person's word against another. And juries don't like that. They want to be presented with evidence. We're handicapped by those old-fashioned notions of people being innocent until proven guilty, and having to establish guilt beyond reasonable doubt. When it's just a question of *"he says, she says"*, there's always going to be room for reasonable doubt. It would take a piss-poor barrister not to ram that point firmly into the heads of a jury.'

'Or a defendant who's not very convincing on the stand?'

Blake smiled. 'Ah, yes. There *are* some people who just look so guilty that jurors will convict them whatever the evidence. But that's the chance you take in a jury system, isn't it?'

'Have you lost many convictions turned over as unsound?'

'Through prejudiced juries?'

'Yes.'

'One or two. The information age is a killer.'

The information age. Fry knew what he meant. For many decades, newspapers had been subject to restrictions on what they could publish during a trial without being guilty of contempt of court and prejudicing a jury. But the internet had changed all that. There were archives of news stories from the time of an offence being committed, or from a suspect's arrest, which could be accessed at the click of a key. For many jurors, it was too much of a temptation not to do a bit of research for themselves. The Court of Appeal had quashed convictions as unsound on those grounds alone. Too much information. A real twenty-first-century curse.

She realized that everyone in the room was looking at her again. Had she been asked a question? She would be a hopeless witness on the stand if her attention wandered from the question so easily.

'So what do you say, Diane?' asked Blake.

'I need time.'

'Of course. All the time you want.'

Fry looked at Superintendent Branagh, and thought she might have detected a tiny hint of sympathy in her eyes. She thought of all the times she'd observed the behaviour of victims and felt a twinge of contempt at their weakness, wanted to tell them that it wasn't so bad as all that, for God's sake, have a bit of backbone and do what you have to do.

And Fry had so often seen people going into court to confront their past. She knew the worst part was waiting in the witness room, and the long walk down the corridor to take the stand. She'd watched people taking that walk. It might only be a few yards, but when you were going to face your own demons, it could seem like a million lonely miles.

For herself, Fry knew that the long walk down that corridor would be the most difficult thing she'd ever done in her life.

41

As Cooper drove through Birchlow towards Rough Side Farm, he noticed that there was now just one car parked behind the village hall. He almost missed it through his rain-streaked window, but for a brief flash of bright metallic blue, which made him stop and reverse a few yards to take a better look. A blue Mercedes. Had the same car been there on Wednesday? He had no idea.

Cooper drew into a lay-by just past the church and called the office.

'Gavin, what sort of car does Michael Clay drive? Isn't it a Mercedes?'

'Yes. Do you want the reg?'

'Please.'

Murfin read the registration number to him, spelling it out in the standard phonetic alphabet.

'Romeo, Echo, Zero, Eight . . .'

Even before he'd finished, Cooper knew he had the right car. And he knew he had the answer to another mystery as well.

'Is Diane around, Gavin?'

'She's just come down from upstairs. But you don't want to talk to her, Ben.'

'Yes, I do.'

'Take my advice, mate. I've just seen her face, and you do *not* want to talk to her.'

'Gavin, put her on, please.'

Murfin sighed. 'Stand by for the nuclear fallout, then. I gave you the four-minute warning. I just hope you've got your tin hat on.'

A moment later, Fry came on the phone. 'Yes, what's happening?'

Well, all or nothing, supposed Cooper.

'Diane, can you come out and meet me at Birchlow, to visit Rough Side Farm?'

'Is that the Massey place?'

'Yes. I think it could be important. I'm sorry if it's a bad time, but there's something –'

'Anything,' said Fry. 'Anything. I'll be straight there.'

Peter Massey wanted so much to talk. It was impossible to tell what had held him back before. Some instinct to put off the moment, a hope that the whole thing might be forgotten? Who could tell? But as soon as Cooper asked the right question, the words poured out of him as if the act of talking made him feel a lot better.

'Mr Massey, did someone else come to visit you last week?' said Cooper when Fry had arrived and they'd fetched the farmer out of his workshop. 'Perhaps to ask about the old ROC post – 4 Romeo?'

'Yes, he was here,' said Massey, not even bothering to ask who they meant. 'Wednesday, it was. I was out in the fields, mending a bit of wall that had collapsed. Too much rain. It washes away the footings.'

'Mr Clay?'

'Yes, Clay. Him.'

He spoke so quickly that there was almost no form to some of his sentences. They broke down into mere fragments of sound – part confession, part recollection, interspersed with snatches of narrated conversation, so that Cooper got Michael Clay's words as well as Massey's own. It was a spasmodic, convulsive purge, as if Massey was being physically sick, vomiting up the guilt and fear.

Fry tried to persuade him to go into the house, but he ignored her, a stubborn expression on his face. Instead, he sat down on an old, blackened bale of straw, removing his cap and turning his face up to the rain.

'I recognized him then,' he said. 'Even after all that time, I knew him as well as I knew myself. His hair was grey, he'd put on weight, but I knew him all right. You don't change the way you move, the way you speak, the way you hold your head. Just looking at him brought back all those memories.'

'Do you want to have a look inside?' I said.

A delighted expression came over his face. 'May I? The hatch is padlocked.'

'Yes, but I've got the key.'

'Do you own it, then?'

'It's on my land, so I suppose I do. No one else wants the thing, anyway. Not any more.'

'To be honest, I was surprised that he didn't know me, the way I'd recognized him,' said Massey. 'But maybe he'd never taken much notice of me at the time. Yes, I suppose that's what it was. He hadn't studied me the way I'd studied him for all those weeks. He thought I was just some fool in the background, not worth bothering about. Well, that was his mistake.'

'So you opened the hatch?' said Cooper.

'Yes. It hadn't been used for quite a while, but luckily it's never been vandalized, unlike some of the other posts, and the hinges are good. There's a bit of water standing in the bottom, though. That's as you might expect – it leaches through the ground and gets in through any cracks it can find. The floor is solid concrete, you see, so there's no way for it to

drain off. I told him that, but he said he had waterproof boots
on. He was really keen to go inside.'

'So you intended . . .?'

'I don't know what I intended, I honestly don't. I watched
him get into the hatch and start to climb down the ladder,
and I wasn't really thinking about anything, except how
funny it was he should turn up like that, out of the blue,
after all those years. I even told him to mind his head on
the counter balance. It can give you a nasty crack, if you're
not used to it.'

'Did he say anything?'

'Oh, yes. He could hardly stop yattering.'

*'You're right, it is a bit wet down here. There's no light in
the monitoring room, of course. It's lucky I've got a torch.'*

'I could hear him splashing about at the bottom of the ladder.
I could see him, too, for a while, poking about at the bottom
of the shaft. He was standing on the grille over the sump. He
tried the pump handle, but it hadn't worked for a long time.
It's supposed to drain the water out through the sump, and I
suppose he remembered that. I lost sight of him when he went
through the door into the monitoring room. But, as he was
getting his torch out, he looked up at me.'

'Aren't you coming down yourself?'

*'No. It's best if one of us stays up here. Just in case. We
don't want any accidents.'*

'I think there was just a split second then, when he almost
knew who I was. Almost. He looked at me a bit funny, as
though he was thinking about it, the way you do when you're
trying to catch hold of some memory that's just out of reach.
I reckon he wouldn't have been able to see my face at all at
that point. He was looking up at me from the bottom of the
shaft, so I'd be against the light. Just a figure on the surface,
a silhouette against the sky. Anonymous. A vague shape he
didn't recognize, the way I'd always been. Maybe it was my
voice that sounded familiar. But, whatever it was, he looked

389

at me strange, not too sure whether I was joking with him, or what.'

'*All right. That's sensible. I won't be long.*'

'And when he was out of sight, you closed the hatch,' said Cooper.

'Not right away. I didn't close the hatch until he was out of sight in the monitoring room. I couldn't even see his torchlight then. It was a bit funny, really. It was as if he'd disappeared, stepped back into the darkness, back into the past. Like he'd never been there at all. I don't mind telling you, there was a moment when I wasn't sure whether I'd just imagined him. I suppose I might have been going a bit mad. I stood on the side of that hatch, and I was completely alone, looking down into a dark hole, with that musty smell rising up towards me. That smell seemed to carry all the memories from the past, memories that I'd kept shut up for forty years.'

Massey looked at them, regarding even Cooper as a complete stranger, intruders he'd never set eyes on before.

'Do you understand? I was looking into a yawning pit. It was like staring inside my own head. It was black and stinking, and I wanted nothing else except to close the door on it again. Slam it shut, before anything got out.'

'You convinced yourself Mr Clay hadn't been there?' said Cooper. 'Just in those few seconds when he was out of sight?'

'I don't know how long it took. I remember thinking that I must look such an idiot standing there with the hatch open, staring down into the hole. So I looked around me. And of course there was no one in sight, not in that spot. There wasn't a soul out walking across the moor, not a car nearer than the road, and that was half a mile away.

'"Well, I'm on my own out here," I said to myself. And then I shut the hatch. Just like that, without looking down again or saying another word. I just shut it, made sure it fit tight, and I put the padlock back on and shoved the keys in my pocket. And then I walked away.'

'You left him down there. With no way of opening the hatch, and no hope of anyone coming along to let him out.'

'Aye.'

'He had a mobile phone –'

Massey shook his head. 'Those things don't work when you're down inside a concrete bunker. A post like this was built to withstand the blast wave from a nuclear bomb.'

Looking at the man, so calm and matter-of-fact, Cooper wondered for a moment whether they would actually find anyone in the abandoned ROC post, or if this was all just a figment of Massey's imagination. Was he entirely sane? Had the old man gone quietly over the edge at some point in the last few years, and imagined the whole incident? Clay's sudden appearance did have a suggestion of wishful thinking – the result of a decades-long desire for vengeance, a hatred so powerful that its object had materialized in the form of a vivid hallucination. They would only know for sure when that hatch was opened.

'We need to get over there,' said Cooper.

'Where is it?' asked Fry.

Cooper pointed across the fields along the edge of the moor, to the raised area with its line of disused telephone poles. The Toyota's four-wheel drive came in useful now as they drove round the edge of the empty field to reach the gateway above Badger's Way.

'It's funny,' said Massey, when he got out and stood by the site. 'If only there'd been someone out on Black Harry Lane, walking their dog or something, it would never have happened. But I suppose the weather was too bad.'

'Does this bunker flood?' asked Cooper suddenly.

'Oh, yes. It was always a very wet post. We had to pump it out all the time. Now it floods right up into the shaft in really bad weather.'

Cooper wiped the rain from his face. 'Like now, you mean?'

Massey seemed to consider the rain, as if he hadn't noticed the continuing deluge until now.

'Aye. Could be.'

With a sense of despair, Cooper looked at Fry, and she began making calls. While she did it, Massey stared at the sky, as if watching for better weather to come riding over the hills to the north.

'I shut my memories away,' he said. 'They're down there in the dark, with the hatch locked tight.'

Then Cooper had a terrible thought. He'd been here at Rough Side Farm himself on Wednesday, around the same time that Michael Clay's phone had gone off the network. While he'd been talking to Peter Massey that first time, he'd noticed the raised area of ground, but hadn't recognized it for what it was. And he'd been here yesterday, too. Had Clay already been shut inside the flooding bunker then? Had he been calling for help, his shouts going completely unheard as Cooper stood around and chatted to Massey about horses and foxes?

He seemed to hear his brother Matt's voice again inside his head: '*I can tell you, Dad would never have done that. He would never have hung back if he thought he might save someone's life.*'

Urgently, Cooper took hold of Massey's arm.

'Quick – have you got the key with you?'

'Yes.'

'Get that damned hatch open, then.'

Cooper was pulling off his jacket, unlacing his boots, shivering in anticipation as the rain began to soak his shirt.

'Ben, what on earth are you doing?' said Fry in horror.

'Going down.'

'We have to wait. This is a specialist job.'

'Saving a man's life?'

'We don't know he's still alive.'

'We don't know he's dead, either. The water might not be up to the top yet. He could have found an air pocket. We can't just stand here while he drowns.'

When they pulled the hatch open, the water was halfway up the ladder. The stink of foul air and dank concrete rose to meet them – a true miasma, so thick that they could almost touch it and feel it. Rain splattered the surface of the water, shattering their own reflections as they stared down into the bunker. For a moment, Cooper experienced that curious illusion of looking at something twice as far away as it really was, because he was looking at his own reflection. And not just looking at himself, but at the grey sky far above his head. It was like staring into the infinite depths, dark clouds like blind sea creatures lurking on the ocean bottom.

Cooper remembered Peter Massey's description of his friend's eyes, looking back up at him like dark pebbles under water, in the last moment before he died. But beyond the surface reflection there were no eyes, no floating body, nothing visible at all in the dark, oily liquid filling the bottom half of the shaft.

Fry drew back from the opening, covering her nose and mouth against the stench.

'You can't do this,' she said.

But Cooper ignored her, concentrating on climbing over the slimy edge of the hatch and feeling for the top rungs of the ladder. As he clambered carefully down, the counterweight for the hatch bumped against his back, tap-tapping like a heavy hand on his spine, on his shoulders, and touching the back of his head as his feet touched the water. Then he looked up again at the light, saw Fry silhouetted against the sky, her coat and hair filmed with rain.

'I know the layout. I'll be OK.'

'How can you know it?'

'They're all the same. A standard design.'

'You don't know what else might be down there.'

'I'll be careful,' said Cooper.

'Famous last bloody words. You're mad.'

Cooper summoned his recollection of the Edendale post.

Beneath him was the bottom of the shaft, behind him an over-hang and a wooden door – the chemical toilet and generator room. To the left would be the other doorway, into the monitoring room. He could see the top of the frame, was relieved to see that the door stood open.

If he had been Michael Clay, trapped down here with the water rising, where would he have made his way to? Where would have been the best place to eke out the last bit of remaining air? The shaft itself, surely? There was a good six feet of space above the water line.

But he touched the walls and felt how wet they were. Slippery with a foul-smelling sheen of mud and mould. So the level of the water was actually falling. At its peak last night, or in the early hours of the morning, the shaft must have been flooded right up to the top, only the locked hatch preventing water from seeping out on to the surface.

So if Michael Clay had known the layout of an ROC bunker, what else would he have done? He would have gone for a ventilation outlet. Of course. Cooper pictured a rusty louvred steel opening in the far wall of the monitoring room. And somewhere in the ceiling was the lower end of the blast pipe, wide enough to detect the pressure from a fireburst explosion, so it must allow the passage a bit of air, too.

Cooper sucked in a long breath and ducked his head under water, pulling himself towards the open doorway. Moving into pitch darkness, he was blinded by the sudden contrast with the light in the shaft and its splintered reflections on the surface of the water. He was so disorientated that he had to break the surface and take a new breath, panicking for a moment that he wasn't going to be able to do it, at the thought that he would have to admit defeat and go back up to the surface, just sit and wait for the experts with their wet suits and oxygen tanks, which could take forever.

He shook his head and clutched at the walls to orientate himself again, feeling the handle of the pump tangle in his legs until he kicked away. The cold was already creeping into his bones and turning his fingers and toes numb. He didn't have very long to do this. It had to be now, or never.

Cooper's head went under again, and then he was in the doorway, pushing against the wooden frame. It was too dark to see anything in front of him. But he could hear David Headon's voice in his head, telling him that the monitoring room was only sixteen feet long. He remembered thinking that it was a small space for three men to spend so many hours in. Seven feet wide and sixteen feet long, like a giant coffin. He could reach the end of it in two strokes.

His violent movements stirred up silt and debris from the concrete floor. Floating objects bumped against him as he kicked forward, like invisible creatures swimming around him in the black water. A plastic bucket, a jerry can that spun away when he cracked his elbow against it. And something rough and fibrous that flapped slowly towards the floor.

Then a long, loosely jointed shape swung into his face. A familiar shape. A human arm. His lungs aching, Cooper grabbed at a sleeve and began to kick backwards towards the door. For a long second, he felt something holding him down, the door getting in his way as he confused the direction of the ladder. In a gleam of light from above, he saw a white face turning slowly towards him, a floating blank-eyed face, staring and staring.

Then his foot found the grille at the base of the shaft, and a rung of the ladder, and he was finally pushing upwards to the light. As he gulped air, he felt hands reach down towards him. Someone had lowered a rope. Voices came down from the sky that he almost couldn't make out.

'Is he dead?'

'Are you all right?'

But he didn't know the answer to either question.

42

Tuesday

Juliana van Doon hovered over the body of Michael Clay, laid out on the mortuary table in Edendale. The body exuded an almost palpable aura of cold, the blue tinge to his skin strange and alien in the mortuary lights.

'No, he didn't drown,' she said. 'There was no water in his lungs. But he suffocated all the same.'

Fry shivered involuntarily. A visit to the mortuary wasn't her idea of the best way to start the day. But today it seemed somehow appropriate.

'Suffocated?' she said. 'How can that be?'

'Oxygen deprivation.'

Tensing, Fry waited for the patronizing remark, but it didn't come. Instead, the pathologist looked down at the body, and wouldn't even meet her eye. Mrs van Doon seemed awkward with her this morning, almost as if she'd heard something that had changed her attitude. Fry told herself she must be imagining things. Yet still the pathologist looked away as she continued to explain.

'He has cyanosis, look – the bluish discolouration of the fingers, toes and ears, and around the mouth. That's caused by a dramatic drop in the oxygen content of the blood circulating through the body. Blood poor in oxygen is purple, rather than red.'

'But he was found in a flooded bunker,' said Fry. 'I assumed . . .'

Mrs van Doon shook her head. 'If this bunker of yours regularly gets wet and dries out again, I imagine there was a certain amount of rusted metal around.'

'Yes, there was.'

The pathologist hadn't even picked up on her slip, her use of the word 'assumed'. *Never assume, it makes an ass . . .*

'Oxidized metal produces carbon dioxide, and that's lethal in a confined space,' said Mrs van Doon. 'Even without the hatch being closed, the victim was at serious risk. He could have passed out fairly quickly, especially if he was panicking, and exerting himself physically.'

Fry looked at Michael Clay's blue-tinged fingers. 'He would have been running up the ladder, trying to force the hatch open. Shouting for help.'

'Of course. No ventilation either, I suppose?'

'A couple of sliding vents, but they were rusted shut.'

'It wouldn't have made any difference if they'd been open,' said the pathologist. 'Carbon dioxide is heavier than air. Without a pump to replenish the atmosphere, he wouldn't have survived very long. As things went downhill, he would have become confused and disoriented, losing co-ordination. His breathing would have progressively weakened, like a fish out of water, and then he would have lost consciousness. Sometimes, people die from cardiac arrhythmia before the asphyxia.'

'So he was already dead when the bunker started to flood?' asked Fry.

'Mmm.' Mrs van Doon tapped a scalpel thoughtfully against a stainless-steel dish, a habit that Fry normally found irritating. Today, it didn't seem to matter. 'Perhaps not when it started to flood. It would have taken time.'

'So he would have lived long enough to see the water coming in?'

'I think so. It's all a bit academic, perhaps.'

'I bet it didn't feel academic to Mr Clay,' said Fry, trying half-heartedly to get a reaction.

'Perhaps not.'

'More like something out of an Edgar Allan Poe story.'

'Poe?'

'He was the writer obsessed with premature burial.'

'I don't remember that particular story,' said the pathologist mildly. 'I was always scared by the one that had the walls gradually closing in. That used to give me serious nightmares.'

Fry shook her head. 'For me, it's drowning slowly, as the water gets higher and higher. Trying to get one more gasp of air, but feeling the water reach your mouth. As far as I'm concerned, it would be a blessing to pass out from lack of oxygen first.'

Then the other woman met her eye properly for the first time. Fry felt a physical shock from the contact. Was there sympathy in her expression? Surely not pity? God, please don't let the pathologist be feeling pity for her.

'We all have to be thankful for our blessings,' said Mrs van Doon. 'However small they may be.'

Cooper knew from personal experience that Fry's smile was worse than any verbal threat she might have made. It sometimes reminded him of a snake opening its mouth to reveal the poison on its fangs. Perhaps it was lucky that E Division hadn't introduced video cameras into the interview rooms yet. Those whirring tapes caught the words being spoken, but not the gestures or the facial expressions.

'So, Mr Massey,' she said. 'Do you still say you don't know whether you meant to kill Mr Clay?'

Massey was very composed now. All that he had bottled

up inside him had come out, and he was facing everything that happened to him now with a quiet resignation.

'I thought about it a time or two over the next few days,' he said calmly. 'I wondered whether to go and let him out. I even walked towards the post a couple of times. But it was so quiet, I just turned round and walked away again. I might have let him out, but I didn't know what to say to him, how to explain it. And as time passed, it became more difficult to explain. After a while, I knew I would never be able to explain it to anyone. I don't suppose you understand what I'm saying, even now?'

'It's hard for us to put ourselves in your position, Mr Massey.'

'Yes, I see that. It's hard for me too.' He looked from Fry to Cooper. 'I'm not a killer, you know. Not really. It was, well . . . sort of circumstances that just came together. The kind of thing I never thought would happen. You just react without thinking when it does happen. It was almost as if I'd been trained for it, had it drilled into me what to do in that situation. I really didn't think about it. I never thought, "I'm going to kill him." So I don't think you can say that I had the intention. Can you?'

'That will be for a court to decide, Mr Massey.'

'I suppose so. What happens now?'

'We're going to have to charge you.'

'Fair enough.'

'Why did you hate him so much?' asked Cooper. 'Was it to do with the death of Jimmy Hind?'

'Of course,' said Massey. 'Les had brought his son to the post that night. He was a new observer, learning the ropes. Strictly speaking, there was only supposed to be a crew of three on duty. Les told me not to mention it. But then, a few days later, I saw Shirley. And I saw who she was with. It was Stuart.'

They both stared at him for a moment, thinking they'd misheard.

'Stuart?' said Fry.

Massey nodded. 'Like I said, Stuart wasn't supposed to be there. But it was him I saw with Shirley a few days later. And I realized he'd been after her all that time. He was Jimmy's rival. It was him that left the loose knot on the siren, I'm sure of it.'

'Stuart? Did you say Stuart?'

'Yes, Stuart Clay, Les's son.'

Fry stared at him. 'Mr Massey, Stuart Clay died last year. He had pancreatic cancer.'

Massey looked completely uncomprehending. 'That's not possible. He was there on Wednesday.'

'No.'

'It was Stuart Clay, Les Clay's son. I knew him – he was with us at the post that night. He killed Jimmy.'

Cooper shook his head. 'DS Fry is right, Mr Massey. Stuart Clay died nearly a year ago. The man who visited you was his younger brother, Michael. Here's a photo of him –'

'That's him: Stuart.'

'No, it's Michael. He was eight years younger than Stuart. Stuart would have been your age now.'

'No.'

'Michael had to deal with his brother's affairs when he died,' said Cooper. 'We think that it was when he cleared out Stuart's papers that he first came across references to the ROC and the post at Birchlow. Then he found other things – there was a cap badge, a photograph of the crew. And, above all, there were a lot of newspaper cuttings relating to the death of Jimmy Hind. That was why Michael came to have a look at the post while he was in Derbyshire. It was part of the process of putting his older brother's memory to rest.'

But Massey still wasn't convinced. It was obvious from the stubborn expression on his face, the distant, unconnected look in his pale, blue eyes.

For one last time, Cooper produced the photograph of the

crew of the Birchlow observer post, Post 4 Romeo. He was confident that he was finally showing it to the right person.

'Mr Massey, do you remember this photo?'

Massey screwed up his eyes, and held the photograph to the light.

'That's us, in the 1960s sometime. There's me and Jimmy. The big bloke is Les Clay. And there's Stuart Clay, Shirley Outram. I know all of them. They're just as I remember them.'

In the photo, Jimmy Hind was wearing round, wire-rimmed glasses, like John Lennon's. He was the only one in glasses, though Peter Massey had also been squinting a little as he looked at the camera.

'Do you normally wear glasses, Mr Massey?'

'Only when I need them.'

'Are you short sighted, or long sighted?'

'Short sighted, I suppose.'

'If I left the room now, would you be able to describe my face to someone? Would you know me again if you saw me in forty years' time?'

'Why would I need to?'

Cooper lowered his head, no longer able to look Massey in the eye. He was thinking of the man who'd died in the underground bunker, starved of oxygen as the flood water crept higher around him.

'Why?' he said. 'So that you don't make a mistake about someone's identity again.'

'He's hopeless without his glasses,' said Cooper later, when he and Fry had concluded the interview. 'He says he doesn't need to wear them around the farm. He doesn't miss anything that he wants to see. But there are some things he doesn't want to see too clearly, anyway.'

'Like people?' suggested Fry.

'Yes, people. He knew me, but he wouldn't be able to describe my face. When he saw Michael Clay, his memories

401

were of a voice, an outline, a way of walking, a series of gestures or mannerisms. The sort of thing that brothers have in common, or fathers and sons. People say that Matt and I have a lot of similar mannerisms, though we don't really look alike.'

Fry seemed distant and detached this morning, as if a great weight was on her mind that prevented her from focusing properly.

'I don't understand why Peter Massey did it,' she said.

'I don't think he understands either,' said Cooper.

'Well, that's not good enough.'

Her tone was suddenly sharp, almost vicious. But Cooper could understand her annoyance. He just didn't know quite how much of it was directed at himself.

Cooper had wanted to see Fry bring her case to a successful conclusion. But somehow he'd managed to take the credit for himself, without intending to. This morning, a congratulatory memo had been emailed to everyone in CID from Superintendent Branagh, singling out the actions of DC Cooper for particular praise. That would do his hopes for promotion no harm at all. The trouble was, he didn't know whether Fry had read the memo yet, since she'd come straight from the mortuary to the interview with Massey. Certainly, no one had dared to mention it in front of her so far.

'I suppose it's in the nature of the job that we always want motives,' he said. 'But people often do things they can't explain the reasons for, even to themselves. We're wasting our time trying to make them give a reason for it, something neat and logical that we can write down and present to a judge and jury.'

'I don't agree,' said Fry. 'Being obliged to explain to another person why you did something can clarify the reasons in your own mind. It's the same principle that lies behind a lot of psychotherapy. If you're never forced to explain yourself, you can just carry on wallowing in denial.'

Cooper thought of some of the real killers he'd seen – the

social predators, people with the glint of cruelty in their eyes. But Peter Massey wasn't one of those. In his own way, he probably thought of himself as being just as noble as William Mompesson, sacrificing his own future to rid the world of a pestilence. A large number of murderers were convinced they were doing the right thing at the time. It often came as a surprise that society didn't agree with them.

Whose motto had been '*Hate and wait*'? Was it one of the de Medicis? Well, Peter Massey had certainly done that. He'd waited more than forty years, nursing his hatred. You'd think that emotions might fade over four decades, but sometimes they just grew stronger.

Cooper realized that Michael Clay's death had taken a hold on his mind. How could it not, when he'd been there himself, in the darkness of the flooded ROC bunker, feeling the debris of the past floating up around him, sensing the presence of death in the water.

This was the sort of thing he would think about at night when he went to bed. His memories would resurface from the mud of his subconscious. The invisible creatures that had swum about his feet; the rough, fibrous thing that had flapped towards the floor. And, most of all, the white face that had turned slowly towards him. A floating, blank-eyed face, staring and staring . . .

Yes, those images he'd created for himself would swirl through his brain, moving in endless spirals until he drifted to sleep. He prayed they wouldn't stay there for ever, haunting his dreams, too.

That morning, Environmental Health officers had visited Le Chien Noir in Edendale. They called Fry to tell her that they had obtained an ELISA kit for detecting animal species content in cooked meat. ELISA wasn't in the police handbook of acronyms, so Fry had to ask for an explanation. Enzyme-Linked Immuno Sorbent Assay. She was none the wiser.

'The testing method is based on antibodies raised to heat-resistant species-specific, muscle-related glycol-proteins. On your information, we used the cooked-horse species kit. They're made in the USA, and we don't use very many that are species specific.'

'And the result?' asked Fry.

'No horse.'

'No horse?'

'Not at Le Chien Noir.'

When Fry put the phone down, she reflected that the people who hadn't put a foot wrong all week were those she'd had the strongest personal reaction against. The Eden Valley Hunt had been above suspicion, apart from one rogue steward. C.J. Hawleys abattoir in Yorkshire was also operating according to all the regulations, so far as she could tell. And R & G Enterprises were a very respectable, forward-looking company, whatever you might think of the purple slabs of meat coming off their packing line.

No, the trouble had been caused by all those individuals with their personal needs and desires, their troubled emotions and hunger for revenge. Peter Massey just happened to have waited a lot longer for his vengeance, for the day when he could finally achieve a form of justice.

As her phone rang again, some instinct made Fry glance up at the other members of the CID team. At least two people looked hastily away. What were they waiting for? What had they been expecting her to do? She was only answering the phone.

'Hello, DS Fry.'

'Diane.'

She recognized the smooth tones immediately, of course. The caller was Gareth Blake. Just the sound of her name from his lips brought back all the feelings she'd been trying to suppress since yesterday. All the activity, the need to respond to Cooper's call from Birchlow, the visit to the mortuary, the interview with

Massey . . . it had all served the same purpose: to avoid the moment that she knew was coming. And to suppress the memories that would now forever bubble up in her mind.

'Obviously, I don't want to put any pressure on you, Diane,' said Blake.

'No. I —'

'But it would be good to talk to you again fairly soon. You know there's a decision to be made.'

To distract herself, Fry stared at her computer screen, saw that she had some emails, and automatically clicked on them to see what they were. It was an instinctive action, with no real thought of finding anything of interest. But she noticed a message from Superintendent Branagh, and opened it.

Blake was continuing to talk, pouring a meaningless noise in her ear, as Fry read the memo from Branagh for the first time.

Cooper had been asked to check through a copy of a statement that Peter Massey had made before his interview. It was a curious document, reading like an extract from the journal that they'd found at Rough Side Farm after his arrest. An odd glimpse into the world of 1968 and the memories that Massey had lived with for the past forty years.

Cooper thought the words were sad and thoughtful, with no apparent attempt at self-justification. It must have been a relief for him to get it all down on paper. There was even a sense of fatalism about Massey's conclusion:

'I thought that what they said must be wrong. At the start, Jimmy and Les and Shirley were all dead. Three of them, just the way it was bound to be. When they told me Stuart was dead, and his brother too, that was all wrong.

'But it seems there's a third, after all. A man I never knew, or even heard of until he was dead. But I suppose he had to die. It's fate, and you can't escape that. Everything happens in threes.'

405

Cooper wasn't so sure about fate himself. He'd never felt that sense of an inescapable destiny waiting for him, making everything he did completely futile. Perhaps he was too young yet. It was possible that you had to reach Mr Massey's age, before you were able to stop and look back on your life, and get that sudden terrifying perspective that convinced you it had all been in vain.

He smiled wryly to himself. Something to look forward to, then. He supposed it was better to enjoy life while he could. Best to appreciate what he had – friends, family, his relationship with Liz, the renewed prospect of promotion.

He felt conscious of Diane Fry's presence on the other side of the room. Without looking, Cooper knew that she'd read the memo from Branagh now. The tension was obvious in the set of her shoulders, the jerkiness of her movements. He wondered what she would say, or whether she would say nothing at all. Perhaps she would store it up and hold it against him for ever more.

One thing Cooper knew. Despite his best efforts, he was no nearer to understanding Diane Fry than he'd ever been.

For some reason, Fry had found herself thinking about rats. In particular, the black, flea-ridden rodents that had brought the Black Death to Eyam. The image of those rats seemed to sum up the past week for her. They were a symbol of disease and death, and the dark, rustling memories that lurked in the disused corners of people's heads. That lurked inside her own, for certain.

Now, a dirty sediment was being stirred up in her life, a spreading black contagion that all the rain of the last few days would never be able to wash away.

Not for the first time, Fry wondered what Ben Cooper knew that he wasn't supposed to. There was no way he could be aware of the reason for DI Blake's visit from the West Midlands yesterday. He couldn't possibly understand what was going on in her mind, the continuous weighing up of pros and cons, the constant running through her head of possible scenarios. He had no idea about the struggle she would face, coping with the pressures she would come under, until she bit the bullet and made a decision.

And, above all, someone like Cooper could never comprehend the painful attempt to balance two powerful urges. The need to keep her most terrible memories safely buried now had to be set against this urge she'd suddenly discovered growing inside – the burning desire for vengeance and justice.

Without being aware of any conscious intention, Fry got to her feet and moved across to Cooper's desk. What she wanted to ask him, she wasn't at all sure. She was just aware of a need to speak to him, to make some form of contact. But the tense atmosphere in the room made her pause, and she forgot whatever it was that she might have intended to say.

On his desk, Cooper had spread some of the items found during the search of Adrian Tarrant's house. She watched him pick up the hunting horn in its plastic evidence bag and turn it over to read the label, its brass and copper length glinting in the light. The sight of it made Fry blurt out the first thing that came into her head.

'You know, Ben,' she said, 'I never did hear the kill call.'

Cooper looked up at her, his eyes intense, his face faintly flushed.

'I was just thinking – we're not even certain that the horn works,' he said.

'We could try it,' suggested Fry, trying to sound more casual than she felt. 'Do you know how to use one?'

Cooper raised an eyebrow. 'Maybe. But trying the kill call? We might contaminate the evidence. It's a big decision to make.'

'I suppose you've given it some thought, though. You're the sort of man who would.'

'Yes, I have.'

'And what's your conclusion, Ben?'

'Well . . .'

Fry waited anxiously on his words, conscious of an overwhelming need for someone to make a decision. One way or another, the decision that she had to take in the next few weeks would change her life, and she needed some guidance. Any kind of direction would be welcome right now. A sign, a portent, a few words of advice.

'Actually, Peter Massey had a thought about decisions,' said Cooper.

'Oh?'

'Do you want to hear it, Diane?'

'Go ahead. Tell me.'

Cooper glanced at her curiously, before turning over a page of Massey's statement and read from the last paragraph:

A finger on the button, or a bundle of cloth on the doorstep. An outbreak of the plague, or the radioactive cloud of a nuclear holocaust. It only needs a second. It only takes one person's decision. And who knows what pestilence might be released into the world?